Martina Cole is the No.
successful novels. Her m
the No. 1 bestselling ha
went straight to No. 1 in
Close was a No. 1 hard
breaking number of wee

Award for Crime Thriller of the Year and was a No. 1 *Sunday Times* bestseller in hardback as well as a No. 1 bestseller in paperback. *Martina Cole's Lady Killers*, featuring the stories of notorious female serial killers, was a critically acclaimed hit TV series in autumn 2008 and *The Take* and *The Graft* are currently being adapted for Sky One. *The Know* was selected by Channel 4's *Richard & Judy* as one of the Top Ten Best Reads of 2003. *Maura's Game*, *Faceless* and *The Graft* shot straight to No. 1 on the *Sunday Times* bestseller lists, and total sales of Martina's novels are now at nearly ten million copies. Martina Cole has a son and daughter, and lives in Kent.

Highly acclaimed for her hard-hitting, uncompromising and haunting writing, as well as her phenomenal success, Martina Cole is the only author who dares to tell it like it really is.

Praise for Martina Cole's bestsellers:

'A gritty tale that will keep you hooked' *Sun*

'Right from the start, she has enjoyed unqualified approval for her distinctive and powerfully written fiction' *The Times*

'The queen of hard-hitting crime fiction' *Bella*

'Martina Cole again explores the shady criminal underworld, a setting she is fast making her own' *Sunday Express*

'Martina Cole pulls no punches, writes as she sees it, refuses to patronise or condescend to either her characters or fans' *Independent on Sunday*

By Martina Cole and available from Headline

Dangerous Lady
The Ladykiller
Goodnight Lady
The Jump
The Runaway
Two Women
Broken
Faceless
Maura's Game
The Know
The Graft
The Take
Close
Faces
The Business

MARTINA COLE

THE TAKE

headline

First published in 2005 by HEADLINE BOOK PUBLISHING

First published in paperback in 2006 by HEADLINE BOOK PUBLISHING

This edition published in paperback in 2009
by HEADLINE PUBLISHING GROUP

1

A Company Pictures and Warner Sisters Production for Sky One
Martina Cole's 'The Take'

Starring Tom Hardy, Kierston Wareing, Shaun Evans,
Charlotte Riley and Brian Cox

Director David Drury, Screenwriter Neil Biswas, Producer Willow Grylls
Executive Producers Lavinia Warner, Charles Pattinson, George Faber,
Helen Flint, Suzan Harrison and Martina Cole

Cover photography by Mitch Jenkins

Cataloguing in Publication Data is available from the British Library

ISBN 978 0 7553 5447 4

Typeset in Galliard by Avon DataSet Ltd, Bidford-on-Avon, Warwickshire

Printed and bound in Great Britain by Clays Ltd, St Ives plc

HEADLINE PUBLISHING GROUP
An Hachette UK Company
338 Euston Road, London NW1 3BH

www.headline.co.uk
www.hachette.co.uk

For
Mr and Mrs Whiteside.
Christopher and Karina.
With all my love to you both.

And for
Lewis and Freddie, my little pair of Kahuna Burgers!

I would like to thank all the people who kept me company through the long nights of writing.
Beenie Man, David Bowie, Pink Floyd, Barrington Levy, Usher, 50 Cent, Free, Ms Dynamite, The Stones, The Doors, Oasis, The Prodigy, Bob Marley, Neil Young, Otis Redding, Isaac Hayes, Janis Joplin, Ian Dury, Clint Eastwood and General Saint, Bessie Smith, Muddy Waters, Charles Mingus, Edith Piaf, Canned Heat, Steel Pulse, Peter Tosh, Alabama 3 . . .
to name but a few.

Prologue

1984

Lena Summers looked at her eldest daughter in abject disbelief. 'You are joking?'

Jackie Jackson laughed noisily. She had a loud laugh that made her sound very jolly. Very happy. It was a laugh that belied the vindictive nature beneath it.

'He'll love it, Mum, and after six years in poke he'll be ready for a party.'

Lena shook her head at her daughter and sighed. 'Are you off your head? A party for him after the stunts he's pulled over the years?' The anger was in her voice now. 'He was still romancing trollops while he was banged up!'

Jackie closed her eyes as if the action would blot out the truths her mother was pointing out to her. She knew him better than *anyone*, she didn't need this constant barrage about her husband.

'Will you stop it, Mum. He's me husband, the father of my kids. It will all work out now he has learned his lesson.'

Lena puffed her lips out in astonishment. 'Are you on drugs again?'

Jackie sighed heavily, trying her hardest not to scream

at the woman in front of her. 'Don't be silly. I want to welcome him home, that's all.'

'Well, I ain't going.'

Jackie shrugged her ample shoulders. 'Suit your fucking self.'

Joseph Summers snapped his head above the newspaper as he growled, 'Don't you talk to your mother like that.'

Jackie stretched her face in comic surprise and said sarcastically, as if talking to a baby, 'Aw, I see, Dad. Need to borrow a few quid, eh?'

Lena suppressed a smile. Jackie, for all her faults, had an uncanny knack of hitting the proverbial nail right on the head. Her husband shoved his face back in the paper and Jackie grinned at her mother.

'Oh, *come*, Mum, all *his* family's going to be there.'

Lena tossed her head and, picking up her cigarettes, said nastily, 'All the more reason to keep away then. Nothing but fucking trouble, the Jacksons. Look at the last time we got together with them.'

Jackie was annoyed again and it showed, her heavy features screwed up as she tried with obvious difficulty to suppress her fury.

'You caused all that, Mum, and you know it,' she said through gritted teeth.

She was clenching her fists now, and Lena stared at her eldest daughter, marvelling at her colossal anger. Even as a child she had been like that, one word and off she went into a frenzy of rage.

There were tears in her daughter's eyes. Lena knew she had to diffuse the anger now or face the consequences, and quite frankly she was tired, tired and more than a little interested to see what prison had done to her son-in-law.

'All right then, keep your hair on.'

'Well I ain't fucking going.' Joe got up and stamped from the room, and they heard him putting the kettle on in the kitchen.

'I'll get him there, don't worry.'

She was regretting her decision already.

'Look at him, anyone would think he'd just got out of prison!'

The men laughed.

They could see their friend's spotty behind pumping away at the small Asian girl they had purchased for him the night before. He had actually been released the previous day from Shepton Mallet, where he had spent the last six weeks. It was an open prison, and his friends had picked him up in a limo with his girlfriend Tracey and a large amount of alcohol in tow. Tracey had been worn out before they had even reached Dartford toll tunnel and he had dumped her at the Crossways Hotel, much to her chagrin. They had then made their way into London where he had shagged anything with a pulse. He was overdue for going home but not one of them had the guts to point that out to him. He was drunk, aggressive drunk, and no one wanted to start him off. Freddie Jackson was a handful, and as much as they loved him he was also an annoying fucker into the bargain.

He had just done six years of a nine-year sentence for firearms, attempted murder and a malicious wounding charge and he was proud of that fact. Inside he had mixed with what he saw as the cream of the underworld and he had come out of there thinking that he was now one of them.

The fact they were all doing in excess of fifteen years made no difference to Freddie Jackson. He was Sonny

Corleone in his mind. He was a man to be reckoned with.

Freddie Jackson had worshipped Sonny, had never understood how they could have killed his character off. He had been the business, far more menacing than that short-arsed runt Michael. Freddie saw himself as the Godfather of the Southeast. Righting wrongs, causing untold hag and making his fortune into the bargain.

No more fucking about for him. He was after the main prize these days and he was determined to get it.

He rolled off the sweating girl. She was pretty and her vacant face reassured him of the usefulness of women.

He glanced at his watch and sighed. If he didn't get his arse in gear Jackie would have his nuts. He smiled at the girl, then, jumping from the bed, he said heartily, 'Come on boys, chop chop, I have to see a man about a witness statement!'

Danny Baxter groaned inwardly but outwardly he looked thrilled at the prospect. He had forgotten how frenetic and dangerous life with Freddie Jackson could be.

Freddie's cousin Jimmy Jackson smiled with the men. He was a watered-down version of Freddie and wanted to be like him. He had visited his cousin religiously and Freddie had appreciated that fact. He liked the kid, he had heart. Plus he was only nine years younger than Freddie. They had a lot in common.

Today he would show Jimmy just what he was capable of.

Maggie Summers was fourteen but appeared eighteen. She had the look of her older sister but she was a tinier, sleeker version. She still had the wonderful skin of extreme youth and dainty white teeth that had not yet been tarred by years of smoking or neglect. Her blue eyes were big, wide-spaced and kind. Like her older sister she could take care of herself; unlike her older sister she didn't often have to. Yet..

At just five feet tall, she had long legs for her height and was completely unaware of how lovely she actually was. In her school uniform of black miniskirt, white shirt and navy-blue sweater she looked as if she was coming home from work instead of school, and that was the look she tried to create.

Lisa Dolan, a sometime friend and occasional enemy, said gaily, 'Your sister having a party tonight, then?'

Maggie nodded. 'I am just going to give her a hand. Want to come with me?'

Lisa grinned happily. 'Yeah!'

If she helped she was guaranteed an invite. They dropped into step beside one another. Lisa, a dark-haired girl with buck teeth, said quietly, 'Here, Maggie, according to Gina, Freddie Jackson got out *yesterday*. That can't be true, can it?'

Maggie sighed. Gina Davis was Tracey Davis's sister, which meant there might be a grain of truth in her claims. It also meant Jackie would go ballistic if she heard about it. Tracey had been seeing Freddie when he had been arrested, but she had had the sense to keep away from the trial. Maggie had assumed it had fizzled out, but it seemed she was wrong. Her Mum had gone on and on about it, hating the way her sister's husband humiliated her all the time. Lena had gone round after the girl herself and been assured it was well and truly over by Tracey's irate father. Tracey had only been fifteen at the time. In the last four years she had produced twin boys and Freddie couldn't get the blame for them as they were only eighteen months old. Truth be told, even Tracey had no idea who the father was, but she was Freddie Jackson's type, big, breathing and with a pair of breasts. Those, according to Lena, were all the criteria needed.

Maggie had a working knowledge of everything and everyone in her world thanks to her mother. Lena had the handle on everyone, and what she didn't know she had an uncanny knack of ferreting out. But she hadn't heard anything about Freddie getting out early till now.

'I hate that Gina, she's a liar and if my sister knew what she had said . . .'

Maggie left the sentence unfinished, getting her point across without too much detail. Lisa would not want to be cross-examined by Jackie, so hopefully she would keep that morsel of information to herself.

Lisa, paler now but forewarned, changed the subject quickly.

Leon Butcher was a small, tubby man with tobacco-stained teeth and a lager belly. He lived in a two-bedroomed council flat with his elderly mother and a collection of jetsam. He was an Uncle, in other words, and he lent small amounts on property, usually jewellery. Today he was looking at an eighteen-carat gold and diamond eternity ring. It was a beauty, first-grade diamonds, lovely setting. He smiled at the young girl in front of him who had obviously stolen it from a relative. She had the sunken eyes of the smack head and he said gently, 'A fifty, that's all.'

It was worth ten times that and she knew it.

He threw it on the grubby kitchen table and removed his eyeglass, then lit a cigarette and pulled on it deeply. He could wait. He had played this game many times before.

After an age the girl said quietly, 'OK.'

He went to the kitchen drawer and took out a wad of money, and as he turned back to face her he saw Freddie Jackson standing in the doorway.

'Hello, Leon.' Freddie grinned drunkenly. 'Is that money for me?'

The girl stood up unsteadily, sensing the atmosphere.

'Hand it over, that's my compensation.'

Leon passed it to him with shaking hands.

Freddie quickly counted off five twenties and gave them to the girl. 'That your ring, sweetheart?'

She nodded.

'Take it with you, love, and forget you were ever here, OK?' He smiled at her and his handsome face suddenly looked friendly, approachable.

She took the ring and left the flat as quickly as possible.

'On our own, eh, Leon?' He walked towards the smaller man menacingly.

'What do you want, Freddie?'

Jackson looked down at him for a few seconds before saying quietly, 'What do I want, Leon? I want you.'

As he nutted Leon, the man dropped to his knees. Then bringing back his leg Freddie kneed Leon in the face, sending his head crashing backwards into the melamine kitchen cabinets. Dropping sideways, Leon curled himself into a ball and took the kicking doled out quietly and stoically. Finally spent, Freddie looked down at the bloody mass before him and said, 'I dare you to press fucking charges, you grassing cunt. Now where's the tom?'

Leon was in agony and a swift kick to the groin had him yelping out, 'In the bedroom.'

Dragging the man up none too gently Freddie threw him across the room. 'Get it.'

He followed Leon into the small bedroom, watching as he pulled a wooden box with difficulty from under the bed.

Opening it, Freddie saw it was full to the brim with wads of money as well as a small fortune in jewellery. He picked up the box and put it under his arm.

'You cost me six years, Leon. You better move away soon because I will always be back, you hear me?'

Leon was still standing and Freddie had a sneaking admiration for him because of that. He had given him a good trouncing, the man would be pissing blood for weeks. But he had made his point.

Leon had only been a witness, through no fault of his own. Filth had made him testify, he was aware of that, but it still didn't lessen Leon's crime in his eyes. He should have gone and done his stir like a man, not served Freddie up as an alternative.

As he left the flat he was whistling. Not a bad day's work by anyone's standards.

Danny Baxter saw him walking back towards the limo with the box under his arm, and grinned as Freddie stopped to chat up a girl with a baby in a pushchair. On this estate there were plenty of girls like that, and they were Freddie's cup of tea inasmuch as they had a little flat and no real life, and if he bunged them a few quid they were eternally grateful.

'He never stops sniffing out strange, does he?'

Danny sighed. At nineteen, Freddie's cousin Jimmy had a lot to learn about Freddie Jackson. 'This ain't got nothing to do with being banged up, Freddie's always been like it. We used to call him "Ever Ready". If you could see some of the sights he's shagged!' Freddie got in the car and said loudly, 'I heard that, Danny boy. Like I told you, the ugly ones are the best – grateful, see.'

They all laughed.

'Let's get up the pub, eh?'

'Don't you think you should go home and see Jackie and the kids, Fred?'

Freddie Jackson laughed loudly at his young cousin's words.

'No, I fucking don't, Jimmy. Fuck me, soon that's all I'll be seeing, morning, noon and fucking night! To the pub, boy, and don't spare the horses!'

It was seven thirty and the Jackson house was filling up with people, the banners were all in place and the sandwiches and chicken legs were waiting to be consumed.

The whole place smelled of Rive Gauche, soap on a rope and coleslaw.

The kids were scrubbed and dressed up, as was Jackie, and there was still no sign of Freddie Jackson.

The ancient stereo was playing 'Use It Up And Wear It Out' by Odyssey and Maggie thought the song title was more than appropriate for her brother-in-law's homecoming.

Where was he, and more to the point where was Jimmy?

Maggie saw her mother roll her eyes in her father's direction and knew that Jackie had seen the gesture too. Jackie looked lovely in a powder-blue top with huge shoulder pads and a long black skirt, and even though both were a little too tight, she was elegant. Her hair was blow-dried around her face and she was wearing too much make-up as usual, but that had always been her style. The glitter on her eyelids made her look sexy, and she had beautiful eyes. If only she could understand just how good looking she could be.

She was also hammering the wine, which was not a good sign.

'Where the fuck is he?' Her dad's voice was loud and could be heard even above the music playing.

'Leave it, Joe.' Lena's voice was lower, trying to prevent a scene.

'You dragged me here, woman, so I have every right to ask where the fucking party boy is.'

'He's just got out of nick, he will be in the pub with his mates where you normally are after a stretch.'

'I always came home first, Lena, be fair.'

He was wrong-footed now and, knowing his wife's knack of causing a major war over a few badly chosen words, he retreated quickly as she knew he would. But he hated the way Jackson treated his eldest child. He used her, he had left her with three kids and enough debt to sink the *Titanic*, and she still treated him like he was something special. When would that stupid girl learn? He was a waster, a user, a fucking leech.

Jackie was bad enough on her own but with Freddie Jackson pressing all the wrong buttons she would be a nightmare. She didn't just love him, she tried to absorb him into her. Freddie was like a cancer eating away at his daughter and her jealousy knew no bounds where he was concerned.

Now it would all start once more, after six years of relative quiet, and he wasn't sure he could cope with it again.

Maddie Jackson was a small woman with greeny-blue eyes and a small cupid's bow mouth. Her slight frame belied a strength of character and a violent temper that even her large daughter-in-law was in awe of. Her only son was the apple of her eye and she would not have one word said against him by anyone. She had lied and perjured herself for him on many occasions from his school to the Old Bailey, and now her baby was coming home she could barely contain her excitement.

She glanced around the small council house and took in every detail. It wasn't her clean but in fairness to Jackie she tried her best. Not that she would ever tell her that of course. Renewing her drink she walked sedately back into the front room and, seeing her husband talking to a young girl, she sighed inwardly. He would never change. All the time he had a hole in his arse, as her mother used to say, and over the years she had seen the truth of that remark many times. He had fathered three outside children and slept with her sister and her best friend yet she still loved him, so who was the bigger fool?

Putting together a plate of food for her husband she walked over to him and saw with relief the girl take the opportunity to get away from him.

Freddie Jackson Senior took the food gratefully and then inspected the chicken leg. He took a large bite and said through the mouthful of food, 'He better get his arse in gear. I ain't hanging about all night for him.'

He didn't mean it, she knew that he was looking forward to seeing his boy. He was, after all, a mirror image of himself as a young man and who could resist that? Who could resist seeing themselves replicated in another human being? He loved his boy even while he was jealous of his youth. Freddie Senior had kept his charm, but drink and debauchery had quickly put paid to his handsome looks. Her son must have inherited one of her genes, though, because no matter what he did Freddie still looked good.

Maddie saw Jackie throw back another glass of wine in seconds and recognised the warning signs of her daughter-in-law's phenomenal temper. Jackie's face sank somehow, as if the life was draining from it, and her eyes became hooded. She looked as if she was on drugs and, knowing Jackie, she probably was.

Maddie watched the girl's mother pushing her towards the kitchen and trying to calm her down. At times like this she was sorry for Jackie, was reminded of herself as a young woman, not in looks but in the bewilderment at the treatment from a man who she adored.

A man who could not even come home to see his children, but had to spend the day with his friends as usual. Six years banged up and nothing had really changed.

The pub was packed, the music was thumping and everyone was treating Freddie to drinks. He was a Face now. He was twenty-eight years old, he had done a lump and he was also a different man to the one who had gone away all those years ago. He was regaling them with stories of people they had only ever heard about but who he assured them were his blood brothers now.

Jimmy was worried about how fast time was passing while his cousin looked like he had no intention of going home at any time. Let alone in time for his own party.

'Come on, Freddie, we got to get a move on. There's a big party at your house in your honour.' Jimmy's voice was high now, it was gone nine o'clock and he knew there would be murders. 'All the family will be there and your mum's dying to see you.'

He knew that mention of his mother would lessen Freddie's anger.

Freddie stared at the younger man for a few moments before hugging him tightly to him and kissing the top of his head. 'You are a fucking good kid, Jimmy me boy.'

Jimmy basked in his cousin's pleasure.

'You're the business, Freddie, everyone knows that.'

It was what he wanted to hear, needed to hear.

'Come on, guys, grab a few bottles, it's back home to the horror of family life for me.' Freddie squeezed a few choice behinds as they walked from the pub, pointing towards a particular girl every few seconds and smiling at them.

Jimmy saw Donny Baxter wink at him with respect, and understood for the first time ever what made his cousin enjoy his reputation so much. Little Jimmy was buzzing, but Little Jimmy was also a six-foot-two man with the want inside him now.

Freddie was home and all would be right with his world.

Maddie saw the girl making sheep's eyes at her husband once more. Time was she would have caused murders, but nowadays she was glad in some ways since it kept him from wearing her out on a nightly basis. She just wished he wouldn't chat them up in front of her, it was humiliating.

What was it that made these men so desirable?

The violence? The feeling of only being alive when you were around them? The danger of knowing they could be gone again in days, hours even?

And Freddie was the same, he was like the spit out of his father's mouth. That was another one of her mother's sayings.

As if Maddie's thoughts had conjured him up her son pulled up outside the house in a large white stretch limousine. As he fell out of the door she could hear his raucous laughter. He was drunk. Happy drunk, but drunk all the same.

Still, she consoled herself, and justified her son's abandonment of his family by thinking no one could blame him. Banged up all that time, he would need to let off steam.

Kimberley, Dianna and Roxanna watched as their father strode up the overgrown garden path and, walking straight past them without even a glance in their direction, burst into the house.

Kimberley, the eldest and therefore old enough to remember the fighting and the arguing, said little. The two younger ones had eyes rounded with excitement. The man their mother harked on about constantly had just breezed past them smelling of brandy, cigarettes and unwashed clothes.

A small retinue of friends followed him sheepishly into the house. Unlike Freddie, they were aware that they should have been here hours ago.

Jimmy's father, James, watched carefully – he, like his wife, Deirdre, had never rated Freddie, and their son's worship of him worried them.

Jackie heard her husband's booming voice and ran from the kitchen on her high heels, her face a bright red mass of anger and also excitement.

'Freddie!' She jumped into his arms and he held her off the ground with difficulty, hugging her tightly before putting her down roughly.

'Fuck me, girl, you weigh a fucking ton! But don't worry, I'll soon shag you back into shape.'

He looked around him happily, proud of his quip, thinking he was the man. After all he was the reason they were all there in the first place.

Jackie's family stared at him in disbelief as Jackie herself beamed with positive happiness.

The King was home, so God help the Queen.

Book One

Woman, a pleasing but short-lived flower,
Too soft for business and too weak for power:
A wife in bondage, or neglected maid:
Despised, if ugly; if she's fair, betrayed.

– Mary Leapor, 1722–1746
'An Essay on Woman'

Do not adultery commit;
Advantage rarely comes of it.

– Arthur Hugh Clough, 1819–1861
'The Latest Decalogue'

Chapter One

Jackie awoke to the electric pain of a hangover, her eyes felt as if they had been sprayed with hot sand and her tongue was stuck to the roof of her mouth.

In seconds she realised her husband was not beside her.

Even after only one night she was aware of him. After he had been sentenced it had taken her a long time to accept that he would not be coming home to her. Heavily pregnant, she had felt his absence acutely. It had been hard losing him like that, but she had waited. Waited and longed for him. While he was in prison all she had thought about was her man, and not a day had passed when she had not missed him and felt almost a physical pain.

But now he was out he didn't even recognise his home any more.

Sighing, she was about to drag herself from the bed when she heard the unmistakable sound of Roxanna's laugh. It was like a fog horn, loud like her mother's but full of infectious humour like her maternal grandmother's.

She could hear her husband's own loud laugh following her daughter's and smiled to herself. The girls were older now, he might find them a bit more interesting. He had never really got to know them before, and she hoped that now he was finally home they could all start being a proper family.

Kimberley came into the small bedroom with a mug of hot sweet tea. At nine years old she was a ringer for her father: dark haired and blue eyed, she had his natural arrogance.

'All right, love?'

It was a question and they both knew it.

'To hear him going on you'd think he'd been at a five-star hotel, not inside one of Her Majesty's holiday camps.'

Jackie knew this was her own dad talking, but then Joseph had been more of a father to the girls than Freddie so what could she expect?

'Don't start, Kim, it's been hard for him away from us.'

'Been hard for us and all, Mum, don't forget that, will you? To hear him talk you'd think he'd had the time of his life.'

At nine she had more wisdom than someone ten times her age, and this was what made her mother angry with her. Kimberley never knew when to leave things alone.

'Well, he's home now, ain't he.'

Kimberley sniffed loudly in disdain as she said, 'And don't we all know it.'

Freddie was surprised at how much he was enjoying his kids, they were good-looking, bright girls. He'd have liked sons though, and after last night's gymnastics he had a feeling he might get one before the year was out. One thing he would give Jackie – she was as up for it as he was. A bit of how's your father was all she needed to keep her temper at bay. A few compliments, a couple of touch ups and she was his.

Once he had her nice and pregnant he could start to take the piss properly. She was a blinder in some ways, old

Jackie. No matter what he did she forgave him. She understood him, and he loved her for that much at least.

But even he saw the need to keep close by for a few days. He was well aware of what happened when you were banged up. People sniffed round, wanted a bit of what you had. As far as he could see Jackie had been a diamond, but you never knew, she liked the old one-eyed snake, so he would keep out a wary eye.

If she had done the dirty on him she was a dead woman.

'Did you learn to cook in nick, Dad?'

Roxanna said this very seriously and he answered her in the same vein, the eggs and bacon in the pan sizzling away.

'No, sweetheart, Daddy could already cook. Why?'

Roxanna said, with six-year-old sweetness, 'I thought we could send Mummy, you cook nicer than her any day.'

Freddie laughed loudly. This youngest child of his was what was known as a case.

He glanced around the kitchen. It was shabby but clean enough, he supposed. He would have to sort out a few quid though, get the place smartened up. He needed a home that befitted his new status in life.

Some of the blokes he had been banged up with had country houses! Acres of land, swimming pools, and what did he have? A poxy semi-detached house on a council estate. Their kids went to private schools, mixed with the best. What was it his old mate Ozzy used to say? 'It's not what you know but who you know.' How fucking true that was.

He had watched them in nick, and what a fucking education it had been. They all had nice fit birds visiting them, all dressed like fucking footballers' wives, with ready smiles and diamond rings. He had been gutted at times when Jackie had turned up in her jeans and her fucking sheepskin coat. But in fairness she couldn't afford any decent clobber, she had been given no compensation.

The thought of compensation darkened his brow.

She deserved it, she should have been worth a few quid, not fucking scrimping on the social.

He would sort that all out this afternoon.

Lena Summers opened her front door and roared, 'You knock like the filth, young Jimmy.'

Smiling, Jimmy walked into the kitchen, nodded to Joseph and, taking a mug from the draining board, poured himself a cup of tea.

'She ready?'

Lena laughed. 'Is she ever? Only just jumped in the shower.'

She was buttering toast and she automatically handed him a piece. He crunched on it happily.

'How did it all end last night then?'

He shrugged, looking too big for the small kitchen. His loyalty to his cousin knew no bounds, but he was also loath to upset Lena or Joseph.

'It was a good night, Mrs Summers, he was just a bit excited, that's all. He's been banged up for yonks . . .'

'Should have fucking kept him there if you ask me.'

Lena turned on her husband. 'Well, no one asked you, did they?'

She turned back to Jimmy. 'Was Jackie all right? I mean it didn't all end up in a fight?'

He smiled then. 'It was fine, honestly. When I left they were slow dancing together, with little Roxanna asleep on Freddie's shoulder.'

Lena smiled, her fears allayed for a few days. The fighting would come, they all knew that. But she wanted her daughter to have at least a few days of happiness first.

If ever two people should keep away from each other it was Freddie and Jackie Jackson. They had courted from school and Lena had loathed him on sight. Jackie had always been a handful at the best of times, but it was as if he had possessed a hold over her from day one. She was obsessed with Freddie and at first the feeling had been mutual. It was only when the kids had come thick and fast that he had started his gallivanting. And like her mother before her Jackie had hunted down and blamed the women. If only Lena could get her to understand that without the men these women wouldn't exist. But she knew herself how much it hurt, how it ruined your self-esteem. How it coloured the whole of your life until you either sank or you swam with it.

Her daughter would never learn to swim, God help her. She would sink a little bit more each time, the bitterness eating her up alongside the jealousy.

Maggie breezed into the kitchen all smiles and Rimmel make-up.

Joe Summers said indulgently, 'Your lift's been waiting ages.'

She grinned. 'My lift always waits ages.'

She grabbed a piece of toast and a mug of coffee and, kissing her mother and father, she walked out of the house quickly. She always left the mug in his car and he returned it when he could. They were nice kids.

Lena and Joe watched as the big, hulking boy followed her as always.

'He's a good kid, Joe.'

Joe sniffed loudly. 'She could look further and fare worse. He dotes on her. And she has got the right idea, that one, keeps him on his toes.'

'As long as he ain't got her on her back.'

Joe eyed his wife scornfully. 'Give her a bit of credit, will you? She's too shrewd, I'm telling you.'

Lena sat at the small pine table and said sadly, 'She's so young, Joe. She's only fourteen.'

'So were you, Lena.'

'And look what happened to me.'

'You didn't do too bad, you got me didn't you?

She laughed disdainfully. 'I won the pools me, did I?'

They laughed together as Lena wondered what he would do if he knew his young daughter was on the pill.

Men, they never saw what was in front of their faces.

Micky Daltry was happy today. His wife was in a good mood because he had bought her a new coat and shoes. His kids were all at her mother's house, and they were going out for a nice slap-up meal to celebrate their wedding anniversary.

She was a good one, his Sheila, and he was sensible enough to know that. She kept the place clean as a pin and the kids were well dressed and well behaved. They all had her looks, thank God, and his nous. A winning combination.

'Come on, Sheila, the cab will be here in a minute.'

She was laughing as she walked down the stairs of their semi-detached house. It was decorated in magnolia matt paint and it was her pride and joy. As was the shag-pile cream carpet that drove the kids mad because they had to take their shoes off at the door. Unlike their mates who wore their shoes in the house until they were put to bed. Then and only then did they take their shoes off along with their coats.

Even their father followed the rule, and that was how they knew they had to.

Sheila Daltry had long blond hair, a slim figure, even

after three children, and a nice nature. She had a quiet, sunny personality, the complete opposite of her husband. Micky was noisy, funny and secretive. He wolf-whistled her and she was thrilled.

A banging on their front door came then and Micky opened it with a flourish.

Freddie Jackson was standing there with a smile on his face and a baseball bat in his hands.

Micky's instinct was to try to shut the door, but after a few seconds' struggle, Freddie forced it open without any trouble.

Inside, he shut the door gently.

Sheila looked at her husband and shook her head sadly. Micky was terrified and could only hold his hands out in supplication towards her. Then he turned slowly towards Freddie, who said brightly, 'I take it you won't be offering me a cup of tea, then?'

Maggie was happy, really happy. She was in love, and it was obvious to all her friends.

Already the story of Freddie's party was doing the rounds of their small world, and Freddie was now like a conquering hero. The stretch limo alone was talked about for ages by the girls and the decadence of it was discussed in serious tones. It was their dream to be like movie stars or pop queens.

'Did you get a ride in it, Mags?'

This from Helen Dunne, friend or enemy depending on who was being slaughtered by the girls at any given time.

Maggie shook her head. 'Nah, but I could have if I wanted to. Jimmy was in it all day, he loved it. Said it had drink in it and everything.' She was lying, but they all chose to believe her.

'That right he beat up Willy Planter?'

Maggie nodded once more. 'Willy was out of order, fucking drunk!'

She toked deep on her Benson & Hedges cigarette. 'Jackie looked beautiful, you should have seen her.'

Maggie's voice was wistful. She loved her sister so much, looked up to her, depended on her.

All the girls sighed.

'That Freddie is a bit of all right though.'

This from Carlotta O'Connor, a well-developed girl who already had a reputation for drink, cannabis and older boyfriends.

They all laughed, scandalised, except Maggie, who said dryly, 'I'd keep that to meself if I was you. My sister is funny where he's concerned.'

It was a warning and everyone knew it. Maggie looked out for anything about her sister she saw as a slight. Jackie had her faults, but she was her sister and she loved her.

Carlotta just smiled, she had her creds, she wasn't scared of anyone. Though she would rather not come up against Jackie Jackson.

'Jimmy seems to be a permanent fixture.'

Maggie grinned. 'He had better be.'

They knew what that meant and started ragging her. She took it well but deep inside she was worried. Now that she had put out she was frightened he would aim her out of it. But she had been unable to resist him any longer, she wanted him as much as he wanted her.

'You all right, Mags?'

She smiled happily. 'Never better.'

Micky was staring at Freddie Jackson in abject terror. Sheila was still standing on the stairs watching the scene before her with resignation.

The cab driver bibbed his horn and Freddie said to Sheila, 'Get that cab, sweetheart, and go to your mum's because me and your old man are going to have a few words.'

She nodded and both men watched as she slipped from the house.

'Nice drum, Micky, you wanna see my house. Right shit hole it is with no money coming in, you treacherous bastard.'

The baseball bat came down on Micky's shoulder in an instant and the blinding pain shot through him, causing him to scream. He dropped heavily to his knees.

'Look, Freddie—'

'Shut your fucking lying thieving mouth, you ponce. My old woman was scrimping and fucking scratching while you and your kids were living the life of luxury on my fucking dough. Do you think I am a cunt, then?'

Micky was crying now and this was annoying Freddie Jackson more than the original affront. Poking his finger in the man's face he raged, 'You cry, you cunt. I done a lump and I kept you right out of it because I am a loyal fucking person. Whereas you, you never even gave my family a drink, no comp, no nothing. I went away for conspiracy to rob and firearms, you sat on your fucking ring with all the dough! You had to have expected me at some point, surely? I want me comp.'

Micky was holding his shoulder painfully as he said through his tears, 'I didn't have nothing to give them, I was only just keeping meself . . .'

Freddie dragged him through to the front room. It was painted in pale greens and creams and had a leather corner unit, nice colour TV and a decent sound system. He threw his one-time friend on to the sofa and systematically smashed the place up with the baseball bat, all the time shouting and poking the baseball bat towards the cowering man.

'Any money you scavenged should have gone to *my* kids, I kept you out of fucking clink, you two-faced wanker, and you *never* even saw them all right for Christmas! I lost my *fucking liberty* and you sat here with your fucking offspring and never thought about my poor Jackie struggling to make ends meet, did ya?'

He attacked the man again with the bat, beating him with his considerable strength. The blood was all over the cream leather sofa and, taking a few seconds' rest, he saw that he had opened up Micky's head. The spray went up the velour curtains and on to the Artexed ceiling.

He took the large bay window out with one forceful blow. He could see the neighbours on their steps listening to the latest palaver, but most of them had already wished him well so he had no fear of the police.

He was gratified to have caused serious damage. He wanted this event to hit the pavement, he wanted people to know that he was back. Back on the street and more than capable of settling scores, old or new. He was going to get involved in some serious skulduggery and he was not going to settle for anything less than complete domination of their world. He had learned a lot in nick, and he was going to utilise that knowledge and his new contacts to their full potential.

Micky had taken the piss big time over the years and Freddie had to stop that now, show him that he was not a man to be walked over.

They had been on their way to a meet with some friends, and the boot had been full of guns. Micky had jumped out of the car to buy a pack of Rothmans when the filth had given Freddie a tug. He had fought them, as was expected, and he had denied any knowledge of Micky

Daltry being with him. Freddie had got the mandatory nine years for the firearms charge and he had kept his head down and his arse up, as was also expected. But Micky should have looked out for his family. Micky had been given a lucky escape and Freddie had not resented that. Why would he? Better only one of them had a capture, and unfortunately it had been him this time. Such was life, an occupational hazard for them.

But Micky had mugged him off. He had not even attempted to do him any favours, didn't even try to get him bail, nothing. Freddie had been a kid then and he had not known any better.

Now though, he more than knew the score.

After fighting anyone, screw or con, who he felt had not given him his due, he had garnered a reputation as a hard nut. He had finally been shipped to the SSB unit in Parkhurst as a double A grade, where he had mixed with the cream of the criminal underworld.

It was a man called Ozzy, a serious career criminal, and dangerous block Daddy who, realising Freddie's potential, had taken him under his wing and shown him not only how to do a lump with dignity, but also how to utilise his strong points.

Ozzy had taught him well, and Freddie had been a willing pupil.

Now he was on the out, he would work for Ozzy, dealing a bit of puff, or debt collecting. He'd work for the Clancys by default, but they were all Ozzy's scams. Freddie was determined to better himself and his standing in life. He had done his lump without any song and dance, and Ozzy had picked him out because of that.

Micky Daltry, on the other hand, had forgotten about him. Freddie had ceased to exist and Micky had believed that he was still safely banged up. Six years seemed such a long time away for the people who were on the outside, and it passed, slowly, painfully and more often than not with the aid of narcotics on the inside.

But, as Micky was finding out, time eventually passed.

Now it was time to settle old scores, iron out any differences. In short make this man understand the error of his ways.

Micky had to understand that no one, but no one, walked over Freddie Jackson.

Micky Daltry, though, would never walk again.

Lena was watching Jackie as she prepared the steak and home-made chips for her husband's dinner. In fairness, she begrudgingly admitted that he had scratched around for a couple of grand for her. He was at least trying.

As Jackie sliced mushrooms and tomatoes Lena saw the happiness on her daughter's face and felt an urge to hug her. She didn't though, she knew she was not a tactile woman.

Jackie poured them both another glass of wine and chattered on, oblivious to the fact that her mother was all but ignoring her conversation.

'He's getting us new furniture, Mum. The new TV comes tomorrow, and the bedroom suites for the girls – oh, Mum, they are gorgeous.'

The excitement in her voice pierced through her mother's reverie.

'Bedroom suites and all, eh?'

Jackie nodded. 'Even Kimberley's happy now, and you know what a stroppy whore she can be!'

They both laughed.

'His mum is going to baby-sit tonight and we're going to the pub for a few drinks. I can't wait, Mum. I am so pleased he's home.'

She stopped slicing and looked into her mother's eyes. Then she said quietly, seriously, 'I missed him, you know. When he ain't around I feel as if a part of me is missing.' She had tears in her eyes as she said it, and without thinking Lena pulled her daughter into her arms.

'He's home now, love.'

Unaccustomed to her mother hugging her, Jackie made the most of it and cried on Lena's shoulder. She smelled of Blue Grass perfume and cigarettes. It was a comforting, homely smell and she was enjoying the sensation of being loved when a voice said loudly, 'Fucking hell, what's all this, then? The Waltons?'

Freddie pulled Jackie roughly from her mother's arms and seeing her tears he said seriously, 'Here, what's up with you? What you crying for, babe?'

He shouted at his mother-in-law. 'What you fucking done to her?'

Lena sighed heavily as her daughter said through her sobs, 'She ain't done nothing. I was upset because I am so glad to have you home again, that's all, because I had missed you so much, waited so long and now you are here . . .'

Freddie looked into his wife's face and seeing the love there, alongside the need and the want so strong she was capable of killing for him. He felt suddenly as if he was inside again and the walls were coming in on him.

He hugged her to him and saw his mother-in-law walk from the room without a backward glance. 'I am home, Jackie. Everything is fine now, don't keep on about it.'

He wiped out in a few words the years she had been alone with the children, her loneliness and her daily struggle. He was telling her that he had had enough of hearing about it, and she knew better than to harp on, so she just enjoyed the feel of his arms around her.

Dianna broke the tension by walking in the kitchen and saying loudly in a mock French accent, '*Ooh là là!*'

Jackie watched as her husband picked up his daughter and kissed her. Dianna was already his favourite, and she could twist her father round her little finger. And all the time she watched the scene, Jackie had to swallow down her jealousy of a seven-year-old child. Her own flesh and blood.

She pulled the child from his arms and, giving her a playful slap on the behind she said gaily, 'Get back in there with your sisters. I am trying to cook a dinner here.'

As her daughter scampered merrily out of the kitchen, she turned back towards her husband but he was already rummaging in the ancient fridge for a beer. The moment was gone and she knew it.

She went back to her cooking, telling herself not to be so stupid, Dianna was a nice child and if she kept him home then that could only be a good thing.

Maggie and Jimmy were in the pub when Jackie arrived. They had got there early and saved a table by the bar. It was already noisy and smoky. Maggie was drinking Southern Comfort and lemonade and even after three she didn't feel drunk. She was already a seasoned drinker, as were most of her friends.

Jimmy was, as always, looking at her. His dark hair and blue eyes were a winning combination as far as she was concerned and she smiled shyly back at him. As her mother said, he looked at her as if she was a great big present he was waiting to unwrap. Then she would remark with her acerbic wit, 'And make sure he don't unwrap too much, girl.'

Maggie would laugh, but now she had been well and truly unwrapped and the fear of losing him was acute. He seemed more enamoured of her, though, and that was allaying her fears for the moment.

She saw her sister walk in and waved her over.

'Where's Freddie?'

Pulling off her jacket Jackie said loudly, 'Give me a fucking chance to sit down will you!'

Maggie's eyes widened. This was Jackie all over. She talked to people as if they were dirt and, luckily for her, people swallowed because of Freddie and his reputation. But Maggie felt it more acutely because this was her big sister and she adored her.

Jimmy's brow was darkening and so Maggie said cheerfully, 'Who's rattled your cage?' She was skating on thin ice because Jackie was capable of turning on her, but she didn't know how else to diffuse the situation.

Looking down into her sister's eyes Jackie felt bad, but the familiar jealousy was once more upon her. Maggie's perfect skin, white teeth and neat figure had bothered her lately. She envied her sister her looks and her youth, she envied her the fact she had no kids and no ties. Freddie coming home had awakened her old anxieties. She knew he would cheat on her and she knew she would be once more plagued with self-doubt and self-loathing and, worst of all, she knew she would eventually accept his philandering because if she didn't he would leave her.

Not the most perfect of outlooks for any marriage.

'Sorry, darlin'. Get me a drink, would you?'

Jackie sat down and, as Maggie and Jimmy knew she would, stared at the door waiting for her husband.

Jimmy noticed that her hands were shaking. As she lit her cigarette he was surprised at how pronounced it was, but then he knew she was pilled up to the eyebrows most days, from slimming pills, Dexedrine to a few Mandrax.

That was when she wasn't shovelling Valium and Norovail down her throat.

She was the proverbial accident waiting to happen.

He slipped from his seat and went outside to the car park. It was already dark and he could just make out the figure of Freddie in the corner of the car park, leaning down to the door of a dark green Granada. He walked over slowly, but he could hear what was being said.

'Ozzy said you could put me right.' The subservience in Freddie's voice was so shocking Jimmy stopped in his tracks.

'You sure you're up for this, Freddie? This is the big time, mate.' The man's voice was warm, friendly with an underlying threat running through it.

'Too right I am ready. I know the score, I can hold up my end.'

'Relax for fuck's sake, it's only a bit of puff.'

The man was smiling, Jimmy could hear it in his voice.

He toked on his cigarette before saying, 'I'll be in touch.'

Jimmy could see Freddie squaring up, could almost feel the excitement running through his veins. 'Thank you, Mr Clancy, I really appreciate it.'

'One last thing, Freddie?' The man pointed to Jimmy and said, 'That nosy little fucker anything to do with you?'

Freddie turned and motioned for Jimmy to come over to him, and as Jimmy got to him he grabbed him in a bear hug. 'This is me little cousin, Mr Clancy, Jimmy Jackson.'

'Little? Fuck me, what did they grow you lot in, horse shit?'

They all laughed.

The driver stuck his hand out and Jimmy shook it nervously. This was Siddy Clancy, and until now he had only ever heard the name. It was the Southeast equivalent of meeting a Hollywood star.

'I'll be in touch, OK?'

Freddie nodded once more and the car pulled away sharply, wheel-spinning out of the car park and nearly causing an accident as it barrelled down Dagenham Heathway towards the A13.

Freddie was puffed up like a peacock. Grinning, he grabbed Jimmy in an arm lock and started singing, 'We're in the money.'

Jimmy was caught up in his enthusiasm, and sang along.

'Fucking hell, Fred, Siddy Clancy. What a turn up!'

Freddie was serious suddenly.

'He's a *cunt*, and I am the man who is going to fuck him up.'

Jimmy wasn't sure he had heard right, Siddy Clancy was a bad man, a dangerous fuck. No one in their right mind would try to have him over, but he kept that pearl of wisdom to himself.

Freddie put a finger to his lip as he said, 'You keep this close to your chest right, and you can work with him alongside me. I'll show you the ropes, son. OK?'

Jimmy nodded as he was expected to. But he felt cold all of a sudden. Those were heavy-duty people and they were not really in his class, but he kept his own counsel.

Inside the warmth of the pub Freddie made his way straight over to a crowd of girls who were drinking at the bar.

Maggie saw her sister's face and sighed.

Jimmy slipped into the booth beside Maggie and, putting his arm around her, kissed the top of her head. Maggie instinctively snuggled in closer to him and watching the little tableau Jackie felt the rage that was always bubbling away inside her well up.

Her eyes were cutting through her husband's clothes and practically stabbing him in the back. He was aware of her watching but he didn't come back to sit with her until he had flirted enough to make the girls uneasy and his wife white faced and drawn.

Chapter Two

Steel Pulse was loud in the quiet of the room, cannabis smoke hung heavy on the air and the three men inside watched each other warily.

Outside the window were the usual summer sounds of kids laughing, traffic moving, and every now and then a car stereo booming its way down the street.

'What is it with him, eh?'

Freddie was shaking his head in disbelief while Jimmy was standing beside him, quietly watching the proceedings.

The black man with relaxed hair and gapped front teeth smiled wider. Jimmy knew that the man was dangerous. He looked friendly, affable even, but there was a steely glint in his eyes, and the unmistakable shape of a machete under his long leather coat. He also had a posse of mates outside the door of his house in South London.

Glenford Prentiss had a large spliff in his hand and he toked on it deeply before saying, in a gruff, smoke-filled voice that intermingled with his heavy coughing, 'It was shit, Freddie, that's the long and the short of it, man, nothing to wipe down. I sold it and you got your money. My boy made a serious fuck-up when he accepted it. I'm just saying in future I do the deals from now on.'

His thick Jamaican accent was interrupted as he tried to clear his throat. He was stoned but still lucid.

Freddie looked at the man before him. He was actually a nice geezer, he liked him, and he was absolutely right. Freddie had weighed Glenford off with some right shit the week before, and now he was learning a lesson.

Freddie prided himself on his ability to learn lessons, learn who could be had over, find out who might put up a bit of resistance. As he was Ozzy's front man he had to watch his step, mind his manners. Ozzy expected him to *cream* something off, not *rip* people off. There was a fine line and he knew that he had crossed it.

He had no choice but to hold his hand up, wipe his mouth and make the best of it.

He grinned, that white-toothed grin that crinkled up the corners of his eyes and made him look for all the world like someone's favourite son.

That grin belied the dangerous personality of its bearer and Glenford Prentiss knew that better than anyone. He had had his say, he was willing to fight his end, but he had a feeling he wouldn't have to. Why shoot the messenger boy? For all Freddie Jackson's hard-nosed demeanour he was only Siddy's puppet.

And Ozzy pulled all their strings.

Everyone knew that.

'It won't happen again.'

Glenford grinned. 'I know that, man.' He embraced Freddie then, laughing that infectious laugh he had. He slipped him a brown envelope stuffed with money, and Freddie didn't count it, he knew it wouldn't be light.

As Freddie pocketed the money Glenford said to him quietly, 'You got to try, man, I know that. I would have done the same myself.'

He passed the joint to Freddie who toked on it deeply,

holding it in his lungs for a few seconds before he slowly exhaled it. Then looking at the joint he said, 'Now that is good grass.'

Glenford grinned. 'Me never smoke what me sell, boy. Especially when it was bought from white boys.'

They all laughed then and Jimmy felt the tension depart the room. He finally exhaled his own breath then. The blacks worried him, but only because they were so unpredictable. He liked Glenford though and he had said the week before that Freddie should only unload the shittier grass on the skinheads who never knew the difference.

In the car a few minutes later Jimmy said as much to him again.

'That was a close one, Freddie. I mean, like I said last week, they know their puff.'

Freddie stopped the car. Turning in the driver's seat he looked into Jimmy's face and said sternly, 'Don't you ever fucking lecture me again, right? We had a touch last week and that's the end of it.'

Jimmy nodded furiously. 'I know that, Freddie. I was just saying—'

'Shut it.'

Freddie was staring into his eyes and the venom was there for anyone to see. Jimmy could feel the menace and he swallowed down the retort he was longing to give.

He was nearly twenty years old and he was a player, and it was getting harder and harder to keep his anger on a leash. Freddie treated him like the hired help and it rankled. He could hold his own with anyone and he wanted the respect that should have afforded him.

Freddie slammed his fist on the steering wheel in frustration. 'I'm sorry, Jim, but look at me, I am still selling shite for Clancy and the time has come to put him wise, whatever Ozzy might think. He is lumped up for the fucking duration and I ain't spending the rest of my life as one of his heavies.'

He started the car up again. 'And I don't need you reminding me, all right?' He smiled then, a sad little smile. 'Let's go and get a drink, eh? I have a little bird on the go in Ilford, you can drop me there and take the car, OK?'

He turned on the cassette player and the sounds of Phil Collins filled the cramped space between them.

Jimmy sighed inwardly. Freddie hadn't been home for days and he knew it was bringing untold aggravation for everyone concerned, except of course, for the man who caused all the upset.

In the last six months he had caused murders with Jackie, and while everyone else suffered, Freddie just did his own thing.

As Maggie's dad always said, Freddie Jackson would never change all the time women had tits.

'Stick the kids in the bath for me, would you?'

Maggie nodded, and, going upstairs, she started to run the bath, putting in a hefty dollop of Matey so the girls would have something to play with.

Once the girls were settled in there she washed their hair quickly and then left them playing with their toys.

In the front room she saw Jackie had opened another bottle of Liebfraumilch.

'Where the fuck is he? For all I know he's banged up.'

Lena, who was in the kitchen making sure her daughter had food in the fridge to feed her children, said loudly and sarcastically, 'They would have informed you by now.'

Maggie could have lamped her mother for her answer. While Jackie could convince herself Freddie was banged up she was, if not happy, then at least reassured that her errant husband wasn't trumping the nearest female he could lay his grubby hands on.

Jackie closed her eyes in distress. 'He's with a bird, ain't he?'

Maggie sat beside her on the sofa and said gently, 'You don't know that, Jackie. Calm yourself down, those kids can feel something's up.' She lit her a cigarette and placed it in her hand, taking the wine glass from her at the same time. 'This ain't going to do you any good, is it?'

Jackie sniffed, the tears near once more. 'It helps me sleep.'

Maggie lit a cigarette for herself. Seeing her sister like this drove her mad. Jackie was so strong in every way, but Freddie reduced her to nothing. Lena came in with two more wine glasses. She poured them quickly and, sipping hers daintily, she sat on the chair and said seriously, 'Sling him out, love, he's no good for you.'

Maggie could have screamed now. Her mother was like a cracked record and even though she spoke the truth it only served to make Jackie even more upset.

'Leave it out, Mum, can't you see she's upset enough as it is?'

She was staring at her mother trying to tell her to let it go. Lena shrugged and sipped at her wine then started once more in a friendly conversational tone.

'He's a fucking piece of shit. Your father was the same, he would track down a bit of strange like a bleeding bloodhound, him. Fights I had over that fat git . . .'

She was smiling now. 'Here, do you two remember that neighbour in Silvertown? What was her name?'

Jackie laughed suddenly. 'Maggie was too small to remember that one, Mum. Oh, your face!'

They laughed together and the sound was happy,

friendly, they were allies now. All Jackie's hurt was forgotten at a funny memory.

'What happened?' Maggie was all ears now, interested in one of the family stories, stories that always involved her father, or her sister's husband and a woman, or series of women. But the tales were told in a funny way, they always saw the humour of their situation and they could make you laugh out loud.

'I heard off me sister Junie that he was trumping a blond-haired woman, she said she was a neighbour. So I'm looking out the window trying to catch the bastard and I see him and this blond bird who'd just moved in our flats, see. I opens the window and he shouts out to this sort, "I'll be over in a minute."'

Lena swigged at her wine, her voice as always getting higher and higher and her hands waving the cigarette and the wine glass around dangerously as she got into her story.

'Anyway, I went down the stairs of those flats like a bullet out of a gun. I go haring over to her place and I really fucking mullered her. Her old man came out and dragged me off, Jackie was giving him verbals, your father was doing his crust. I had handfuls of that poor whore's hair, there was claret all over the pavement . . . The neighbours were all out watching.'

They were laughing together now.

'So what happened?' Maggie was grinning at the way her mother and sister were roaring with laughter.

Then, wiping her eyes, Lena said, 'Well, it weren't her, was it.'

Maggie's eyes were stretched to their utmost. 'You're joking.'

They cracked up.

'Straight up, your father had borrowed a hammer

off the woman's husband a couple of days before and they wanted it back. I could have fucking died on the spot.'

Jackie polished off her wine in two gulps and rubbed the tears from her cheeks with her fingers, laughing her head off.

'Oh, that was funny, Mum.'

Lena nodded then she said quietly, seriously, 'It weren't really. We make it funny, but it was terrible. The poor cow was battered like a Friday night cod. I see her up the Bingo sometimes, and I still feel bad about it. I battered the fuck out of her in front of her kids and she was a nice woman. Might have been a good mate even, you never know.'

Maggie could hear the sorrow in her mother's voice and felt a sudden urge to cry for the wasted years she had spent chasing a man who didn't want to be chased. Waiting for a man who had no intention of coming home. Jackie was her mother's daughter all right.

Then Lena said flatly, her voice husky from too many cigarettes and late nights, 'You'll learn, Jackie, just like I did, love, they ain't worth it. When you get to my age they only stay home because no one else wants them. If I had a pound for every time I followed him, fought over him, argued and screamed over him, I would be a rich woman. I dragged you kids all over the country visiting him when he was banged up and he never appreciated it, not really.'

She swallowed down her wine.

'My mum used to say to me, don't assume because you want him everyone else does. I wish I had listened to her because she was right.'

Jackie stood up unsteadily and walked out of the room.

Lena sighed then. 'You'll have to stay with her till

he deigns to come home. Who knows what she's capable of.'

Maggie nodded sadly. 'Do you regret marrying me dad then, Mum, really?'

Lena smiled and her washed-out good looks were evident in the kindly light of an evening drawing to a close.

'Every fucking day, sweetheart, every day of my life.'

At first Maggie thought that she was dreaming, and putting up her arms protectively she tried to push the offending hands away.

They were still there. Opening her eyes she saw in the dimness her brother-in-law Freddie Jackson trying to lift up the nightie she was wearing, all the time kissing her neck and shoulders. Realisation hit her then and she sat bolt upright on the sofa, the fear apparent on her face.

'Stop it.'

She was whispering, even in her fright she was aware that her sister would rip her head off, would blame her if she saw this sight.

Freddie gave his usual lazy smile. He had Jackie where he wanted her and they both knew it. He was trying to force Maggie back into the cushions once more, smothering her with his mouth, the wet stickiness of him making the girl want to heave. He smelled of beer, cannabis and sweat. He had been on the missing list for a few days and she was staying over with her sister to try to keep her company and, more importantly, to keep her calm. Now here was the man of the hour trying it on with his wife's little sister, and the worst of it was that Jackie would never believe her husband capable of anything so low. Even though low behaviour was normal behaviour to him, Maggie knew the blame would be put squarely on her.

She was pushing him away more aggressively now.

'Fuck off, Freddie.'

He was digging his fingers into the flesh on the top of her arms and she felt tears stinging her eyes. The fear was enveloping her now, fear of him and fear of her sister mingling. She punched him in the chest as hard as she could.

'Will you fuck off.'

He still hadn't spoken. But now as she writhed in his arms he looked down at her and she saw he was determined.

'Shut the fuck up, you stupid little bitch, do you want fatty down on top of us?'

Somewhere in his drink- and drug-addled brain he knew that what he was doing was wrong, but he had been after this particular piece for a while. She wouldn't even accept a lift home from him any more, preferring to get the bus. She knew her sister had her suspicions but could prove nothing. As always, everyone involved with Jackie saved her feelings, yet she walked over people at the drop of a hat and expected total loyalty even though she didn't know the meaning of the word.

The only person Jackie was loyal to was this drunken beast who, at this moment, was trying to shove a heavy knee between her slim thighs.

It was the baby Rox's voice that seemed to break into his head like the blow of an axe.

'Auntie Mags?'

Maggie saw the little girl in the doorway and, feeling Freddie's grip loosen, took the opportunity to slide from beneath him on to the shag-pile carpeted floor.

'Come here, sweetheart. Do you want a drink, lovie?'

She scrambled to her feet and then, picking the child up, she walked quickly into the kitchen. Her heart was still beating a tattoo in her chest and the revulsion was still in her mouth. It tasted tannic, like tin, or lead. She wanted to clean her teeth and bath herself. Wash the feel of him off her.

She sat the child on the draining board and made her a drink of orange juice. Rox gulped at it gratefully. She was a dear child, with beautiful blue eyes and thick curly hair. Maggie hugged her and rubbed her face in Rox's soft curls. If she ever had a child she hoped it would be just like this one, she was perfect.

She heard Freddie stirring a few minutes later, knew even at her young age that he was waiting for her to return to the front room. She stood in the freezing cold kitchen and cuddling the child to her she waited until she heard him stumble up the stairs to bed with her sister.

Maggie waited another ten minutes until she heard voices, and then she deemed it safe. She brought the child into the front room and settled her beside her so they were both comfortable. Rox wanted a story, and as Maggie spun her a yarn she could hear the bedsprings above her creaking.

She lay there for hours, and the dawn was breaking before she dared to close her eyes and sleep. It had been a close shave this time, but she was determined to best him. She always kept it to herself because of Jackie. Freddie used that knowledge and she lost a serious amount of respect from him because of it.

There was no one to confide in because it would cause too much trouble. Her father would cause a war, her mother would cause a bigger war and the family would be smashed apart in nanoseconds.

The worst of it all was she couldn't even tell her Jimmy. He idolised the man who in turns frightened and disgusted her on a daily basis.

She was almost fifteen years old and already her life was becoming a series of deceptions.

* * *

'What's the matter with your arms, Mags?'

Her mother's voice sounded worried. 'Has that fucking Jimmy been pushing you about?'

Her father was up and out of his chair in seconds. 'You what, Lena? What's wrong with her?'

Maggie pushed her mother away. 'For crying out loud, we was mucking about that's all, he don't know his own strength!'

Lena looked into her daughter's lovely face and saw the confusion there.

Maggie turned to her father. 'Tell her will you, Dad. Jimmy would never hurt me in a million years.'

'She's right, Lena, he worships her.' He picked up the *Sun* from the table and laughed as he said, 'He is a big lad for his age, be fair.'

He went back to his chair and his television, happy that his younger daughter was OK.

Lena wasn't so convinced. 'You ain't been yourself lately. Everything all right?' She nodded, pointing with her head towards her daughter's tummy. Realising what her mother thought, Maggie's eyes stretched to their utmost. 'Thanks a lot, Mum! I ain't like me sister, getting a belly full before I have even had a life.'

Lena knew by the scandalised tone in her daughter's voice that she was wrong about that much at least.

Jackie burst through the door, her eyes red rimmed from crying. 'He's gone.'

Lena rolled her eyes at the ceiling as she filled the kettle with water. 'What, he on the missing list again, then?'

Jackie was lighting a cigarette, and didn't even bother to answer her mother's question.

'The airing cupboard is full of puff and the stink is

going right through the house. I'll fucking skin him when he finally turns up.'

She was opening a brown vial that contained her Dexedrine and swallowed them down without a drink of any kind. Almost immediately, she picked up the bread knife and started to cut herself a sandwich.

Lena took the bread knife off her and put the bread away. 'How can you eat on those things?'

Jackie laughed. 'They take a while to work, but I smoked a joint on me way over and now I have the munchies.'

Joe was almost catapulted from his chair then. 'You what? Drugs is it now, you dozy mare!'

Lena was trying to calm her husband down but he was roaring and swearing now in pure anger.

'Fucking Persian rugs now, not just the slimming pills, and the slimming injections. Oh no, she has to start smoking the Jamaican Woodbines.'

He pushed his face into his daughter's and bellowed, 'What about them poor kids of yours, eh? Bad enough they are lumbered with that useless ponce as a father, now they have to contend with you and all. He was higher than Halley's Comet last night in the pub with that skinny little Hutchins girl hanging off his arm . . .'

Maggie and Lena both closed their eyes in utter hopelessness at his words. As usual they had kept that gem of information to themselves.

'What, little Bethany Hutchins? But she's only a kid.'

Jackie felt a wave of humiliation wash over her. The girl was well known. Bethany's father, Alex Hutchins, and all her brothers were louts, drunks and thieves and Bethany was only seventeen. A young-looking seventeen, with high breasts and a shock of red hair. Her father would cause the Third World War over her and Freddie knew that.

He wouldn't?

She looked at her mother and mouthed the words out loud.

'He wouldn't.'

Lena sighed. 'He already has, love.'

Then she turned on her husband, who was quiet now, realising what he had just caused. 'You couldn't keep your trap shut, could you. Now look what you've done!'

Jackie snapped to life then. 'How long has this been going on, then?'

Maggie sighed audibly. 'A couple of days, that's all. He was drunk in the pub, you know what he's like.'

'But I'm pregnant!'

Jackie was silent once more, the shock had hit her at last and her secret was out. Her father started ranting again and Lena let him go because what he said was right.

'And you are still pumping those Dexies down your throat when you've got a child cooking inside you? Have you no fucking care for anyone or anything, girl?'

Jackie was wrong-footed now, but she was too angry to care. 'Everyone knows that stimulants can't hurt the baby—'

'That's an urban myth, Jackie, and you know it. You should be fucking ashamed of yourself.' Maggie's voice was hard and even Lena was taken aback at the disgust it held. 'Whatever he is or he ain't, you married him and you keep taking him back. No wonder he walks all over you and has no respect. He'll skin you alive if he thinks you've been taking pills while you are in the club and I for one won't blame him.'

Jackie turned on her little sister then, because the truth of the words hit her like a cold shower. 'Don't you fucking lecture me, madam. I know what you and Happy Harold get up to on my settee.'

For the first time ever Maggie wasn't frightened of the

woman towering over her. Instead she was so angry she felt as if she could fight her own end if needs be.

She shouted into her sister's now shocked face. 'Oh shut the fuck up, Jackie, me and Jimmy are courting. You should be ashamed of yourself!'

'She ain't got no fucking shame. If she did she wouldn't be with him!'

Jackie turned on her father then.

The screaming was reaching crescendo when Maggie picked up her bag and coat and left the house. She was shaking with anger at the knowledge her sister would take any kind of drugs while carrying a child, even if the child was fathered by a piece of shit like Freddie Jackson. It was wrong, so very wrong. And if she stayed near Jackie she would not be responsible for her actions.

Outside she breathed in the cold air to try to calm herself down. Freddie had been home for eight months so Jackie could be a few months gone. She had always had a big stomach and since the last one it was even harder to tell, plus she still didn't stop eating even with all the pills she popped.

Maggie lit a cigarette and started to walk to her friend's. She needed to distance herself from her sister for one night at least.

Jimmy would know where to find her if needs be.

Siddy Clancy was laughing and Freddie laughed along with him even though he didn't think the joke was funny. But he knew how to play the game, he knew the score.

Siddy had heard about the rip-offs and Freddie had been expecting a tug, he had just expected it sooner.

In fact the reason he had lost so much respect for Siddy was because he had swallowed it for so long. Freddie was guessing, rightly, that someone up the food chain had finally collared Siddy for a word and now he was doing his Doris Day act.

They were both drunk, drinking heavily to prove a point. Freddie was aware that he had sunk one too many vodkas for his own good. But then he looked at Siddy and realised the man was gone. He was completely out of his box and this was made even more apparent by the fact he was talking too much about Ozzy and Ozzy's business.

Freddie looked around the small saloon bar and noticed that it was nearly empty, then he remembered they were on afters and it was an Ozzy-friendly pub. One he had bought and managed many moons ago, before he had been sentenced for armed robbery and conspiracy charges. The murder had never been proved, however, but he could still be brought to book over it, everyone knew that.

Filth wanted him to stay where he was for the duration and at this moment in time so did Freddie. He saw an opportunity and he was determined to take it.

'What are you trying to say, then?' He frowned. 'You insinuating that Ozzy ain't straight up?'

His voice was loud and he knew the conversation was being listened to by Paul Becks, who ran the pub, and his wife Liselle, a pretty girl whose demeanour hid a psychotic personality.

In his drunken state Siddy had let his guard down, and now he was playing the big man, playing the part he had always played thanks to his inexhaustible supply of brothers and his natural aggressiveness.

'All I am saying is Ozzy has been away a long time, and this is my fucking manor now.' Somewhere in his drink-addled brain a small voice was telling him to go home, that Freddie was not the man to boast to. But he was enjoying himself, he was enjoying bigging himself up even though in reality he didn't need to do it.

Siddy lit a cigarette with difficulty and when he finally puffed on it to get it alight he started coughing.

Freddie looked at Paul and shook his head sadly. 'Get home, Siddy, you are talking too much.'

It was said with contempt and Freddie knew that he had in effect thrown down a gauntlet. He planted his feet firmly on the floor ready for an attack.

Ozzy had always told him, 'You give people the bullets and they will fire them'. How right he was.

'What do you fucking mean!' Clancy was annoyed now he had been caught out. He had assumed Freddie was up for the gossip and now he knew he was wrong he wanted to shut him up.

'Fucking Ozzy is a nice bloke, I don't dispute that, but he's been away ten years and he still has a big lump before he's eligible for parole. It's me who's run the fucking streets for him, me and my brothers.'

He swallowed down his drink in one gulp.

'Don't you fucking come the old woman with me, mate. I knew him when we was kids.'

Freddie laughed then. 'Well, I was banged up with him, and he is straight up, he is doing his bird with a smile. And a cheery wave. You can't even imagine what A grade is like, mate, let alone a double A cat prison. You never been inside, have you? Not even a remand.'

It was said contemptuously as if there was an underlying reason for it, and even in his cups Siddy knew he was wrong-footed. 'What do you mean by that? You fucking wanker . . .' Paul Becks walked closer to the counter where he always kept a loaded shotgun for events such as this.

Freddie held up a hand in a gesture of friendliness. 'Go

home, Siddy. We are drunk and you are getting mouthy about Oz and he was fucking good to me in stir. He looked after me and I can't stand here and let you bad-mouth him.'

Freddie was keeping a wary eye on his protagonist and Paul and Liselle knew that. They were for Ozzy, who had also been very good to them. Consequently, at the moment they were with Freddie. For all Clancy's brothers they knew it was Ozzy who called the shots. Even from the SSB unit in Parkhurst.

They also knew that the only reason Freddie had ended up there was because he was a lunatic who had had more fights and arguments with screws than any other person in the prison system.

He was an unmanageable, someone who everyone was wary of, screws and cons alike.

Chapter Three

'How far gone is she?'

Maggie shrugged. 'She never said. Me dad let the cat out of the bag about that Bethany and she went ballistic. Then she said she was in the club, and we had all seen her just drop the Dexedrine. If Freddie knew . . .'

Jimmy nodded. He could understand the fear in her voice. 'Fucking hell, he'd go bonkers. He has his faults but he does love them kids.'

Maggie looked at him incredulously. Freddie could afford to love the kids, he hardly ever saw them. Whatever her sister was or wasn't, she had looked after them all from day one to the best of her ability.

'Are you having a laugh or what? Loves them kids? He is never home. He don't even know them.'

Jimmy sighed as if it was all too much trouble for him, and he looked so much like Freddie then that she felt a chill go through her.

'Take it from me, he loves them girls. He just wants a boy, that's all.'

He said it with such aplomb he could have been talking about himself, and this was not lost on Maggie. She had had a glimpse into the future and at the moment it did not augur well as far as she was concerned. Jimmy was spending too much time with Freddie, but that could be rectified.

Maggie tossed her long blond hair as she snorted in derision. 'Who's he think he is, Henry the Eighth? He wants a son?'

This was lost on Jimmy who had no knowledge of history unless it involved the lineage of someone he knew about.

'What are we going to do?'

Jimmy shrugged. He had tracked her down for no other reason than he fancied a quick tumble with her before he picked Freddie up from the Becks' pub. He loved her, but sometimes he just wanted a bit of the other with no aggravation. With her sister and his cousin, though, that was nigh on an impossibility. He adored her, he could not imagine life without her in it, but every now and again he just wanted a faceless fuck, and like all men of his ilk he saw it as his due. So, taking a deep breath he answered her as he knew she wanted him to. 'Fucked if I know, babe.'

He was putting the ball back in her court, because the way things were she was going to call the shots. He was supposed to be at the pub by now but he had waited for Maggie instead and it had been a waste of time.

Now he was gutted, and he was sick to death of Freddie and all he entailed as well.

Paul and Liselle looked at the two men warily.

Siddy looked ferocious, but it was Freddie their money was on. Plus, Freddie had Ozzy's best interests at heart. And for all Siddy's family connections no one in their right mind would attempt to have Ozzy over. Even Siddy's brothers would take a step back if they knew what he had been mouthing off about, and knowing Freddie they would hear about it sooner rather than later.

He would need to justify any violence and back up any claims of Siddy being disloyal to Ozzy. That is where they would come in and they were willing to do just that. Ozzy might be banged up but his finger was still firmly on the pulse of all his enterprises.

'Go home for fuck's sake, Siddy.'

Once more Freddie was mugging him off and Siddy knew it. Even through his drink and his drugs he knew he had entered a lion's den of aggravation and there was nothing he could do about it, he was too far gone. If he walked away now he lost all respect from his peers, and yet if he stayed and fronted it out he would also lose respect because he had caused it, he had created the situation in the first place.

It was the ultimate insult, but Freddie said it so nicely that anyone who wasn't in the know would not understand the seriousness of it.

Siddy was losing all reason now because of the way Freddie was talking to him. He could hear the disrespect in his voice, see the arrogance in his stance and almost smell his own humiliation. He was drunk, he was stoned and he was about to make the biggest mistake of his life.

Out of the corner of his eye he could see Paul watching him warily, knew he had his hand on the shotgun under the counter and also knew that he would shoot him without a second's thought before he would shoot Freddie Jackson.

Freddie was flavour of the month with everyone lately, even Siddy's own family. He had taken over so much it was only now, with the situation in hand, that he finally understood he had been played like a fighting fish and Freddie Jackson had reeled him in.

He picked up a pint pot by the handle and gathering all his strength he attempted to smash it into Freddie's face. Pint pots could do serious damage, they were heavy glass and they were a good weapon.

'You fat cunt.'

Freddie sounded as if he was waiting for it, which Siddy conceded he most probably was. Siddy knew when he was beaten.

Freddie had stepped back and grabbed his wrist, which held the pint pot, then, smashing Siddy's arm down on the bar, he waited until he had dropped the pot before he began systematically beating him with closed fists, and eventually finishing the beating with his feet. The pint pot was smashed over Siddy's head for good measure.

As Siddy lay on the dirty carpet he could smell beer, sick and his own blood. He should have gone home, but it was too late now. He knew he had walked into this fight without any kind of redress. Freddie had repeatedly asked him to leave and in the cold light of pain he knew he was finished.

Freddie, for his part, was euphoric. He had done what he had set out to do, he had witnesses to Siddy's utter disregard for Ozzy and his predicament, and he had the goodwill of all Ozzy's workforce, many of whom were sick and tired of Siddy and his crew.

Freddie was out of breath now he had finished his business with Siddy, and he looked at Paul and Liselle in mock distress as he was handed a double brandy. Knocking it back in one gulp, he was surprised that he suddenly felt as sober as a judge. Extreme violence could do that to you, he had found out over the years. It was as if the adrenaline cancelled out the alcohol somehow and left you feeling more alive and alert than you had ever felt before.

He kicked Siddy in the head a few more times, holding

on to the bar so he could use all his considerable strength for the attack.

Siddy was groaning, and throwing up beer and vodka all over himself and the floor.

'Throw that cunt out, will ya? Fucking wanker, he is.' This from a small man in the corner who was playing cards with his brother-in-law. It was a measure of Freddie's newfound credibility that the man felt confident enough to call a Clancy a cunt in public, though they had all said that and worse in private over the years.

Paul looked into Freddie's eyes and grinned, and his grin told Freddie he had just found himself a friend for life.

Now all he had to do was find a few more, and he would be home and dry.

Jackie was frightened. Her secret was out and her father had been more than vocal about what he thought of her and her *antics*, as he kept referring to her drug taking. Her mother, for once, had not attempted to keep the peace and Maggie walking out had not helped the situation. That her Maggie had walked away from her had hurt. No matter what she did, Maggie had always stood beside her. Maggie idolised her and she needed that adulation, everyone else mugged her off over the way Freddie treated her, if not to her face then behind her back. Maggie was the only one who really cared about her whatever.

She loved Maggie, really loved her, but sometimes her feelings veered towards hatred as she saw her little sister enjoying her life so much. Maggie really didn't know just how lucky she was. Jimmy thought the sun shone out of her, everyone adored her. She had no idea what life was really like.

Not like Jackie did.

Her own life was so difficult that she had trouble getting out of bed some days. Everything had been on hold for so long, and she had put so much store on her husband finally coming home, that she had forgotten that the reality of Freddie was so much different to her dreams.

In her dreams he was perfect. She had seen him coming back home, grateful to her for waiting so long. She had seen him loving her like never before, seen his grateful look as he saw his children all clean and cared for, saw him telling her he loved her more than anyone else in the world. This fantasy had kept her going for all those long and lonely years. When she was rock bottom, struggling to make ends meet, or lying alone in her bed going mad for the touch of a man, that fantasy had been what had kept her alive.

But instead, he had walked back into her life a day late and then he had managed to destroy her all over again. And the worst of it was, she knew she had let him.

Would always let him.

That hurt more than anything: the knowledge that he *knew* he could do what he wanted and she would *let* him.

If she had so much as looked at another man he would have taken care of it from inside the prison, he would have seen her maimed, in pain and even seen his children motherless if it meant he kept his reputation in hand. There was no way he would have stood for the humiliation of his wife going on the trot with another man, even if he had got a twenty. She would have *had* to wait for him. Freddie was lucky because unlike a lot of the wives it had been what she had *wanted* to do.

In some ways she wished he was banged up again. When he had been away from her and away from everyone around him, it had been the only time she had felt he was wholly hers.

He had loved her with letters and visits, though even then he had still had his birds visiting him as well. As the years had gone on, she had been his only constant and that had made her happy for a while.

She had seen them off, all the girls who had loved bragging that their bloke was banged up, that he was a dangerous criminal, that he had a reputation. Of course, eventually nature will out and the girls had dropped away from him. Who could blame them? A banged-up bloke can't keep you interested without taking you out, giving you sex and buying you things, which was all his birds had wanted deep down. They had exchanged his letters for a real live man who they could actually have physical contact with. He had loved her then, because he knew she was the only female company he was going to get.

Then he had come home, and he had gone on his usual busman's holiday trumping anything with a pulse and a pair of tits. And she had swallowed it all, until now. Now she had the added humiliation of Bethany Hutchins. Bethany, who had tits like lumps of warm cement and a reputation that made her sex life a who's who of criminals from the local manor. Jackie closed her eyes tight in distress. She hated him when he did this to her, she knew he didn't care a toss about her feelings, or the fact she had to see these people on a daily basis. Up the shops, in the pub, at friends' flats and houses – this was a small community and he would fuck his way through it if she wasn't careful, like he had before he went away. Even her mates weren't off limits to him, as she had found out over the years.

Yet for all his faults, real and imagined, if he knew she was pregnant and dropping pills he would kill her. She had learned many years ago that the best form of defence with Freddie was attack. So she put her coat on and, leaving the girls alone in bed, she walked from her house.

Bethany Hutchins was about to get the shock of her little life.

Maggie was upset but she had finally accepted her boyfriend's haphazard loving. She knew he had a lot on his mind and she allowed for that. Jimmy would always love her for the way she understood his feelings without him having to explain himself over and over again.

Jimmy adored her. He needed her, but his work was taking his life over because Freddie was so unstable. Jimmy for his part had a feeling that Freddie was going to piss all over their fireworks if they weren't careful. He was off the rails, looking for fault with Clancy. In short he was after his pavement. He wanted all that Clancy had, and knowing his cousin like he did, he was going to get it whatever.

Freddie was so dangerous, yet he was also in his own way astute. He knew how to tap into people's fears, knew instinctively what scared them. Jimmy was his cousin's number two. He loved being trusted so much, and he knew Freddie would do whatever was needed to keep them both in the manner they had become so accustomed to.

Life was catching up with him even at his young age and he had the sense to see that. He also knew that whatever shit Freddie brought to their door he had to fight it with him side by side.

That was the law of their world. But it didn't mean he had to like it.

Jeannie Hutchins was in her late forties but looked older, not that anyone would ever have said that to her face, of course. She had the deep-grooved skin of a woman who had smoked and drunk herself old before her time. Her hair was cut short and blow-dried into a halo around her head. Her heavy green eye shadow and liner made her look demented, her lipstick was Burnt Orange by Max Factor, a colour she had worn since the sixties. Her thin body was wiry looking and she could have the proverbial row when necessary.

She wondered if she would have to defend herself this night because as usual her husband was nowhere to be seen. That could be a good thing, though she would have to wait and see the outcome before she decided that.

When she had opened her front door and seen Jackie standing there, her heart had sunk down to her boots, even though she had been expecting her.

Because in her day she had *been* Jackie. She also knew Jackie well and liked her. They were two of a kind, both had men who were villains, who were quite happy to walk all over them and who expected them to wait until they were released from prison. No matter what.

Bethany had made a big mistake, and she had inadvertently upset her mother. Because Jeannie had been on the receiving end of women and girls like her youngest daughter all her married life, her Bethany was going to get the hiding of *her* life. It was long overdue, and she was quite happy to dish it out herself if Jackie was not up to the job. Jeannie felt that her daughter was on the slippery slope of becoming a villain's bird and she knew it was hard enough being a villain's wife, let alone being the number two in the equation.

Now as she looked at herself twenty years earlier, her resolve was strengthened. 'I've been expecting you, Jackie love.'

This was not what Jackie had been expecting and she found herself smiling into the eyes of a kindred spirit.

Inside the flat the smell was overpowering, Jeannie was

a housework dodger and the place looked like a tip. In the small lounge a large colour TV took pride of place and even though it was sticky from children's hand marks and covered in dogs' hair it was still bright enough to light the whole room up. Bethany was sitting in a large Dralon chair and the look on her face was priceless to the two women.

Jackie knew immediately that Jeannie was giving her daughter a lesson in life and secretly thanked whatever God had decided to smile on her this night.

'Hello, Jackie.'

Jackie grinned nastily. 'Hello, Bethany, long time no see.'

The atmosphere in the room was electric and Bethany was staring at her mother now as if she had never seen her before in her life. She was aware she had been served up to Jackie and the knowledge was terrifying her. That her own mother would take an outsider's part was unheard of. They were a family and family stayed together no matter what happened.

Wait until she told her dad about all this!

As Jeannie put the kettle on she heard the first sound of fist on skin. It was hard not to interfere but she knew one day her daughter would thank her for this night. At least she hoped so anyway.

Her granny used to say if you lay down with dogs you got up with fleas. Well, her daughter's fleas had well and truly come to bite her.

She could hear the screaming and crying as the kettle boiled.

'You took your fucking time!'

Freddie was not as annoyed as Jimmy had thought he would be, in fact he looked euphoric. He also looked sober, though he was just about to snort a line of amphetamine off the counter.

He automatically cut one for his little cousin.

Paul and Liselle were grinning and as Jimmy was handed a drink they filled him in on the night's excitement.

As Jimmy listened, the smile on his face got more and more frozen because the Clancy family might not be as amenable as they all seemed to think about Siddy's injuries. He kept this to himself, though, because he knew that there would be no reasoning with Freddie while he was like this.

In truth there was no reasoning with him at any time.

But Jimmy needed to think, to digest the information and to gather up a plan of attack in case they might need one.

As he listened to Paul explaining to Freddie what he was going to do the next day, however, his heart got lighter by the second.

'Me and Liselle visit him every month and bring him up to spec, see, Freddie. We knew that Siddy was having him over like, but there wasn't much we could do without proof.'

Paul poured them all another drink as he continued. 'But it's the houses we need the help with and I reckon you'll have to take them over as well. Liselle won't let me near the brasses, as you can imagine.'

The three men laughed, much to the chagrin of Liselle who was too sensible to let them know that her husband was about two inches from having his balls removed without any kind of anaesthetic.

Freddie knew nothing about the houses, but this did not show on his face. He was already wondering how much he could earn from it all. He had never seen himself as a ponce, though he had been called it more than once during the course of his life. He knew all about it though, he had picked up a lot on his sojourn inside.

'Tell Ozzy to put me cousin down as a visitor. He ain't ever had a capture and that will take the onus off you and the wife. Ozzy can deal directly with him then, can't he?'

This suited Paul right down to the ground. He hated being the go-between and he was always frightened it would all come on top, which would leave Liselle and his kids without any back up. The problem with skulduggery was that there was always someone waiting in the wings for all your glory, and he was in truth just a bread-and-butter Face. He liked to know there was someone higher up the food chain to take the flak. That person was now Freddie Jackson and Paul was thrilled about that fact. He had been in on Freddie's first foray into leadership and he would subsequently never forget it.

He liked Freddie as well, in his own way, and he knew Freddie was mad enough to keep most of the pretenders off his turf.

For Paul it was a win-win situation.

Later, after Siddy's brothers had been to the hospital they returned to the pub to see what they could salvage from the situation with Freddie Jackson. Their jobs were OK for the moment but they knew they had the hard wait until Ozzy decided what their fates should be.

In fairness to Freddie, Siddy had by all accounts asked for what he had received and they were not about to rock anyone's boat, least of all their own. At the end of the day, no one knew Siddy like they did and so they had an understanding of the trouble that could help them salvage, if nothing else, their reputations.

They were nervous but friendly and Freddie could not fault them.

Dawn had broken before any of them thought about going home.

Jeannie was lying across Bethany, trying to stop her husband Alex from killing her. She had already stood by and seen her daughter take one hammering, and she was not about to let her take another.

'She is only young, he swept her off her feet, you know what Jackson's like . . . He'd shag a fence if it was all that was available.'

She was trying now to push her husband towards the bedroom door.

'Jackson is now Ozzy's main dealer and this mad bitch has caused murders with his wife,' he shouted. 'He took out Siddy. Fucking Siddy, my mate, my old mucker is shitting it over that cunt and now I hear my daughter is his main squeeze.'

Alex was losing his anger now as she knew he would, so she carried on pushing him out of the room as gently as she could. Providing he couldn't see Bethany his rage would subside, although hearing it being replaced by fear in her husband's voice meant she was getting scared too.

'I stood by and let Bethany get a slap from his fat wife, it is *sorted*. Now all she needs is you after her and all. She has learned a valuable lesson, so let it go for fuck's sake.'

'Paul was willing to shoot fucking Siddy rather than have any hag off Freddie Jackson, do you understand what that means, woman? I work for Siddy! So where does that leave me?'

Jeannie didn't know but she was too shrewd to say that.

'It leaves you where you were *before*, running your scams until you are *told* different. Now when you see

Freddie you act nice, you congratulate him on his promotion and you keep your trap shut and you hope against hope that he ain't a one for holding grudges.'

Her husband was nodding now, but she could almost taste his fear and it was communicating itself to everyone in the house. Even the music that was normally a constant source of irritation seemed to have stopped.

Bethany was quiet as she listened, wishing with all her heart that she had not drunk so much and that she had not been so welcome in her father's local pub where she had been taken on a daily basis since a babe in arms. Where she had been petted over after cutting her first tooth and where her holy communion had been held in the back bar. She was too comfortable there, even she had come to realise that.

But that was all academic now, that trouble was over, and new trouble had come to take its place.

Such was her life since she had been a small child.

Maggie and Jackie were holding hands.

Jackie had miscarried her baby at four o'clock that morning, and now she was back in the fold with her family and her husband.

No one had mentioned anything to Freddie about her drinking or her drug taking and he had been magnanimous with his wife as he had not been around when the accident had happened. She had slipped down the stairs and that had caused it all.

It had been a five-month foetus and he had been shocked that she had been so far gone. It had also been a male child, and this had affected Freddie more than he would have thought possible.

He had heard through the grapevine about his wife's visit to Bethany and because he put the blame down to himself he was being especially attentive towards her. He felt responsible inasmuch as he had fucked the girl in question. His wife's interference had frightened her away, which had actually done him a favour.

Now Jackie was at home with her sister, pale and wan, determined to diet and also determined to give Freddie another baby, a son.

She knew he wanted a son so badly that if she produced one she would be safe. Safer than she was now anyway.

He was virile, he was a slag and he would give a baby out to anyone who opened her legs and was pleasing on the eye. And that was something she could not take. The only thing she had going for her was that she was the mother of his children and he loved those kids. A boy would be the icing on the cake, and she was willing to use whatever she could to keep him beside her.

Maggie smiled as she placed another mug of tea beside her sister. 'Can I get you anything, mate?'

Jackie grinned, happy they were back on an even keel once more. 'Light me a fag would you, babe, and then maybe make me a salad sandwich, eh?'

Maggie nodded. She had not long made her a stack of bacon rolls. 'Still on your diet, then!'

They laughed together, they knew each other better than anyone would ever know them and they were once more happy with that situation.

The upset and row was forgotten.

Until the next time.

Freddie looked around the house in Ilford and could not believe his eyes.

Wall-to-wall birds, all shapes, all sizes and all for the taking. Black ones, blonde ones, Chinese ones, even Asian ones. He felt as if he had died and woken up in pussy heaven.

They sat about the large lounge in various states of undress, leaving nothing to the imagination. And they were all looking at him expectantly, all watching him warily, all waiting to see who he put the moves on first. As usual his reputation with the ladies had preceded him. And the best thing was he didn't even have to buy them a drink.

Well, their question was easily answered: the tall blonde with the cheap home perm but a pair of Bristols that looked so large they should have had their own passports. She had nice teeth, too. He was funny like that, could never knob a bird with, as he put it, rusty railings. He was always telling anyone who would listen that personal hygiene of the North and South was a requisite for his amours.

As he grinned at Stephanie Treacher and she beamed back, he felt the first stirring of interest inside his pants.

Then a tall woman with short blond hair, piercing green eyes and a deep husky voice walked into the room. 'You must be Freddie?'

He looked her over as he did all women, and said jauntily, 'And you are?'

She smiled then, a wide, white-toothed, even smile that he was quick to notice didn't reach her eyes.

'Your boss, darling. I am Ozzy's sister Patricia. Follow me through to the office.' As she walked out of the door he noticed the girls were all smiling at him, not *with* him but *at* him. He had heard about this woman but he had never seen her before, and she had the same rep as a lot of the men he dealt with. Fair but hard was the general consensus.

It suddenly occurred to him that she really was his boss.

Pat, as she was known, had a long lean body, almost boyish, and incredibly long legs. She also walked with shoulders back and the air of someone who knew what they were about. As he followed her he glanced around the room at all the girls, and the look told them they could wait.

Stephanie raised her eyebrows in a friendly fashion and he winked at her. Confident she was on his list of things to do, she went back to filing her nails. She had scratched a customer earlier and he had not been best pleased. As a school teacher the man was worried about his wife's reaction to a scratch that ran the length of his back, a scratch he would never had experienced if he had not grabbed her by the hair and nearly choked her with his idea of oral sex.

The men that came into this place had watched one too many films, and *Deep Throat* had a lot to answer for. The men really thought that all women could swallow that much cock without gagging. And she *had* been gasping for breath, had been nearly collapsing with agony, and he had acted as if she had deliberately caused *him* trouble.

Consequently she now felt that if she could pass an afternoon with Freddie Jackson now and again, then it might make the job a bit more bearable.

Chapter Four

'All right, Ozzy?'

Jimmy felt the iron grip of Ozzy. No matter how often he shook this man's hand he was always amazed at the sheer strength inside it.

Ozzy grinned, or at least his crinkled-up face expressed the fact he was smiling, but it was so hard to tell. He had to be one of the ugliest cons ever from his bald head, that was scarred from his youthful career of bare-knuckle boxing, to his overweight body that was solid as a rock despite making him look sluggish and heavy.

But it was his voice that Jimmy loved, it was deep brown, like syrup, and it was a voice that was made for a good-looking singer, or a man of refinement. Not the lump of meat that sat in front of him.

Jimmy loved Ozzy and he'd got the impression over the last year that even if the feeling was not exactly mutual, the man liked him. They got on like a house on fire. He sometimes gave him requests to Patricia which even Freddie didn't know about. Ozzy's sister was everything to him, and Jimmy liked her and respected her a lot. As Ozzy said, she thought like a man, and that was high praise indeed from someone of his calibre.

Jimmy enjoyed the prison visits. From the first time he had walked through the security clearance and stepped into the SSB visiting unit in Parkhurst he had felt as if he had come home. The prison fear was gone from him now.

He knew he could hack this environment if he had to. He *didn't* want to, but knowing that if it all came on top he could hold his own without fear made his life so much easier, as well as being a constant reminder to Jimmy of how life could change dramatically, overnight, in their chosen profession.

Ozzy had two Kit Kats and two mugs of tea delivered to their table. He was the only inmate afforded this luxury and the POs turned a blind eye, understanding his need to be treated with respect. It made his life easier and it definitely made theirs easier. So it was a small price to pay.

Most of them were crunching extra wages from him anyway, whether it was for a bottle of Scotch to mellow out his Saturday nights or a few ounces of coke to mellow out his evenings while he plotted and planned his empire. He also made sure there was enough smack in the prison to keep many of the lifers higher than a jumbo jet while they pissed away valuable years of their life.

Seeing the respect made Jimmy feel fortunate, made him feel a part of the big picture. He was unconsciously modelling himself on Ozzy. He liked the way the man never shouted to make himself heard. Liked the way he smiled and joked his way through trouble, and so sorted things easily and amicably.

He used violence as a last resort, and it worked for him because when he did use it, the violence was so extreme the repercussions were felt for many years afterwards. He would cripple or maim, and anyone on the receiving end knew that they deserved it. But the reputation he gathered each time was what made him the legend he was.

When the violence finally arrived, it was far more than should have been expected. It never really fitted the alleged crime, it just shocked even the most hardened of cons in its savagery.

Never lose your temper in public. That was Ozzy's best advice, and he had been repeating it to Jimmy now for twelve long months. His education was nearly complete. Ozzy asked for, and more importantly respected, his opinions.

As they sat together now, Jimmy could feel the respect of all the lags and their families around him. He drove a new BMW and he dressed properly, and he was also learning how to play the crook's most dangerous game: how to keep out of stir.

And he had the best teacher in the world sitting right in front of him.

Patricia O'Malley was a little bit annoyed with herself. Ozzy would go ape shit if he knew, but even that fact could not disguise the thrill of what she had allowed to happen.

Freddie Jackson was scum, he was the lowest common denominator, but she had felt the sexuality off him from the first time she had laid eyes on him. It had been years since she had felt that much excitement over a man.

She liked deep down and dirty sex, always had, ever since she had lost her virginity to a bank robber at fourteen. The next day he had copped a fifteen and she had copped off with her games teacher, another older man who had been kind enough to show her what her mother and every other woman was missing.

He had shown her how much sex could be enjoyed without love of any kind – she thought like a man in that respect. She liked sex for what it was, a good feeling, a release of tension. Nothing more, nothing less. She couldn't understand how women fucked up their whole lives over it, wasted it on one man.

And she had dropped to her knees for a man she could crush without a second's thought if he upset her, and who would now think he had one over on her. Freddie Jackson was all she hated in men, and he was also all that she loved. She would enjoy bringing him down, enjoy making him sweat. If he was stupid enough to believe that a roll in the hay was going to bring him any favours from her then he was in for a big shock. He wasn't the first man to think that, and she knew he would *not* be the last.

When Freddie walked in a few minutes later she was ready for him.

He entered the room like he owned the place, like it was already his through last night's sexual activity. His smile told her he thought he was on the ball, on top of everything. He was thrilled with himself, thought because he had made her moan he was now her boss. He was washed and dressed better than usual, she would give him that much. He had made an effort.

'How are you today?'

Even his words were like a drawn sword.

She pulled herself up to her full height, five feet seven inches, and she grinned at him sarcastically. 'You talking to me, you fucking prick?'

She dripped ice, and she looked him over as though she had not seen him naked and panting only hours earlier. She could see the pupils of his eyes widen with the shock of her words.

Pat was determined to keep this as a business arrangement, and to keep him under her heel just in case she felt like another roll with him at a later date. The main thing with people like Freddie Jackson was never to give them an inch. She would have to watch him like a hawk.

* * *

As Ozzy was always saying, you learned only by experience. And he was passing all his considerable experience on to a young lad who he sensed had an aptitude for greatness. For the first time in his life Ozzy loved someone, really loved someone, and it was not in a sexual way. Sex had never been very high on his agenda anyway. Which was exactly the reason why he found it so easy to be banged up. He wasn't much for female company, never had been really, yet he wasn't gay, and if he had been he was hard enough to swallow his knob over it. He was far too respected to let his sexuality get in his way.

He had just never had the libido of the men he had known over the years. As they had got older the women had got younger, with no logic as far as he was concerned. Ninety-eight per cent of sex was in the head, whoever you were banging at the time.

After all his years inside, and all his years alone, he saw this young lad as the son he could never have. Had never wanted until now, when he was looking his fifties square in the eye and the knowledge he might not be around for the duration had hit him on the chin. He wanted to leave his empire to someone who would appreciate it, keep his name alive and maybe father enough sons to deal it out to on his death. He saw himself in Jimmy, though obviously the boy was a much better-looking version.

Ozzy had learned very early that good-looking people got more out of life, they didn't have to try as hard as their uglier counterparts. And this boy was handsome, but he was unaware of just how attractive he was. It could only be a good thing, because at the end of the day good-looking men always squandered what the good God had given them. Beautiful women used their bodies, that was accepted since women were only good looking for a short time and without a personality they were forgotten in seconds. Once the stretchmarks and the hanging belly took hold they were no more than memories. A good-looking man could have fifteen kids and no one would be any the wiser. It was this fact that told him God was indeed a man. A female God would have given women stretchier skin and the sense to understand business.

Women walked away from their lives the minute they fell in love. A man could love a woman but she would never be his be all and end all, though a clever man might let her *think* she was, of course. But nature would always out. The mother of the main children must be taken care of at all costs and a man had to know that any children he was bringing up were his own. No cuckoos in the fucking nest to grow and betray you at some point. You had to be careful. Women could lie to your face and smile while they did it, every sensible man knew that.

Now Ozzy was happy to be passing all his wisdom on to this nice little fellow with the handsome face and the mind of an accountant. A young man who was quick to learn and who could fight his way out of a German prisoner-of-war camp.

Freddie was a good front man, Ozzy respected that, but Freddie would always need to be led by the balls. This Jimmy, he would lead and no one would ever realise what he was doing. It was the difference between a detached residence and a council flat, it was that clear to Ozzy. Freddie for all his big talk would always be just a tad below the average lifer, but this lad was going places.

'How is Freddie getting on with the houses?'

'He's doing marvels.'

The fact the boy was so loyal to a man who could barely count without taking his socks off made him all the more endearing to Ozzy.

'That's not what I heard.'

Jimmy grinned. 'Look, honestly, I keep me eye out, he is a good investment. Everyone listens to him. He is as mad as a brush, but he keeps things running smoothly.'

Ozzy was pleased with the answer.

'He also shags every bird in the houses, don't he?'

Jimmy smiled again. 'Yeah, but he ain't the only one to do that, is he? Anyway, his wife is ready to drop anytime. He's a family man at heart.'

'A family man? Are you having a tin bath, son?'

'You know what I mean. She is convinced it is a boy this time. A little lad would sort him out, no trouble.'

'If not, you tell him a big lad will be sorting him out if he ain't careful. Tell him the armed robberies are too close together and that's a recipe for Old Bill to start pissing all over him.'

'I'll relay the message, in me own words of course.'

Ozzy laughed loudly. 'You'll do, Jimmy me boy. Just keep him on a short leash, OK, he is upsetting people.'

Jimmy nodded. 'He is a really good enforcer you know, and in his own way he is fair.'

'I understand that, mate, but he also brings a lot of attention his way and that is what we want to avoid.'

'I know that, Oz, but he is loyal to you.'

Ozzy smiled then, the boy himself was too loyal really, but then family ties were closer than any other kind.

He snapped open his Kit Kat and ate it slowly, as always digesting everything that had been said before continuing.

'Now, an old mate of mine is getting out of Durham soon. Give him a job and keep your eye on him, OK?'

Jimmy nodded once more, knowing that whoever this was would be more likely to be keeping his eye on them.

'What's his name, Oz.'

'Bobby Blaine.'

Ozzy watched the colour drain from Jimmy's face.

Bobby's name was synonymous with lunacy and also with violence. It was why they had been such good mates.

Bobby B, as he was known, could instil fear into the meanest of hearts. Bobby was also a laugh, he was the funniest man that Ozzy had ever met, and he had met a few in his time. Bobby could smile and joke as he slit your throat, which of course was his downside, and the side that Ozzy wanted to use.

Jimmy decided he wouldn't give him too much responsibility until he had to because, knowing Bobby, he would only be out a year, if that, before he was once more at Her Majesty's pleasure. While he was home, though, he would use him.

Ozzy used people like he used his Kleenex, and when they ceased to be of any use, he binned them.

Simple as that.

Lena watched her daughter drag herself from the kitchen chair.

'My back's killing me, Mum.'

She looked awful. Lena would be very surprised if Jackie went full term with this child. Her belly was heavy and had already dropped, even though it wasn't due for another few weeks.

'It's all the weight you're carrying. That baby must be like Man Mountain Dean.'

They both laughed at the thought.

'I hope so, Mum. I like the name Dean, it's a manly, happy name.'

'You're not naming it Freddie then, after its father?'

This was said slyly to annoy her.

'Of course it will be called Freddie, but a second name

should reflect the child's family background and character.'

Lena grinned. 'Better name it fucking Looney Tunes Jackson then, and be done with it.'

They laughed once more.

'Or how about calling it Radio Rental!'

They were shrieking with laughter now.

'Stop it, you rotten old cow. Want another cup of tea?'

Lena nodded and lit a cigarette. Giving it to her daughter she said gently, 'Sit yourself down, love, I'll make it.'

The kindness in her mother's voice was nearly Jackie's undoing, and as usual they had gone from hysterical laughter to verging on tears in seconds.

'Has he been home?' This was said quietly.

Jackie beamed as she answered. Drawing heavily on her Kensitas cigarette she said gaily, 'He is really excited, Mum, can't wait.'

Lena smiled once more, glad to see her daughter happy. The pregnancy was keeping her on an even keel for the moment. She prayed daily that Jackie would be delivered of a boy, it was what she wanted so desperately that she had spent huge amounts on seeing tarot readers, psychics, and any other fortune teller she could find in the local paper or through word of mouth.

All had said the same thing, it was a little lad. Well, it had better be.

Freddie was out and about a lot, but with her pregnant he was at least touching base more often. After the miscarriage he had been contrite and had blamed himself, but that wasn't going to last for ever.

'You are keeping off his back, aren't you?'

Jackie sighed. ' 'Course I am. It don't do me any good getting upset, does it? Like you always say, it won't bring him home.'

Lena decided not to pursue that line of conversation. The last year had been touch and go with Jackie and Freddie, especially since he had started working the houses along with the other businesses. She had been at the mercy of the houses herself a long time ago when her husband had been a pretender to the throne, and her Joseph had not had half the looks of Freddie. But then, brasses were a breed apart, everyone knew that. They looked out for the main chance and who could blame them?

Lena had sat it out for years, and now her husband was all hers. It was a hollow victory, she admitted, but a victory all the same. For Jackie, leaving Freddie was not an option and she knew that, but she still dreamed that one day her daughter would get what she wanted from her husband. From what she had heard, though, he was still pole-vaulting with anything in a short skirt. As her husband had remarked so often about his son-in-law, no change there then. And as her husband and Freddie Jackson were like two peas in a pod, she also knew that he was speaking from experience.

Maggie was smiling her usual sunny smile as she washed hair and made endless cups of tea. Her job as a trainee hairdresser was everything she had wanted and more, and her life revolved around Jimmy, work, *Dallas* and her family.

The fashions suited her, the glamorous looks were made for her wide-spaced eyes and thick blond hair, and as such she made a striking contribution to the salon where she worked. Even with the thick make-up she still looked young and fresh, and that was her attraction.

Her dear little face and happy-go-lucky charm worked wonders with the clientele and she made a fortune in tips.

The owner of the salon, a tall woman with high hair and a pseudo French accent, knew a find when she had one, and treated Maggie with the right amount of respect and caring.

This little girl was a quick learner, a kind-hearted and available listener, and did not see anything to do with the hairdressing or the salon beneath her. Madame loved her, and so did anyone who came into her orbit. All the other young girls she had trained up had smiled and worked and waited until they could go on the trot – a hairdresser's in Bethnal Green was not their idea of sophistication. Maggie was grateful to be there, and it showed in everything she did. Most of the week it was perms, older women who had had the same styles since the fifties. They had their hair done once a week, it was lacquered so much it would not have moved in a hurricane, and they gossiped and laughed as they drank tea. Three days later they came back for a 'combout'. And Maggie did these with her usual smile.

But it was the Friday nights and the Saturdays when Maggie came into her own. The new styles were second nature to her, and she managed to make the girls feel at ease in the old-fashioned salon. She played her own music on the record player: Simply Red. 'Holding Back The Years' and 'Money's Too Tight To Mention' always went down well, and she also made sure they had Thunderbird wine to drink. The place was buzzing, and Madame enjoyed having the youngsters back again. Maggie had done the business a big service just by being there. She was dreading the day she walked away like all the others. Maggie Summers was a grafter, and coming as she did from a family of wasters, that, in itself, was a touch. She also sensed that Maggie was not going to follow in their footsteps. This girl would go places, or die in the attempt.

Only sixteen and already she knew what she wanted from life.

Maggie for her part thought Madame Modèle was the greatest thing to hit the earth and was determined to emulate her. She saw the way Madame was with the customers, and she instinctively understood that was the secret of good business. Even the lowliest of women were made to feel special in Madame Modèle's and Maggie loved her for that alone.

As she washed an elderly woman's hair she imagined the day when she would have a salon of her own and a bevy of pretty young women working underneath her all dressed in mint-green overalls and with their hair in French pleats. That had always been her dream, and like everything else she did, she threw herself into it wholeheartedly.

Maggie, unlike the rest of her family, was a person who thought of a goal and then moved heaven and earth to achieve it, and with Jimmy behind her she knew what she wanted was getting closer and closer by the day. He was already earning fortunes, and he was only twenty-one, it seemed that life was determined to give them both a break. Unlike her sister, she had no problem with her man working at the houses because she knew she could trust him. Unlike Freddie, her Jimmy didn't need strange at every opportunity and she could tell by the way he talked about the brasses that he had no interest in them. He saw them purely as a means to an end – at least she *hoped* he did.

She pushed the thoughts from her head.

Thanks to Ozzy they were set, and she knew that Jimmy and Freddie were going to be in work for many years to come. Already she and Jimmy had substantial savings, and even though most of it could not be put in the bank, they were now in a position to buy a small house.

Maggie was so happy she felt like she could sing from the rooftops. All she prayed for now was that her sister's baby was the boy she so desperately craved, then everything would be fine. She was already blow-drying and doing basic cutting. Before she knew it she would be the 'free' hairdresser to her family, but even that couldn't dampen her happy spirits today. Nothing could.

Life was getting better and better and soon she and Jimmy would be married and she would be able to relax. They were getting engaged in a few months and the wedding would be six months later. Even though she would only just be hitting seventeen, she knew there would be no opposition from the families. In fact, they were all looking forward to it. Everyone agreed that Maggie and Jimmy were a match made in heaven.

It was early evening and Freddie and Jimmy were in the office of the main house. It had become their hang-out, and it was all because of Freddie and his pursuit of strange. The house was situated in Ilford and was a large, spacious Victorian house that held a variety of women and a variety of drugs.

Freddie, unlike his younger counterpart, had embraced the emerging drug culture with both hands. Where Jimmy was content to maybe have a few joints when the night was over, Freddie was unable to let the night end. Never knew when enough was enough, never wanted to go home unless he had to.

He was snorting as much amphetamine as he could lay his hands on and as he was now dealing in large quantities that was a lot of speed. He also dropped blue ones, Dexies and Tenuate Dospan, slimming pills that added to his paranoia and often to his unpredictable temper.

As they sipped at cheap vodka and chatted about

Ozzy's plans, Jimmy could see the tell-tale signs of a mounting rage coming from Freddie. His hands were shaking and his eyes were unfocused, he also had the sweats that heralded an amphetamine rush.

In short he was wired.

'You all right, Freddie?' This was said nonchalantly but carefully so as not to upset the large, overbearing man who was so obviously looking for trouble.

Freddie stared at him for long seconds. Jimmy could see him practically talking himself out of the fury he wanted so badly to unleash. It was like watching a boxer who had a hammer instead of a boxing glove. He knew he shouldn't use it but the temptation was too strong.

'You and Ozzy seem tight these days.'

Jimmy sighed inwardly. This was becoming a recurring theme and in a way he could understand the logic behind it. Freddie was the number one, and he had trouble sitting around waiting for Jimmy to relay everything.

His visits to Ozzy had become a bone of contention between them. But as Jimmy had never had even a parking ticket or a caution, he was the only person who could visit the unit in relative peace.

To visit A cat or double A cat prisoners you had to go through a rigorous and unnecessary police check. This entailed having passport photos taken, filling in a form to make sure you were who you said you were and resided where you said you resided, and finally having a bored PC come to your home to verify you looked like the person on the photograph.

This was fine on paper but, as Jimmy was proving with every visit, all the police checks in the world could not stop messages or even orders being exchanged between the prisoner and their visitor. Freddie knew this and it had been his idea that Jimmy be the go-between, but Jimmy had become aware that his cousin was not too happy about the situation now.

However, that was something he could do nothing about. Ozzy called the shots and that was that. He understood his cousin's feelings, he was after all the man who had set this up. Freddie had been put in Parkhurst after he had been deemed unable to rehabilitate. This was due to the fact that he had maimed and fought guards and prisoners alike. He had not taken kindly to being locked up, and his natural anger had been unleashed at the littlest provocation. It was only on the unit that he had felt at ease, and in a way it had done him the world of good. He had tasted serious skulduggery and he had loved every second of it.

His six weeks in Shepton Mallet acclimatising for his release had been fantastic since Ozzy's arm was long and it was respected everywhere. Freddie had been given a hero's welcome and he had also had a single cell, a few quid and as much drink and fags as he could manage.

Now, though, he was starting to resent Jimmy being the only means of communication with Ozzy. Freddie being Freddie couldn't help thinking that he wasn't being told the whole story, which in fairness was often the case. It was hard for Freddie to accept that Jimmy was a doer, he was a thinker and worst of all he was *liked*.

It had suited Freddie when people pretended to like him. When he was younger he had seen it as a form of respect, but now he was seeing another side to life, which was being shown to him by a young man who was beneath him, not only in age but also in stature.

A young man who owed him not only his daily bread but his whole life. He had made Jimmy into the man he was, and the fact that he was doing so well should have made Freddie happy. He was ashamed of his jealousy, but nonetheless it was still there.

Jimmy understood that, he knew Freddie better than he understood himself though Freddie for his part didn't know him at all. Freddie never really tried to *know* anyone. As long as they were useful and toed the line, he was happy. At least he had been until now.

Jimmy knew he had to tread warily, because as much as Freddie loved him he was too competitive for his own good. Even more so now he was making gigantic fuck-ups left, right and centre.

'Come on, Freddie, you know the score. If you want to get someone else to schlep to the Isle of Wight and listen to Ozzy, you go, boy. You're the one who made me go in the first place.'

Jimmy sounded contrite enough to stop a war, and he was looking worried enough to placate the man he loved more than any other on the earth. This was becoming a regular mantra, and it was starting to get on his nerves. He worked hard and if Freddie couldn't see that, he was a fool. Jimmy carried him a lot of the time, though that was never mentioned. Jimmy was walking a fine line and as he was getting older and more involved in everything, he was starting to resent it all. He implemented a lot of Ozzy's demands because it was easier than waiting for Freddie to get around to it. But he had to do it in such a way Freddie felt that he was doing the legwork. Freddie was lazy, always had been and always would be, although he was great at the threatening, at the bully-boy end of the business, because he enjoyed it. But the day-to-day matters got on his nerves, Freddie would let things slide, and all because he couldn't keep off the gear and off the birds.

Jimmy was sensible enough to know that his own particular forte was the fact he could *placate*, he could *talk* people down, and he could avoid a lot of the confrontation that their job entailed. From the robbing to the collecting, the dealing, right through to the clubs, the pubs and all the other sundry businesses that they were supposed to oversee for Ozzy, it was Jimmy who kept it all running smoothly.

Freddie was aware of this, but his personality could not, and would not, allow for anyone else being in the frame. Jimmy was quicker than him at the mathematics of the jobs, at the scheduling of the workforce and at liaising between the different people who worked for them. He was his blood and he was good at what he was doing, but it galled him, even though it was because of his cousin's acumen that he could breeze through each day.

He stared at the younger man before him, and saw, as he always saw, *himself* if he had only been granted a small modicum of sense. In his heart of hearts he knew he should sort himself out before it was too late, cut down on the drinking and the drugs, take more of an interest in what was going on around him, but that was easier said than done.

And as he looked into Jimmy's face he felt the familiar shame wash over his thoughts. The kid was good and he was the only person Freddie Jackson really loved, other than himself. He grinned then, the affable, raffish grin that had got him into more beds and more fights than he could count.

He leaned across the beer-stained desk and grabbed Jimmy's chin. It was a painful grasp but Jimmy swallowed it, though deep inside he wanted to tell this man who he revered and adored the truth of his situation. But he didn't, he couldn't.

'You clever little fucker, Ozzy must think all his birthdays and Christmases have come at once with you!'

Jimmy pulled his head from Freddie's grasp. 'I only tell

him what he needs to know and I relay his messages on to you, Freddie. Why do you do this to me?'

It was a plea, and they both knew it.

Freddie knocked back his drink in one gulp and then shrugged. 'Just don't ever think you can overtake me, all right? Never try and mug me off.'

Jimmy smiled then, the most difficult smile of his life. 'Why would I try and do that to you?'

The question and the answer hung in the air.

Chapter Five

'Oh shut the fuck up, Jackie, and come here!'

Her pretence at cleaning was annoying Freddie. She had been walking in and out of the room, emptying ashtrays and tidying around in general, trying to attract his attention. Now he was ready to give it to her.

Freddie was smoking a joint and listening to Pink Floyd on the stereo; he had been singing 'Wish You Were Here' to himself for two hours. Unlike his friends Freddie liked his music low and interesting.

Freddie watched as Jackie waddled over to him. She was a lump this time, so big even he was getting worried. 'You sure there ain't about four kicking away in there, girl?'

Jackie was laughing now. She loved it when he took notice of her, but the backache she had been suffering from all day was starting to interfere with her pleasure.

Her long dark hair was cut to perfection and brushed to a sheen. Thanks to Maggie's obsession with hairdressing the women of the family had never looked so well groomed.

As Jackie slumped down on to the brown Dralon corner unit, Freddie pulled her into his arms and said gently, 'Your hair looks triffic.'

He knew the compliment would please her, and it was true, her hair did look nice. It was the rest of her he had a problem with. She was so scruffy looking, as was the house.

'You always had a lovely barnet, Jack, and it looks nice like that.'

It had been cut into long layers and backcombed within an inch of its life. She was thrilled with it, more so now her husband had not only noticed it, but had admired it.

He had also once said she looked like the poor man's Joan Collins on PCP, but no one had ever had the heart to pass that remark on to her.

'A woman's crowning glory, I remember that from school when I was a kid. It's the first thing a bloke notices, apparently.' He was a tit man personally but he knew better than to say that to her at the moment. Her sense of humour had been on the missing list for a while now.

'I try and keep meself nice for you, Fred, you know that.'

As he looked into her face the yearning was there, stifling him as always. But he swallowed down the urge to do a runner and instead he called for Roxanna, who came into the front room all red faced and cross.

'I was playing with me dolls.'

Her voice was as usual autocratic when talking to her father and as ever this made him laugh. He was half stoned and Jackie could hear it in his voice. It was a regular occurrence now, and she hated it because she *daren't* smoke dope in front of him, but the smell was driving her mad.

'Bring me coat in, babe.'

'Go and get it yourself!'

He was laughing at her once more, the stoned-over

laugh that annoyed his kids because they knew what had caused it, and it wasn't them.

'Get me coat, you lazy little cow.'

Roxanna made a cross face and stormed from the room. Seconds later she dragged in his long leather coat, pulling it along the floor behind her, then letting it drop in a crumpled heap by his feet.

'One coat!'

The sarcasm was evident and she sounded like a little old woman, not a child.

'You lairy little mare.'

She grinned then. 'Takes one to know one.'

He was still chuckling as Roxanna walked silently from the room, the animosity coming off her in waves. 'She's her mother's daughter, her!'

It was said proudly, and Jackie was thrilled by his tone. This was the Freddie she loved, the Freddie she craved, the man she adored, not the obnoxious bully he became in drink or while speeding out of his box.

He rifled through the long pocket inside the lining of the coat and brought out bundles of cash. Dropping them into her lap he said gently, 'Put that away for junior here. Anything you need, you just let me know, OK?'

'How much is here?'

He loved the reverence in her tone as she grasped the bundles of cash to her greedily.

'About seven grand, but don't worry, there's plenty more where that comes from.'

He said it in his big 'I am' voice, the voice he used so she would know just how good he was to her. How he risked life and limb for his family, without a thought for his own liberty.

She fell for it every time.

Kissing him softly on his lips she looked into her

husband's eyes. The complete and utter trust and love she held for him told him he had now gained himself a few nights out on the lam. He had iced twenty-five grand that morning from a wages snatch in East London, he was still feeling the rush from the job and he was enjoying his pregnant wife's adulation. He needed it, because for all the strange there was floating about in his orbit, there was only one woman on his mind and she was beginning to take over his every waking moment.

Patricia had used him, and that had never happened to him before in his life. Usually he was the conqueror. *He* used women, they did *not* use him, consequently he was absolutely besotted with her, and to make matters worse he had a feeling she knew it and was enjoying his discomfort. The way she smiled at him, then ignored him, before finally speaking to him in that animated way she had, making him feel like he was back in with a chance. Then blanking him for days, as he spent his time trying to think of excuses to talk to her.

But their encounter had blown his mind. Never before had a woman taken *him* to bed, enjoyed him without even talking to him before or after, and then acted as if he didn't exist. He thought about her constantly, her boyish body that she was so confident with, her small breasts that he had adored. Patricia had taken what she wanted from him and he had loved it.

As he thought about her his hand slid towards his wife's swollen breasts and he caressed them gently. She was so unlike Patricia. Jackie resembled a cow, with huge udders and that milky smell women got when they were ready to drop. Patricia was long and sleek, and she could move like no woman he had ever bedded before.

Jackie felt his hands on her and as always was willing to give in to him. Like her mother before her she believed that if you never refused a man he would not want to stray. Her father had proved the lie to that statement and so had her husband.

She, like Lena, didn't understand the logic of womanising men. It was all about power, and like a rapist, they used women as a means to an end. It wasn't really anything to do with the sex act, as far as they were concerned that part was just a bonus for all concerned. It was about the chase, and once the women had succumbed they were history. They were another story to be told in the pub, another conquest that made the men concerned forget the futility of their lives. They never once cared, or really desired the woman in question, who were just a pawn in their game of life.

'You be careful, Freddie. I'd rather scrimp than see you banged up again.'

He smiled at her, the smile that made every woman think she was the only woman in the world who mattered to him. 'You're my girls, ain't you? I have to take care of my girls. That's why I work all the hours God sends.'

The answer annoyed Jackie as he knew it would.

'What? In the whore houses . . .'

He clamped his hand across her mouth roughly, all the time speaking in a low, determined whisper that brooked no argument. 'Don't start, Jackie, you know it's me job. I have to keep an eye out, mate, see that the punters don't rip anyone off and make sure the girls don't try and pick anyone's pocket. Especially Ozzy's.'

She was struggling to sit up now, had moved away from his embrace. Then, pushing his hand from her mouth roughly, she lit a cigarette to control her breathing, before saying scornfully, 'The *girls*? Is that us girls, as in me and your daughters, or the whore girls?'

He sighed, his long-suffering sigh, the sigh he used to

make her feel stupid, make her feel that she was in the wrong, was *always* in the wrong. It was the sigh that told her if she kept on there would be trouble.

'Shall I stay at home then?' His voice had risen and she knew the kids would be able to hear him from their bedrooms, which was another of his psychological weapons. 'Shall I sit here and watch the flock wallpaper with you, eh? Drop a trip, shall I? At least that way I would have a bit of entertainment and all.'

He was getting aggravated now. She wonders why he ended up practically lamping her one, and then she causes all this! He took a few deep breaths. He had to talk her round, at least until she had dropped the new chavvy. Then he could do what he liked.

'You can kiss goodbye to all this if I stop doing me work.'

He looked around the over-furnished, untidy room, and waved his arms about in disdain. He was playing her and she knew it, but they also both knew that the money would always take precedence over everything else. She loved lording it up to the neighbours and she loved the feeling of spending. Her spending was astronomical lately, and unlike her sister she was never one to think of the inevitable rainy day. Never thought to make the money work for her in case he ended up on another six-year holiday courtesy of the judicial system. After all the years alone and scraping a living she was going mad, and the money also told everyone in her orbit that he *must* love her. It was the balm on her sore heart, it was her defence against the world.

He watched as she eyed the seven grand and knew he was home and dry. He hugged her tightly then, and she enjoyed the feel of him as she always did. She craved his attention as she craved his good will.

'Well, try not to make a night of it, eh? Remember that you have a family here.'

Her voice was still uptight and they both knew that it was not real permission. She was more or less telling him she wanted him home with her. Trying to make him feel guilty for abandoning her.

With her pregnancy, he needed her to smile as he walked out the door. The last time, when she had lost the baby, he had felt guilty, had been made, for the first time ever, to question his actions. He was determined never to feel like that again.

She had used it for so long, even his own mother had warmed to her, had silently blamed him. He was only amazed that Lena, who would normally blame him if it rained on the day she cleaned her windows, had not stuck her oar in. In fact, she had not said anything about it at all. Now he made sure Jackie and the girls were well looked after, both in public and in private. He had heard a whisper that his treatment of his wife had been leaked all the way to the Isle of Wight.

He had been banged up with Ozzy and his mates for a long time and he wanted their good will. If looking after this fat bitch would guarantee that then that was what he would do. He still resented her though, and once she was delivered, she was going to get the shock of her life. If it was another split arse, she was doomed for eternity as far as he was concerned.

But his image was his all, and at the end of the day image and reputation was what paid his wages. In their world it was all you had. So he kissed the tip of her nose gently, then looking at his brand new Bulova watch pointedly he said heartily, 'You get a bit of sooty and sweep and lay off the fucking drink. That poor baby will be born half pissed if you ain't careful.'

It was said in a joking way but the underlying edge was there. He was warning her and she knew it. She wondered briefly if her mother had tipped him the wink but dismissed the idea immediately. He had eyes, and a sense of smell. It wouldn't take a blind dog long to sniff her out.

She looked at his handsome face and was amazed that someone who looked like a Greek God, and who could smile in a way that could melt the hardest of hearts, was capable of such cruelty.

And he *was* cruel, but even though she knew that, the pull of him was still as strong as the first time she had seen him. With him she was never happy because he made her feel ugly, like second best. Yet without him she felt bereft, as if her life had no meaning, had no purpose.

He was going to start a row with her if she didn't let him out of the house without a fight. He had as usual presented her with two choices: either he goes out and she smiles, or he stays and fights and then storms out leaving her angry and upset. If she let him go happily, then he may be inclined to come home sooner rather than later.

A few seconds later, he got a beer from the fridge and placed the bottle of cheap Liebfraumilch she kept there on the kitchen worktop with a bang. 'Chilling it now, are we? Not necking it straight from the bottle?'

His voice was telling her he was ready to row, and as Jackie looked through the doorway into the small hallway she saw Roxanna, all big eyes and nervous twitch.

Closing her eyes she said as gaily as she could, 'You better get a move on, babe, it's getting late.'

He snapped the beer open and took a deep drink. Then, putting the can on the cluttered draining board, he ran into the hall. Grabbing Roxanna he threw her to the ground and pretended to bite her. She was shrieking in delight and the noise was going through Jackie's head.

'Who's her daddy's girl then, eh?'

She was screaming, 'I am, I am,' when he stopped and, kissing her gently, got up and with a small wave and a blown kiss to his daughter he was gone.

Roxanna got up and ran to her mother, her happy face glowing. Jackie pushed her away none too gently and barked, 'Get off me, for fuck's sake. You're like a fucking leech, you are.'

Roxanna was upset and, her natural belligerence coming to the fore, she shouted, 'Don't take it out on me because you made him go away.'

The girls always blamed her. He charmed them and he gave them what they wanted, and she was relegated as usual to nothing in their eyes, and her own.

The slap was loud and it was painful when it came and, as Rox ran crying from the room, Jackie felt the usual guilt and devastation at the turn her life had taken.

The first glass of wine took the edge off her anger, the second stilled her racing heart and the third saw her go up the stairs to try to make peace with her girls.

Jimmy was sitting in a pub with a man he really did not want to be with, and until Freddie and Bernie Sands arrived he had to smile and provide large Scotches for someone he instinctively loathed.

Jimmy was anxious about the whereabouts of Freddie and his new crony Bernie. They were an hour late already. Bernie had been banged up with Freddie for a couple of years, and now he was home they were both making up for lost time. Much to the detriment of wives and families.

Kindred spirits, they were hardly apart and even though this was a cause for celebration as far as Maggie was concerned, it worried Jimmy. Without a stabilising influence Freddie was as mad as a brush – that had been proven time and again since they had taken over from the Clancys. Now Freddie had Bernie, and the last thing Freddie needed was someone geeing him up even more than he did himself. Bernie was a short, fat man with shaggy blond hair and a face that belied his friendly reputation. He looked miserable even when he was ecstatically happy.

Bernie was a bank robber and a collector, he could get a debt off a dead man, or so his reputation said. And even on short acquaintance Jimmy felt this was an understatement. Jimmy knew that they were out robbing on a daily basis and this was what was giving him sleepless nights.

Since the rise in armed robberies in the seventies, security firms had upped their own security measures in defence of their cargoes, until now, in 1986, the only security vans without bullet-proof windshields were Group 4's. They were being targeted because with a well-placed sledgehammer, a few choice words, a handgun, and enough bottle, their vans could be knocked over in less than ten minutes.

The adrenaline rush alone was enough to have made Freddie already addicted. They had been averaging two a day, every few days, one in the morning, and one in the afternoon for the last few weeks. It was so easy that they were unable to even contemplate getting a capture.

The blags, as they were referred to in the appropriate circles, were excellent bread winners and they were also something that could be done on the spur of the moment and without the usual elaborate planning of, say, a proper bank job or jewellery heist. For example, the money they had blagged that day was for a reason, it was like bunce, it was for sundries, it was to them pocket money. Some people popped security vans for bail money, or just for a decent stake.

The man sitting opposite Jimmy held up his empty whisky glass and shook it at him. His eyebrows were raised and his red-veined cheeks were stretched in what Jimmy assumed was a smile. His thoughts interrupted, Jimmy got up and went to the bar once more, aware of the looks he was getting because of the company he was keeping, and wishing with all his heart that Freddie would arrive. Even though he had his creds and could take care of himself, he didn't fancy his chances with some of the blokes sitting around, looking at him suspiciously, if they decided to come at him en masse.

Paul filled the glass with ice, and then, surreptitiously spitting into it, he filled it from the drunks' optic. The drunks' optics were the watered-down shorts. They were not used until the end of the night, then used only on people who were well gone and could have a fight, but still insisted on drinking. People who could not be told enough was enough, and who might be armed, or were nursing a grudge.

They were the optics they made money from by keeping their stocks up, and the ones that stopped murders from being committed.

The phlegm looked like normal bubbles on top of the whisky and Jimmy felt his stomach rebelling as he handed the glass to the tall skinny policeman with the sarcastic smile and the air of someone who was under the impression he was far too good for the place he had landed up in.

DI Halpin was a tame filth, but he was not tame enough for Jimmy. In fact he was a flash prat until he had accidentally got himself on to the Serious Crime Squad through severe boot licking and serious amounts of cash provided, naturally, by people like Freddie and Jimmy. He was making the mistake all treacherous people eventually made. They believed their own press, they saw themselves as not only above the law they had sworn to uphold, but above the people they traded with, and they always got the fright of their life when they finally realised just how deeply they were entrenched in the shit of their own making.

They were quite happy to lie and cheat old friends and colleagues, were comfortable with their double dealing and the fact that violent criminals, as well as the usual blaggers, walked free and clear while they fitted up someone they either had a grudge against or who they had once more been paid serious money to take off the street.

Consequently, the criminals they dealt with saw them as the lowest of the low. When he was a humble filth, if Halpin busted a dealer with five weights of dope, the dealer knew that only two weights would be taken into evidence, the other three would be back on the street within hours. He helped himself to monies and firearms located on searches, which he also recycled back on to the streets. He honestly believed he was above the law.

It was this greed that had brought him to the attention of Freddie and Jimmy in the first place, and tonight he was going to find out the real reason they had bought him. For the last six months he had been courted by them, had taken a luxurious holiday, and pleased his wife no end because he had finally agreed to the conservatory she had been desperate to have built on to the back of their mock-Tudor, four-bedroomed detached house in Manor Park.

Halpin was flavour of the month at the moment and he was loving it. He did not see what he was doing was wrong in any way, he saw it as a means to an end. He was still young enough to feather his nest, and after talking to colleagues he was determined that he was not going to end his days on a police pension, reminiscing about a bygone era when he was useful, and when he was still being listened to.

He had seen that time and time again with colleagues, and it frightened him. His own father had seemed like a god to him but now he saw him for the man he really was, a small man who had lived for work. Well, Halpin was determined that he would work to live. He wanted a good life, wanted money in his pocket, and if it meant he had to bend the rules to achieve that goal, then so be it.

He had married above him, and he was painfully aware of that fact. He loved his wife and his kids and he wanted them to have all the things he felt they were entitled to. He had loved being in the force, but as the years had gone on he had come to understand that there was not only a ceiling to what he could earn, but also, that to get on properly he had to court the right people. Drink in the right pubs and ignore the flagrant bending of their rules.

The feeling of pride he had felt in his job had gradually been eroded. It was on a drugs raid a few years earlier that he had finally burned his boats. Until then he had taken the occasional drink, meaning he had received money for turning a blind eye and leaving people to ply their trade as long as they were not too blatant about it. The attitude being they were better off with the devils they knew.

Then he had been teamed up with an older man who had tipped him the wink on their way to the raid. He told him that they had a deal with the man in question, and that they were to go to the pub for a couple of hours before the raid took place to give him plenty of time to sort himself out. It was stepping over the line, and this had bothered him.

But it had been the dealer's house that had convinced

him he was a mug. It had blown him away, from the kitchen that looked like something from NASA to the glass and chrome lounge. It had been a learning curve, the sheer luxury of it, the way the man's family had been dressed, and the kids in their private school uniforms.

The dealer, a close friend of his governor's, had opened a bottle of Scotch and sat down to chew the breeze with them. It had been an enjoyable afternoon and the beginning of his double life.

He had gone home that night and as he had let himself into his semi-detached in Chigwell, with its cream-coloured nets to stop the neighbours peering in, and its constant smell of damp, it had occurred to him that crime did pay, and it paid a lot better than he had first thought.

Now his wife was happier than she had ever been, as were his kids. Money *did* buy happiness in its own way, he was proof of that. As for the adages about money *not* buying happiness, well, he had proved that was utter crap. They were sayings to keep the poorer parts of the population quiet, mainly those without any real money. It might not buy good health but money bought the best doctors in the world. Money might not make your relationship better but it certainly kept the relationship going, because it was the lack of money that caused most of the rows in most of the households.

Halpin's whole concept of life had been challenged and he had finally found the solution to his worries. A decent holiday built a marriage, the break gave them all a chance to recharge their batteries and the hot sun did wonders to break down barriers between man and wife. The strolling along a beach, the few drinks before bed and the smiling children crashed out from a day's swimming and playing went a long way to making people happier.

His life was better than ever, and he felt he had a

hold over the people he had to deal with. At the end of the day he was a policeman, they needed him and he held all the cards. It was this belief that allowed him to show his disdain for these people. It was also the reason he was going to be brought down to earth in the next twenty-four hours.

He heard Freddie before he saw him.

As was his wont, Freddie came in the pub like a conquering hero, smiling and laughing, a word for everyone and a drink offered. He knew his job, he also knew it was important to keep good relations with people because you never knew when you might need them. The Clancys had found that out, and it had been a lesson well learned for all concerned.

Freddie was still smiling as he sat opposite the DI, who watched warily as Bernie Sands eyed him for long seconds before drifting over to the bar.

'Hello, mate, all right.'

It was a greeting, not a question.

Freddie snapped his fingers towards the bar. 'Drinks all round, please.'

Paul nodded. He liked old Freddie. Since he had taken over, trouble in the bar had all but ceased, even the lairiest among them were wary of Jackson. Even Bernie Sands said please and thank you, that alone was a touch.

Freddie knew his job and he kept everyone, except himself, on an even keel. He was worth every penny, and he knew it.

As he looked at the policeman with the beer gut and the weather-beaten look of a man who had drunk too much too soon he said happily, 'You and me need a talk, mate, because tomorrow me and you have to sort out a bit of skulduggery at the Old Bailey.'

Jimmy noticed that the man's smile was now frozen on

to his face. It was funny, but they always thought they were never going to be called on for anything serious.

But Halpin was about to find out that they owned him, and that he owed them far more than he had thought possible.

Maddie Jackson and Lena Summers were in the waiting room of Rush Green Hospital in Romford, waiting for news. Jackie's backache had been the onset of labour, and she was now causing untold aggravation to everyone in her orbit.

Rush Green had a special baby unit, and they were both concerned for their grandchild. It seemed that the child might be breech and Jackie, being Jackie, was screaming the place down.

For the first time ever the two women were in accord, they both felt that Jackie was making far more of it than there actually was. Both women had given birth at home, then got up and cooked a dinner within twenty-four hours.

Like their mothers before them, they saw childbirth as a natural occurrence, unlike the girls of the day, who saw pregnancy as some kind of illness. Saw it as an excuse not to work, not to do anything *heavy*.

And Jackie acting like she was the only person ever to have a child was irritating them both no end. Her screams echoed the length and breadth of the hospital, and, as they both agreed, it wasn't like she had not done it before.

'Can you hear her?' Maddie's voice was angry and even though Lena was in agreement she had to show some kind of loyalty.

'She wants her husband, that's what wrong with her.' It was said in a nasty, arrogant, 'your son is in the wrong' kind of way.

Maddie laughed then and said. 'Wants her husband? Didn't we all?'

The truth of the statement made Lena want to smile. They were both thinking of lonely births with husbands who had gone out to celebrate and not come home for three days. That was, to them, how it should be. It was women's work – why try to make the men interested in something they could never be interested in by their very nature? The two women started to laugh then, and a few minutes later when a nurse brought in a pot of tea they drank it together in peace.

Even Jackie's screaming and swearing didn't affect them, as they had decided to pretend they didn't know her until the child was delivered.

They wouldn't do that, of course, but for now they were both enjoying the respite.

Chapter Six

Tommy Halpin was nervous, and this was a completely new concept to him.

He had always felt in charge of his life. Every decision he had ever made was for a reason, either to further his career, or to squeeze as much money as he could out of the low lifes he used for his own ends.

Until now, even though he had mixed with these people on a regular basis, he had always felt that as he was the major contributor to their little arrangements, he was safe. They *needed* him far more than he *needed* them.

He had felt important enough never to consider the way he treated them. Unlike his governor, who had a rapport with those he dealt with, Halpin had always felt that he was letting himself down by associating with these people, let alone making out they were friends. Even though these were the men who, after all, were paying his real wages. The wages that provided his family with all the little extras they had come to expect from him.

But tonight the atmosphere was different, it was charged somehow. From the minute Freddie had sat down opposite him Halpin had sensed something was off kilter. Suddenly he felt like an outsider, like the kid at school who tried to be in with the main crowd and could only achieve it by selling out his friends and ultimately himself.

This was not a good feeling for him, it was too close to home. Plus he had drunk a lot of Scotch while he had been waiting, so he was also worried that mentally he was not the full ten shillings. He felt unable to control the situation, something that had rarely happened to him in his life. He was, as his wife said in private, a control freak.

The sad thing was that he was disliked by most of the people in his orbit. Police colleagues and the criminals he dealt with all had that in common. Tommy Halpin was an arrogant bully who had never listened to anyone's advice and had always considered himself far too clever by half to listen to anyone else's opinions.

When his governor had shown him the ropes, he had always stressed the main rules: *never* get pissed on the job, no matter how comfortable you felt with the people you were with; never forget you were dealing with criminals and that they lived by a different set of rules to everyone else; and no matter how nice they were to your face, you could never really be a part of their circle by the very nature of the job you did. To them you would always be a filth, and a bought filth at that.

He knew what he had said was true and he had listened accordingly, all the time thinking that his boss was stating the obvious. He wished he had listened to him properly. He had also told him, watch your back, and *never* put moody money in the bank, it was too easy to trace. Never leave cash in the house and never buy a car that was under two years old. His main chant, though, had been, never relax, remember who you are dealing with and treat them like you would a rabid dog. You are only useful to them while you can provide a service that they need. His governor had made a big deal about it all, because if he had a capture he would automatically take all his work mates down with him.

The enormity of this was only just seeping into Halpin's consciousness, the extent of his treachery was finally sinking in. If he had a capture, no one he associated with would ever be trusted again. It was this one fact that made his governor so paranoid. Every honest collar they had felt would automatically be suspect, if they were proved to be on the take. Now, he finally understood his governor's paranoia about what they were doing and his constant reminders of the seriousness of their situation.

He had forgotten the golden rule, that he was only a means to an end for these people. That there were plenty more where he came from.

Maggie had arrived at the hospital and had automatically taken over from Lena and Maddie. Maggie could handle Jackie and her sympathy was in place, it had not been worn out yet by her sister's constant swearing.

'Where is that fucking bastard!'

Maggie didn't answer her, instead she folded up the bedding from the floor and placed it on a chair.

When a doctor came in another volley of abuse was spewed at him and he retreated without saying a word.

Maggie sighed. 'You have to be the stupidest cunt on the planet, Jackie, do you know that?'

Jackie's head snapped towards her little sister in shock. 'What did you call me?'

Maggie sat on the chair. The bedding was more comfortable than the plastic seat and she appreciated that. She had been on her feet all day at the salon and she was tired out.

'Oh, don't give me the shocked looks, it's your

favourite word, you've called all the nurses and the doctor it. When are you going to grow up, Jack?'

She pointed at the dishevelled woman angrily. 'That baby is in distress. If it's breech then they need to sort it out and if anything happens to it because of your antics, Freddie will go mad.'

She waited while her sister digested this bit of logic before she carried on. 'We are trying to track him down, but whether he arrives or not, that child has got to be born so why don't you shut up, stop all this showing off and let the people here get on with the jobs they are paid to do?'

She was calmer now, and Jackie was listening. Maggie knew that the mention of her husband would bring her round.

'But it hurts, Maggie.'

Maggie smiled sadly. ''Course it hurts, it hurt the other three times and all, remember? So let them help and for fuck's sake act your age, not your bloody shoe size!'

It was a silly saying of Maggie's and they both smiled then.

'There's a young girl in the room next door, and she is only seventeen and your screaming is terrifying her.'

Jackie wiped her running nose with the back of her hand. She felt bad, she was hurting and she needed a drink. Not that she would say that out loud of course. She knew Maggie had a bottle of champagne in her bag and she wished it was all over so she could neck it and settle her nerves.

She wished that just once Freddie would be there for her, see the child born. She had read somewhere that it gave the man a better bond with his children. She couldn't see it herself, *she* had been at her children's births and it had not made any difference at all. They still got on her wick.

'You have been out of order and if you ain't careful

they will refuse to treat you, Jackie, and your threats will end up with Lily Law at the end of the bed. Now just once in your life, Jackie, stop thinking about yourself, think about someone else.'

The fact that Jackie took it from Maggie told her she was nearly home and dry. But Jackie always caused ructions when she was in labour and she had always got away with it before. This time the staff were not willing to swallow it and Maggie didn't blame them one iota. She wouldn't have taken it either. They were threatening to call Old Bill in, and that automatically brought social services. Jackie was such a mess, and if she wasn't careful she would end up with social workers breathing down her neck again. Maggie loved her sister but at times she really didn't like her.

'You are going to let the doctor examine you now, because if the baby's breech they have to get it sorted.'

Jackie nodded then, digesting her sister's words. Even she knew she had gone over the top, but it was in her nature. Everything with Jackie had to be a fight, had to be a drama, she couldn't help it. She had to have the spotlight on her, and her bad behaviour had always guaranteed that she got it.

Now, though, Maggie's sensible words had made her think about what she was doing. She had threatened one of the nurses with her water glass and she knew that, unlike years before, that could now get her a court appearance and Freddie would not be impressed if that happened.

'Bring them in.'

Freddie was watching the different expressions on the man's face and he knew they had him by the short and curlies. He had seen it before so many times with the tame filth and he loved the feeling it gave him.

People like Halpin had to be brought down gradually, it was a psychological thing. For a while you had to make them feel that even though they were the takers, they were the ones who were actually in control of the situation.

It was easy to do, you just pandered to their natural vanity. Halpin had been under the illusion he was in some way the aggressor in the partnership forged by his old boss, who had in effect served him up to Freddie Jackson as a favour. This manipulation of anyone weaker than yourself was something the likes of Freddie Jackson learned very early in life. Where he had come from you had to learn what his father had jokingly called psychological warfare.

From a kid, Freddie had understood that if you weren't clever enough, or strong enough, to beat people at their own game, you made sure you either cultivated an innate cunning or learned to use a weapon and developed a good rep as a nutcase, otherwise you became someone else's gofer.

Halpin was his gofer now and he was going to enjoy explaining that to him. Halpin, like most of the police who were on the take, had been on the receiving end of people like Freddie all their life. It was the main reason he had turned to crime fighting. The natural respect for the uniform, the very nature of the job, it was an automatic choice for a lot of people, because it was the only way they could ever be in a position of authority. But the Halpins of this world didn't just want the respect from Joe Public, they also wanted inside the wallets of the criminals.

They were so easy to bring into the fold, they were like lambs to the slaughter, and they were also what made Britain so great.

There was a fine line between the robber and the filth, and in most cases the robber would rather have a capture off a decent Old Bill. Not off a taker like Halpin. In its own way that was an insult to them and their craft. It was hard to get to the real strong policemen, they were decent men who were quite happy to live their lives on the right side of the law and they did not see the dealers' or the bank robbers' lifestyles as something to emulate. They saw it as something to destroy.

Now Halpin, who could sense the change in Freddie and young Jimmy, was just beginning to understand that the people he thought he controlled, actually controlled him.

Freddie loved this bit, it was what he lived for. Freddie Jackson loved to bully, it was instinctive and it was what got him out of bed every morning.

Jackie was in agony, real agony and Jackie being Jackie was letting everyone know that once more. At least now she had good reason, as she was well on for the birth itself.

'Oh, keep your noise down, you silly mare.'

Her mother's voice was not as sympathetic as she expected. It was upsetting for Jackie to hear her mother talk to her like that, considering her mother-in-law was also in the room with them. Maddie was not impressed and Jackie could see that, but Jackie was the one having the baby and she was determined to make the most of her time in the limelight whatever her mother thought.

Maggie had shot off somewhere and Jackie's good intentions had flown out the window again. It was late and no one seemed able to track Freddie down. She was convinced he was with a prostitute. The picture of him with some young girl with tight skin and no stretchmarks was becoming larger in her mind by the second.

A young Chinese nurse was trying to get her to sip at

a glass of water, and Jackie was abusing her loudly, trying to knock the glass from her hand. Lena was ashamed of her daughter and the way she was acting. From her bad language to her racist comments to the nurses, she was a disgrace.

The young nurse, who had been brought up in Upney above her parents' chip shop, was losing her patience.

'Fuck off, and leave me alone, you fucking Chinky bastard!' Jackie's voice was loud, determined and full of hate.

The girl, a superb nurse who was already sick and tired of her job and the abuse she had to take on a daily basis, said angrily, 'Sod you, too. You want to make it harder then you go for it.'

As she left the room in a huff, Lena smiled at her apologetically. At least the girl had a bit of spunk, which is more than could be said for her daughter.

She walked over to the bed, where Jackie was kicking the bedding on to the floor for the umpteenth time, and writhing around as if she was possessed. Anyone would think this was the first child ever to be born. She knew the child was OK, the doctor had already assured them it was a normal delivery, so now Jackie was back to her normal obnoxious self. She had alienated all the nurses and all the doctors again, so even a cup of tea was now out of the question.

Lena felt she was just about ready to blow herself. 'You have to stop this, Jackie, you are making a fool of yourself. It ain't like it's your first, is it?'

Jackie was clenching her fists once more, in temper, but her mother's voice was telling her she had pushed them all to the limit and she knew when to let things go. Freddie's mother was looking at her like she was nothing as usual, and it was hurting her. But Freddie loved his mother and if it took Maddie Jackson to get him here then she would do whatever it took.

'Has anyone tracked him down yet?'

Lena shook her head and said in exasperation, 'What do you think? What do you want him here for, anyway? He would only get in the way.'

Jackie was not listening, she was at the end of her tether with the thought of her husband out enjoying himself while she was in agony giving birth to his child.

'He would rather be with those whores in that brothel than with his wife. Has anyone rung the place in Ilford?'

They had rung everywhere, Freddie knew where she was, there was no way he had not heard about the situation. Liselle at the pub had indicated that he was there, and that he had already been apprised of the situation regarding his wife.

Freddie could not give a flying fuck and they all knew it. Why didn't Jackie just accept that he would not come until the child was delivered? Maggie had just left to cab it over to the pub, so hopefully he might deign to make an appearance, but no one was holding their breath.

Maddie sighed heavily, and Lena followed suit. For once the two women were united, and it was this sudden friendliness that made Jackie take notice of what they were saying.

Lena started in first. 'That fucking child has got to come out, right? So stop fucking about and get on with it. If the baby is born Freddie might be more inclined to get his arse over here.'

Jackie was crying. Her big moon face was red, covered in a heat rash, and shiny with her tears. Maddie stared at her for long moments. She looked awful, and the way she was lying with her legs open, the purple stretchmarks on show, and her toenails ingrained with dirt did not help her one little bit. In her heart Maddie didn't blame her son for wanting to keep away, she was more amazed that he had impregnated the dirty bitch in the first place.

Jackie's crying was getting louder now. She wanted her husband and the fact he would not be coming made her want him all the more. She sounded like an animal, but not a nice animal like a cat, mewling gently as it gave birth. She sounded like one of the animals where Maddie had grown up. And the worst of it all was she looked like one of them. From her bloated face to her dirty feet. Her mother had always referred to the dirty women around their estate as animals, it was an Irish thing. Maddie's mother judged people by the way their children were turned out and how well they managed their money. She had followed suit, and still felt that a woman's kids said more about her than anything else. If the children were clean and cared for, fed and watered, the woman was classed as decent. Jackie's whole way of life disturbed her. Her son's wife should be a reflection on him, and she had a terrible feeling that this girl was.

Jackie was groaning once more, and her face was screwed up in pain. She was only having a baby, anyone would think she was dying of cancer or something the way she was carrying on. How her son had ever seen fit to mate with her was beyond Maddie's comprehension. Yet she loved his girls, and they in their own way loved her. But she found it difficult to go to the house, because Jackie made it all so hard. Jackie was jealous of *her*, his mother. She had never tried to make a friend of her, even when Freddie had been banged up she had not attempted a modicum of friendship. The prison visits had been timed so they would not meet.

It grieved her that her favourite son had married this baggage, who, even now, could not keep herself clean and tidy for the hospital. To Maddie, appearances were everything, and how the world perceived you and your wifely skills was of tantamount importance. Yet all she ever heard about Jackie was how she was making a show of herself. When her Freddie had been put away, she had had to step in when Jackie had overspent on catalogues and then not even attempted to pay, and deal with the embarrassment of finding out that Jackie had gone all over the place ordering stuff and then threatening women with her husband's family if they tried to get what they were owed. To top it all, she'd had her own husband telling her that she had better sort it all out because the embarrassment was killing him. Then, after all she had done for her, she had to contend with Jackie looking at her in that disrespectful way she had, the girls sitting there all scruffy, with their pretty faces stained with sweets.

She remembered Jackie telling her that she needed help now Freddie was gone, that she needed clothes for the kids and food on the table, when everyone knew any money she laid her hands on went on drink and drugs. Expensive hobbies that once more put her daughter-in-law in debt.

Another one of Maddie's foibles was debt. She could not understand spending what you didn't have. When she had found herself paying off her daughter-in-law's debts it had been the final straw. Hundreds of pounds on clothes for her and the girls, clothes she wasn't even going to look after, that ended up in a washing pile and stayed there. It was all wrong, everything had gone all wrong.

Now, though, what else did she have, other than her children and her grandchildren? And a husband who was suddenly in love with a twenty-two-year-old girl.

The humiliation was still smarting along with the

knowledge that this time it was different. Over the years he had tried to save her feelings, but this time he was not bothered about her at all. Had lost all respect for her, because he was enamoured of a child, a girl who already had two children by two different men, and a mouthful of expensive teeth that had been paid for by the man Maddie had loved all her life.

A girl who he took everywhere with him, like she was some kind of trophy, like a prize that said he wasn't getting old. It was laughable, and she would have laughed if it had happened to anyone else but her. Freddie Senior was staying with this girl most nights and he was parading her around the place without a thought for her. It was as if he had gone mad overnight, and now she was reduced to seeking out her son's mother-in-law, someone who she had prided herself on avoiding for all those years. She knew Lena was aware of the situation, but then it was nothing new to her, she had lived with it all her life. She also knew that Lena, knowing the score, felt for her, because she understood just how hard this situation was. To think she had looked down her nose at Lena for years and now, when life was overwhelming her, it was to Lena she was turning.

Once, Maddie would have caused murders, she would have fought him every inch of the way. But not any more. She was past fighting now, because she knew in her heart that if she pushed it, he would actually leave her this time. He was older, and he needed the reassurance of youth more than ever. She also knew he was working for his son, and experiencing a renaissance of his younger days and the skulduggery he had loved so much.

Freddie had given his father a new lease of life and she would never forgive him for that.

'I want my Freddie. Where's Freddie?' Jackie wanted

her husband, she wanted him beside her as she produced his son. It was what she had dreamed of for months.

Maddie rolled her eyes at Lena. In the waiting room they had already consumed a large amount of brandy, courtesy of Maddie Jackson's emergency supply that she kept in her large, mock-crocodile-skin handbag. Maddie liked a drink occasionally, when life was getting her down.

She had only come to the hospital because her husband was on the missing list with his young girl, and her son was nowhere to be found, but for the first time ever she was warming to Lena, a woman she had always seen as below her, mainly because Lena and her brood had never moved on from the estate they had all grown up on. Whatever her husband was, he had moved them away. It grieved her that Freddie was still more comfortable in the council house he had with Jackie than she would have liked. All the money he had earned, and he still had nothing.

But they were both spendthrifts, they both saw money as something to use unwisely. She had hoped that Jackie, at least, with three kids, would have learned the value of a pound. It was not to be, now the girl was sweating and groaning out another child that would be brought up on the rock and roll. Because her son and his wife were claiming benefits, she knew that for a fact. Jackie was still getting her social security every Monday, she saw it as her bunce, as *her* money. When Freddie had been banged up it had been a necessity, now she should be making ends meet without bringing in government agencies and everything they entailed.

The word Jackie always used when she approached her about it was *entitled*. But more people had been captured over claiming benefits than was realised. Once they started poking their noses into your business, the law nearly always followed.

Maddie closed her eyes and tried to forget about the circumstances of her family because she was worried, more worried than she had ever been about her life. Freddie Senior was reliving his youth, and this had made her realise that she had never lived hers even when she had had it. She had not known *how* to be young, and suddenly this was important to her. Her life had been wasted, and it was only now she was becoming aware of that fact.

It was this more than anything that was playing on her mind. All her life, since her first child at seventeen, she had been a mother or a wife, and now she was being discarded. Her husband's leaving was only a matter of time, of that much she was sure. And the knowledge hurt, it was like a physical pain.

All her anger at Jackie was being suppressed now, because without the girls and this new baby her life would be over. Her husband had been everything to her for so long, and had always respected her and cared about her. She had never thought for one moment that he would stop. Now, though, her life was off kilter and she had a lot more in common with Jackie than she had ever thought possible. So she had no option but to concentrate on her family, and, like many another woman before her, she was finding out that at the end of the day that was all you really had.

For a proud woman like her, it was harder than she could ever have believed.

'Tomorrow we have a couple of mates up at the Bailey for a bail hearing, we want to make sure they get it.'

Halpin nodded warily.

'How can I do that?' His voice was quavering and he knew that Freddie and his sidekick could hear it and were enjoying it.

Freddie grinned, and pushed a new drink towards him. 'It's easy, see. We have done this loads of times.'

He lit himself a joint and then, blowing the smoke in Halpin's face, he coughed heavily before continuing. 'We need you to explain to the judge, quietly like, in his chambers, that my two mates have been a great help to you in solving other cases and so they deserve a break. But obviously it all has to be on the hush hush, as they can't be seen to be helping anyone with anything, that goes without saying.'

He could see the beads of sweat on the man's face and thanks to the cannabis he wanted to start laughing, but he knew he couldn't.

'Stop worrying, this kind of thing is done all the time.' Freddie motioned to Jimmy, who took a sheet of paper from his pocket and laid it on the table. 'These are their names, and what they are being charged with. The judge has already been given a large drink, so he will be ready for you and then it's just a formality. They *will* be granted bail.'

Halpin sipped at his Scotch to gain himself some time. It was one thing turning a blind eye, or relocating drugs and firearms. But to walk into the Old Bailey and lie to a judge was asking for trouble. It was putting yourself in the frame, in the public eye. It was making yourself visible to your own.

'Who were these blokes nicked by?'

'South London filth, it's all on the paper. They have all been ironed out by some friends of ours, but that's nothing for you to worry about. They know the score and they are willing to back up your story.'

Halpin saw a way out of his predicament and the relief he felt was almost tangible. 'But I am Serious Crime Squad, why would I be a part of that? It doesn't make sense.'

Freddie was getting fed up now. He wanted out of the pub, he wanted to celebrate his baby being born. He hoped it was a boy, he was sick of daughters. They were more trouble than they were worth, like all women.

'Look, mate, just do what the fuck you are told. They have a lot of form between them, they need to be seen to be helping out the big boys. You are one of those big boys and it's about time you earned your fucking keep.'

Jimmy was impressed. This was Freddie's forte. He had been born to intimidate, and no one could do it with such quiet menace or screaming terror as Freddie Jackson.

The next step with Halpin was to get him to recruit for them and he would do it. He had no choice in the matter. As Jimmy watched the policeman down his Scotch in one nervous movement, he knew they had him and he also knew that Halpin was just beginning to understand what he had got involved in.

Chapter Seven

Maggie watched the little performance from the bar, and as always when she saw Jimmy at work, it made her nervous.

She was not in the mood to go back to the hospital just yet, and she was hoping she might be able to shame Freddie with her continued presence. She didn't hold out much hope though. Freddie was already off his face and looked set for the night.

She guessed that the man with them was being shaken down for something, and as she observed Jimmy's and Freddie's body language she felt a prickle of fear. She didn't like this Jimmy, she knew she would never be comfortable with this side of him. Even her father treated him differently nowadays, she had seen the respect he afforded him. The way he listened carefully to everything he said, as if overnight he had become the fountain of wisdom. The overblown gratitude, when Jimmy slipped him a few quid for a bet.

One part of her was thrilled, she knew better than anyone that in their world it was his standing in the community that would ultimately get them a better life. Her sensible side, though, also knew he was into serious business now and that could mean serious prison time.

She pushed the thought away. Jimmy was too shrewd. As young as he was, he had Ozzy watching his back, he was as safe as he was ever going to be, and she had to stop worrying. The worry blighted the good times, and it was always there in the background. And watching her sister in the hospital bed being delivered of another child, she had seen how her own life with Jimmy could end up if she wasn't careful. Even though he loved her, and she knew he did, he adored her, she also knew that Freddie had once loved her sister in the same way. Now that feeling was all one-sided. Jackie still worshipped her husband, Freddie only stuck around because Jackie was his legal. But even that didn't guarantee anything these days. Men walked away from long marriages, something that had been unheard of not that long ago.

Her mother had always said that, once the kids arrived you were on your own. Maggie had not understood that statement until now. She was too young to know so much about life, and she was acutely aware of that. But she had made a promise to herself a long time ago. If Jimmy ever slept with anyone else, she would never let him near her again.

They would be finished for good, for ever. She would never let him talk her round, make her feel less than she was. Once they fucked you over, if you let them talk you round it was as if you were giving them permission to do it over and over again.

It was imperative that he never lost her respect, she was cute enough to know that much. She was not going to have the life her mother and sister had, she saw herself above that kind of treatment. She was better than that and she was never going to let herself forget it.

'People only do to you what you let them.'

How many times had she heard that old chestnut? Her

granny had said that to her mother a hundred times a day. Her mother had not listened to her advice, but Maggie would. Her father would chat up women in front of her mother, and she could still remember the fights they would have about it. Her father even used to take her round to his girlfriends' houses when she had been a kid. Her mother had believed that because she was with him he wouldn't get up to any of his usual tricks. Not with his daughter in tow. Her childish presence was supposed to have made him remember his responsibilities. Her mother had tried everything to keep him true to her and what had it got her?

Maggie still had vague memories of cheap perfume, and strange houses. Other kids to play with sometimes, or being given sweets and plonked in front of a TV set. He had always made a big fuss of her, made her feel special. She knew now, of course, that that was second nature to him. She was a female and he loved women, especially his youngest daughter who had thought he was a god. Her father would tell her not to tell Mummy where they had been because it was a surprise. She had believed him at first, then she had sussed him out. She had finally refused to go with him, even though her mother would tell her to. Her mother, who had still thought his daughter would keep Joe on the straight and narrow.

They had never discussed it, but he had guessed that she was on to him. It had changed the dynamics of their relationship somehow. Even as a little kid she had sensed that it was all wrong, that her father had wanted her with him for all the wrong reasons. Not because he couldn't bear to be away from her, but because she was his blind. She also knew that if they ever discussed it, it would destroy them both. He had used her, and she was determined that no one would ever treat her like he had treated her mother.

Overnight, her mother had become the bigger, more important person in her life. Until then her father had been her hero, and her mother had just been there. But it was a learning curve and she would never let herself forget what men were capable of.

As she watched Freddie and Jimmy, the similarities between them were uncanny, they were like twins born years apart. Freddie, though, was the alpha male, he was the one you looked at first. His size and looks were more striking than Jimmy's. Darker, his hair was thicker and blacker, and he had the deep Irish colouring that women loved, from his blue eyes to the five o'clock shadow. Even Maggie could see why women were attracted to him and *she* hated him. But he was very handsome, and his air of danger only added to his attraction.

Jimmy was the younger, sleeker version, but he was catching up with Freddie every day. He was taller than Freddie now, though he didn't have the heavy build that Freddie had cultivated in prison. Freddie had been in the gym for the best part of his sentence and he had done what many a man had done before him. Built up his body, to take his mind off his predicament. But now he had been home for so long, he was starting to run to fat.

As she watched them together she pushed all her doubts from her mind. Jimmy had been the love of her life since they were little kids, and she had to keep reminding herself that he was not like Freddie.

When the man they were with finally rose to leave she walked over to them. Freddie looked at her intently, his eyes roamed over her body as if she was standing there butt naked. He made a point of doing it, and she still felt uncomfortable under such intense scrutiny, especially when her sister was there. He knew she was frightened of Jackie sensing that he watched her, that he wanted her. She was too young to have to deal with sexual politics, but she had grown up on a diet of rage and sexual indiscretions. And she hated him for making her life harder than it already was.

At least he didn't try it on so much any more. At one point she had been frightened to be near him. Even if Jackie was in the next room he would make a play for her, try to grab her breasts. And then he would laugh at her when he saw how scandalised she was. Now though, Jimmy's rise in the world had put paid to that.

Freddie seemed to be aware of the way Jimmy was progressing, and if this kept him off her back then she was all for Jimmy's rise to power. But the underhanded way Freddie came on to her, made sure she was always wary of him and what he was capable of.

'She dropped it yet?'

Freddie sounded bored. Until he heard the word boy he was not going to let himself get excited.

'Don't you think you should come to the hospital, Freddie? Jackie is having a rough time of it.'

He raised his eyebrows and then, smirking, he winked at Jimmy who couldn't help grinning at his antics. Freddie was funny, there was no getting away from that.

Then Freddie started to laugh. Maggie hated his laugh, it was the ultimate insult. He laughed at you, rarely with you.

'You mean to tell me you hung about all this time thinking I was going to go to Rush Green to hold her fucking hand?'

Jimmy watched them both. They were natural antagonists and he understood how Freddie got on Maggie's nerves, he just didn't fully understand what the problem was with Freddie. He knew Freddie fancied her, that was apparent, but then he knew any man in their right mind would fancy her, and it went deeper than that.

'Want a drink, Maggie, or do you want me to run you back to see your sister?'

Jimmy's words told her she was wasting her time and even though she knew it, she still had to try. If Freddie would only go and see his wife then Jackie would calm down.

She used her trump card and hoped it would work. 'I had better get back to the hospital, your mum looks tired, Freddie, as if she hasn't been sleeping. I'll try and get her to go home.'

Freddie was amazed that his mother was there at all, let alone staying till all hours. Maddie loathed her daughter-in-law, it was one of the main things they had in common these days. He wasn't stupid though, he knew his father was making life intolerable for her with this new bird. It was a bit full on, even he had noticed that. The little bird was taken all over the place with him, and his father was besotted with her.

He had not seen his mother for a few days and he knew his father had not been home for over a week. He was holed up round the girl's flat, with her two bastard kids and her speed habit that Freddie was inadvertently financing, because his father was not bothering to do any actual work. He was disrespecting the woman who had brought up his son, and who had made sure he was clean and fed.

He was suddenly worried about her. She had been a good mother, the only woman he had any respect for at all. He stood up.

'Come on, let's go and see how the old bird's doing,' he said. 'She better have a fucking boy after all this.'

Jimmy was relieved. He had not wanted another night of it in the pub. He wanted to be with Maggie, and just relax.

Freddie was feeling good about himself now, he could be delivered of his son and heir this very night. The thought excited him, he wanted someone to carry on his name. It would make his life bearable. He loved his girls, especially his Dianna, but a son would be the ultimate.

His mother would love him to be there, anyway, she needed him and he knew that. It wouldn't hurt him to make her happy, and turn up at the hospital for five minutes. She was big on family stuff, always had been.

Jackie watched her husband as he gazed down into the handsome face of his son.

He grinned at her then and she smiled bravely. She was feeling OK but she was determined to milk this for all it was worth.

He was perfect, nine pounds seven ounces of dark-haired Jackson. Lena and Maddie were over the moon, and she was experiencing the pride she had felt after all her births. She loved the babies when they were brand new and it was only when the novelty had worn off and everyone stopped coming round that they started to get on her nerves.

But with this child, from the first time she had looked into his eyes it had been different inasmuch as she had felt a physical tugging inside her chest. It was like looking at Freddie. The baby was the living image of his father and she felt the exhilaration of knowing she had at last given Freddie what he wanted.

When Freddie had arrived she had been triumphant. Her mother-in-law had insisted she tidied herself up and brush her hair and she was so glad she had done it. He had taken one look at the baby, and she had watched in sheer amazement as his face had lit up, and for a few seconds he looked seventeen again. All the love she had for him was once more to the fore. The hurt he had caused, and the neglect she had felt over the last six months was all forgotten as they both shared the miracle of their little son.

Maddie and Lena had looked on with relief as they had observed the little tableau, mother, father and son together.

Lena, as thrilled as she was with her grandson, was worried at how fast her Jackie was knocking back the champagne. Her eyes were glassy and she was talking loudly, but thankfully no one else noticed that she was already half pissed and the child was not yet an hour old.

'What a handsome boy, eh?'

Maddie smiled her agreement and enjoyed the look of pure happiness on her son's face. It was so rare these days.

'Maggie said she kicked off in the hospital.'

Maddie nodded. 'It was embarrassing, I wish she wouldn't carry on like that.'

Freddie sipped at his cup of tea and watched his mother's face, scowling now. He knew that for someone like her, his wife's way of carrying on was scandalous. He had to admit that he was coming round to her way of thinking more and more as time went on. No matter how much money he gave Jackie, she was always skint, no matter what they bought for the house, the place always looked like a tip.

Sitting like this, in his mother's lovely front room, he missed the orderly cleanliness of his childhood. He missed the feel of crisp clean bedding he'd had as a child. Maddie had starched the sheets and he had loved the feel of them, the smell of them. She would pop a hot water bottle in for him when it was cold, and he had snuggled down into the warmth and felt safe.

With Jackie, he was lucky if she bothered to sling the duvet on the bed about five minutes before they got in it.

He had been proud of his mother and father when he was growing up, from their lounge diner to the York-stone fireplace. He had felt different from all his contemporaries because his home had been superior in every way.

Now he was working for Ozzy, he felt that his home should reflect his standing, but he also knew he could never trust Jackie with a mortgage. If he got banged up it would all go pear-shaped in no time, since she didn't even pay the rent until they threatened her with eviction.

He picked up money for Ozzy every month from people who owed him for a variety of reasons, and through this collecting he had been given an education. The way some of the people lived had opened his eyes to a life he had never known existed. But the most amazing thing was that they were all like him, they had come from council estates. The difference was that they had made their money work for them.

Ozzy had made him see what he called the big picture. He had sat and listened to Ozzy explaining about this new order, about how Thatcher was going to put money in everyone's pocket, starting with a housing boom. How it had never been cheaper to borrow money, which for people in their game meant easier laundering of their profits. He loved Margaret Thatcher, he saw her as the saviour of Britain, and Freddie had listened and he had learned.

Freddie wanted to be a part of that world, because he knew people treated you differently when you had money and possessions. It was human nature. When he went inside the great big gaffs and saw the way they were decorated and the way they were kept, he respected the people who lived there because they had achieved that status.

It wasn't like when you saw rich ponces on the telly who had never done a day's collar in their life, and inherited fortunes and then pissed them away. Who could respect people who had never earned a penny in their lives? It was not the way of his world, you earned shed-loads of dosh, so you earned respect.

As he sat in his mother's house, and watched her as she plumped cushions and brought in biscuits, he could not believe that once he had thought this little semi the height of sophistication. His father had been an earner all his life. A grafter, and yet now he realised that if his old man had used his loaf he could have been drinking his tea in a drum worth fortunes.

Even Jimmy was saving up for a deposit on a house, and he knew the boy would get one as well. When Ozzy had explained to him in prison one boring Saturday afternoon about how you worked your way up the housing ladder he had been fascinated. Until then it had never occurred to him, he had thought people who got in debt for a house had to have been off their heads. He had never understood the logic of making money work for you long term.

Freddie's world had been so small, but now he had a son and he was determined that he would have everything a son could possibly have.

'You all right, Mum?' She looked distracted, this woman who had always had a perfectly made-up face, who no matter what happened had always been above hysterics, who was as cool and calculating as a two-ton-an-hour barrister.

She smiled, and he saw the new lines around her

mouth, the papery thinness of her skin. She had got old and he had not even noticed.

'Not really, Freddie.'

For the first time in his life she wasn't being strong. He had always relied on her strength because it was what had got him through his darkest hours. No matter what he had done she had been there for him. She had lied, cheated and committed perjury for him and he saw for the first time that she might actually need something back from him.

He sat up and said magnanimously, 'Whatever you want, Mum, it's yours.'

He really meant it and Maddie felt the urge to cry. Her big, blustering son, who like his father was so self-centered he would only give himself a kidney, was trying to be there for her. It was in some ways too little too late. But she was desperate, if she hadn't been she would not be asking. She knew he would understand that.

'Can I ask you a favour, Freddie?'

He smiled. He was being charming, he had a handsome new son whose birth had made him realise that he loved this woman with all his heart. She had gone through that pain to bring him into the world. She was his mother and he was suddenly aware of what that really meant.

She seemed embarrassed and he noticed that her cheeks were flushed. Her eyes were pleading with him to help her out, help her say what she wanted to say, and his immediate thought was that she was going to mention his father's latest amour. So he kept silent. He didn't want to start a conversation about his father that they would both regret. Once things were said out loud you could not take them back. It had to come from her and he had to listen and then make a decision over what steps he was going to take to relieve her of her worries.

After a few minutes his mother said quietly, 'I have no money, Freddie, could you please lend me a couple of pounds.'

The shock of her words was like a bucket of ice water hitting him in the face.

Maggie was cuddled up to Jimmy in the back of his car.

It was not ideal but it was warm and roomy and they had made it as comfortable as they could. Jimmy kept blankets in the boot and they snuggled under them together, happy just to be in each other's company.

Jimmy loved the feel of her against him, when they were together like this he understood how men could kill for a woman.

'He's a lovely baby, ain't he?'

Jimmy shrugged and then kissed the top of her head.

'He's a baby, they all look the same to me. At least Freddie's happy, anyway.'

He felt her body shudder against him as she gave a loud snort of derision.

'Fucking happy, he'll make a fuss for a week and then get fed up with it like he always does.'

'That's their business, Mags, don't let it interfere with tonight.'

She wanted to laugh, he was always trying to keep the peace. She understood Jimmy and Freddie were close and she knew he didn't like the way Freddie treated Jackie, but his loyalty was one of the things she loved about him.

In fact it was his loyalty that she would have to depend on in years to come. When she had a couple of kids and the relationship was older. She knew that as time went on and he made his way in their world he was going to have young girls throw themselves at him. You only had to look at Freddie and his father to see how life could develop.

'Let's get married soon, Mags, eh?' He squeezed her to him. 'I have enough to buy a place, we can go looking at the weekend. I want us together like this all the time, I am sick of having to take you home and pretend we ain't shagging at every available opportunity.'

She laughed. 'I am ready when you are, mate.' He kissed her on the lips, and she felt the urgency in him once again.

Sooner rather than later suited her, she just wanted out of her mother's house and into a place of her own. She had it all planned, and she was determined to see that her plans did not go awry. No kids for at least six years, and a nice little business to see her through the future. She felt so lucky, and she prayed silently that they would not end up like Freddie and Jackie.

If he ever stopped loving her like this she knew that she would die inside, and it was this knowledge that helped her understand why her sister and mother acted like they did.

Freddie Senior was in his element. He was experiencing a high the likes of which he had never thought possible.

Kitty Mason had just blown him off and it had left him weak as a kitten and feeling like Tarzan.

She was now rolling herself a joint. She sat cross-legged on the floor, her naked body shining like marble in the lamplight. All the years he had been married he had never seen his wife in the nude, and though he had sown his wild oats he had never had a woman so at ease with herself and her body like Kitty. Even after two kids her body was like a well-chewed Blackpool whelk, not a mark on it!

He could watch her for hours, there was something about her that made him want her like he had never wanted any woman before. He had always had his sidelines, and he had enjoyed them, and then he had left them. They had known the score and that had been their attraction. He took them out and he wined and dined them, gave them a seeing to as and when it suited him. They, for their part, had the opportunity to be seen with a well-known Face and experience the criminal lifestyle of money and long nights out.

It was an arrangement that suited everyone and this state of affairs would carry on until the relationship died a natural death.

But from the moment he had seen Kitty it had been a totally different experience. He had been besotted within seconds.

This was an alien concept to him. Never in his life had a woman affected him so strongly. He knew he was setting himself up for a fall, that the thirty-odd-year age gap could only bring him grief, but he was drawn to her. When he wasn't with her he wondered constantly where she was and what she was doing. Drove himself mad wondering if she was with someone else, more to the point, if she was sleeping with anyone else.

Freddie Senior knew in his heart the way he felt about her was unhealthy. She was like an addiction, yet he could not bring himself to try to give her up. Her little flat was lovely, and even though she had two kids she kept the place spotless. It was nicely decorated, and her kids were well behaved. Kitty was a free spirit, and he was attracted to that. She looked after herself, paid her own bills, had even done her own decorating. She had a strength of character that wasn't apparent to most people and it was that independence that most attracted him.

The downside of Kitty, though, was she never knew when to shut her mouth. She opened it without ever once thinking about what she was saying. In his world, women were rarely afforded that luxury and she had put a lot of backs up with her outspokenness. When she had a drink she got very loud, and she also had a problem with any other women around her. It had not taken her long to see that it was her involvement with him that allowed her to say more or less what she liked. But he knew he was going to have to put the hard word on her soon and he was dreading it.

Kitty was capable of having a knock-down, drag-out fight, and afterwards giving him the most amazing, mind-blowing sex he had ever had in his life.

He lay back on the sofa as he listened to Sade. He had a dry mouth and his heart was beating fast, the sound of it loud in his ears, and he knew he was getting the rushes from the amphetamines he had snorted earlier.

He felt sixteen again and he loved it. The feeling of being completely free was like a drug in itself. He snorted, he smoked dope and he listened to music that until Kitty had turned him on to drugs had sounded like shit. He had been an Elvis fan, had loved Sinatra. Now he was listening to 'Papa Was A Rolling Stone' and actually liking the stuff.

The drugs had been a revelation to him, he had not been turned on or tuned out in the sixties. He had been a fifties man, a man who saw alcohol as his only vice. He had loved his wife, who he now saw as nothing more than a brick gradually helping him sink into his old age. Maddie was a decent woman, and he respected her. But all his married life she had been respectable, he had never had a decent shag or a decent conversation in thirty-four years. His generation had stayed married whatever. They had consciously looked for decent women who they knew would take care of the home and any kids they might accrue. They had married their mothers and felt honoured to be doing so.

Now, though, he wanted excitement, he felt the sap rising inside him and he knew that Maddie, God love her, would never be enough, had never been enough. Even before the kid, when she had been well stacked and had a face like a movie star, she had been cold. He knew that people from their background believed that women who enjoyed sex were wanton, were untrustworthy, and he felt cheated because of it.

Freddie Senior had spent the best part of his life looking for what this girl gave him, belief in himself as a man. Not as a giver of children or a provider. Kitty lay back and let him take her. She would howl her enjoyment out and he got off just watching her as she came.

She passed him the joint now and he toked on it deeply. The speed was making his heart beat erratically and he wanted to come down a bit.

As Kitty got up and slipped her dressing gown back on, he heard a knock on the front door. It was the middle of the night and Kitty, being Kitty, did not even think it was unusual. He jumped up and pulled on his trousers and shirt.

'Who the fuck could that be?'

Kitty laughed at him. 'Probably a mate, Fred. Relax, for fuck's sake.'

Kitty was used to people coming round at all hours. She had a flat and she had gear, so it was a natural occurrence for her.

She opened the front door a few minutes later and Freddie Senior was surprised to see his son walk into the room.

'All right, Dad.'

Freddie was smiling, the picture of friendliness and camaraderie. He heard a child crying and the low voice of Kitty as she went in and hushed it. As he looked around the room he was surprised at how nice it was and this showed on his face.

'She keeps this place lovely.' Freddie Senior was explaining himself away and they both knew it. 'So, what brings you here?'

Freddie could hear the nervousness in his father's voice, he knew the fact he had come here would throw him.

'Jackie had a boy tonight.'

Freddie saw the smile on his father's face, the genuine pleasure he was feeling for him, and he grinned back.

'Handsome fucker he is, built like the proverbial, a Jackson through and through.'

Freddie Senior shook his son's hand and hugged him tightly. 'Sit down and I'll get you a beer.'

Freddie sat on the sofa, observing the room. In spite of himself he was impressed. He would not have put Kitty and this flat together in a million years, and she had certainly gone up in his estimation. He clocked the speed that was lying in neat lines on the smoked glass coffee table and the half-smoked joint in the ashtray.

His father came back with a bottle of Scotch and two glasses. 'Let's have a proper drink.'

Freddie accepted his whisky and downed it in one gulp, then he knelt on the floor and snorted a line of amphetamine quickly. Sniffing loudly, he held his forefinger to his nose for maximum effect. The speed was good and it hit his brain in seconds.

'Might as well have a party, eh.'

His father laughed and poured them out more Scotch.

Kitty came back in. She had put on a pair of jeans and a cheesecloth shirt. She looked very young and very pretty. Freddie Senior was grateful to her for getting dressed, it seemed wrong somehow for her to be in a state of undress in front of his son. She sat on the sofa and poured herself a glass of wine.

'Nice little drum.'

She smiled at Freddie then, and he saw why his father was like a dog with three lampposts.

'So you've got a boy, then?'

He grinned again, and Kitty was reminded of how good looking he was. She felt she was looking at his father at the same age – the resemblance was uncanny.

Freddie stood up and said gaily, 'Yeah, me son and heir. Can I get a refill?'

She nodded happily. The fact he was here said that he accepted the relationship with his father. To her this was progress indeed.

Freddie picked up the bottle of wine that Kitty had placed by the whisky, and turned and slammed it with all his might over his father's head. He then stabbed at him with the broken bottle five times, leaving the man a bloody mess.

Kitty saw the blood everywhere, spurting all over her new cream carpet and spraying her walls. Stoned, she was unable to move from the chair. She just stared at the seeping blood in morbid fascination wondering if this could really be happening.

Freddie Senior was lying there, the skin on his face open in gaping flaps. He was literally trying to hold his face together with his hands.

'You cunt! You'd treat my mother like she's nothing? She ain't got a fucking pot to piss in and you're here with your fucking slag?'

He started to punch his father in the head then, heavy, thudding punches that left his hands covered in his own father's blood.

Kitty started to shake, the shock of what had happened

was finally kicking in and she tasted the bile as vomit filled her mouth. She swallowed it down and she shouted in horror, 'What the fuck are you doing? I have got kids in there!' Her voice sounded to her as if it was coming from miles away.

'Fuck you, you ugly fucking cunt, and fuck your fucking kids. You ever talk directly to me again and I'll ram that dope up your box and then use you like a fucking bong!'

Freddie turned back to his father.

The children were crying now, loud sobbing cries that told their mother they were frightened. The noise had woken them up. Kitty ran from the room in terror, worried now for the safety of her kids. Neighbours were banging on the walls but she knew they would not phone Old Bill. They just wanted the noise to stop.

'My fucking mother ain't got a fucking bean, you useless cunt.' He watched his father groaning in pain without any kind of compassion. 'You fucking ever treat my mum like that again and I will fucking kill you.'

Freddie Senior, who in his day had been classed as one of the hardest men around, who had worked with the Krays and who was still revered for his past reputation as a bare-knuckle boxer, looked at his son and saw the future of their world.

He wanted no part of it.

Life had changed drastically, their world had changed dramatically, but he had never believed that this day would ever have come.

He watched his son snort another line, take a drink from the bottle of whisky, and finally pick up the half-smoked joint, and then he passed out.

Freddie washed up in the spotless bathroom. He liked the colour scheme and decided he might go for something like that when they next decorated.

When he left the flat and the sound of Kitty sobbing and the children's distressed voices a few minutes later, he had a spring in his step and a light heart.

Chapter Eight

Jimmy watched his father's face. It was puce, and it was riddled with bewilderment and genuine disgust.

James Jackson Senior was livid, and Jimmy could understand that. His brother had not only been beaten badly, he had also been publicly humiliated.

It was hard for anyone of the old school to get their head round what had happened. It was unheard of, it was breaking every unwritten law and the worst of all was, the jury was out until Ozzy's feelings were known.

Freddie's attack had reverberated around the manor in nanoseconds, thanks to Kitty and her big mouth. Jimmy understood his father's ire but he wanted him to keep out of the aftermath if possible.

Unlike his brother, Freddie Senior, James had never been that entrenched in the business. He had been a heavy, still was a heavy if needs be, but basically he liked a quiet life. He had never had the acumen to make it to the top, he was a drone, a day-to-day worker. He had never wanted the spotlight. Why would he? The spotlight was for people who needed to feel validated. James was quite happy with who he was.

Freddie's attack on his father had blown everyone

away, not least young Jimmy who had not believed it until he had seen the man for himself. As disgusting as it was, in a way Jimmy understood why it had happened – not that he would voice that opinion out loud, of course. But in a strange way he knew that Freddie was doing what he thought was right. He had, though, as usual gone about it the wrong way.

Freddie Senior had left his wife without any means of support and that was a definite no no. Husbands and sons were there to protect the wife and mother. It was how things worked in their world and Freddie Senior had to be reminded of his responsibilities. No one had a problem with that, it was the punishment meted out that had caused the uproar.

Jimmy also knew that Freddie Senior had pushed his luck over the last few months. When you considered the facts, mainly that he had never in his life had such an easy ticket and was consequently milking it for all that it was worth, you might get an understanding of just how the whole episode had occurred in the first place. If he had just once tugged his forelock the whole chain of events might have been avoided.

But Jimmy kept his own counsel. His was not to reason why, his job was to clear up the shit as and when it fell on them all from a great height.

Maddie, for her part, was devastated at the turn of events, but had taken her husband back with quiet dignity. Yet, in reality, what choice did she have? He would be scarred for life and he was blind in one eye. It would be a reminder every time he looked in the mirror of what his son had done to him, and it would remind him of why. It was a reminder that they could all have done without.

Freddie, meanwhile, acted as if nothing had happened

and refused to talk about it. Jimmy had garnered the truth of the situation from Maggie who in turn had got it from her mother.

Maddie and Lena had become bosom buddies overnight.

The child had been the catalyst for that friendship and they both spent every waking hour near the baby. Jimmy almost hoped he had a brood of girls, if boys meant it brought the witches' coven down on them.

Jimmy's mother, Deirdre, a small woman with a pretty face and a slim figure, was cooking as usual. No matter what time of the day or night, she cooked. If you walked into her kitchen at four in the morning, within five minutes a hot meal would be placed in front of you. She had done it enough times for him, and he had been grateful for it. He knew she would not give an opinion either way on the events of the last week and he, like his father, would have been surprised if she had. She was old school, this was men's business and she would leave the men to sort it out.

She watched and listened, but kept her own counsel.

'You and him are tight, so tell me, what's the fucker had to say to you about it?'

Jimmy knew his father hated the closeness he had with Freddie, and he sighed. 'He ain't said a dicky bird, but I heard it was over him leaving his wife high and dry, not a penny piece or a bit of grub in the house, while he shagged that Kitty and snorted drugs.' Jimmy knew he was trying to justify what Freddie had done.

James Jackson Senior was annoyed. He loved his brother and though he knew his faults better than anyone, what Freddie had done was wrong. It was out of order and, worst of all, in their world there was no precedent for it. He had attacked his own father, left him maimed for life and to compound that act it had been on the night his son was born.

'Nothing warrants what he did. Freddie will find out soon enough that people will not tolerate that kind of behaviour, no matter who they fucking work for.'

It was a veiled threat and Jimmy felt his heart sink down to his boots at the words.

'You keep out of it, Dad.' His voice was sharper than he had intended and his father looked at him in abject shock.

'Don't you fucking talk to me like that, I ain't me brother. I'll rip your fucking nuts off, boy, you disrespect me like I am a fucking cunt!'

Jimmy could see the fright on his mother's face and hastily tried to make amends. 'Look, Dad, just let it go. I would never disrespect you and you know that. All I am saying is that Freddie must have had his reasons, and at the end of the day it is nothing to do with me or you.'

James Jackson was on the point of hysteria as he listened to his only child's words. Then he was bellowing out at the top of his considerable voice, 'Nothing to do with me? My fucking brother looks like the Elephant Man and you say it's nothing to do with me? His own child fucking mugs him off and leaves him for dead, and you think it's a private fight? What fucking planet are you on?'

He looked at his wife for confirmation of this statement. Jimmy knew they hated Freddie and all he stood for, but she shrugged as if in complete bewilderment at what she was hearing. She had done this many times before, she knew how to play the game.

James Senior was a shouter, he shouted at the least provocation. It was something that had irritated his wife and son for many years. Yet while he was shouting they were safe. When he finally stopped shouting, trouble was sure to follow. Thankfully, nine times out of ten, he shouted himself out. Jimmy was hoping against hope that that would be the case now. Freddie would take Jimmy's own father apart, without a second's thought, and he had a sneaky feeling that James knew that. He was depending on him to make sure that if it all went off, he would protect him from a similar fate, and Jimmy would do that. His father was safe, safer than he realised.

This was a worrying time for Jimmy, he knew that everything could collapse around them if this was not handled properly. And if it all came on top he would have to take Freddie out. That would mean out of the ball game, out, once and for all.

Because Freddie was not a person you could fight and beat, and then expect to be left in peace with a cheery wave and a handshake. Freddie would hunt you down like a dog until he had wiped you off the face of the earth. It was his nature, it was why he was so good at his job. It was what was frightening everyone in their orbit. Everyone was thinking like his father, but no one actually wanted to do anything about it. They were all hoping someone else would do the dirty work for them.

Anyway, Jimmy wasn't sure he could beat Freddie in an out-and-out straightener. If it went off with Freddie, he knew he would *have* to kill him stone dead. He hoped it wouldn't come to that, but at the end of the day, family was family.

He left the house a little while later, and, going in the shed at the end of their tiny garden, he took out a small handgun he had hidden there. If necessary he would use it without a second's thought. Freddie was a man where a gun was mandatory if you needed to explain anything serious to him.

Deep in his boots Jimmy knew he was just waiting to

see how Ozzy took this latest turn of events, because no matter what anyone else said or did, he knew it would be Ozzy who would decide what the final outcome was going to be.

The new baby was being adored by his mother, his grandmothers and his sisters. He was a happy child who was never alone.

All the females in his orbit were absolutely thrilled with him and he was thrilled with them. He was ruined. Only a week old, and already he was crying every time he was laid down. The grandmothers were convinced that this cleverness on his part denoted a brain the size of Albert Einstein's.

His father, however, was impressed that his little son was shrewd enough to already have women running at his every beck and call. Even Jackie was still enamoured of her child, although her nerves were shot with the events of the last few weeks. He allowed for that because he knew that women and hormones were a lethal mix. Jackie had the brain capacity of a gnat, and he was not about to turn her into a fucking gibbering idiot. He would leave the drink and the drugs to do that to her. But either way he would not be blamed for that as well.

She had given him a son, and he was quite happy to give her a pass until she pushed him too far once more. He knew it would happen, Jackie was the kind of person who always fucked things up for herself. It was what she was good at.

Since the turnout with his dad, Freddie had stuck close to home. He was being father of the year, and who could denigrate a man who wanted to be with his new-born son? It was the perfect alibi, it was the perfect excuse and he was determined that no one would ever put two and two together.

He knew he was being discussed from one end of the manor to the other and he didn't give a flying fuck about that. He was worried, though, about how Ozzy might perceive what he had done. He would swallow his knob if Ozzy took umbrage, but even then he knew it would only leave him with a grudge against Ozzy, and he held grudges like other people held bags of shopping.

No one scared him. He was not so much proud of that fact, as he accepted it as the truth. There was not a man walking who could put any kind of fear in his heart. He was completely confident of his capabilities. He was always focused on the job in hand, he never deviated from anything he decided to do and he would die before he admitted he was wrong.

At the end of the day he had seriously injured his own father, a man he had loved and revered, because he had crossed the line. His dad had left his wife without even the price of a packet of biscuits, left the woman who had visited him in prison, kept the home going while he sat on his ring doing fuck all, or spent most of his time with his birds. This was the same woman who had never once made his father ashamed of or embarrassed by her. She was respected around and about for her clean-living ways and her devotion to the church.

How dare he think he could abandon her for a slag like Kitty Mason? Freddie would not have given a shit if he'd had a hundred birds on the go, so long as he took care of his business beforehand. His mother should have had first grab at his wallet, then what he did with the rest of his poke would have been his business.

Freddie knew he was trying to convince himself, as well as everyone around him, of why he had taken his father out. If he was completely honest, he knew that the confrontation with his father had been a long time coming.

He had needed to make the man aware of *who* he was now. Freddie Senior had still treated him like a kid, had talked over him when they were in the pub. Expected Freddie to finance him and his legion of hangers-on. It was all wrong. He was due the respect of everyone, his father included, and over the months it had been eating at him like a cancer. Even his father was competition to Freddie, and he should have bowed down to the superiority of his son's new status.

His mother had inadvertently given him the perfect excuse. He had defended her honour when in actual fact he had been defending his own.

Maddie brought him in a mug of tea and, as she put it on the small coffee table beside him, he grabbed her hand and kissed it.

'You all right, Mum?'

It was more a statement than a question.

'Never better, son.'

It was what he wanted to hear and they both knew that.

'I love him, you know.'

She smiled sadly and nodded, unsure if he was talking about his father or his new young son.

Joseph Summers was in the pub and he was being bought drinks left, right and centre. He knew it was because people wanted the SP on Freddie and his father, and he made a point of not discussing it. No one had asked him outright, and he knew they never would. They were hoping he would come over all indiscreet, and the amount of beers he was being bought were to hasten that happening.

Joseph was a lot of things, but stupid was not one of them.

He saw Paul and Liselle eyeing him and smiled in their direction. Like everyone else they didn't know what to do. It was an unheard-of situation and they were waiting to see how the main man himself reacted. After all, Ozzy had the final word on everything.

Jimmy walked across the pub and was aware of the people watching him. Joseph grinned at him and he motioned to Paul to refill his glass.

Paul brought them over two pints, and Joseph noticed how everyone was gradually moving away to make room for his daughter's boyfriend. He loved this boy like his own, and he was over the moon that at least one of his daughters had got herself a decent bloke.

'How's everything?'

Jimmy shrugged. 'How do you think?'

His voice said to drop the subject, and Joseph did not need to be told twice.

Paul gave Jimmy a small envelope and he slipped it into his pocket. He made small talk until he had drunk his pint and then he slipped out of the pub with everyone's eyes burning a hole in his back.

Liselle automatically poured Joseph another pint and gave it to him on the house. He smiled his thanks and looked around the pub. He was glad to be in Jimmy's good books because this thing could come on top at any moment, and he was interested to see what the outcome was going to be, though he didn't want any actual part in it. His daughter's husband was a piece of shit and in one way he hoped that he would be brought down a peg or nine. He certainly needed it, but Joseph had a sneaky feeling that Freddie Jackson, as usual, was going to get a pass.

Ozzy needed him. He needed him because he was a lunatic with no scruples or morals or conscience. The law of the land might take a dim view of what Freddie had done, but if Ozzy said it was OK to nearly murder your own father, then that would unfortunately be that.

Freddie and Jimmy were at the house in Ilford, the girls were all busy and Patricia was making sure that the ones to be cabbed to punters were all given their times and addresses. They always gave them a time, and if they were late they were looked for. It was one of the reasons they worked a house.

The law was peculiar in that if the girls solicited on the pavement they were breaking it, but if they were cabbed to an address and got out of the cab on to a private property they were as safe as houses. It was laughable really, but the girls liked the cabs because they made a change, got them out of the house for a few hours and also meant they could take their time and maybe have a drink or a coffee before getting back to the fray.

Patricia smiled at Freddie in a friendly way for the first time in weeks, and he felt his heart lift. He knew she must have heard about the altercation with his father and her smiling told him that she must believe he was in the right. It heartened him that someone he respected could see the justice in his actions. He needed her approbation at the moment.

'You know that you have a call coming here tonight, don't you?'

He nodded. 'Jimmy relayed the message, don't worry.'

His voice told her he felt that Jimmy passing on the message to him was out of order, but he would swallow because it was from Ozzy.

Patricia smiled once more. 'I am sorry for your troubles.'

It was an Irish saying, something that was said at

funerals. She was telling him she agreed with his actions, agreed with what he had done. He had not been imagining it, she liked him really. The world was once more an exciting place to be. He loved the chase and this bird would make him chase her all over the show. He couldn't wait.

Suddenly there was a crashing sound from upstairs. Two of the girls ran towards the sound through force of habit. They tried to get up the narrow staircase together, and Jimmy lifted them backwards bodily as he rushed up to the bedroom with Freddie.

The girls were good at taking care of each other, especially if there was trouble from a punter. They might fight, argue and try to muscle in on each other's action, but if one was threatered they knew they were safer in a pack than they were on their own. They needed each other because of the loneliness of their occupation. When you were alone with a complete stranger the danger was astronomical, and they all tried in their way to see that they were as safe as possible. They looked out for one another and they set aside personal grudges if one of them was at risk. Most of them could fight, but even the hardest had trouble fighting a big irate man.

The small crowd of half-dressed females huddled together at the bottom of the stairs and listened out for what was happening. They knew it would be Ruby who had the trouble, it was always Ruby because she was tiny, and she was innocent looking and she had a mouth like a docker and never tired of using it.

Freddie was first into the room and he looked around him in shocked disbelief. The room was a small back bedroom, it had old-fashioned wallpaper with big pink roses, and a princess-sized bed with pink nylon sheets. There was a small dressing table that held baby oil, Durex and Johnson's Baby Powder, these items being the mainstay of a prostitute's trade. A large man with a beer belly was sitting on the grubby blue shag-pile carpet holding his head in his hands.

The girl was nowhere to be seen. The room looked tidy enough, and Freddie guessed the noise had been the dressing table being smashed back against the wall because the mirror was cracked.

The man was fat and had sparse grey hairs all over his chest and shoulders, home-made tattoos and thick, wiry grey hair. The stench in the room was overpowering, and wrinkling his nose Freddie shouted, 'Where the fuck is the girl?'

It was more than a question and they all knew it. The doorway was now jammed with Patricia and the girls, whose eyes were round and full of bewilderment.

No one could understand what had happened, and they had seen everything in their time. The man was crying, an ugly, guttural sound, and Freddie proceeded to drag him up bodily from the floor.

'Where is she?'

Freddie was looking round the room, demented now. How could the girl have got out without them seeing her? His sensible head was telling him how, but he did not want to believe that. It was too outrageous even for this place. But he turned and motioned with his head to Jimmy, who he could see had already sussed out the situation.

Jimmy stepped carefully across the room and popped his head out of the open sash window. Ruby was lying across the dustbins and the angle of her neck told him she was dead.

He turned to Freddie and said quietly, 'She is down there. He must have slung her out the window, the cunt.'

Freddie did the unexpected. He threw the man across the bed and, without looking at him again, he walked from the room and Jimmy heard him taking the stairs three at time. Ten seconds later he heard the first of the screams from the girls and all hell breaking loose.

He threw the man's trousers at him and said in a loud voice, 'Get dressed, me and you have to take a ride.'

The man was still crying and Jimmy was reminded once more why he hated men who used brasses. There was something lacking in them, something radically wrong with a man who needed to rent a hole to vent his spleen.

Ozzy was walking with the vicar towards the chapel. He made a point of going to Mass at every opportunity. It was worth the time. In the lifers' unit the born-again were the majority because of the different treatment they received. They were always looking at parole, and if that meant becoming a God-gobbler then so be it.

The vicar was a nice man, but very gullible. He also had a lot of the different weaknesses he talked about in his sermons.

Patricia's doctor had rung that morning from a psychiatric unit in London explaining to him that she was suicidal and needed desperately to talk to her brother. This phone call had been backed up by another reputable doctor who had assured the vicar that Ozzy talking to her would be a big help in her recovery. They had arranged for the phone call to be at seven o'clock that evening.

This was classed as an act of God, it was what happened when men's wives or children died, when some kind of access to the outside world was important to the wellbeing of either prisoner or family. It was also very rare, and Ozzy knew the favour he was being done. The vicar knew he would get a serious drink for this little day's work. He was a gambler, and he was into local bookies for a small fortune. Ozzy had made it his business to find this out and now the vicar, who thought he was doing a one-off favour, would become their lifeline to the outside world. No one had pointed that fact out to him yet, they would let it dawn on him gradually.

Ozzy was given a cup of tea and the vicar was very solicitous, making sure he had plenty of sugar and a plate of biscuits. Ozzy smiled at him as he slipped from the room quietly to enable the poor man to have some privacy. The vicar's phone was never tapped. It was what was called an open line and Ozzy was going to use this to his advantage now and in the future.

On the other end of the phone was Patricia, who took a few moments to fill him in on recent events. He listened quietly and then waited while the phone was passed over to Freddie Jackson.

Maddie placed a large plate of steak and chips in front of her husband, and he nodded gratefully.

She hated him like this. He kowtowed to her, he agreed with everything she said, it was as if all his strength had been taken away from him. She forced herself to look at his face because she knew it was important that he did not look hideous to her.

The pain was bad, she knew that, and he looked awful even now the swelling had gone down. He had had over sixty stitches in his face and if it had been inflicted by anyone other than his son, he could have borne it. But the fact it was their only child – the son he loved, the son he had brought up to be just like him – that had annihilated him, the fact it was his son who attacked him so viciously, made it so hard to accept.

Yet her husband was the man who had made the monster, he was the man who had taken him on his robberies, who had taught him to fight. Had made sure his education had been sparse, but also that he could work out a bet to the last half point.

He had made sure there was food on the table and that their home was nice. He had always had his outside women, and she had accepted him for what he was. Yet the monster he had created was the only person she had ever really loved in all her life. Her son had become everything to her, because his father had never really been there since his birth. Freddie Senior had been her life, then his son had been her life.

She wasn't sure how she felt about any of them any more. But this man who sat at home and tried to please her just got on her nerves. He was like a caricature of the man she had known. He was polite, he was agreeable, he was the antithesis of the man she had loved.

She did not know this man. He disappeared into the bedroom if there was a knock on the door, he refused to see anyone, even his brother, and he had no interest in anything that was going on around him. He ate whatever she put in front of him, he nodded and smiled in thanks, and he frightened her.

It was hard for her to accept that Freddie had in effect emasculated his own father. It was harder for her to understand how her son could have justified the violence of the attack, even though what he had done had made her, in the eyes of every woman she knew, the luckiest of mothers.

Her friends were actually jealous of a son who would look after his mother in such a public way, though their husbands thought it was a disgrace. Not that any of them would say that to Freddie Junior's face, of course.

Life was strange. You never knew what was going to happen to you and you never knew what was going to be the outcome of the most normal and simplest of days.

Jimmy watched as Freddie spoke to Ozzy on the phone.

He watched the changing expressions on his face and knew instinctively that Ozzy was with him on the event that had caused so much bad blood. He could practically see him puffing himself up with his own self-importance.

Freddie Jackson had been given permission to do what he wanted.

Now that Freddie had the big man's approval he was back in the fold. No one was going to say a word about him, or to him. Ozzy had just made what Freddie had done *acceptable*.

It was about women being taken care of, it was about men being reminded of their responsibilities, but it was mainly about Ozzy keeping everyone sweet. He needed a nutter and Freddie fitted the bill. More than fitted the bill. Ozzy knew that Freddie would never be trusted after what he had done. That no one would ever forget the breach of etiquette, or the fact it had been condoned by Ozzy.

Freddie for his part had no idea that he was actually working for someone even more slippery than Old Bill.

Jimmy waited until the call was over, then he went out with Freddie and in silence they disposed of two bodies.

Poor Ruby was found three days later on a rubbish tip in Essex. The man was burned away, he would spend eternity in a school furnace just south of Brentford. He had been disposed of with the usual rubbish collected in and around a school yard. In this case that consisted of needles, wraps and empty condom wrappers.

The school really livened up after dark, a bit like Freddie and his cronies.

Chapter Nine

Maggie opened her eyes and looked at the badly Artexed ceiling in wonderment.

She would end this day as a Jackson, she would be a married woman. The excitement was filling her body and affecting her senses. All her life she had wanted this one thing and now it was here.

She could never remember not wanting to be joined with Jimmy Jackson, as his better half, as his wife. Today it was going to come true.

She looked around her bedroom, at the pink lampshade, at the dark-green candlewick bedspread and the posters of Chrissie Hynde, and was euphoric that she would never wake up in this room ever again.

She stretched, her arms were over her head and she wiggled in happiness as she surveyed her little world. Then she knelt up in the bed, and looked out of the bedroom window at the same view she had seen for the best part of her life. The other flats, the same curtains, the rain-stained concrete and the underground garages where no one would dream of keeping a car because it was too dangerous.

She had loved this view. It had always been there, it had

been her world. Now she was ready for a different world, and their new little house was never going to be like this. Her kids would have everything. Their rooms would be themed, they would be beautiful little palaces for her little princes and princesses. Her children would have an environment fit for them. They would not have to fight their neighbours to get to the ice-cream van, they would not have to listen to people arguing when they were drunk, or see people fighting outside their bedroom windows.

They would have the best that could be offered to them, the best that could be bought. Not like this place. This place was concrete hate. It was what was wrong with the world they lived in, and the worst of it all was, in her own way, she loved it. It was all she knew. Yet it was everything she wanted to get away from.

She and Jimmy had already bought a house to live in, and she would only ever come back here to visit. It was a small, semi-detached place in Leytonstone. It had a lounge diner, it was decorated in browns and creams, and it was beautiful to her. It was also a bus ride away from her family, which was eventually the deciding factor.

She leaped off the bed. It was six a.m. and she felt as if she was a newborn, as if the world was waiting for her to become a whole person.

She was eighteen in three weeks. Before then she would be a married woman, and she would be the happiest girl alive.

Jimmy saw the girl beside him and groaned.

The night before was a complete blank, and he knew that was how this was meant to be. He had been drinking brandy and port, a lethal combination, and he felt as if someone had hit him over the head with a billiard ball in a sock. Even that scenario was not too off the wall, given the company he kept most nights.

The girl was young, he could see that much, and she was also snoring, which had woken him up. She sounded like one of the seven dwarfs and he grinned to himself. Trust him to end up with fucking Sleepy. Yet he knew if she woke and tried to strike up a conversation he would then have to change her name to Dopey.

He sat up and sighed. He felt terrible. His clothes were nowhere to be seen and the window was shut tightly, which was why the smell of sex was so overpowering in the tiny room.

He had woken up with a tom, and at a glance he couldn't see any condoms anywhere. He could be clapped up to the eyebrows on his wedding day, and no one would think it was funny other than Freddie.

He got out of bed and stepped gingerly on to the carpet. It had the tacky feel of a tom's carpet. Covered in everything that was disgusting, it had the stickiness of what was commonly known as crud, and it smelt of cigarettes and punters.

He felt as if twenty Paddies with hammers were knocking holes in his skull. It was only after he had spent five minutes trying to open the window that he realised it had been nailed shut.

He groaned. It followed that the door would be nailed shut as well. The heating in the house was full on, which accounted for the heat and the smell, and he would lay his next paycheque on Freddie already being home and dry and laughing his head off at the predicament he was now in.

This was Freddie's idea of a joke.

If it had happened to anyone but him Jimmy would have been the first person guffawing. As it was he couldn't just see the funny side. That Freddie had done it to him made him feel as always where Freddie was concerned – that there was an underlying nastiness behind it.

His only glimmer of hope was a used condom glistening in a green glass ashtray. He breathed a sigh of relief and then tried to escape.

Patricia had been woken at five thirty, by a phone call from one of her girls.

She walked into the house in Bayswater all sheepskin coat and Chloe perfume. The elder, a girl of thirty-five with a bad tit job and crooked teeth, was panicking, and Patricia had to talk her down for twenty minutes before she could ring round and locate Freddie.

She then walked into the bedroom of a black girl called Bernice. The girl was nineteen, looked thirty, and was one of the best earners they had ever had. Unfortunately, one of her regulars, a managing director of a multinational company, had chosen her bed to have a heart attack in an hour earlier. It was put down to amyl nitrate and Patricia thought that this was probably an accurate diagnosis.

He was over fifty, overweight and overdue a medical.

Bernice was calm, for which Patricia would be eternally grateful, and the other girls were keeping a low profile.

This had happened before and so they had a protocol.

She covered the man with a bright green sheet, and, pouring herself a coffee, she waited for Freddie and Jimmy to come and sort it all out with the minimum of fuss.

Freddie Senior was lying in the bed staring at the ceiling.

It was eight months since the attack and he had been out just once. That was only to have the stitches out. Now his wife was expecting him to go to young Jimmy's wedding, and he had no intention of going anywhere near the place.

Every time he tried to leave the house he felt hot air rushing to his head, he felt physically sick and he knew that if he stepped outside the door he would faint. He looked at his suit hanging on the back of the bedroom door and felt the familiar waves of nausea washing over him.

Maddie had great hopes for this wedding. She assumed he would go and everything would automatically be back to normal. Women were complete cunts when it suited them. She had caused all this and she was now trying to make out like it was nothing, that his son had only committed a misdemeanour. That it could all be put behind them.

He had been broken in the most public way possible and there was no way he could ever get even with the perpetrator. He fantasised about killing his son, but he knew he would never actually do it.

He could hear the familiar sounds of his wife in the kitchen. She didn't sleep either these days. He heard the kettle boiling, the cups rattling and, closing his eyes, he wished the biggest heart attack ever experienced on his wife of thirty-five years.

Anything, to get him out of this day.

Joseph Summers was over the moon, and even though his wife had stopped him having his first celebratory drink of the day the moment he had opened his eyes, he was still happy at the turn of events.

His daughter was about to marry the man of his dreams. The fact he was also the man of her dreams was just the icing on the cake. He would never have to do a day's collar again in his life, and no one could say a word.

He was set, settled and he was about to begin a whole new way of life.

If only his other daughter had had the sense to marry a man like Jimmy instead of that useless prick she had settled for, how happy life would be. But he was shrewd and he knew that little Jimmy was one day going to be big Jimmy, and it was that day he would dream of until it came to pass. He had wanted to take Freddie out so many times, but he knew he would never have the guts. But if life had anything left to offer him, then it would be that he lived long enough to bury the bully his elder daughter had tied herself to.

His younger daughter brought him in a cup of tea and he smiled at her like a man who had won the pools and then found out his son-in-law had died.

Happy could not even begin to describe it.

This was the new order and it was not before time.

Freddie and Jimmy were tired, but they had to finish what they were doing. It was imperative that they made sure their tracks were covered.

As they carried the man out of the house they started laughing. Jimmy knew it wasn't funny, but Freddie's eyes as he looked at the inert form between them had made him crack up.

'When I saw he was dead it shit me right up. At least it got me out of that fucking room, though!'

Freddie laughed again. 'He's fucking dead all right. But what made me start laughing just now was remembering your face when I finally opened the bedroom door. You did not even hear us nailing it shut, you mad bastard.'

Jimmy grinned. 'Thanks to you I was out of me fucking box!'

'Too right.'

They laid the man in the boot of the taxi they had purloined. He stared up at them with a half smile and milky white eyes

Slamming the boot shut, Freddie smiled. 'I'll deal with this. You get yourself home and ready for the last walk. The condemned man, that's what you are today.'

Jimmy shrugged. 'No I ain't.'

He was serious and Freddie watched the boy's anger as it rose to the surface.

'I have the best little bird in the world, she is good and kind and decent. She would stand by me through anything and she is a little grafter.'

' 'Course she is, mate.'

It was said as if he had never heard such tripe in his life, and as he walked round to the driver's seat, Jimmy followed him and grabbed his arm.

As he pulled Freddie round towards him, he said quietly, but with enough menace to start a real argument, 'Don't mug her off, Freddie, she is everything to me. No one will ever take her place. She is my life, she is everything good that I have, and no one will ever talk about her without respect.'

It was a threat, it was a starting point for war. It was the most truthful thing he had ever said.

Freddie took a deep breath. Looking into Jimmy's eyes he saw real love, and it wasn't just for Maggie, it was for him. Jimmy was asking him not to ever make a crack about Maggie when she was his wife. He was asking him to afford her respect in every way possible, he was asking him to remember they were blood brothers, that they had ties that went beyond everything they had ever known.

Freddie was in a quandary. He knew that this was tantamount to mutiny, but he also understood where

Jimmy was coming from. He loved the little whore, and she was a whore. He only had to sit it out and wait for her to blot her copybook, because she would. They all did in the end.

So he smiled and said gently, 'It was a joke, mate. You've got a little fucking blinder there. Ease up, boy, it's your fucking wedding day.'

Jimmy watched the way Freddie avoided his eyes, and in that moment he saw him properly for the first time in years. *Really* saw him. From his gold snide Rolex to his diamond signet ring. He saw the ragged nails on his hands and the stubble on his chin. The rough silk suit, and his hand-made shoes. Even with all the money he was earning he still looked dilapidated, he looked seedy and worst of all, he looked what he was.

A cheap hood.

They were a lot of things, but cheap hoods should not be one of them. They were the best you were going to get in their world and Jimmy had made a conscious effort to reflect that in his manners and his dress. Freddie, as always, just expected everything to come to him because of his attitude and his fearsome reputation. The drugs and the loans were just coming into their own. People who had never had the money before now wanted recreational puff, or cocaine. Speed was for the cheapos, the Giro generation. The new designer drugs were for the new generation of people who worked hard and played hard.

This new world was going to give Jimmy everything he had ever dreamed of or wanted, and he knew at that moment that this man, the man he loved more than any other, would always be his Achilles heel.

Their world was changing and they had to change with it.

Freddie was what Ozzy called a romancer, and Jimmy

finally understood what that meant. He suddenly felt depressed, but he drove back to his mother's house and forced himself to get into the enjoyment of what was to be his wedding day.

Jackie was dressed in a blue Ossie Clark trouser suit that had walked out of Maison Riche in Ilford High Street hidden underneath a sheepskin coat, and had then made its way to her house at half the asking price. It had bell-bottom trousers and was hand-stitched. In baby-blue crepe, it was cut for a woman with large breasts and Jackie's spilled over the neckline and made her look sexier than she had in years.

The kids all looked lovely, dressed like little angels in their bridesmaid dresses, and Freddie was nowhere to be seen.

Jackie had already drunk a bottle of wine and it was only eleven o'clock in the morning. The car was picking them up in an hour and she was sorry now that she was so early for once. Normally she'd be late for everything, including her own wedding.

Baby Freddie was gurgling away and little Rox was helping hold his bottle of tea for him even though he was more than capable of holding it himself. He loved tea and Maggie, being the fussy bitch she was, had dropped off a new bottle the day before, one that didn't have tea stains inside it. Jackie smiled as she opened another bottle of cheap German wine. Wait until marvellous Maggie had a few fucking ankle biters, see how she got on then!

At the moment she was like all new brides, dreaming of her lovely home and her perfect kids. Well, she had news for her – they all dreamed of that. Reality unfortunately made you see the error of your ways. Marriage was like war, and if you were lucky you managed to win a few battles.

She had watched her sister the last few months, with her wedding lists and her swatches, and now she looked at the girls in their peach-coloured bridesmaid dresses and stifled the urge to laugh once more. Madame Modèle had been there at eight that morning and put all their hair up, and she had then decorated the French pleats with little peach-coloured flowers.

Jackie's own hair looked stunning and she was grateful for the woman's light touch.

She could not help feeling jealous because this was so different to her wedding. That had been a quick marriage when she had been five months pregnant because Freddie had not been sure it was what he wanted to do.

The humiliation still stung.

It was only the way Freddie had ridiculed all these arrangements that had made her feel better about it all. He had taken the piss from day one, and then when Maggie and Jimmy had bought the house he had slaughtered them.

Deep inside, however, she knew that it was not funny, in fact it was wonderful what they had achieved, considering their ages. But even though she knew that, her natural antagonism and feeling of inferiority stopped her enjoying what they had achieved with them. Her sister had eaten, shat and slept this wedding, and she had not even tried to help her, not really. She had taken her cue from Freddie as always, and even the bridesmaid dresses had only come about because the woman who was making them lived locally and had been happy to come to her house.

She was drunk now and she knew it. The world was suddenly taking on a rosy glow and the kids were looking at her with that look they had but she was determined that no one was going to piss on her firework today.

Freddie still wasn't home when they got into the wedding car and left for the church.

Joseph walked up the aisle of the Holy Trinity Church in Ilford and felt so proud he wanted to burst.

Jimmy was watching from the front pew and he could see the worried expression on his face. It was only then that he realised they had no best man.

Freddie was nowhere to be seen.

He felt Maggie tense beside him and automatically slowed down. The wedding march was playing and the rest of their family and friends were there. No one, not even Freddie Jackson, was going to ruin this day.

As they approached the altar he heard the sighs of the women. They were all remarking, he was sure, on how beautiful his daughter looked.

And she was beautiful. She was stunning and she was his heart.

He could hear Lena crying and smiled to himself. Bless her, at least this time she was crying for the right reasons. Last time she had been crying because she had known her elder daughter was about to make the biggest mistake of her life. That had been proved time and time again. Where was her prick of a husband, anyway? He should have been here by now. Since the boy had been born he had been a bit better. At least he came home more often than he ever had before.

Personally, Joseph couldn't take to the child, not that he would ever say that out loud. His wife and all the other women in the family thought baby Freddie was the second coming. But he had his father's shifty eyes, and he was a lazy little fucker. Blood will out, as his old father used to say, and he had always been right.

Joseph was annoyed that even on his daughter's big day Freddie somehow managed to overshadow it. Maggie smiled at him as he lifted her veil over her head, and out of the corner of his eye he saw a skinny black man with dreadlocks and a morning suit moving along the front row and sitting himself next to Jimmy. He guessed this was the new best man, and held back his anger that Freddie, as usual, could not be depended on.

Maggie was finally married, and even though she had not expected Glenford Prentiss as the best man he had done an admirable job at such short notice. Jimmy had become very good friends with him, and she liked him a lot. He was nice, his girlfriend Soraya was a star, and they had had some great nights out together.

Jimmy was acting as if nothing was amiss but she knew he must be really smarting, because unless Freddie had been nicked, he had more or less snubbed them both on the most important day of their lives. Even Jackie was looking sheepish, so it showed Maggie how serious this breach of etiquette was.

In her heart of hearts, though, she hoped he didn't turn up. He was a loose cannon and she wanted the reception to go off without a hitch, a fight or drunken brawling. Without Freddie there, the odds of anything like that happening were cut by ninety per cent. But she was happy – he was finally her husband and so for her Jimmy's sake she hoped that Freddie would turn up just to put his mind at rest and make his day.

Jimmy kissed her hard on the lips outside the church and everyone cheered, but she could feel the tension in him and cursed the man who even on her big day could take the shine away without a thought. She smiled her best smile, though. Whatever she felt inside she was not going to let anyone see it. They were husband and wife and that was all that mattered.

Maddie was sipping a brandy and Coke and watching her grandson being taken round the room and shown off. It was a lovely reception, and she wished her husband could have been persuaded to leave the house to enjoy it. She had told everyone that he had the flu, and this flu had been around for so long no one expected anything else. It was like he was dead, but she had not buried him.

Freddie's absence from the church had been noticed and, she was sure, commented on. But inside, like Maggie, she hoped that he kept away. He ruined everything he touched, he was like the Jonah in the old myths. He was her son and she hated him these days.

She sighed and swallowed down her drink in one go. It was difficult, this constant smiling and pretending everything was hunky-dory when in reality all she wanted to do was place her head on the table and cry until she had no more tears left. But she couldn't. It was all about the con, all about how you were *perceived*. She was too old for this game. She had lost the urge for it many years before, and now all she wanted was to go home and sit with the husband she loved and who smiled at her and agreed with everything she said.

She hoped that young Jimmy and his new wife had a better shot at marriage than they had. She had a feeling that they were going to fare better than most because, as young as they were, they were so obviously in love. But then so had been the majority of the people in this room on their wedding days. It was a matter of whether that love survived the trials and tribulations of everyday life.

As Lena told anyone who would listen, Maggie wasn't

even pregnant, they were young and in love, simple as that.

If only things could stay that simple.

Freddie and Patricia were in bed, and even though he was out of order, the chance to be with her was too good to miss. At least that is what he told himself, though really he knew she was an excuse.

He had dropped the taxi off at a scrap-metal yard in South London and watched as it had been crushed with Hapless Harry in the boot, then he had gone back to the house to make sure they had cleaned away everything to do with the man. He knew the girls would not be able to resist using any credit cards that might be floating around. He had disappeared, and that was that. The last thing they needed was his cards being kited around Brentford shopping centre.

Then Patricia had offered him a lift, because he had no car and had been dropped back at the house by one of the men from the scrappy who was after a freebie with the girls for his time and effort. He had realised then that the wedding was a no go, and in fact he'd known all along that he was not going to show up. He would have started a fight with a complete stranger if he'd had to in order to keep away.

Something inside him had berated him, told him that nothing should keep him away from Jimmy's big day. That it would cause bad blood, because Jimmy had put a lot of store on his wedding, and he also put a lot of store on Freddie being his best man. It was an honour, and on one level he was gutted that he had let him down, but he also knew he would now be the talk of the wedding, and, like Jackie, he needed to be the centre of attention no matter what.

Patricia got out of the bed and lit a cigarette. She sighed and yawned. 'You had better get your arse in gear and show your face, hadn't you?'

He sighed. 'Bit late now.' He grinned lazily at her and patted the sheets. 'Come back to bed, I've fucked meself now anyway.'

His arrogance, as far as she could see, knew no bounds. She stood up and said nonchalantly, 'No way! I am invited to the reception and I am going, mate. I like little Jimmy and so does Ozzy. I have to give them their wedding present, Ozzy spent ages agonising over it.'

With those few words Freddie finally realised exactly what he had done. He would have to justify a blanking of this magnitude with something big.

The Irish club was packed now, and the reception was in full swing. Even the priest was drunk, and leading a private singsong of Irish rebels' songs in the corner by the bar.

Maggie was still wearing her long ivory dress and her hair was still perfect, and Jimmy gazed at her in wonderment. She was finally his, and they were going to be together for ever.

There was plenty of food, the drink was flowing freely, everyone was having the time of their lives, yet for all his smiling and joking Jimmy had never taken his eyes off the door.

Freddie had been a complete no-show.

He felt in his pocket for the keys given to him by Patricia. They were the keys to a small hairdresser's in Silvertown, and he was astonished at Ozzy's generosity. He had yet to tell Maggie but he was saving it for later, for the right moment. When he had explained that to Pat, she had understood his reasoning and told him he was an old romantic at heart.

He had responded with a smile. 'I hope so. I want her to have all the romance and love she can handle.'

Pat had walked away then, and he would have laid money that she had tears in her steely green eyes.

Glenford was talking about his Irish grandfather and everyone around him was in stitches. He had made the day for them, had stepped into the breach, as they say, and Jimmy would be grateful to him for that until the day he died. The wedding had been a success, but to him it had been marred by Freddie's absence. He also knew he would never forgive Freddie for this humiliation.

Maggie went to him then, and she slipped into his arms comfortably. He held her tight and they swayed together to Teddy Pendergrass's 'Love TKO', a record they had made love to so many times. Feeling his disappointment over Freddie's disregard for them she whispered, 'I love you, Jimmy Jackson.'

It was heartfelt and, looking into her deep-blue eyes, he decided then and there that he was not going to let Freddie ruin this moment, this day, or this wonderful journey they were about to embark on. He would look after this girl, and he would try to ensure that she never knew an unhappy day in her life. And if she ever did, it would not be because of him.

'Maggie, I love you, girl, and I promise you will never know hurt from me.'

Jackie was dancing nearby with Joseph and, hearing the words, she wanted to cry. Not just for them and their obvious happiness, but because she was alone and she was living a lie. She saw Jimmy kiss her sister gently on the lips, his arms protective as he held her, and her sister's eyes so trusting and so bright as he whispered in her ear.

'Ozzy sent you something wonderful, baby.'

Maggie was nonplussed and she laughed as she said, 'What? What you on about?'

Pat was nearby now because Jimmy had motioned to her to join them. Jimmy placed the keys in Maggie's hand and she stared at them in bewilderment.

'What are these for, then?'

Pat took her cue and said happily, 'It's a salon, babe, and it's yours. Ozzy has also earmarked ten grand for you to do it up exactly how you want.'

Maggie's scream could be heard all over the Irish club. People snapped their heads in her direction and then smiled as they realised she was squealing with happiness. She was hugging Patricia and then jumping up and down with glee as she told everyone what had just happened.

Jackie stood back. Unlike her father, who was congratulating his daughter profusely, she felt the usual jealousy and antagonism. As always, Maggie had been given it all on a plate.

The news went round, the congrats were given, and Jimmy was once more proud that Ozzy had seen fit to reward them so generously. It set the seal on a perfect day and he took her back into his arms to the strains of The Temptations and 'My Girl'.

As they swayed together, Freddie walked through the door. He was in his morning suit and he looked dishevelled and drunk. Sighing, Jimmy watched as he strode purposefully over to his mother.

Maddie stood up and greeted him, but the smile did not reach her eyes.

Then Freddie began walking her out of the room. He shrugged at Jimmy, who, against his better wishes, followed him outside with his new wife in tow. He knew the eyes of the room were on them and wondered if he was going to have to fight him this night, of all nights.

'What happened to you, then?' he asked.

Freddie held out his arms in supplication. 'I am so sorry, Jimmy, but me dad's topped himself.'

It was Maggie's, 'Oh my God,' that started Maddie off. She was wailing like a banshee, a terrible, lonely sound like a wounded fox, high and filled with such pain it was almost unbearable to listen to. It was this terrible keening that brought everyone outside to hear the terrible news.

But even as he commiserated with him, spoke all the appropriate words, Jimmy was sure that it was not the real reason for his blanking his wedding, and he knew that Freddie was well aware of that.

Book Two

Thou shalt not steal; an empty feat,
When it's so lucrative to cheat.

– Arthur Hugh Clough
'The Latest Decalogue'

Proprium humani ingenii est odisse quem laeseris.

It is part of human nature to hate the man you have hurt.

– Tacitus
Aricola, 42

Chapter Ten

1993

Jackie watched as her son demolished another Easter egg, stuffing it into his mouth and barely chewing the chocolate before grabbing another one. He would be sick soon and he would cry, then the whole cycle would start all over again.

As usual there were too many eggs, too much chocolate, and she did not have the energy to tell him to wait until he had eaten his dinner. He never ate real food, not in this house, anyway. He ate crap, and she had stopped trying to make him do any different.

His tantrums were legendary, and his sisters had gone ahead to their aunt's house rather than sit and listen to it all. He had been calling them names since he had awoken at five thirty that morning. He had sat up all night watching videos, and had not deigned to go to bed until gone two.

It was *Driller Killer* that kept him quiet at the moment, and the more violent the movie, the more he became engrossed. Jackie knew she should stop him from watching them, but it was the only time they got any peace. He loved the blood, and as Freddie and Jimmy were now the main people involved in video piracy, it was only natural that the boy should want the films that were so easy for them to locate.

Little Freddie thought it was funny when he watched the blood and gore, but it was as if he had no concept of pain because of them. If he had a hammer, he would hit you with it and laugh. She knew this because he had done it countless times. It was like living in a nightmare.

Pouring another glass of vodka, she sat down and wondered if Freddie was going to be back in time to go to Maggie's for their dinner. It was Easter Sunday and the whole family would be there. Maggie's was now the place where everyone got together on high days and holidays. Maggie with her dinner service and her tablecloths. Maggie the cook and the golden girl. With her top-of-the-range car and her fucking beauty salon. She really thought she was something special.

Jackie glanced at the clock and knew she would have to get going soon or she'd be late for dinner. One good thing with Maggie: at least there would be plenty of drink and grub at her house.

If Freddie didn't come quickly then she would go on her own, she was used to it these days. She had stopped expecting him, had learned to just wait and see when he arrived. It was easier for her in the long run because it meant she could have a drink in peace.

He acted as if she had some kind of *problem* – this from a man who was drunk and drugged every night of his life, and all day as well if he could get away with it. He had even hinted, in their more antagonistic rows, that it was her drinking that had caused their son problems. It couldn't be the fact that his father never came home and treated them all like dirt when he did, could it. He was blaming her for the way Little Freddie was, when he was a replica of himself, from the temper, to the single-mindedness and the complete and absolute disregard for his safety, or anyone else's for that matter.

To call her a drunk was one thing, but after the first visit from social services, he'd asked if she thought maybe Little Freddie had foetal alcohol syndrome? Where would he get a term like that from? It was something she had never heard about, had never even known existed. That jibe had hurt her because, deep inside, she had a terrible feeling there just might be a grain of truth in it.

She gulped at the drink. It was her anaesthetic against the world, against her family who pitied her on the one hand, and who blamed her for her problems on the other.

Little Freddie, as he was known, even though at seven he was already wearing the clothes of a ten year old, stood up and walked to his mother. 'Are we going?'

He was getting irritated. He hated being alone with her. He liked it when he was surrounded by people, when he was the centre of the universe. But even his doting sisters were getting fed up with him and his attitude, and he was finally learning to act lovable now and again to keep them interested.

He kicked his mother on her shin, and she leaped forward and slapped him hard across the side of his head. She caught his ear with her ring and he screamed loudly, 'You fucking bitch, you fucking whore.'

He started grabbing at her then, trying to pull her hair and punch her face. She put her glass down quickly and, smacking him once more across the head, she threw him away from her. 'Fuck off, you mad bastard, before I fucking knock you out.'

He lay on the floor then, screaming and swearing at her. She picked her drink up again and took a deep swallow. The tirade would soon reach a crescendo, then he would just lie there and swear at her until she hit him again. Jackie sat back in the chair and closed her eyes. He was like an animal, and she knew it was her fault.

When he had first done it they had all laughed. He had been eighteen months old and he had attacked poor old Kimberley because she had told him off, and his language had been ripe. They had all sat stunned for a few minutes and then started rolling up. The words coming out of his mouth, and his dear little face while he said them, had been so outrageous they had roared. Then the girls had told him to repeat it, because it was so funny, and it had caused them all to crack up again. Little Freddie had soon sussed out that it was an attention-getting device and before they knew it his whole speech was peppered with effing and blinding.

It had set the tone for him and now at nearly eight it was his main vocabulary. He had been ejected from two playschools because of it. Now the school was refusing to take him back again, but that was also because he attacked anyone in his radius if they did not let him do exactly what he wanted.

It had brought the social workers into their life and she could knock him out because of that alone. If that Mrs Acton mentioned her drinking one more time she would scream. Fucking social workers, if she had that mad little cunt all day and night she would have a bastard drink herself! And Jackie had told her that in those very words, enjoying the woman's shock at her turn of phrase and feeling as if she had finally scored a point.

But he *was* out of control, there was no doubt about that, and as the only person he was even remotely civil to was his father, he would stay that way until Freddie came home regularly and took him in hand once and for all.

Fat chance of that ever happening.

Jackie sighed and then poured the dregs from the bottle of cheap vodka into the glass. He was still swearing and calling her names, but she ignored him as best she could, just saying, 'Get your coat on, and I'll call the cab.'

Maggie had been cooking all morning, and the smells coming from her kitchen were driving everyone mad. Lena and Joseph were already there, all spruced up and filled with pride at the lovely home their youngest daughter had created around her.

She and Jimmy had moved into this place a few months earlier. According to Lena, it was a brand-new, large, detached, four-bedroom mock-Tudor mansion, with a *huge* garden and en-suite bathrooms. Lena *never* stopped going on about it to anyone who would listen. Her pride in her daughter knew no bounds.

It was a nice place, but for Jimmy and Maggie it was just another stepping stone. Unlike Freddie, Jimmy had taken Ozzy's advice and he had invested in property. It was the best thing he had ever done in his life. He bought early, waited and then they moved on again, with their tidy little profit ploughed back into a new house that was always a bigger and better place for them to live.

This was their first brand-new home, though, and as much as they loved it, they missed the character of their last place. But they had bought that for a song. A builder friend had owed Jimmy a big favour and this was his way of paying him back. They'd done it up and then sold it because it was too good an opportunity to miss.

They would have the character house once again, only bigger and better next time. This place would do for another couple of years. It had a big garden which wasn't overlooked, and they had the kitchen and bathrooms of their dreams.

Maggie looked up at Jimmy as he walked into the large kitchen to refill his father-in-law's glass.

'All right, babe?' he said.

She nodded. ''Course I am. Are Paul and Liselle here yet? I heard a car pull up.'

Jimmy walked out into the big entrance hall. A few seconds later, he saw them coming through the front door, and waved them into the kitchen.

Liselle looked around in admiration. 'This place is lovely. I wish you well in it.'

Maggie kissed her on the cheek. 'Take your coat off, mate. We're lucky with the weather, anyway.'

Jackie's girls were all laughing and joking in the front room, putting on music, and Maggie smiled as she heard an old soul tape going on. The girls loved all the old songs, thank God. As Sam and Dave blared out of the sound system, she walked through to the garden and was grateful to finally have a sip of her white wine.

Maddie was sitting quietly on a garden chair. She was always invited, and she always sat by herself, smiling, but rarely joining in. Her husband's death had hit her hard and Maggie always remembered the awful feeling on her wedding day when the news had been blurted out by Freddie.

His father had lain in the bath and slashed his wrists, and the thought of it still made her blood run cold.

It had been such a traumatic thing for them all to have to deal with on such a happy day. Freddie had found him, and had not wanted to ruin the wedding. He had waited until the body had been taken away and the bathroom cleaned up, so his poor mother had not had to face that on top of everything else.

Maggie knew that Jimmy, like her, felt awful for the way they had assumed Freddie had just blanked them. She pushed the thought from her mind and went over to where poor Maddie sat on a garden chair.

She sat beside her and chatted for a while, but she knew the woman was waiting for her son, and if he arrived it would make her day. If he didn't then she would go home and sit alone and wait for him there. At least he took care of her. Maggie couldn't take that away from him.

'I wish you would just listen to me sometimes, Freddie. I knew they were fucking ice creams.' Pat's voice was heavy with annoyance because she knew Freddie was still not listening to her.

The South London warehouse they were standing in was full of snide. Though Jekyll and Hyde was the proper term for all the goods stacked around them, it had been shortened to Jekyll or snide. The warehouse was chock-full of snide booty and swag. A lot of videos, most not yet on general release. Disney videos were where their money really lay. Disney only brought their films out every seven years, so there was always a new market for them. One year it might be *Bambi*, another year *Dumbo*, but the main thing was, once the film was released it would not be brought out again for a long while. This worked to their advantage since all they needed were a couple of master tapes and they were off. They could knock them out for a couple of quid and the one-parent families could treat the kids *and* buy a carton of fags, and still be quids in, as opposed to going to Woolworths and paying what they termed the full bifta.

There was also plenty of hardcore porn, otherwise known as old Bluey. They made fortunes from that too. It was easy to bring it in from Denmark and Sweden, where you could watch what the fuck you liked without having to justify your shagging preferences to anyone but your old woman.

Then there were knocked-off Fila tracksuits, run up in Korea and shipped over for the benefit of the unemployed and anyone who used a local market. The designer stuff was worth a lot of money, and it caused a lot of aggravation because there was so much competition around trying to flog it off.

'How long did they say they would be?' Patricia tapped her foot in annoyance, and Freddie checked his gold Rolex. It was definitely not a Jekyll nowadays. Patricia had seen it before and knew it sweeped not ticked, but they had boxes full of snide watches for the discerning punter. From Rolex to Cartier, it was one of the best scams ever. Everyone suddenly wanted to be a film star, wanted to look worth a few quid, and they were tapping into that market.

'They should have been here by now, Freddie.' Patricia lit a cigarette, also snide. These were knocked up in China and they had everything from the right boxes to the right import dockets. They were ten pence a pack, and they knocked them out in the two hundreds all over the smoke for fortunes. It was like having a licence to print money.

'They had better get their arses in gear, right?' she said.

Freddie heard a van pull up outside and sighed theatrically. He knew how to play the game and Pat was getting on his wick acting like he was her fucking ball boy.

The men he was meeting were two brothers from Liverpool. They were young, ambitious and basically braindead.

They had been taking a lot of the merchandise from them and relocating it up their end of the country. All well and good, except the brothers now owed Freddie a lot of money and after repeated requests for payment, and outrageous and insolent excuses for the lack of moolah travelling back down the M1, they were about to get what was known in their game as a severe warning.

The two brothers were called the Corcorans. Shamus and Eddie were in their twenties and were loud, funny and good company. Now they would have added to their résumé, piss takers.

As they walked into the dimness of the warehouse they were both smoking cigarettes and, as usual, laughing. Seeing Freddie, they both slowed down. He was not supposed to be there, and they had believed they were meeting with his minions, Des and Micky Fleming, and Bobby Blaine.

'Hello, Freddie, we didn't expect to see you today.'

Freddie grinned, all white teeth and camaraderie. 'I know. How are you, boys?'

They shrugged simultaneously. 'Great, yourself?'

Shamus was the brains of the outfit and he was uneasy. He knew Freddie was going to have to have a word, and he tried to pre-empt him. 'We've got some of your money in the van.'

Pat laughed. 'That makes a fucking change. We thought we were giving out to a new charity, the Liverpool ponces' society. You a member, eh?'

Freddie laughed then, a genuine, friendly laugh that relaxed the two men. 'How much you got for me, then?'

He sounded all right and the brothers relaxed. Freddie smiled. In his tracksuit pocket he held a set of knuckle-dusters. They were custom-made and spiked, and they would do a lot of damage in the minimum of time.

Shamus flicked his hand over his shoulder in a friendly way. 'We've got ten grand out there.'

Shamus was a large lad, but he did not have the presence he needed to intimidate. His brother did have the presence, but he lacked the killer instinct. They would always work for someone and that someone would always leave them to take the flak. It was sad, but it was a fact of life.

'Go out to the van, Pat, and have a rummage, see if you can locate any poke. I'll meet you outside in a minute.'

She nodded to Freddie and walked sedately away from the men.

Shamus knew what was coming and braced himself. He had taken the piss, he knew that, but his brother was not the sharpest knife in the drawer and he wanted to protect him.

'Look, Freddie, let me brother go, mate. I'll take whatever is coming . . . it was me who pissed the money away, not him.'

Freddie admired him for his loyalty. He understood that the younger brother was obviously not a contender for *The Krypton Factor*, so he made a snap decision. He brought his hand out of his pocket and attacked Eddie with all the force he could muster. Shamus jumped in but Freddie knocked him to the ground.

Freddie took Eddie's face off in under two minutes.

Then, once he had dropped to the floor, he turned to Shamus and grinned at him as he kicked the boy's ribs into mush.

Exploit any weakness to your advantage. Freddie had lived by that rule all his life and it paid off. Shamus's weakness was this poor boy who would spend the rest of his life with breathing problems, due to a punctured lung, and a face full of Mars Bars, courtesy of his knuckle-duster.

He also knew his money would be there within the week.

Freddie had already taken care of the Liverpool end, so he had not stepped on anyone's toes. Shamus would find that out soon enough, so he decided not to add to the boy's burden today by telling him he had nowhere to go for retribution. This was an out-and-out straightener.

He shook hands with Shamus before helping him sling his brother into the back of the van and giving him directions to the nearest hospital.

'No hard feelings, son, but you remember to pay on the nail in future if you want to carry on doing business with me, OK?'

He was being magnanimous, he was being the big man and letting the lad know that it wasn't personal, it was just business. He was trying to help him with his future endeavours, giving him a lesson in the big boys' way of trading.

After all, it was Easter Sunday. He could afford to be nice one day of the year.

Jackie was rocking, and her loud laugh was getting even louder. She was taking the piss out of Maggie as usual, calling her Mrs Bouquet in one breath, and reminding her of her beginnings in another.

It was a pattern and Maggie was used to it, but she knew that Jimmy never would be, that he was on the verge of throwing her out. He wasn't worried about Freddie's reaction to his aiming Jackie out the front door, though, he was more worried about hers. Freddie was always urging him to send his wife home, telling him it was his house and he should not let Jackie mug them off in it.

But Maggie understood her sister's disappointment in her own life, and knew that every time she saw her she was reminded of a youth she had thrown away on a man who had no real care for her and who, for some strange reason, she could not live without.

Joseph stared at his eldest daughter. She was so far gone he knew it was a miracle she was still able to talk. They were all in the dining room. The meal had been perfect, and the kids had been good, even Little Freddie who always underwent a personality change at Maggie's house. They were now enjoying port and brandies and the cheese platters Maggie made up so beautifully, and Jackie was getting personal and vindictive.

'Why don't you shut your fucking trap for once?'

Joe was pointing at his daughter with a cheese knife, and Lena was trying to pull his arm down all the while saying quietly, 'Leave it, Joe, you'll only make her worse.'

Jackie poured more brandy for herself. 'Well! Who does she think she fucking is, with her fucking family dinners and her fucking big house, looking down her fucking nose at me?'

Maggie sipped her port and sighed. She had been here many times before, and as ever she would sit it out until Jackie went into the lounge and fell asleep.

'Well, let me tell you something, lady,' Jackie poked herself hard in her ample chest. 'I am a better person than you, remember that. I am a better fucking person than you will ever be.'

She was now pointing at Maggie with a long fat finger. The nail varnish was chipped and her hands were chapped and sore looking. 'I don't need cars and fucking houses to make me feel good about meself.'

This was a familiar rant and Maggie ignored her, waiting for her to get it out of her system, but Kimberley shoved her head towards her mother and said nastily, 'Why would you need cars to make you feel better, Mum, you've got fucking alcohol.'

Somewhere in Jackie's head the words penetrated and she knew the girl was speaking the truth, but the thought of her daughter saying that to her was like a knife in her chest.

Lena was nearly in tears. She dreaded this and every time it happened it upset her more. She knew it was all their own fault. They had allowed Jackie to get away with it, and consequently she now believed she could do and say what she wanted whenever she wanted. This should all have been nipped in the bud years ago.

'How dare you talk to me like that? I am your mother.'

Jackie had the self-righteous tone off pat, and she also had the look of a woman who had been whipped once too often. She'd been a complete manipulator of everyone around her, and as the years had gone on she'd become unable to see that none of it was working any more. Especially with her girls, who knew her too well.

'You are a piss head, Mother, and you ruin everything because you can't stand to see anyone doing well, can you?'

'Stop it, Kim, leave her alone.' Maggie's voice was calm and she handed her sister a cigarette and then lit it for her.

It was what Jackie wanted – if Maggie wasn't annoyed with her then she was still in with a chance of redeeming herself. She puffed on the cigarette as if her life depended on it and looked out of the sparkling clean patio doors into the garden.

Everyone was talking again in low voices, and Jackie felt the urge to cry that always came when she was with her family. Opposite her chair was a long gilt mirror and she could see her reflection. At first she had wondered who the hell it was, the dark-circled eyes, with their bitterness and hatred burning out, and the heavyset body and hunched shoulders encased in a white frilly shirt that made her look even bigger than she actually was. Despite her denial, on one level she knew it was her, and seeing the destruction of herself just made her angrier, because it showed her the abortion her life had become.

Jackie glanced back out of the window and stared at the green lawn and the small summerhouse that was freshly painted. It was a lovely day, warm and bright, with the sun glistening down on the ornamental fishpond. It looked so nice, so normal and it was this normality that frightened her.

This should have been her, this should have been her house, her home, and Freddie should have been sitting with her and loving her like Jimmy did Maggie. They showed her life up for what it was, and she couldn't bear it sometimes.

Even her children only tolerated her. As the girls had grown up they had grown away from her, further and further by the week. Maggie and Jimmy still didn't have kids, they were waiting for the right time. They planned everything and they made sure they had enough money and enough time to bring their plans to fruition. Even Maggie's little shop was now one of five hairdressers and beauty parlours she had spread all over Essex and the East End. Jimmy had a pub, a garage and a night club, and that was without his hot-dog vans and the houses they rented out. And they worked them all together, they did everything together. They even had a place being built in Spain.

They were a constant reminder of what she didn't have, had never had.

Jackie hated them for that.

Freddie had dropped Pat back at her house and stayed for a couple of hours. They were an item, he supposed, except she still acted like she was a single woman.

He loved her house. It was bright, clean and quiet, so bloody quiet. Her sound system was the best that money could buy, and like him she listened to it down low, not blaring out and blasting your eardrums the way Jackie and the kids preferred. Pat had a chocolate fridge and a fridge for beers – it was like a different world. She was also so independent. Even though over the years this had annoyed him, he liked it about her now, especially since one of his little amours had given him an ultimatum.

He was going to pop in to see her before going to Jimmy's for his dinner. Jimmy knew he had a bit of business so he wasn't expecting him until late.

Freddie drove on to the Thamesmead estate and parked outside a tower block. Locking his stacked-head Mercedes, he sauntered over to the main doorway and observed the kids hanging around like little clones of one another.

Jimmy had recruited a few kids off this estate when he had started doing the flowers years ago. He had got a couple of boys from here to work the plants for him, and they had been sound little workers. He had driven them all over the place and settled them in lay-bys with a flask of tea and their flowers all bucketed up in water. Freddie had thought he was mad until he saw the money he was pulling in, then he had worked them with him.

Nowadays, of course, it was all taken care of for them and they just picked up their poke at regular intervals, but it had been the catalyst for him listening to Jimmy's ideas. He had a good business brain, and so did little Maggie. Look at how she had turned those shops into gold mines. Seven years on, that girl had a small empire and, in fairness, she had built it on her Jack Jones. And she hadn't even dropped a chavvy yet, she still had her tits in the right place and a stomach like a washboard. Jimmy was a lucky fucker.

Freddie still had an ambition in life, and fucking Maggie was it.

She looked at him and he knew she was looking down her pretty little pointed nose, but the time would come when he would bring her down a peg. Like his father always used to say, wait long enough and you'll get what you want from life. Just make sure it was worth the wait.

He walked into a flat on the ninth floor. The door was open, the door was always open. The flat was occupied by a nineteen year old called Charlene, who had thick blond hair and green eyes framed by thick dark lashes. There was no doubt about it, she was a looker, and her neat little body was made for Freddie Jackson's large, brutish lovemaking. However, she had a kid called Deandra, a name she had heard on a TV show and loved. The child was a nice little thing, and she was also at Charlene's mum's, as it was a weekend.

As he walked into her tidy front room he was smiling. Charlene, however, was not.

'You took your fucking time.'

Freddie was doing his best not to laugh at her. She really thought she was something special. What was it with these girls? Did they really believe a few fucks and a couple of Indian meals represented a relationship?

Pat was getting suspicious, and if he cared about any woman it was her. This whore had actually phoned her house and then threatened him with exposure, not only to her but also to his lawful wife!

Now that was a melon scratcher as far as he was concerned, and he knew he had to shut this fucker up once and for all or she was going to be one of those girls who caused more trouble than they were worth.

'Hello, Freddie, good to see you, Freddie. Ain't that what you are supposed to say to me?' His sarcasm was lost on the girl, who all her life had been fêted, first by her father and mother and then by everyone in her orbit, because she was so beautiful.

She had got pregnant by a no neck at sixteen, and he had gone on the trot without a backward glance. He was now doing an eighteen for armed robbery and drugs offences, so he was definitely out of the picture. She had latched on to Freddie because he was good looking, he had plenty of poke, and he was also the number one diamond geezer in her vicinity.

She had what he wanted – a lovely face, a good body, and she knew how to make a man feel like a king in the kip. Now she was flexing her little muscles. She wanted him full time, was not happy with his erratic style of courtship, and she was under the impression that he was as up for this fairy tale as she was.

He looked at her dispassionately. She was lovely, really lovely, but she had about as much conversation as a junkie in a holding cell. Her only allure as far as he was concerned was that she had her own drum, clean knickers, and made a decent cup of tea in the morning: his criteria for a good shag.

Charlene was sitting upright now, on her second-hand three piece, and looking at him daggers. She really thought she had enough nous to keep a man like him interested in her. It was unbelievable the way these young girls kidded themselves when they were there for the taking for men like him.

They were in every pub and club he frequented, they were like leaves on the ground. When you dumped one, another one would be standing in the same place in the same bar a few hours later.

They wanted him, they wanted what he was, and what he had to offer. They were like those young girls who married old geezers who were caked up with dosh. When one of them married some old fucker with no poke, except his pension, and moved into his sheltered accommodation, he would believe it was love.

Until then, bollocks to them all.

This girl would spout love if he wasn't careful. He had been there, done that.

'You can't treat me like some fucking tart, I won't have it.' She was all on her dignity and full of her own self-importance.

Her eyes were made up and her lipstick was perfect. She had been expecting him and he knew she had been dolled up to the nines every day waiting for him to arrive.

She really was a lovely little thing.

She was about to experience one of the worst days of her life and he was sorry for her because of that. But needs must when the trollop drives!

He walked to her and dragged her up from her seat by her thick blond hair. Pushing his face close to hers he said quietly, and with deliberate menace, 'Who you talking to?'

He was so close to her face she could smell his breath, and the sweet aroma of the grass he had smoked earlier.

'You are going to tell my old woman about us, are you?'

Charlene was trying her hardest to shake her head but he was holding her like a vice.

'No one threatens me, lady, and anyone who does, man or woman, is a cunt. Do you understand what I am saying to you?'

She was terrified. Her lovely green eyes were filled with tears, and she was thankfully speechless with terror. This was going to be easier than he thought.

'If my wife or kids ever hear about my little wander

into your flat, I will blow this fucking place off the face of the earth. Do you hear me?'

She was desperately trying to nod her agreement.

He let her go then and, smiling at her with that charming dead smile he had, he kissed her on the forehead and said, 'You know it makes sense, darling.'

Then he pushed her back on to the sofa and left.

She could hear him whistling to himself as he walked back towards the lifts.

Chapter Eleven

Jackie had drunk herself sober by the time Freddie arrived at the house.

As he pulled up outside he was impressed despite himself. This was his idea of a nice place, not like Jimmy and Maggie's last one with its pantiled roof and all the old-fashioned fireplaces. He liked the newness of this house, the clean lines, the integral garage. He would love a drum like this, and he could have one if he wanted to.

He always reminded himself of that when he was around them, and he always promised himself that it would happen sooner rather than later. If Jackie wasn't such a dirty bitch he would have gone for it years ago, but no matter how much he weighed out, no matter how much they decorated, their place was still a shit hole.

Dirty, scruffy and in constant need of redecoration.

Young Jimmy had always bought for cash and then remortgaged, that way the money was clean. It was a perfect way of laundering their robbery and drugs cash. Freddie had missed the boat in a lot of respects. It was getting harder to do that now, unless you bought really cheap. But his money went through his hands like water. He would put on large bets, lose the money and then recoup and lose it all once again. He was constantly out and about. He would make the night last as long as possible because there was nothing to go home to. He ended up paying for everyone, not just with the drinks but also with the gear. He attracted hangers-on, the piss heads and the druggies who knew he was always good for a night out because he could never let the night end.

Jimmy would have a couple of beers and say his good nights. He was happy to go home to Maggie and their nice bed and their nice life. Freddie had never been able to do that, even when the kids had been young. Maybe it was a personality trait, or something missing in him, he didn't know. But he had sat for twenty-four hours at a time and spent huge amounts of wedge on people he didn't even really like.

The money just disappeared. He had no real back up if there was an emergency, and he knew he was ashamed of that because they had earned real money. Most people would kill to earn like they had, and he had pissed it all away.

And with Jackie having their place decorated on a regular basis he knew he was just throwing good money after bad. Jackie had nagged at him until, a few months ago, she had been delivered of a new white wood kitchen, and already it was rotten. Even while the men were fitting it she had not bothered to clear her dirty dishes away, or make it habitable. He had seen the men tiling the walls and having to move used plates and mugs out of the way themselves.

He had been so embarrassed he had caused ructions. But Jackie, she was a lost cause and they both knew it. He told himself that was why he didn't bother, he was trapped with her and he had accepted it. Since his son's birth he had been tied to that place. The worse his son behaved the less he wanted to be there, but the tighter the hold she had over him. He hated his life and yet he didn't know what to do about it.

If it wasn't for Patricia he knew he would lose it completely. Even though he wanted her more than he had ever wanted anyone before, he knew it suited him that Pat was not the clingy type. Jackie would completely fold without him. Although he knew they were not healthy together, if he left her it would be the end of her world. He was the only thing she had ever really wanted until his son had been born, and now Little Freddie had to try to make up for his father's absence.

Jimmy let him in to the house and they hugged. This was a new thing with them which had started a few months before when they had been drunk, and now it seemed right to show the deep feelings they had for one another. And the feelings they had for one another did run deep, even though as time was going on it was becoming harder for Freddie to ignore Little Jimmy's success.

In the dining room he saw that Paul and Liselle had already gone, but the usual hangers-on were still there, his family included. He kissed his mum, said his hellos and sat down. He barely glanced at his wife, but as Maggie put a plate of food in front of him he smiled at her nicely. 'Thanks, mate.'

She smiled back. It was a game they now played.

Maggie looked beautiful, her hair was now dyed a deeper blond, and it had white highlights that made her look even more angelic than usual. It was her teeth he really admired, though, straight and a startling white. But then she was always tanned these days. She was the epitome of the nineties woman, independent and well groomed, and she was sensible enough to make sure her husband was fed and watered and shagged into submission into the bargain.

He envied Jimmy his marriage as he envied him his peace of mind.

The turkey was moist and the salad was crunchy, and as he watched Jackie trying to focus as she spoke to him he sighed inside. Even Little Freddie was good when he was with Maggie, and his girls worshipped her. She made sure their hair was perfect and that they knew how to dress for their builds, and she gave them a safe haven when Jackie's drinking got too much for them.

As much as he was grateful for all that, his nature also made him resentful of her. Like his wife, inside he felt this couple showed up the uselessness of their existence together, and no one liked to be reminded of that.

'Will you answer me, for fuck's sake.'

Jackie was shouting at him now and he turned towards her and smiled. 'I heard you the tenth time, Jackie. I told you this morning, if you had listened to me then, I had to go out and do a bit of business, all right?'

She was placated because he had spoken directly to her.

Little Freddie came in and he sat him on his lap and let him feed off his plate. He knew the boy only ate proper food if it was given to him in this manner.

His daughters were all watching a film and he could hear them laughing and chatting together. They would wait until he went in to see them. They were getting big girls now and he knew he had to keep an eye on them, especially his eldest. Kim was built like a thirty year old, and knew more than the brasses who worked for him. She was ripe for the picking, and he was determined that she would get a better crack at her life than they had. Maggie was taking her into the salon business with her once she finished her college course in health and beauty, which pleased him. She would still be in his orbit, and that was important to him.

Joseph started to tell a long convoluted story about when he was a young man and had got his first job. As he watched him spin the tale, Freddie finally relaxed. He would sit it out for a while, and then he and Jimmy would have to get going. But he could manage an hour or so with this lot.

He glanced at his mother. She was so lovely to him, and he worshipped her in his own way. But she depressed him. Her whole life was spent waiting to die, and it annoyed him. Life was for living and the worst life was worth fighting for. Even Jackie would go out kicking and screaming, he was sure of that much.

He was proud that his mother was still well groomed, but since his father's death she had become as mad as a hatter. He knew it was only him and the kids that had kept her going. Her advice about Little Freddie had been to give him a good hiding, and he had a feeling she was right about that much at least.

Maddie saw him looking at her and she winked at him. She had always winked at him at Mass when he had been a kid and he had loved it, so he winked back. He saw Lena had noticed the gesture, and she smiled at him kindly.

He liked Lena. She was a nice old bird, and she looked out for his mum, which saved him a job. So if for no other reason than that he would have liked her anyway. But she was also a shrewd old bird and she helped keep Jackie together, which Jackie needed these days because, thanks to the drink, she was gradually unravelling at the seams.

If Jackie knew exactly what he and Jimmy were now involved in, she would go completely over the edge. Her biggest fear was of him getting another capture, even though he knew in other ways she would probably welcome it, just so she could be certain where he was of a night. He wondered if Maggie knew the half of it. Jimmy told her most things, but he had a feeling even Jimmy would think twice before discussing this lot with his wife.

If they worked this right it would be the pinnacle of their careers in skulduggery. It could also be the reason why they spent the remainder of their youth in a maximum security prison.

Maggie had washed up and put nearly everything away, with her mother happily helping her. She poured them both a large Scotch before saying, 'Leave it now, Mum. I'll finish unloading the dishwasher in the morning.'

'It won't take a sec, darling.'

Maggie let her mother do it, she knew she loved this part of the day. Lena enjoyed her houses even more than she did.

'Oh, I love this place. Stay here for a while, love, it's gorgeous.'

Maggie grinned. 'We'll give it a while, Mum, don't worry.'

Lena sat down heavily on the stool opposite her daughter. She was so enthralled with this breakfast bar she felt she could sit there all day. Just looking around her at her daughter's home, at her life, made her happy. If only Jackie could find that kind of peace she would finally feel she could relax and stop worrying about them all. But right now she had an agenda, and even though it was the last thing she wanted to bring into their conversation she did not know who else to turn to for advice.

So lighting yet another cigarette she said quietly, 'Something's got to be done about Jackie, you know that, don't you?'

Maggie sighed then. She had been expecting this, it was a conversation they had frequently. 'What do you suggest, then? She ain't going to stop drinking, until she really wants to.'

Lena nodded in agreement. 'Someone needs to talk to her about it . . .'

Maggie held up her hands in supplication. 'Well, it ain't going to be me this time. I've tried it before and she nearly ripped my head off. It's an illness, Mum, and she doesn't think she is ill.'

Lena had looked old lately, and as Maggie watched her sipping her Chivas Regal she saw the lines that had gathered around her eyes and her mouth. They made her look as if she was permanently unhappy, which she wasn't. Considering the life she had been given, she was a relatively happy woman. It was Jackie who worried her, who gave her sleepless nights.

'That child is out of his fucking tree,' Lena said. 'Did you hear about yesterday?'

Maggie shook her head. 'What's he done this time?'

She sounded bored. Little Freddie was always doing something, it was him, it was how he lived. He was his mother's son, a drama queen. Not that she would ever say that out loud, of course.

'He had been accused of touching that little girl across the road, that little Karen. You know who I mean, Sammy's daughter.'

'What do you mean, touching her?' Maggie's voice came out sharper than she had intended.

Lena was pink with embarrassment. 'You know what I mean. What do I have to do, draw you a picture?'

Maggie swallowed hard. What her mother was saying was too outrageous even for that little sod. 'I don't believe it . . .'

Lena interrupted her. 'Neither did I, but now I ain't so sure. There is something radically wrong with that child.'

'Oh, Mum, leave it out. He's a little boy, a fucker, I admit, but he's only seven.'

She didn't want to believe it.

She was dismissing her mother's words and Lena was aware of that. Looking down at the floor, she said, 'One of his sisters saw him, and stopped it from going any further.'

Maggie sat back on her stool, and as the words penetrated her brain she felt as though someone had punched her in the tummy.

At her old house, Little Freddie had stayed over one night, when her neighbour was holding a party for her daughter, who was turning four. She had never got to the bottom of why the child was screaming but she had guessed it was something to do with her nephew. Everyone had gone home suddenly, all saying the same things. The kids were tired, they were whacked out. But in her heart she had known it had been something to do with Little Freddie. The neighbour, a pleasant woman with two kids and a nice home, had basically blanked her after that day. It had been nothing you could put your finger on – she had been OK, she said hello, asked how they were, gossiped on the drive – but Maggie had never been invited inside that house again.

When she had mentioned they were moving home, the poor woman had looked relieved, she would have sworn to that on a stack of Bibles. Maggie had assumed she had found out about Jimmy's other businesses, which would not have been too far off the wall because he was a Face in the neighbourhood. But now she wondered if it was something far more sinister.

'Was anything done? Was he brought to book over it?'

Lena shook her head. 'Jackie doesn't know, at least I think she doesn't. You know what she's like, she wouldn't believe it anyway, not about her golden boy. But it happened, and it was a serious assault. That's what Kim said anyway, and she ain't a spinner.'

'He's *seven*, for fuck's sake. If he did do something bad, then he must have seen it somewhere, must be copying something he's seen.'

Lena looked defeated, she was nearly in tears. She lit another cigarette from the butt of the previous one. This was the first time Maggie had realised that she was chain-smoking these days.

'Have you seen the films he watches?' Lena asked her. 'Jackie doesn't police him, no one does. He sits up all night watching videos, watching filth and violence. They let him do what the fuck he wants.'

Maggie was more than aware of that but she decided not to mention it. She was guilty of it herself. Little Freddie was a nightmare of a child and she had a feeling in her bones that what she had been told was true. Kimberley didn't make things up, as her mother had pointed out. If she said it had happened, then it had happened.

She felt sick suddenly. This was something that she had never dreamed happened to people like them. But then Jackie was not like them, Jackie thought she was a law unto herself.

'What's Sammy said about it?'

Lena shrugged. 'What can she say? Who in their right mind is going to accuse Freddie's boy of noncing? But, as bad as this may sound, I believe it. I think he is more than capable of doing something like that.'

Maggie knew her mother would never say a thing like that unless she was absolutely sure there was truth in it.

She heard her father laughing with the girls in her

lounge, where they were watching a film. The girls were all staying over, they usually did of a weekend. Jackie and Little Freddie were long gone, otherwise they would not be having this conversation.

She glanced at the clock and saw it was nearly midnight. She was not expecting Jimmy home for a while yet but at this moment she wanted him more than ever.

'You know what we want, so why are you stronging it?' Freddie was flexing his muscles, and everyone in the room was aware of that fact. But he was also dealing with his counterparts, Joey and Timmy Black. They were from Glasgow and they were hard men who had fought to get to the top of their game. They wanted a merger with London. Drugs were now their staple diet, so it was natural that they should merge with Ozzy's crew.

Between them all they could become the biggest distributors in Europe. They had the money, the brains and the acumen. They also had a friend who, while on the run, had made contact with some very nice Russians who could smuggle in live rattlesnakes dressed as geisha girls and get away with it. In short they now owned most of the customs officers in the southeast ports.

It was a doddle really, but Ozzy and the Blacks knew that they would be more powerful if they became partners. Between them, they could sew the trade up. As it was, with so many different firms plying their trade at the one time, it was inevitable that they would eventually step on each other's toes. When that happened, it would cause ructions and bad blood between the warring parties.

At the moment, the Scots had the second-largest handle on the drugs trade, since even though they had more heroin addicts per square foot than anywhere else in Great Britain, there was still a booming market for every other kind of narcotic. The coke and amphetamine market was mainly English. The Welsh were still dependent on magic mushrooms and LSD, while the Irish were more puffers, cannabis smokers. But the trade was changing rapidly, thanks to the club scene and a new drug from the States called ecstasy. PCP had never really taken off in the UK, mescaline had made a small inroad, but this new drug was everything anyone could want. And because everyone wanted in, these mergers were now becoming quite frequent across the European union.

Ecstasy was a feel-good, high-inducing dance drug, and although it was expensive and currently hard to come by, they knew that soon it would be everywhere. This was the money-making time, when they could charge the earth for it. They needed to hunt down anyone with a factory and bring them on side.

This needed to be well planned and well thought-out. Then they could all distribute it wisely and make sure it was only peddled by their people. It was in reality no different to a large organisation wanting to bring in a new product. It would be advertised and talked about, and then all the different retailers would eventually want to stock it.

This merger was about to bring in more money in one go than anything ever before. It was Mickey Mouse money, Monopoly money. It would be in huge quantities and it would all be in cash.

The only bugbear was that Freddie and Joey had bad blood between them. They had both been banged up in Parkhurst and they had fallen out over contraband. Freddie had run the tobacco and alcohol for Ozzy, and when Joey Black had arrived, with a body full of tats and the Glaswegian head-butt, it had caused them to go head to head.

Freddie had won hands down and Joey had always given him the credit for it, but that did not mean that he did not want a rematch at some time to reestablish what he felt was his rightful position. He had swallowed his knob in prison, you had to, and he had also known that he could not ask for any kind of replay because it was all done and dusted as far as everyone was concerned.

In prison he had been able if not to forget, at least to put it out of his mind. On the street, however, he knew it was discussed and talked about. For his own peace of mind, and to make sure that people still saw him as the undisputed king of his world, he needed to take Freddie out.

This would be difficult because they needed each other at this moment in time, and so although their meeting was fraught with undercurrents and hidden agendas, it would all be put aside in the pursuit of money.

But once the money started rolling in, the borders had been opened, and they had become legends in their own rights, there would still be the little matter of Joey Black and Freddie Jackson.

The clever money was on Freddie, but the outsiders were of the opinion that maybe he might be the better bet. Unlike Freddie, Joey had something to prove.

'Are you sure this is not going to get you a capture, Jimmy?' She asked this every time, and he smiled at her concern. She really was looking out for him and he loved her for that.

'Look, Mag, anything I undertake has a risk and we've always known that, right? This is no different, except we will be settled at last, we will never have to do a hand's turn again unless we want to. Just relax, if I did get a lump you'd be all right.'

She smiled at him as she always did. He needed to feel she was behind him, and she wasn't. Not really and she never had been. But this was her Jimmy, and she wouldn't go against him and what he wanted to do. He thrived on his work, he was always careful, and he was always honest with her. She knew that if Freddie knew just how much he told her he would panic. But Jimmy trusted her and he had good reason to. She would never, ever do anything to harm him or their life.

'Can anyone connect you to the factories?'

It was a fair question and one he had been expecting. 'Nah, to be honest the Blacks will take care of that side of it once we have established the trade runs. Our main interest at the moment is getting the stuff out to the distributors. So stop worrying, woman, it's all under control.'

This was her cue to let it go. He had that inflection in his voice which told her he had said enough now, and wanted the subject changed. She knew him so well.

He was pouring himself a glass of cold milk, and she watched him as he glanced around the spotlessly clean kitchen. 'The girls in bed?'

She nodded.

'And that mad little fucker's gone home, I trust.'

She grinned, then remembered what her mother had said about him. She decided not to mention anything just yet.

'Did you hear the latest about him?' Jimmy asked.

Maggie shook her head and tried to look innocent. 'No, what?'

'According to Freddie, who thinks it's hilarious, the child, if he can be called that, has been dumping outside people's houses. If they try and tell him off, he drops his kecks and dumps on their doorsteps.'

Maggie shook her head sadly. 'He is out of control, Jimmy. I think he should be put away.'

Jimmy shrugged and finished his milk. 'That might be closer than anyone thinks.'

She frowned. 'What do you mean?'

'According to Freddie, the social workers want him to go to a special unit. It's for troubled kids and although he would be the youngest one there I think even Fred sees that something has got to be done.'

Maggie didn't say anything, though she hoped the boy did go away. If what she had heard was true the sooner he got professional help the better. But she also knew Jackie would never countenance it.

'Is me mum still getting her hair done tomorrow?'

Maggie yawned slightly. It had been a long day. 'She's popping over in the morning.'

Since the day they married, and Freddie Senior topped himself, Jimmy's father rarely had anything to do with his son. He never visited them, and no one ever mentioned it.

Jimmy nodded and rinsed his glass under the cold water tap. He didn't look bothered but she had a feeling he was. He would choose Freddie over anyone, except maybe her.

Though sometimes she even wondered about that.

Freddie was in bed with Stephanie. She was a good-hearted whore and he liked her. She was as thick as two short planks and her sense of humour was childish, but they had a rapport and best of all she never asked him for anything, ever.

If he turned up he turned up, if he kept away for months she never batted an eyelid in his direction. While Pat had worked out of the Ilford house he had kept away from her. Now, though, she was back on his list of things to do and she loved it.

As they lay together smoking a joint they heard the bedsprings in the next room creaking. They started to laugh.

'She don't half get some poke next door,' Stephanie said.

'In more ways than one!'

Stephanie was rolling up now, because she was so stoned and because, when Freddie was like this, he made her happy. He was being his most charming, and his most sexy. She loved the darkness of his skin, the whiteness of his teeth. He was always chewing gum or mints, so his breath was always fresh. She appreciated little things like that, in her job some of the clients' bodily hygiene left a lot to be desired.

Freddie cuddled her to him and she felt safe, safe and happy.

Then he flipped her expertly on to her tummy and, lying on top of her back, he bit her on the back of her head. As she struggled he pushed her face harder and harder into the pillow. As he entered her from behind she was grunting like an animal, and the pain in her head and thighs brought flashing lights into the blackness of the pillow. She could feel her chicken takeaway from earlier in the evening rushing into her mouth, and clogging up her nose as she tried desperately to get it out of her mouth so she could breathe.

She was choking, and the overpowering feeling of helplessness was terrifying in the extreme. She could hear him calling her names, and telling her that she was nothing, a whore, a slut. The words were merging together into one and as she lost consciousness she felt the burning of the food in her nostrils, her mouth open in a silent scream.

* * *

Little Freddie heard the front door crash open and still didn't take his eyes off the film he was watching. *The Texas Chainsaw Massacre* was his favourite video at the moment, and the blood and gore were just starting to spurt everywhere. He saw his Uncle Jimmy flash by in his peripheral vision, and stayed watching the TV.

Freddie was asleep in bed with his third woman of the night – first Pat, then Stephanie and finally his wife. Hearing the noise he opened his eyes blearily. Jackie was still snoring beside him and the duvet had come off the bed, showing her fat body sprawled across him like a beached whale. Her breath was rank and he pushed himself away from her. Then he realised that someone was stomping up his stairs and heard Jimmy's voice swearing and shouting, and it occurred to him that something terrible had happened.

Freddie had smoked some cocaine earlier and, mixed with the brandy, it had badly affected his reaction times. It wasn't until he was dragged bodily from the bed by Jimmy that he started to wake up properly.

'What the fuck's going on!' Jackie was sitting up in the bed, clutching a pillow in front of her to hide her nakedness and watching in amazement as Jimmy started to attack Freddie.

'You fucking vicious cunt! You wanker!'

Never had Jackie seen Jimmy sound so angry nor heard him shout so loudly. What frightened her more was that Freddie was not attempting to fight back in any way. He was just lying on the floor taking it.

Jimmy was kicking him, and when he was finally spent, he looked down on Freddie. Shaking his head in obvious despair, he rubbed his eyes and face, and Jackie saw the tiredness that had come over him.

'You went too fucking far this time. She's dead, Freddie. Dead.'

Jackie heard the word *dead*, and her whole body went cold. The fear had hit her now. This was serious, really serious and she was terrified that she was going to lose her husband over it.

'Who's dead? What the fuck is going on here, guys?' The fear in her voice communicated itself to her husband, who seemed suddenly to come out of his stupor.

Freddie got up off the dirty floor, and as Jimmy looked around him at the squalor that was Freddie's life and the mess that was his closest relative, he felt himself fighting back the urge to cry. 'Look at the way you live, the way you exist here with this lot. You're like a pack of fucking animals in a lair. This ain't a life, Freddie, you live like fucking parasites, the lot of you.'

The words penetrated Jackie's consciousness and even in her drink-fuddled brain the insult took residence, and a feeling of hot shame swept over her.

'This could destroy us, all we've worked for, everything, and all because you can't fucking control yourself.'

Freddie saw his wife trying to comprehend what had happened. She was staring at them both in horror, then Jackie was kneeling up on the bed and screaming, 'Who is fucking dead, for Christ's sake tell me, will you.'

And a little voice said, from the doorway, 'All the people on the telly, Mum, they're all dead.'

Chapter Twelve

Now Maggie knew exactly what had happened, the fear inside her was growing by the minute. She had gone to the house on Jimmy's direction and taken the girl's belongings and she had then dumped them on a landfill in East Essex. But just the thought of what had happened to that girl made her feel ill.

She understood better than anyone what Freddie was capable of, she just didn't believe that he could really have killed that poor girl in such a mindless, savage way. She had fought him off enough times as a girl, but even she would never have believed this of him.

She still had flashbacks to the times he had tried to corner her in her own home, and she had felt the unease as he stared at her sometimes, with that vacant look she knew meant he was thinking about her in a sexual way. If Jimmy knew the half of it he would have a seizure, and it would cause so much trouble that the reverberations would be felt for generations. Her own father would not take it very well, either, and that was without her mother's attitude. And Jackie, well, if she knew, she would blame her, like she always blamed everyone else except her husband.

Now this had happened, and Maggie had seen the pain and confusion in her sister's eyes this night, she knew that this was going to be in the forefront of her mind for a long time.

If it got out in their own community it would be hard enough for them, but if the filth took him in over it then everything they had worked for would be in vain. It would destroy everyone Freddie had come into contact with, it would taint them all.

Ozzy must never find out about any of it, and she knew from Jimmy's worried expression that this was going to be the make-or-break time.

As Maggie drove back to her house she had the windows open because she felt physically sick, and her head was clammy. She could not believe what she had just done and she wished that Jimmy had kept her out of it. It showed how worried he must be to involve her in this.

She remembered that she was supposed to be doing his mother's hair this morning and sighed. As she pulled up at the traffic lights two young men stared at the beautiful woman in the Mercedes sports car and tried to catch her attention. Even though this happened on a daily basis, she was suddenly convinced that they were following her. She wheelspinned away, and left them in her wake and wondering what the hell was wrong with the blonde in the brand-new Merc.

Jackie was drinking white wine mixed with vodka. It was eleven o'clock in the morning and so it was early even for her. Little Freddie understood that something momentous had happened and was for once in his life being quiet, and it was this that made everything seem even more surreal.

The alcohol was her painkiller, it was her crutch against

the world and it was also the reason she got out of bed these days. She knew Freddie didn't want her, not really. The only thing keeping him near her was their son, and now the girls were growing he was suddenly taking an interest in them again. They had trundled along OK until this last event, but now she was frightened, seriously frightened of what this could all become, what it could all cause.

Freddie had killed a brass.

The words kept going round in her head and even though she knew it was true she was still having trouble coming to terms with it. Her hands were shaking and she wasn't sure if it was her usual morning unsteadiness or because she was in shock.

Jimmy had accused him of rape, said it had to be rape because no one would willingly be treated like that. But she was a brass, so she was used to being treated like shit. It was how brasses earned their money, wasn't it? They did what the wives refused to do for their men, at least that is what Freddie had always told her.

They had disposed of her belongings, according to Jimmy, but he had also said they had called an ambulance and pretended that she had been topped by a customer. In her heart she knew this was a load of crap, that this story was for her benefit, concocted by Jimmy when he had calmed down and seen how the news had affected her. He had been brought back to earth by her crying and screaming. But how could she believe this of the man she had loved for so long, who was the only reason she was even sitting at this table, who was everything to her no matter what.

She wasn't that stupid, she could work the truth out for herself, and it was the knowledge that he had done exactly what he had been accused of that frightened her so much.

They had dumped the body, they would have *had* to.

She wondered how they had shut up the other girls in the house. It must have cost them fortunes. Well, she didn't care how much as long as Freddie was going to walk away from it.

If this Stephanie, or *whatever* her real name was, had been topped by a punter, she still would have been disposed of. The last thing they needed was anyone scrutinising their working practices.

She gulped at her drink, and as she glanced once more at the clock she wondered if the girls would be back today. She had a feeling that they would be left at Maggie's or her mum's until Easter was over and this could all be sorted out.

She burped, and tasted the tannic cheapness of the wine, then she topped up the glass and drank once more. She needed oblivion and she knew that today of all days it was not to be hers. This was far too serious to anaesthetise with wine or vodka. This needed brandy or even whisky.

As usual, all she could think about was her and her needs. The dead girl was not really anything in her mind, she was just a brass, and who cared about brasses? She hated the woman who had caused all this, and she was sure it had just been an accident. Freddie wouldn't hurt a woman for no reason. A man, yeah, but not a female, not a *woman*, it was not feasible. He was a womaniser, she knew that much, and womanisers *liked* women. A man who'd harm them didn't like women. It stood to reason, didn't it, really?

She closed her eyes on her thoughts. She didn't really know what to believe; she only knew what she *wanted* to believe, what she *needed* to believe. And that was that her husband could not be the monster that everyone seemed to assume he was. She knew him, had given him four children. If anyone knew about her husband then it was *her*.

She knew that people thought she was a mug, but that was OK as far as she was concerned. No one knew him like she did. No one saw the kindness that was inside him when he dealt with his kids, or the way he tried to be a good person. The drugs and the drink got to him like they did her. It was an illness.

She clung on to this new thought as if it was a lifeline, which for her of course it was.

She heard the front door open and she turned in fear towards it.

Freddie knew he had fucked up big time. He also knew he had got to get back into everyone's good books and he had to get back into them sooner rather than later. He could suffocate that silly bitch all over again, she was nothing but trouble. Was he going to have to pay for this for the rest of his natural? So he had *accidentally* topped a brass, a fucking brass, a woman who, for a C-note, would shag a fucking doorpost. He knew Steph, she would shag a Rottweiler for a score and a large lump of dope.

Why hadn't he just gone home? He had asked himself the same question over and over again.

Now he was being made to feel like he was a *criminal* or something. Anyone would think he had hurt a civilian the way they were all carrying on, and if Pat found out, well, that would be the icing on the cake. Patricia would walk away from him and all that he stood for without a second's thought. As hard as she was, she liked the girls and in her own way she took care of them.

He had been out of his nut, it could have happened to anyone. It wasn't like it was planned or something, it was an *accident*.

If only he had not smoked the cocaine. Why couldn't he ever leave well alone? Why did he have to always be out of it? The brandy had already softened the edges, so why he had carried on drinking and coking, he didn't know. But Steph was as up for it as he was, only no one was interested in that fact.

She had wanted him there, she was always happy to see him, so why should he be given the bum's rush over a fucking brass? Well, this just all seemed outrageous and over the top as far as he was concerned.

He had enjoyed it, that was the real truth.

But he would swallow, he had no choice really, and when the time was right he would make sure that they all understood once and for all who really was the daddy.

Paul and Liselle watched Freddie as he downed drink after drink. The gossip had reached them, and they were doing what everyone else was doing. Waiting to see what happened before they decided on any action they might take.

The pub was empty except for Freddie, and they were glad about that. But when little Maggie walked in they both knew that trouble was going to come at any second. It was in her eyes, in her walk, in her very demeanour.

'You fucking nutter, you make me sick!' Her voice was low and husky, and Liselle pushed her husband towards their living quarters. She would deal with this. She knew that, no matter what, Freddie would not touch a hair on this girl's head. Not today anyway.

Liselle placed a large Scotch and Coke on the bar in front of Maggie, but she wasn't interested.

'My Jimmy has to sort out your shit all the time, but you have gone too far with this. My sister might fucking think you are the dog's knob but I know you for what you are, and my Jimmy does as well now.'

'Fuck off, Maggie.' He sounded bored, but there was an underlying fear in his voice and both Maggie and Liselle picked it up.

'Go home and have a few kids, might shut your fucking big trap up once and for all.'

'My Jimmy is a decent man, and he is bailing you out as usual. You are a joke, mate, but I warn you now, Freddie. One more fucking stunt like this and he will walk away, and if my sister has any sense she will do the same. You have no respect any more, you have no real rep, you are a *bully* boy, a fucking ice cream and you have finally gone too far.'

He looked at her, imagining how it would feel to punch her lights out and fuck her until she screamed. But he just smiled and said to Liselle, 'Hark at her, eh? The cunts are in control, the split arses are on the rampage.' He moved towards her quickly and she jumped in fright, which just made him laugh louder.

'Go home, Maggie, before I forget you are a relative.'

'I am no relative of yours, mate. You are fucking scum, and it's only Ozzy's wrath that is keeping you out of the courts. You do realise that, don't you?'

'Piss off, go and cut someone's hair, it's all you are fit for. Go and suck Jimmy's cock, put a smile on his face for once, eh?'

He was laughing once more, and she wondered at a man who could kill someone and not care about it.

'If you ain't careful, Mags, your husband will be bedding the brasses again. He has had his fair share, I can tell you.'

She knew he was lying to her and she spat at him then, and the globule of phlegm hung off his chin.

'Go home yourself, *cunt*, Jackie's looking for you as always and you never know, you might need an alibi.'

He smiled at her once more but she knew she had scored a major point. He was a real enemy now and she didn't care. That girl was dead, and because of her husband this man was going to walk away from it all. This grieved her.

She left the pub with her head held high and her heart nearly broken.

Freddie wiped his face with his hand and licked off the spittle with relish, much to the disgust of Liselle.

The point had been made and Liselle admired young Maggie for that much at least, even though she knew Freddie would never forgive her.

Jimmy was sitting with Pat, and they were discussing the events of the night before. Both were aware that there was no way Ozzy could ever get even a hint of what had really happened. He would go ballistic and he would be within his rights, they were all aware of that, so this was a serious case of saving their own arses.

Freddie did not know that Patricia had been alerted by one of the other girls, and the fact that he thought he might just walk away from it really annoyed her. She was the main boss, her brother's hologram for when he wasn't there, and he had not been there for a long time thanks to his natural aggression and the judicial system.

'We can't have this ever get out. I have threatened all the girls with death, pain, torture and destruction if they ever open their mouths, whether it is to each other or to their pimps.'

'Pimps?'

Pat wanted to laugh, even Jimmy was a fool where brasses were concerned. Brasses loved their pimps, because every man in their orbit used them for money. At least with the pimp they had a level of respect – all the time they were earning they were treated with decency. That was why Jimmy would never be a good brothel boy. He didn't have the innate cunning needed by pimps to keep the girls in line, or in love, however they looked at it, or the complete disregard for other people that was the main requisite of a man who lived off women. She knew he hated the fact they had the houses, saw himself as above all that. But it was a decent money-spinner and the sooner he accepted that the better off he would be.

'I think he has learned his lesson, Pat, I think he is as frightened as we are about what happened.'

His loyalty knew no bounds. If only Jimmy could hear the way Freddie cunted him when he had had a drink. The way he laughed about his *perfect* life with his *perfect* wife. The jealousy was there, and even though she knew in another way Freddie loved and admired his younger counterpart, at times she understood how hard it was for him to see the boy who had looked up to him actually making more of his life than he ever would.

The world they lived in was a funny place. You could be the biggest piece of shit but if you achieved and did not tread on anyone's toes you were fêted. If you fucked up, or someone decided to take what you had and succeeded, then you were forgotten about. It was the way things worked. No one gave a toss who they were earning with as long as they were earning.

Jimmy, she knew, had never understood her relationship with Freddie, and she could not explain, even to herself, the excitement a truly dangerous man generated inside her chest. The knowledge of his exploits and the fact that he treated her with kid gloves was a heady package. Every time she stripped him off and saw the want in him, it made her almost come there and then with the thrill of it all. He was like a wild animal who she had tamed. And now, although of course she would not say this out loud, she practically owned him. She would hint that she knew about the event, make him realise subtly that she had him over a barrel, and watch as he tried his best to make her want him even though he had fucked up big time.

And want him she did, like she had never wanted anyone in her life before.

She liked to be in control, money did that to a body. When you could keep yourself, make your own decisions and most of the men you met were wary or even scared of you and your connections, it was a natural progression. Now she used the men, they did not use her. She needed sex, nothing more and nothing less. There wasn't a man walking who could give her more than she could give herself, so why bother?

She would have Freddie again. She knew without a doubt that he actually cared about her, and it was probably the nearest that bastard had ever come to loving a woman. She was willing to give him another whirl, and this time he would be so far under her thumb she would leave an imprint.

But until then she had to talk Jimmy round and let him believe that she was only swallowing because of him, that she was willing to keep Freddie on the firm because of all the money they had invested. After all, as she would remind him, Ozzy was her brother and it would mean lying to him, at least by omission if not to his face. He would owe her, Freddie and Jimmy would owe her big time.

She wondered if Jimmy would see through her. He was a clever little fucker and she respected that in him. She was also wary of him because her brother thought the sun shone out of his every orifice, and that included his arse.

She knew that Ozzy had a good head for people and she also knew that as long as Ozzy wanted him, then she wanted him as well.

She knew how to play the game. She wasn't stupid.

'You all right, love?'

Freddie was holding a crying Jackie and she was letting him hold her. Enjoying the feel of him as his strong arms tightened around her.

This was what she wanted, what she needed. He poured her another generous shot of vodka and still holding her he motioned with his head to the glass. Deep down she knew that normally he would have been telling her not to drink, accusing her of being a piss head, a drunkard. Today, she knew it suited him to get her drunk, to get her on his side and as always she was quite happy to let that happen.

If only he knew that no matter what he did she would be there for him. She always had been in the past, hadn't she? No matter what he had done, she had stood by him, defended him, cared about him. Why would that change, unless of course he had really murdered the girl and now he was frightened?

She pushed that thought from her head. He was a man and all men chased strange. Her own father had chased enough of it when she was growing up.

She saw a picture of Jimmy flash into her drink-muddled brain and forced it away again. Freddie joked at times that Jimmy was a bit Stoke-on-Trent, well, maybe he was. That would explain why they were so happy. Her sister and Jimmy were like some kind of parody, like a fucking advert for happy families, or Kellogg's Cornflakes.

That might be why. If Jimmy *was* a bit of a shirt-lifter, then that explained a lot.

She knew what she was thinking was all wrong, and even worse, she was being completely disloyal to a sister who had *always* supported her, who had always cleared up her messes. But she needed to think it so she could feel better about herself and her husband's latest escapade. Jackie would sacrifice anyone for her own peace of mind, or her husband's.

She was so pleased that he was with her, trying to make her believe in him. This was exactly what she needed in her life. Freddie knew where his bread was buttered and it was buttered with her and by her.

Freddie held his wife, knowing that the more he was with her the more chance she would believe his side of the story. Also, love her or loathe her, Jackie wouldn't blank him even if she had seen him do it with her own eyes. Whatever he said she took on board.

'You didn't do it deliberately, did you, Freddie?'

He had been expecting this question, it meant that he was nearly home and dry. This was where she convinced herself he was telling her the truth. He had been there, done that so many times that he could have nodded off and still given the correct responses.

He pushed her away from him, making sure she felt vulnerable, making sure she felt his upset by his anger. Felt rejected. He looked as innocent as the day was long, he was all wide eyes and broken heart. She knew she had just done a wrong one and she would have to pay for that.

'Please, Jackie, are you trying to hurt me or what? Are you deliberately trying to make me feel even worse than I do already?'

He was picking up his cigarettes now, and his lighter, he was telling her with his body language that he was going to walk away from her, leave her, maybe for good. He was capable of doing that, even over this, he was capable of leaving her high and dry for days or even weeks on end. He had done that so many times, just walked away from her, from the kids . . .

He sighed heavily. 'I can't do this any more, Jackie, I just can't take this any more, you know. I try and be honest, be straight . . .'

She was clinging to him now, her whole body was trying to hold him to her, near to her, keep him in his seat so she could look at him, be with him all night. It had been so long since they had loved properly, since she had felt this good about herself.

She loved it when he needed her, and he needed her so rarely that when he did she would do anything to keep the feelings only he made her feel.

Ozzy had no idea what was going on. He had problems of his own. A new screw had appeared as if by magic on the SSB unit and was under the impression he was there to do a job or something.

He would not be bought off, he would not be told and, worse than that, he was under the mistaken apprehension that he had some kind of *sway*.

That he might even be *listened* to.

This was an anomaly for all the men on the unit, who had thought he might just be holding out for a few extra quid. That was not unheard of in the prison system, after all they were all after what they could get and the cons and screws alike understood that.

This guy though, this Harry Parker, really was the *unreachable* screw. They had all heard of them but this was the first time they had ever come across one. He was rude, arrogant and he could not be bought. It was time for them to do what had to be done and it was Ozzy who decided to do the dirty deed.

When young Harry, as he had become known, walked into the recreation room at seven thirty in the evening, ready to tell everyone to go to bed and have sweet dreams etc, he found the place empty except for Ozzy.

Ozzy smiled at him in a friendly but threatening fashion, and said, 'I think it's time we had a meet, don't you?'

Harry shook his head. The more the screws told him he was a mug the more he was determined to do what he thought was right. His arrogance knew no bounds, not yet anyway.

'No, I don't. I think you had better get your fat arse off the chair and get your fat body into your cell. I am bolting down in –' he looked at his watch then – 'fifteen seconds.' He smiled at Ozzy with that infuriating smile he had, the smile that had made his wife leave him, his family endure him and his friends avoid him.

Ozzy didn't move for a while. He stared the man down before saying reasonably, 'So this can never be resolved, is that what you are saying?'

Harry nodded once more, then he said sarcastically and with the voice of a winner, 'At *last.*' Pointing at Ozzy, he said in a most disrespectful manner, 'You don't scare me, none of you. You're all villains and you're all banged up. I am going home to my house and the telly. The sooner you understand that on my watch you all take care and look out for yourselves, the better off you will all be.'

Harry was still smiling his maddening smile he had. It never touched his eyes and it held no real mirth.

'Is that right, you obnoxious little cunt.'

Harry was shocked at the language, even though he had heard worse than that over the years. 'Get up, Ozzy, and don't you ever talk to me like that again. If you do you will be on report.'

Ozzy still sat there quietly and without any thought of moving anywhere.

This threw Harry, who was now getting frightened. The other screws should have been there by now and it occurred to him he might be on his own. He was a bully, but only when he was assured he could be one without ever getting any kind of comeback. He was the man in the pub who caused a fight and then stepped back as someone else finished it for him.

Ozzy understood him, probably better than he knew himself, and getting up he walked to Harry and with a lightning movement he chivved him. The shank he used was very sharp and had been made in the machine shop a few days earlier. It was a Stanley knife blade embedded in a piece of wood that was supposed to have been the bow of a model boat being made for a charity auction.

It was a lethal weapon, and it was also a handy little tool.

Ozzy watched as young Harry put his hand up to his throat, and he watched as he saw the complete bewilderment on the man's face. He really could not believe he had been chivved, he had actually believed that he would not get any retribution whatsoever.

It was amazing, really. Someone should have given him the unofficial rulebook. It was down to the screws to take care of each other, it was not the cons' job to make sure they looked after their own.

There was a horrible gurgling noise coming from old Harry. Ozzy had done this enough times to know it was the end of the line for him, he was going to die on the filthy floor of the rec room. Well, he wouldn't be the first, and definitely not the last.

What a pointless death, and what a pointless cunt to come into a drum like this and really believe that he could get the better of them all. Bring back Esther Rantzen and her jobsworths.

He knelt over the dying man, making sure not to get any of the rapidly growing pool of blood anywhere near his shoes or clothes. Harry's eyes had not glazed over just yet. He was still trying to call out, and the blood was coming out of his severed windpipe in little bursts of red mist.

Ozzy grinned at him then. 'Ta ta, son.'

He stood up and walked sedately from the rec room. Outside the screws were nowhere to be seen, but he expected that. It was as arranged, and if he arranged something then it happened. If only that little fucker had understood that, then things might have been very different.

He was whistling away to himself as he sauntered back to his wing and he waved at friends and pretend friends, who were all aware of what he had done.

He went into the toilets and dropped the chiv in the sink. He was followed seconds later by a gofer by the name of Paulie who poured a kettle of boiling water over it. Then he took it in a clean towel to the top landing, where he dropped the whole thing into the tea urn where it would be boiled and cooled overnight, making sure there was nothing on it that could be traced back to Ozzy or his counterparts.

For a few weeks there would be almost a seg time, which meant a segregation feel to the wing, a serious lock down and investigation. After all, a screw had been panhandled. But then it would all go back to normal and life would resume as before, minus one arrogant little fucker and minus any kind of retaliation.

Jimmy and Maggie were sitting with Stephanie's mother. Jimmy watched as his lovely little wife explained how sorry they were for what had happened to her daughter. They had brought the woman ten grand for her expenses, and the mother, who had sold herself until her daughter had been able to go out and earn for the both of them, was over the moon.

Stephanie's youngest son, a big, hefty four year old, looked suspiciously like Freddie and Jimmy knew that Maggie had noticed this as well. The boy was not a head-case like his father, in fact he was a kind, dear little boy, and Maggie felt the urge to cry as she saw the way he cuddled his grandma and kept asking where his mammy was.

She got the impression that Steph had been a good mother in her own way, and she also had the feeling that the grandma would dump the kids into care without a by-your-leave.

Maggie poured another cup of tea and sighed heavily. She felt annoyed that she had been dragged into all this, and also that her sister seemed to think that this girl's death meant nothing.

As she looked around the scruffy but clean kitchen it was as if the poor girl was in her sights. She had grown up in a kitchen like this, and in a different world this could have been her, her life, and maybe even her death.

She knew, unlike the majority of women on the planet, how easy it was to get caught up in the world of prostitution. She always laughed as she watched women in her salon talking about their lives, women who were literally kept by married men and still did not equate their lives with those of the women who were doing the same thing for any poor fucker with a few quid. And so many of the young girls she saw were the girlfriends of local villains and did not ever think that they were going to get older and might be traded in. In her mind they were no better than the Stephanies of this world, but she had the sense to keep that gem of wisdom to herself.

She had told Freddie exactly what she thought of him, and she knew that he would not let that go, not in a million years. She also felt all the better for saying it to him and getting it off her chest.

He had laughed at her, and she knew that he felt he had got one over on them all. Oh, he might look like he was contrite in the future but he wasn't. Now the shock had worn off he was back to his old self. They had saved his arse and it was all over as far as he was concerned. He had walked away, he always walked away from everything. And she had seen the way her sister had looked at him, as if he was a god.

Maggie had called him scum, and she had told him that if it wasn't for Ozzy she would have seen him rot in hell for what he had done.

Now Jimmy knew what she had done and she didn't care.

Then they had come here to this house full of sadness and hurt and she would never forgive either of them, Freddie or Jimmy, for dragging her into all this.

Freddie saw the murder on the news and smiled. He had known that Ozzy was going to take out the little bastard, and he was only glad that it had been now, and not another day. As luck would have it, he would be all segged up for a while and that meant no visits, no nothing.

He was a lucky man in more ways than one, in fact at times he wondered if he should change his name to Lucky Jackson. If he fell in shit he would come up smelling of Old Spice and dead whores. He laughed at the thought, and Jackie turned around and looked at him askance. He smiled at her, his most charming, his most innocent smile.

As he lay on his sofa, drinking vodka and wine and watching another serial-killer film with his son and wife, he was feeling almost back to his normal self.

The old whore was dead and that was that. It was all about protecting the living now, and he was alive and he was kicking. She was a fucking brass, a tom, she was lucky to have lasted as long as she had. In fact, he had done the world a favour, she was a fucking blot on the landscape of life. His dad used to say that about him, well, he was dead and all. He had learned the same lesson before he went, and that was not to push him too far because he was not going to let anyone take him for a cunt.

Life was a series of kicks in the teeth, as his old mum had always said, and she was right. But that bitch Maggie was going to pay for the way she had spoken to him, and for the way she had looked at him, and she would pay with change to spare.

He had no reason to let them walk all over him because of a fucking brass, but he was shrewd enough to know that at the moment he had to swallow and wait his turn.

Because his turn would come, he was sure of that, and when it did she had better watch her well-tanned little arse.

Chapter Thirteen

In the time since Stephanie had died everything had slowly got back to normal, at least to all outward appearances. Anyone who could be bought off had been bought off, anyone who cared was already a thing of the past and the girls were all too frightened to open up that particular can of worms.

Jimmy had never been the same, and Freddie was more than aware of that. He didn't even stay for a drink with him any more unless he had to, and Freddie was fed up with it all. It was a brass, so what was the big problem? It was certainly a melon scratcher as far as he was concerned, anyone would think it was a real person who had died, someone with a life, or at least a life *expectancy*.

Jimmy was blanking him. He knew a blank when he got one, and he was getting a bit miffed with it all. It seemed young Jimmy could be one awkward ponce, an observation he had made many years ago. Now, though, it seemed Jimmy was under some kind of impression that what he thought actually mattered.

The atmosphere between them was still rife with accusation and even though they had never once discussed it since the fateful night, the blame was there whenever

Jimmy looked at him and it was starting to really give him the hump.

This friendly mugging off had to stop, and Freddie was now ready to address it.

Since the night Jimmy had come to his house all testosterone and anger, he had made a point of keeping his trap shut. He knew that Jimmy had a point and he'd been quite happy to play the game. Now, however, it was over and time to look through the round window. Freddie was aware that it was still too soon to flex his muscles, so he smiled and shook hands and wished Jimmy well.

Outwardly at least.

But he did not have 'wanker' tattooed on his forehead, and he was tired of being treated like one. Inside, he was fuming.

And now he had exactly what he had been waiting for. The fact it had come at such a timely pass just made it seem all the more enjoyable.

The Blacks were kicking off over every little thing, he had seen to that himself. He had been having little digs at every available opportunity, and had made sure they were now both sick of him.

Their main supplier was over from Amsterdam and, oh dear, it seemed he was in Glasgow, which meant little Jimmy had to get his arse up there quick smart. The man was *supposed* to have been in London, where the main action was to take place. The Blacks were doing their nuts, as was the Amsterdam bloke, and now poor Jimmy had to go and smooth it all over. Well, such was life, eh? He grinned to himself. He had made a point of fucking up the arrangements and the Blacks and he didn't augur well, so Jimmy would have to go.

Maggie was doing her crust because she wanted to go out for their *anniversary*, and now that was all gone skew-whiff and, judging by the telephone conversation Jimmy had just had with her, she was not a happy bunny.

Well fuck her, and fuck Jimmy.

Freddie smiled again. As Jimmy left to pack a bag and get a flight to Scotland, he stayed in the pub with Paul and Liselle, happier than he had been for ages, and started the serious drinking of the night.

Maggie was fuming, and she made sure that when Jimmy got home she would not be there. She knew he hated coming home to an empty house. He liked her being there all of the time, and she also knew that Jimmy, being Jimmy, had no real idea where his clothes were kept. So she drove to her mother's and smiled grimly at the thought he would have to drag the dressing room apart to find his underclothes.

Well, let him. She was sick to death of him always being available for everyone else in the world, except her. She was so angry with him that she had no interest in his trip, or anything else for that matter. She had talked to Pat, who had been her usual high-handed self about everything. She was another one who thought she was the dog's bollocks and she was *nothing*, without her brother *she* was *nothing*. Like Jackie she was only as good as the man they were embroiled with.

Well, Maggie had her own life and her own businesses . . . but deep inside she knew she needed Jimmy just as much. They were trying for a baby, and somehow she'd felt sure it would finally happen. This was to have been their special night, and when he told her he had to go to Scotland she had felt like launching him into outer space. She had new underwear, a bottle of champagne being chilled and strawberries and cream waiting to be consumed. All the things the women's magazines told her would make the night sexy, romantic and ultimately exciting.

She smiled wryly. Pity the magazines never allowed for when the man in the scenario was a fucking drug-dealing shit-bag who would have to fly to Scotland at the last minute because another couple of drug barons had made a fuck-up of momentous proportions. She supposed they assumed everyone reading their crap were like them, middle class, married to bankers or advertising men, people in suits. No doubt the nearest they got to the criminal fraternity was if they published the crime figures.

At this moment in time Maggie really envied them. Sometimes, when the women came into her salon and talked about their lives, she really loathed them. Not the ones from her world, with their bleached hair and their permatans, but the ones that came in over the weekend. The execs, they had nicknamed them, the ones who talked about their holidays and their jobs. The women who didn't think it normal to discuss a friend's husband's court case, or his latest encounter with the female sex. Who saved up for things, and wanted to get promoted at work because the money would mean they could start a family.

Women whose husbands were not called away at a second's notice, or who didn't put their lives on the line every day and risk a hefty prison sentence.

She had wanted to give Jimmy an ultimatum at one point this night, but she suddenly knew she would be wasting her breath. It had taken this to make her see her life for what it really was.

Nothing she said would stop him going, so she decided that just for once she would not be there like a good little girl. He could sort himself out and he could see how he got on without her doing everything for him. She was being silly, probably being petty, or at least that was what her husband would think. She rarely kicked off and so the fact she had now would mean fuck all to Jimmy.

She knew he had to go, because the bad blood between Freddie and the Blacks stopped him from being able to take any real part in the deals, but it still rankled. Freddie walked away from everything, it was what he did, the ponce. He was a fucking waster, he pulled in serious wedge yet he always had an excuse never to do any of the real collar. She wished he would just once do what he was paid for. Instead of always leaving it to her Jimmy.

Jimmy was Ozzy's right-hand man. He earned well for them and she really loved him. She tried to imagine herself with someone else and she couldn't. There had never been anyone else, never would be, and she knew that was also true for him. She felt bad suddenly, felt disloyal, and in her world loyalty was everything. Her Jimmy was a good provider, and they were young, they had plenty of other nights.

As she pulled up outside her mother's she was sorry she had not stayed behind to see him on his way. Bless him, he was a lovely man, really. The guilt was starting to eat into her thinking now, and she was calming down. She didn't really want him to go off on his own, without her even throwing him a kind word. Anger was a terrible emotion, it made you do things you knew were wrong.

She sat in her Mercedes Sport and she wept for a few minutes. She knew that Jimmy would ring her from Glasgow and she would answer his call, and then everything would be all right once more. But she couldn't let him get on the plane without making her peace with him. Supposing something happened to him?

She loved him, would always love him, and she knew that she was wrong to make him suffer like this. But she wanted a child so badly, and this was their time for making one, making a perfect, gorgeous little Jackson.

She plastered a smile on her face and, turning the car around, she raced back home as fast as she could.

The Blacks were fuming. Freddie had made a point of causing a row and they were now at screaming point.

Freddie had always caused more fights than John Wayne, and now he had made sure that the chemist had come to them instead of coming to London. London, where the fucking gear was going to be made and distributed. According to Freddie, they were also going to be given first dibs on the best gear.

He was a wind-up and he'd been about to find out that they were not going to be mugged off, and what did they end up with?

Little Jimmy.

Now, they *liked* and *respected* Jimmy, but they *wanted* Freddie. They wanted a straightener with him, they wanted him off his home turf, and they wanted him without weapons, because everyone knew he was a weapons master.

They had also heard a rumour that he had taken out a poor working girl, and a working girl with his kiddie, no less. Even without the aggravation already between them, that on its own was enough for them to have a row with him.

He thought he was better than everyone around him, and he was also under the mistaken apprehension that they really had swallowed over the last lot. They were also aware that Freddie was on his last chance, not just with them, but with everyone he had ever come in contact with. The Blacks were decent men, with wives and girlfriends, and kids outside the marriage as well as inside.

They took care of their dependants, which is more than they could say about that fucking wanker Jackson.

Word on the street was that even Ozzy had the pox with him. If that was so, then they would not only settle a large score, but get a few Brownie points into the bargain. This was a mission now. Both the brothers were up for it and if that meant taking on Jimmy then so be it. He was a nice lad and a hard lad, but he was also related to that piece of murdering scum. They were wary of Jimmy, however, because by all accounts he was right up Ozzy's arse. Ozzy might be gone but he would never be forgotten.

•

Looking up from the mess he'd created in the dressing room, Jimmy saw his wife's headlights hit the wall and smiled. He had hoped she would come back. He understood her anger, and he was sorry, but at the end of the day, work was work and he had to sort it all out. It was what he got paid for, what bought their houses and provided their way of life.

She was aware of that, and he knew she was upset because they had already made arrangements. But Ozzy was their employer, and he had to make sure everything went along according to plan with the minimum of fuss and the maximum of efficiency.

He heard Maggie walk into the house and run up the stairs, and he went to the bedroom itself. The dressing room looked like a bomb had dropped on it and he knew she would be angry with him over it.

She was standing there with that dear little face. Her blond hair looked immaculate as ever, and her make-up was not heavy but as always made her look healthy, made her look like the girl next door. The really good-looking and sexy girl next door.

'I am so sorry, babe.'

She knew he meant it.

'So am I, but I was so looking forward to tonight. I really wanted us to have a good one.'

'We will, babe, when I get back from Jockland.'

He was making her laugh, 'Jockland? That's a new one.'

He pulled her into his arms. 'The Blacks are up in arms and it's all because that useless cunt Freddie . . .' He didn't finish the sentence, he really didn't need to. 'He has wound them up from day one, and now I have to make a point of going there and sorting it all out.'

Maggie looked into his handsome face, saw his deep blue eyes and his dark-skinned handsomeness, and she wanted him like she had never wanted him before.

He kissed her hard on her lips. 'You know I don't want to go, and that if I had a choice I would be here with you, so please, babe, give me a break, eh? This is work, heart, just work and you know thanks to that cunt I am the only one that they listen to.'

She smiled then, a real smile. This was the man she loved, the only man she had ever loved. In her life there had never been anyone else she had ever wanted to be with. Even as a girl, when her friends had spent their time dreaming of pop stars, she had only ever been interested in her Jimmy.

He was everything she had ever wanted and everything she would ever need. As he pushed her on the bed she allowed him to take her as she had always allowed him to take her. Grateful that he wanted her, grateful that she had him in her life and grateful that he was as in love with her as she was with him.

She often wondered if he took a flier with other birds. She knew they stalked him, and why wouldn't they? He was a fucking god in more ways than one. But she pushed the thoughts from her head. What the heart didn't see . . .

'Sweetheart, we will have the most beautiful baby ever, right? A handsome lovely little baby and it will look just like you.'

'I love you so much, Jimmy.'

He grinned then and kissed her on her lips tenderly. 'You will never know what love is until you feel the love inside me, darling.'

Her heart was swelling up inside her chest with pride. He meant it and she knew he meant it. He was her love, her only love as she was his. He was like the Barry White record she adored. It was their record, they had danced their first dance to it in the youth club. He was her first, her last, her everything.

And he always would be, it was just the way they were. Without him she was nothing, she felt nothing. She was his, and he knew that better than she did.

Freddie was watching the clock, and Liselle wondered what he had going down. After all the years she had run the pub with Paul she could tell when someone was waiting for something to go down. It was a knack she had acquired.

She had watched bank robbers as they waited to go on the *off*, she had also seen murderers as they waited until their victim left. And more than a few murders had been conceived on these premises, not to mention perpetrated, she knew that better than anyone. She had lied to the filth enough times for her regulars.

This was a rough old pub, and now as she watched Freddie Jackson she knew that he was going to do something he was ashamed of. It was in the cut of his jib, a favoured saying of her father's. He was up to serious skulduggery. People like Freddie did not know any other kind.

Jackie tried her best, there was no doubt about that, but her kids were the biggest bastards in recorded history. Deep in her heart she hated them. They were such hard work.

Her house was far too hot as always. It was also very dirty, and it was extremely smelly. They had eaten fish and chips earlier and the house stank of vinegar and cheap cod. In addition, Little Freddie often urinated where he sat, and consequently every time the heating went on the smell was overpowering.

Now Jackie sat at home and watched her daughters as they watched their favourite movie, *Pretty Woman*, and she felt like screaming. Why did they love a film about a prostitute? She felt at times that they were mocking her, that they knew what their father had done. Especially Kim, who would look into her mother's eyes and bring her shoulders up to her head in an innocent yet knowing way. Jackie drank her drink quickly. This was all she needed, this lot reminding her of how shit her life was.

Sometimes she wondered why she bothered with any of it. Little Freddie was off his shopping trolley, and it took all her wits to keep him out of care. The girls had no real interest in her whatsoever, and she knew that when they were old enough they would be off. Out of it, and who could blame them?

They would rather be at Maggie's, anyway. They loved it there, thought the house was *cool*, thought it was the best place in the world. Anyone would think Maggie was their mother the way they carried on about her. About her salons and her clothes and her fucking regular tanning sessions. Who the fuck did this lot think they were?

She was their mother, *she* was the one who had given

birth to them, *she* was the one who had brought them up. When Freddie had been banged up, she had done everything she could for them all.

But did they thank her for it? Did they fuck. They were the most ungrateful bastards ever to walk the earth, and she had given birth to them all.

Little Freddie spat at her as he walked past to go and get himself some sweets from the kitchen. He often spat at her, he spat at everyone and thought it was funny. But when her hand shot out and slapped him hard across his buttocks he yelped out loud and then, as always, when he was hurting, he attacked her.

Pulling her hair and spitting and screaming at her, calling her names.

In the end she punched him with all her might in the tummy and winded him. He crumpled to the floor, and just once, for the first time ever, he shut the fuck up.

She finally felt the sense of victory he usually felt when he pushed her to the limit of her patience.

His next attack knocked her on to her back and it took all the girls to drag him off his mother.

And the worst of it all was, they were laughing at him as always.

The house was quiet, and Maggie lay in the bath, luxuriating in the absolute happiness she was feeling.

She was glad she had not stayed at her mother's house. Even though the house felt far too big for her when she was alone, she was so glad she had come back to her husband. She knew *husband* was not a word the women used these days, it was almost a derogatory term, but she was proud that Jimmy was hers, glad he was her husband, her old man, her bit of all right, as her mum would say.

She sipped her wine and lit herself a cigarette, and as

she pulled on it she felt the fluttering inside her that she often felt when she remembered making love with Jimmy. It felt like she was going over a steep hill in her Merc, that exciting feel of his hands on her. His tongue, his heavy body on top of hers as he brought her to climax.

She closed her eyes and pulled once more on her cigarette. She had Barry White on the player in her bedroom. His deep baritone was sneaking into her en suite and she was thinking of her Jimmy and his lovemaking when she felt a hand touch her shoulder.

Her eyes flew open and she dropped the cigarette on to her chest. Sitting up in pain and terror, she looked into the laughing face of Freddie Jackson.

'All right, Mags?'

He was grinning at her, and she was astonished to see that he was undressed.

She felt the bile in her stomach rise up as he licked his lips slowly and then, laughing once more, he said, 'What's the matter, sweetheart, you all tired out?'

She felt vulnerable, frightened and worse than anything she felt the utter loneliness of a woman who knew she was completely alone, and completely at someone else's mercy.

She sank under the bubbles, ashamed of him seeing her naked, ashamed that she had not protected herself enough and ashamed because she had known in her heart that this day would come and now it was here she wasn't sure she had the strength to fight him off.

And the fact she had not asked him what he was doing there or what he wanted told him all he needed to know.

'Please, Freddie, go home, leave me alone . . .'

'Oh fuck off, Maggie, you want this as much as I do, and you've made me wait. I ain't waiting any longer.' Then he dragged her from the bath by her hair, lifting her up as if she was nothing, a featherweight.

She screamed, knowing her screams were a waste of time. No one was going to hear her, that was the downside of large, well-built houses. She could feel her feet dragging across the floor, and she was twisting and turning, trying to get free from his grip.

But as she squirmed he was laughing harder and harder, and when he threw her on the bed, the bed she had lovingly made not two hours earlier after the lovemaking with her Jimmy, she was still trying to cover herself up, cover her nakedness, cover her perfectly toned and very attractive body. That only her husband had ever had access to.

He was pushing his knee between her legs, opening them, and she was really crying now, sobbing and begging him to stop and leave her alone before it all went too far.

'Ah, what's the matter, then? You telling me you don't want a bit of cock?'

She could smell him, he stank and she knew instinctively that he had been with someone else already. He had the stink of a dirty woman on him, and she knew it was a deliberate ploy, he wanted her to feel like nothing, and he had achieved his objective.

As he entered her, the burning sensation was like nothing she had ever felt before, it was like he was using an object. The hardness of him, the stench of him, was overpowering. He was above her, and as he tried to kiss her she kept pulling her face away, until he grabbed her hard by the chin and then he kissed her and forced his tongue into her mouth. It tasted horrible, of beer and brandy and dope. His spit was thick from the cocaine and it clung to her lips, making her gag.

It was so invasive she started to retch and she knew he was finding it all hilarious, she knew he could not see what was wrong with her. To him this was just a quick fuck, a way to teach her a lesson. And he had planned it so he could use her and then walk away, knowing she could never tell her husband. Daren't tell her husband, daren't tell anyone.

As he started to pummel into her, she could feel his arms tensing as he got ready to ejaculate, and she tried to force him off her, but he held her down and he talked filth into her ears as she felt the hot wetness of him inside her. She felt his rancid breath and, as his sweat mingled with her tears, she felt him shudder to a halt.

He lay on top of her, he was panting and he was also making sure she could not move away from him just yet.

Never in her life had she felt so disgusted or so used.

'You needed that, didn't you?'

She could hear the laughter in his voice, could hear the triumph, and the complete and utter satisfaction as he kissed her on the tip of her nose before he spoke once again.

'You're not regretting this, are you, Maggie?'

She tried to tip him from her, tried to get away from him, but he was too strong and he was also enjoying himself too much.

'Anyone would think you'd been raped, the way you are carrying on.'

He was goading her, and it was then she realised that she could not win, that he was far stronger than she would ever be. That Jimmy would not understand any of this, that Jimmy would never want her again, not really, no matter what he believed or what she told him.

She knew that Freddie was completely aware of what he was doing, he was loving it, enjoying every second, and he was going to get away with it for no other reason than he sounded so reasonable. Even after what he had done to her, he was sounding like it was a game or something they had planned. He had been so nice to her for so long, they had a kind of truce, and now this would be used against her. She could not compete with that, and she knew it.

This was payback time.

He was staring down at her, and even in her distress she could see how good looking he was, how he would look sheepish and sorry as he blew her family apart. If Jackie ever found out about this, there would be a war.

As if reading her mind he said gently, 'Imagine what Jackie would do if she heard about this, eh?'

He was kissing her forehead this time, as if she was a favoured child. He squeezed her breast hard, making her wince. Then he was pulling himself downwards, she could feel his tongue between her legs, and that was when the vomit finally found its way out of her mouth.

She threw up all over him, all over the bed and all over the brand-new cream-coloured carpet.

She saw him kneeling above her, saw his heavy body, his hairy legs and his yellow toenails and the vomit came up once more. Projectile vomiting. It was all over them both and he was laughing as if it was the funniest thing he had ever seen.

He jumped off the bed. His nakedness made her feel ill, his complete maleness was so at odds with the way Jimmy made her feel. He had violated her, he had taken her strength and turned it against her. She sat on the bed in utter despair, every shred of decency taken from her, and then the phone rang.

She stared at it as if she had never seen a phone before. She knew it was Jimmy, probably phoning her before his flight so he could tell her he loved her. Tell her how much he would miss her. And here she was in her own home, covered in her own vomit and looking at the only person in the world her husband loved as much as he loved her.

'Shall I get that, Mags?'

She was shaking her head in disbelief. He was mocking her, enjoying the fear she was feeling, and she knew there was nothing she could do about it. The phone was still ringing, and she watched as he went to answer it.

Scrambling across the bed she picked it up first. The line was dead and she felt pure relief at knowing she would not have to try and talk to her husband.

'You're a funny little one, ain't you, Maggie. I knew you'd be a good fuck, you had the makings of a fuck bird even when you were a kid. I used to fuck Jackie and think of you. Well, now I don't have to fantasise, do I?'

She caught sight of herself in the wardrobe opposite her bed and then realised that Freddie had watched himself as he had raped her.

She was covered in sick, her breasts were bruised as were the tops of her legs. He had bitten her shoulder, and as she stared at herself she felt the humiliation wash over her once more.

Freddie was sitting on the bedroom chair, the chair she had sat on with Jimmy, where they had made love and watched TV together.

'You look like shit, Maggie. Jackie had a good shag today and she didn't throw up, in fact she loved it. I was thinking of you, I often think of you when I am fucking Jackie, because you are a fucking flash little whore, a flash *cunt.* You thought you were better than me, didn't you? Well, now you know you ain't.'

'Get out.' It was so hard trying to talk to him, she was shaking inside. 'Jimmy would kill you for this.'

He was laughing again, fondling himself leisurely, shaking his head as if she was a comedian.

The phone rang once more and the sound was loud in the room.

'Shall I get that, then, tell Jimmy you and me had a bit of a drink and it all got out of hand?'

She was shaking her head in terror, and he knew he had her then.

'Please go. Just go.'

She could smell herself, the vomit and the unmistakable smell of Freddie Jackson, a stench she knew would never leave her nostrils.

The answerphone kicked in this time and they could hear Jimmy's voice as it came up the stairs from the hallway.

'Sleep well, my darling, I'll ring tomorrow. Love you, babe.'

Chapter Fourteen

Jackie was fuming. She felt betrayed and the feelings of hatred were overpowering.

'You stupid cow, I never said a fucking word.' Freddie was sitting up in the bed smoking a cigarette, and his smirk was sending her off her head. He always thought things like this were funny.

'You called me Maggie. How would you like it if I called you Jimmy?'

He shook his head and stifled a yawn. 'You know what's wrong with that logic, don't you, Jackie? You wouldn't have a cat's chance with Jimmy, but I reckon your little sister would be up for it with me. Ain't you noticed the way she is always nice to me? Always polite and friendly. I married the wrong sister, I should have waited for Maggie to grow up, eh?'

Jackie was temporarily speechless with rage and shock. In her heart she knew he was talking rubbish, but her jealousy was all-consuming and she felt the rot set inside her for ever.

'She wouldn't touch you with a barge pole.'

It was said with all the confidence she could muster.

He stubbed the cigarette out and said loudly, 'If you

say so, Jackie, but I have me moments, as you know very well. Women like me, always have. Still, while we are being so honest, I often go round there for Jimmy and think, how lovely to be married to someone with firm tits, no stretchmarks, and a good little business head, because her salons make fortunes.'

Jackie was as quiet as he knew she would be. Once he pointed out her failings she always shut up, because experience had taught her that he would get really personal and vindictive if she didn't.

'You bastard,' was all she said.

He grinned.

After five minutes of painful silence he said conversationally, as if they were just two friends chatting together, 'Jimmy said they are trying for a baby. Do you think they will get one after all this time?' It was an olive branch, he was giving her the opportunity to let the conversation go. Even though he had deliberately called her by her sister's name during sex, he knew the chances were she would shut up to keep the peace and try to talk normally with him. As always, she was more frightened of him walking out on her than of him staying and fighting.

Jackie knew the middle ground and she grasped at it like a drowning man. 'Maggie came off the pill ages ago, eighteen months now. Jimmy doesn't know that, but she said the quack told her it can take a year to get it out of your system. I mean, she ain't getting any younger, is she?'

He smiled once more. Only Jackie would come out with a gem like that.

'Where does that fucking leave you then, Jack? She is gorgeous, old Maggie, and from what Jimmy says she likes the old one-eyed snake.'

'Stop it, Freddie, she is my sister.'

He laughed. 'I know that, mate, but I wish you had a bit of her nous, and a pair of Bristols that had not gone fucking south, and a tight little fanny that wasn't like a fucking gaping wound.'

She went for him then as he expected. He was too tired to wind her up any more, but he knew that now he had put the thought into her head, she would let it take root, and when it finally began to grow the jealousy would do his job for him.

He would pop round to Maggie's and then mention it in front of Jackie, make out like they were close, watch the two of them squirm. He was looking forward to it.

He held Jackie at arm's length until she calmed down and then he did what he always did, he cuddled her until she fell asleep.

Maggie was going to learn the harsh facts of life and Jimmy was going to find out that his little wife was not as happy as he had thought. She wouldn't tell, he knew she wouldn't, she was too scared of the consequences.

Unlike him of course, who would relish them.

Jimmy had taken his crown, and he had taken the only thing Jimmy really cared about.

Maggie looked at the clock. It was six thirty in the morning. She could hear the birds singing and see the light creeping across her bedroom floor. She was still in the bath, the water was stone cold but she could feel nothing. She was numb.

She had changed the bed, disposed of all the bedding, cleaned up and remade it. Washed the carpet, cleaned the room, and scrubbed herself raw.

She was in shock at what had happened.

Freddie had forced one final act on her, and she knew

that would haunt her dreams even more than the rape. She could still smell him on her. It was a cloying stench of hate and when the tears finally came, she couldn't stop them.

She knew in her heart she should report him, stop him from ever doing it again, should not collude in this secret. But she also knew that if she did that, her marriage would be over in no time.

Anyone else, a stranger, an aquaintance, and Jimmy would have swallowed. But not Freddie. Jimmy would never be able to get over that. Forced or otherwise, it would cause a death and she was aware that that death could even be hers. Jackie would lose her mind, would never believe this of Freddie. She couldn't, if she did her own life would also be over and there would be no going back for the sisters.

Maggie felt beaten, demoralised and totally defeated, and she was shrewd enough to know that this was what Freddie wanted, and that she was in effect playing into his hands. He had won, and he had beaten her in more ways than one. She would have to play a clever game from now on, make sure she was never alone with him, and make sure he never got the opportunity even to talk to her without other people present.

Her life had gone from pleasure and enjoyment to a fearful journey in a few hours, and she just did not know what she should do for the better. She could only try to save whatever dignity she could, and salvage her life in the aftermath of all this hate. And it was hate that had caused it all. Hate. She had felt it coming off him in waves.

But it was her feeling of utter helplessness that was the worst thing, of knowing she had no way out of her problems, knowing she was in effect owned by someone she hated.

She was still sobbing an hour later when the milkman delivered her milk.

Jimmy was worried. He could not get Maggie on the phone.

The Blacks were being stroppy, the chemist spoke little English and all in all he was fed up. But as always, he was trying to be positive.

Being positive was another one of Ozzy's lectures. He reckoned that the great thinkers had all debated whether positive thinking really worked, and it seemed it did.

'Be serene. It is not what happens to you, it is how you deal with it.' Now that was one of his Maggie's old dear's sayings. Her mother was full of shit, but he liked that one and when he had quoted it to Ozzy they had laughed together.

He felt the rage subside then. He was trying so hard to stay positive while all the time he wanted to be at home with his wife and watch her face as she opened her anniversary present. He had left it for her in the garage, on the seat of her car.

He pictured her going in there all smiling and smartly dressed – she always looked good, old Maggie – and seeing the leather box on the passenger seat of her Merc.

He knew she would be over the moon.

He wished now that he had got a mobile phone. A lot of people were getting them these days. Like Ozzy, he was worried about them since they were too much like evidence, but if he had one now he could phone his Mags and tell her he loved her. No court could hold that against him, surely.

Maggie had a car phone, but he had never called it because it cost a fortune and also because he could never remember the fucking number.

He was not really a gadget person, but he had a feeling that the sooner he became one the happier he would be.

He had left messages on all the answerphones for Maggie, at his home and at the salons, with his number in Glasgow. She had still not rung and he knew she must have found her present by now.

There was no way she wouldn't like it. Maggie loved a bit of tomfoolery, and this was top-notch gear. Hatton Garden, nothing skanked or off a fence. He had never had a dodgy item in his home in his life. Another Ozzy warning: never, ever put skank in your house or your motor, always keep receipts for proof of purchase, and try to make a scene while purchasing anything, nicely if possible, so you were remembered if ever anything came on top.

Also: never live beyond your means, always stash cash away from your drum unless you could prove where it came from, and never, ever get into any kind of dialogue with Old Bill or other lags you didn't know personally or who had a wanker's recommendation.

It was sound advice, and he realised that now more than ever.

If they raided his drum this morning there was nothing in there that could be used against him. Maggie's salons justified their earnings, as did his rented properties and his legitimate businesses of fifteen court bailiffs and two separate security businesses. These were run by a couple of blokes who had come highly recommended, and who were as bent as a corkscrew but who had never in their lives had a serious capture. They were strictly small-time and he gave them a good living, a better living than they could ever have dreamed of, and they were seriously grateful to him because of that.

Ozzy was a wealth of wisdom and he loved him and his sayings.

Never have a dog and bark yourself – ergo, why threaten someone when you could get someone else to do it for you. Unless it was personal, of course.

Never shit on your own doorstep, you only slipped in it and broke something eventually.

And his favourite, like the Hollywood moguls always said, and which was true for the modern-day criminals, never get caught with a dead girl or a live boy.

That one had made him roll up. Until of course Freddie had made the truth of that statement apparent.

He just hoped this latest drama would all be sorted in the next few days so he could go home and have a nice night with his wife.

He loved Maggie and he knew he was lucky to have her. But he wished she would ring so he could relax.

The locksmith was leaving as Lena pulled up outside the house in a cab. She saw her daughter paying the man, and was surprised that she looked so haggard. Maggie wasn't ill surely, she had looked great yesterday, and they were supposed to be going over Lakeside to do a bit of shopping.

She hoped Maggie was OK. She fancied a day out, and she liked Lakeside. It pissed all over the high street as far as she was concerned.

She paid the cab, miffed that Maggie had not come bowling out with the money as usual. In fact she could have sworn that her daughter had not even noticed her. She walked up the drive. This was a lovely place and she never failed to enjoy its splendour. Jackie was a lost cause, a pain in the ring, but Maggie, she was like something from a film, a celebrity or something. She had made such a success of her life and Lena never failed to remind herself that one child at least had managed to wash off the taint of the council house. It was glory by association for her, and she loved every second of it.

She had to knock on the door, which showed her just how preoccupied her daughter must be.

'Who is it?'

Lena was perturbed. 'Who do you think it is, you stupid mare? We had a date, remember. Open the fucking door and get the kettle on.' She was laughing loudly as always, then she stopped, remembering she was in a nice street now and that Jimmy, even more than Maggie, frowned on the effing and blinding she was so used to. She looked around her and then relaxed. This place wasn't overlooked so she was safe.

The door opened slowly and Maggie smiled wanly.

'You look like death warmed up!'

Maggie could have cried. This was the last thing she needed, but in her confusion she had forgotten her mother was supposed to be coming over. 'I feel really rough, Mum.'

'Anniversary hangover, more like!'

Maggie shook her head sadly and she looked on the verge of tears. 'You know Jimmy had to go to Scotland, remember.'

Her voice was quavery, and she sounded blocked up, ill.

Lena was concerned. She *looked* rough, bless her. She looked awful, in fact.

She bustled about taking her coat off and getting her cigarettes and lighter out of her bag. In the large kitchen she put the kettle on herself, and then sat at the scrubbed pine table. Once she had lit up, she was ready to rock and roll. 'You got the flu, mate, you can see it from here.'

Maggie tried to smile once more. 'I have a really bad headache, Mum, I don't think I can cope with shopping.'

Lena was disappointed but her daughter looked terrible, and she said gently, 'Go to bed and I'll bring you up a cuppa and a bit of breakfast, eh?'

Maggie shook her head. 'Just the tea, thanks.'

'Why was a locksmith here, anyway? You lost your bleeding keys again?'

Maggie sighed heavily, and Lena looked at her in concern once more. The girl was obviously sickening for something, and she seemed worn out and depressed. It was in her eyes, they were dead somehow. Her daughter looked uncannily like her sister, wiped out and grey skinned, and that alone was enough to alert Lena to trouble of some kind. She suddenly felt really worried. Her baby looked very ill, from the dark circles under her eyes to the pasty pallor of her tanned skin. She looked yellow, like she had not slept for days.

'Well, answer me, why change all the locks? What's going on? You ain't had an intruder, have you?'

Maggie broke down crying, tears silently pouring out of her eyes, and she didn't even attempt to stem the flow in any way.

Lena was scared now. She rushed to her daughter and pulled her tightly into her ample arms. 'Here, hold up, girl, you all right? You been burgled or something?'

Her voice was soft, caring, and it was Maggie's undoing. The sympathy on top of the way she was feeling made her start sobbing, low at first, then after a few seconds loud and harsh. She sounded like an animal in pain.

Lena rocked her daughter and tried to whisper the loving words that all mothers used to placate their offspring. Finally, after what seemed an age, Maggie began to calm down, but she still remained with her face buried in her mother's brand-new Marks and Spencer twinset.

'What on earth is wrong? Tell me, love, tell your old mum.'

Maggie was still sobbing, shuddering as if she was cold, even though she was calmer.

'Were you burgled, my love? Did someone break in?'

'No! Don't be silly, Mum.'

Maggie's voice was hard, and Lena was taken aback at the tone of it.

'I just lost me keys, that's all. For fuck's sake, Mum, give it a rest, will you?'

Lena swallowed down her retort. The so-called lost keys were on the hall table, she had seen them as she had come in. Maggie had a distinctive, heavy brass key ring that, on close inspection, spelled her name.

Lena kept her own counsel and made the tea. She knew that once her daughter was ready she would get some kind of explanation. She hoped it wasn't to do with Jimmy, then she dismissed the thought out of hand. Whatever this was, it would not be about him. They were sound as a pound. No, this was something completely different. Maggie looked like shit, and Lena decided that if she had a bad head then maybe that was the cause of her upset. She had had a migraine once, years before and she had never wanted to repeat the experience.

But why the change of the locks? If she had anything happen she would get Lily Law. No reason not to – they were all legal. Not a nicked thing in the house, they were far too shrewd for that.

Lena was nonplussed, but she was also sensible enough not to pry just yet. Maggie was still upset and needed to calm herself down. But this frightened her, this was so out of character for her daughter, and she hoped it was not something too awful, something that could not be rectified.

The only person who could make her daughter feel like this was Jimmy, but he would never hurt her in any way, of that much she was sure.

She sighed deeply, then lit another of her endless cigarettes.

Well, as her old nana would say, it would all come out in the wash.

Jackie was looking at herself in the full-length mirror in her bedroom. She had just had a bath, and she knew that the bath was long overdue.

The drinking stopped her from doing the everyday things, but by the same token she had always been lazy. When her husband had gone away she had lost interest in herself, and she had drunk to blot out her struggle with the children and her struggle with her loneliness. Freddie had never understood that, he had been surrounded by people in the same boat, while she had been too frightened to go to the pub, talk to a man or be seen in any situation which could be misconstrued. Her world had gradually imploded and her best friend had become her drinking partner. Her best friend was vodka when she was flush, wine and cider when she wasn't.

She closed her eyes and savoured her drink once more. It gave her a lift, even more than the pills, although the Valium she also took on a regular basis always ironed out the little wrinkles in her life. It smoothed the edges, made life that bit more bearable.

She had soaked herself for ages, knowing the grime in her toes would take time to dissipate. She had decided that she was going to start looking after herself, and so at eleven thirty in the morning she was sipping white wine mixed with vodka and attempting to put on eye shadow and lipstick.

She could hear the girls whispering in their room. They were laughing, really laughing and the noise was grating on her brain. She had a sneaky feeling they were laughing at her.

'Stop pissing about, for fuck's sake, and go out!'

She could hear the high-pitched anger in her own voice and she hated herself for it.

They were good kids really, she knew they were. She also knew they spent their time living down her drinking, and her fighting. She popped another little yellow pill and swallowed it dry.

The laughter had stopped and the music went on. Even the noise of the Spice Girls was preferable to their skitting and laughing, which always made her feel paranoid, as if they were mocking her. She knew they most probably were. Shouts of 'happy birthday' had been rife earlier when she had got in the bath, which had not helped with her bad humour at all.

Kimberley strolled in a little while later. 'You look nice, Mum, where you going?'

The fact she assumed she was going somewhere depressed Jackie even more. Was this how bad things had got? She looked at her daughter. Kim was turning into a lovely girl and she was poking out in all the right places. They all were, and her jealousy knew no bounds. 'Who are you, the fucking police?'

As she looked into her daughter's eyes she saw the girl's confusion, saw the wonderment at seeing her mother tidy and in make-up when she would normally still be in bed shouting her orders in a raspy voice as she coughed up the cigarettes and vodka from the day before.

'I only asked!'

'Well, fucking don't. Do I have to have a reason to get meself tidied up, then? Is it such a fucking big deal in this house if I decide to look nice?'

Jackie wanted to shut up, but she couldn't. She always had to justify herself to these young people who were watching her, judging her and finding her sadly lacking as a mother, a person, and as a human being.

'Well, shoot me for asking a question, why don't you.'

She flounced off in a temper, and Jackie swallowed down the urge to call her back, to hug her. They hated being hugged by her, and she knew it was because she stank of drink, of despair, and worst of all she stank of hopelessness. Her world had imploded a long time ago, and now she was waiting for it to explode, for Freddie to finally leave her. When that happened she knew it would be the end for her.

Freddie had frightened her the night before. The faceless women she could cope with, but her own sister? Her Maggie, who was probably the only person she had ever trusted around her husband. Because she had never been able to trust him with anyone else, but she had trusted her sister. She had known that no matter what he might want Maggie would not do that to her, but now she was not so sure.

And Maggie was not only young, she was beautiful. She was stunning, and she took great care of herself. At times the envy Jackie had felt towards her had been almost visceral, and she had felt great dismay about her youthful body, and her tight skin.

But Maggie wouldn't touch him with a strangers, would she? The thing was, Jackie wasn't sure any more. Her self-esteem was on the floor, her life was in the toilet and her head was all over the place. She was a mess.

When Freddie wanted something he went all out to get

it, and no one knew just how charming he could be when the fancy took him. He would go on an all-out assault, and Maggie would not know what hit her. Jimmy was her world, but if there was trouble between them she knew Freddie would use that to inveigle his way in there. He would see it as a laugh, think it was funny to sleep with Jimmy's wife. Freddie saw all women as fair game and he saw all their men as mugs who were finally shown the true colours of the women they professed to love.

But Maggie? Maggie and Jimmy were set like a jelly, and anyway, Maggie was too shrewd, far too shrewd, surely? Maggie had at least a modicum of loyalty, she was sure of that much.

Or was she?

She knew about that Patricia, knew all about their so-called affair, knew that it was more on his side than hers. Now the Patricias she could cope with, because they was going nowhere. He was great in the kip, but even Jackie knew he was a type and most women did not want his type for any length of time. He was dangerous, he was a fucker, but at the end of the day he was generally hers. The Patricias would finally send him home with his tail between his legs when he stepped over their imaginary line, and then she picked up the pieces.

He needed her then because he felt like she did now. Useless, unwanted, nothing.

Her head was gone, the pills were taking over and she was actually enjoying listening to a Spice Girls record. She lurched into the bedroom and asked them to crank up the sound on the stereo, and they all laughed as Little Freddie mimicked her every word.

As she started to tell him off, he did a pretty good impression of her, and she was getting more and more annoyed at every word he uttered.

Then he jumped off the bed and did a passable imitation of her walking when she was drunk.

She tried to smack him, but Roxy dragged him on her lap and the girls were all roaring at her once more. Little Freddie was pretending to stick his fingers down his throat and pretending she made him sick, which once more set the girls off in hysterics.

Christ, but at times she hated that fucking child.

Freddie was watching Patricia and she knew he was.

She looked lovely, and she knew that as well. Even though she was not really that good looking, her confidence, immaculate dress sense and air of leadership made her more than attractive in the eyes of most of the men in her orbit.

Used as they were to women being totally dependent on their men, she was an anomaly, and also a fuck-off businesswoman whose brother was madder than the maddest person who was ever declared mad. This same brother gave her carte blanche with most of his business dealings, which in their world made her an honorary man. It also made her rich as Croesus, and once more that was something that held an attraction in itself. Her reputation as a good fuck who wanted no emotional ties was also a big draw in their circle. Most women wanted to be the new bird, the overtaker, while she had no interest in filling anyone's shoes. So a lot of men wanted her, and they wanted her for a variety of reasons.

But none wanted her more than Freddie Jackson, who would see her on his arm as a reflection on himself. Would see her as a step-up, and who would walk away from Jackie and even Little Freddie if that was what it took to get her full time.

She played him, and they both knew that. She let him

think it was a possibility, then she would make him more than aware of the absurdity of the situation.

But today, Freddie looked like the cat who had got the cream and she knew by his whole demeanour that he was full of himself, puffed up like a third-rate brass on a bender with the army.

Patricia's flat was fantastic, and Freddie loved it here. It was new, a penthouse and he liked it so much he imagined himself as its lord and master. It was spotless, and the fridge was always full of beer and decent food, and the bed was always sweet smelling and crease free.

She had a nice drum, and he envied her that. He also envied the fact he was not the only man in her life. But he consoled himself with the fact that of them all, he was the most constant.

She made him shower before they slept together, and even though he knew it was an insult to him, he did it. If any other woman had ever asked him to do that he would have decked them. But with Pat, you either did it her way, or not at all.

It made such a change from the whining cunts he was normally involved with, who wanted sexual gymnastics and then wanted his loyalty and his love.

As if.

Yet he would give it to this woman without a second's thought, he would watch his step and even give up the strange, because the Patricias of this world did not believe in second chances. Once you fucked up it was over, and that was that.

If she knew what he had done the night before she would freak. She liked Maggie, everyone liked Maggie. In fact, Maggie was a lot like Pat – she was a grafter and she knew her own worth.

It was strange that he wanted to bring Maggie down

but not Pat, but he understood the reasoning behind destroying Maggie. It was because, between them, Maggie and Jimmy were everything he wanted to be. He had spoken the truth the night before when he had told Jackie that he should have waited, that he had married the wrong sister. But it went deeper than that. He saw the way they lived, the way they interacted, the way they were admired and respected by their peers.

Jimmy was Ozzy's eyes and ears. It was Freddie who had been banged up with Ozzy. But Jimmy was now Ozzy's blue-eyed boy, little Jimmy who he had schooled and loved.

Maggie was also a law unto herself, with her salons and her fucking high-handed ways. Even his girls looked up to the two of them. To a man younger than him by nearly a decade. They all treated them like they were visiting royalty and he was like the fucking hired help.

Well, he had started a train in motion and now he was going to sit back and watch what happened. Maggie was his and he knew it. Jimmy was an unknown quantity, but she would never spill the beans on their little encounter.

He also knew that the fact she would hide it would be her downfall, because once she lied to her precious Jimmy their whole life would begin to collapse.

Jimmy worshipped her. Mug that he was, he saw her as the most important thing in his life, and their life was good. They had the life Freddie had expected, but thanks to Jackie and his kids, and his drinking and his drugging, and his disregard for anything and everyone in his orbit, that life had never materialised.

Ozzy, he knew from little things Patricia had let slip, saw him as the underdog now. He was no more than a heavy, it was little Jimmy who called the shots. Well, Jimmy was getting far too big for his boots, boots which, incidentally, Freddie had fitted him with many years before.

He had come out of nick full of hope and dreams. He had spent night after night in his cell planning his new life, and he knew in his heart that he had thrown it all away. He had fucked everything with a pulse, he had ponced off everyone he knew and he had basically handed the reins over to a young man who had once seen him as the epitome of everything he had wanted to be himself.

Freddie had blown it, and he was aware that it was far too late to regain any kind of foothold. He was just a heavy now, a well-respected and well-treated heavy, but a heavy all the same. His father had pointed this out to him all those years ago, when Jimmy and Maggie had married with all their pomp and ceremony, and he had known then that what his father said had been true. Well, he had shown him!

He had been due his pension, he had been due his lifestyle, and he had let it slip through his fingers.

Knowing he had fucked it up himself did not make his little cousin's rise to power any easier. All the contacts they used were *his* friends, all the main people were their social equals. He knew he was now only *tolerated*, and it was this that he could not take any more.

Hatred was preferable to toleration, and the worst of it all was that even little Jimmy barely tolerated him these days. Yet for all that, it was his rep, *his* fighting ability and his ruthlessness, that kept the pretenders to their thrones at bay.

Jealousy was a terrible force. It ate at people and it made them dislike and distrust the people they loved. It caused the unsuccessful parties to question their own lives, and look too harshly at their families and their so-called friends. It made for paranoia and it made for dangerous bedfellows.

Well, Jimmy Jackson might be making a name for

himself, but his little love nest was now tainted and that would have a domino effect on the rest of their lives.

He would bring the flash little fucker down from the inside, and watch as he saw his life crumble, much the same as he had himself.

'Are you all right, Freddie?'

Pat's voice was coming from far away, and he knew he was on a coke trip. He had been snorting it for hours like a man with a nose bigger than Barry Manilow.

He sighed and said sadly, 'I think things are a bit off at Chez Jimmy's. Maggie has been fit to be tied since he had to go up to Jockland.'

'Well, you can't blame her, it was on their anniversary.'

She dismissed him and once more he felt the anger rising inside him. He swallowed it down and said, with as much kindness as he could muster, 'I think he is firing blanks. Jackie was telling me Maggie stopped the pill eighteen months ago and there's still no sign of a baby.'

Patricia looked at him in absolute amazement. 'Who are you now, fucking Marge Proops? Who gives a fuck!'

But he knew this would be relayed back to Ozzy, and that was exactly what he wanted. In future, he was going to become the stable one, the one who sorted things, even if it meant being nice to that pair of wankers otherwise known as the Blacks of Glasgow.

Jimmy would soon find out. No one mugged him off, and he didn't care who they were.

'Please, Mags, tell me what is wrong with you, mate.'

Maggie shrugged. 'I am just tired, that's all.'

She walked past her husband and looked out of her office door. She watched the goings on in the salon as if they were of paramount importance. She had no interest really, the salons pretty much ran themselves, but if it took her eyes away from Jimmy's then that was OK as far as she was concerned.

She could not look him in the eye any more.

If he touched her she wanted to cry, and if he didn't she wanted to cry.

Jimmy observed her warily. She had not been the same since he had gone to Scotland. He had explained over and over again that he had not really had any option. The Blacks spent their time dreaming of taking out Freddie, and so he was the natural choice as go-between. Thanks to him, Jimmy, the Blacks and the poor little chemist from Amsterdam, who now resided in Ilford with a young girl called LaToya and a bad crack habit, they were all quids in.

But she had not recovered, and no matter how much he tried to talk to her, or tried to love her, she was different. It was as if she was in another dimension, and it was starting to frighten him. He didn't know what to do about it.

'I am all right, Jimmy, for fuck's sake leave me alone, will you!'

He sighed heavily. 'You sure you are all right?'

She didn't answer him and he didn't know how to break the crashing silence between them.

Chapter Fifteen

Glenford Prentiss smiled his gap-toothed smile and Jimmy returned it. They had become good friends over the years, and they were close, as close as they would ever be to anyone, considering their line of work.

'Come on, Jimmy, you need to talk to someone, man. You looking stressed, you looking like a man with a problem he can't resolve by himself.'

Glenford knew he might be overstepping the mark but he was worried about Jimmy. He looked terrible. This man had gone down in drug folklore. He had flooded the market with ecstasy. From the raves all over the country to the blues on the Railton Road, he had made it accessible to everyone. The price was low, the product was good, and the money was rolling in. Jimmy should be over the moon, and yet here he was with a face like a wet night in Montego Bay.

Jimmy was stoned. This was not a usual occurrence for him and he felt the dragging heaviness of the skunk. He had never really been into skunk, it was a heavy, potent puff. He was more a Lebanese gold kind of man. He liked to mellow out, chill out, and finally go off to sleep.

Skunk, however, was a different thing altogether. It

could make you hallucinate if you smoked enough, it was a chemically controlled puff, and he usually avoided it. But everything was a massive fuck-up at the moment, and as he was spending the evening with Glenford he decided to have a blow and maybe sort his head out.

It was a mistake.

'Come on, man, a few Red Stripes and you will become loquacious, the words will be tripping off your tongue.'

He was laughing. Glenford had done a serious lump as a young man, and he had spent his time with a dictionary and his right hand. That was his favourite story, and even though Jimmy had laughed like everyone else he knew there was more than a grain of truth in it. When Glenford was in the mood he could talk for England. He used words that were so alien to the people listening but were said with such aplomb, and in such circumstances, that they were almost like listening to music.

He was a wordsmith, and he had once confided to Jimmy, while very stoned, that his hero was, of all people, Les Dawson. The man, he assured Jimmy, had been the most exciting wordsmith of them all. He said that this man had been underrated, and was in his opinion the last great humorist and talker other than Spike Milligan.

This had caused Jimmy to laugh himself nearly unconscious, but then when he had watched the tapes with Glenford he had been inclined to agree. Les Dawson was humorous, and he was also imaginative. Like Glenford, Jimmy had realised the man's total command of the English language. Without the puff though, Jimmy wasn't so sure. Glenford was also a Monty Python aficionado. He could repeat any sketch, any line from any film and he also knew every anecdote about the Python team that was in the public domain.

Now Jimmy wanted his friend to start on about Les

Dawson, or his new idols Bill Hicks and Eddie Murphy.

Anything was preferable to thinking about his own situation.

'Maggie ain't right, and she ain't been right for a while.'

Lena was voicing the opinion of everyone around her, but unlike everyone, she was saying it out loud.

Jackie shrugged as always when faced with any kind of problem that did not involve her or her life. Consequently, she was exasperated as she cried out, 'She's all right. Fuck me, Mum, she's *coining* it in, so she can't be that fucking in a state, can she?'

Lena regretted speaking now. She knew Jackie was so jealous of her little sister that anything said about her was derided, or just plain dismissed. But Lena was worried, very worried. Her youngest had gone from a happy, caring woman to a nervous wreck seemingly overnight.

It was as if all the joy had been milked from her, along with her happiness and her natural energy, and all that was left was a husk, a living, breathing husk that was like a pale imitation of the girl she had been.

She went through the motions, she smiled, she worked and she did everything she had always done. But somehow, it was like she had been replaced by a clone.

The girl was not right, and Lena was terrified that something very sinister was going on. So she tried once more in case her elder daughter might have noticed something.

'Has she said anything to you, Jackie?'

Jackie sighed, then said sarcastically, 'Like what exactly, Mum? How you are getting on her fucking tits because you are never off her fucking doorstep? Do you think that maybe you might have overstayed your welcome there?'

Lena closed her eyes and suppressed her anger, as well

as the urge to smack her eldest daughter right across her fat, bloated face. Instead she goaded her with words, because she knew that words hurt this daughter more than a baseball bat across her thick skull.

'You are a bitter pill, ain't you, Jackie? You jealous fucking mare. She ain't crossed this door for weeks and you don't even care, do you?' Lena got up and, putting on her coat, she left without another word. But she felt Jackie's anger and she knew it was misplaced.

Jackie knew that she should have swallowed the criticism, and that her mother had an actual point. They were family after all. Instead, she was just glad that her mother had gone and left her in peace.

Since Freddie had become so enamoured of her Maggie, she had been grateful for her sister's absence from her life. Jackie still went there at weekends, and ate her food and drank her drink, but the fact that Maggie didn't come to her house any more didn't really bother her. She had only come to spy anyway, spy and give her lectures dressed up as the ramblings of a worried sister.

Jackie closed her eyes and stopped herself from yelling out loud that her husband was lusting after Maggie, and she was frightened that maybe Maggie might be lusting after him back.

All she heard these days was how he had popped in to see Jimmy, and how Maggie had made him coffee or a sandwich, and how *well* she looked, how *lovely* she was. How *nice* she kept the house. Each compliment was said in a nice conversational way. No one listening would realise that he was on a love job, and each compliment stabbed her like a hot knife because she knew that he wanted Maggie.

In Jackie's mind, most of the women in their world wanted a Freddie, so it stood to reason that Maggie with her safe life and her boring husband would want him too. In her darker, more honest and sober moments she brushed these feelings away, knowing they were stupid and completely unfounded. She loved Maggie, and she knew that Maggie was probably the only person who genuinely loved her, the only person she could really trust.

She knew she had treated Maggie like shit over the years. She had put everyone else above her little sister, she had borrowed money off her, and then she had run her down, often to people who she knew were doing the exact same thing to her. Justifying their own existences. Who, like her, could not comprehend a woman in their world who seemed to have it all sussed, who was happy with herself, and who was with a man who was not trying it on with any woman with a pulse or a social security book.

Jackie trusted people who she knew in her heart had no real regard for her, were not really *friends.* They were disloyal, they were all without jobs, lives or any kind of structure to their days, but what they did have going for them was that they were *like* her.

They were aimless, and full of their own self-importance. They relied on the men in their lives for their self-esteem, and they had no real concept of friendship or honour. Most of her so-called mates were only still friendly because they knew too much about one another and they were frightened to fall out in case the loose lips and two-faced talk suddenly became about them and their lives.

Maggie had once said, in a rare moment of anger, 'At least with my friends I ain't afraid to be the first to leave.'

That had hurt Jackie, because she knew that it was true. As soon as one of her cronies left her house she was pulled to pieces, run down shamelessly and spoken about as if she was a dire enemy. It was their way, and Jackie knew that she was saved from the worst of that treatment because her old man was a nut nut.

So she was a big fish on their estate, and she revelled in the fact she was more or less safe from it all. She also joked about Freddie, ridiculed him, and that made her an important part of their infrastructure. Jackie was the pivot that their world needed to turn on, she was a friend by association with most of her estate. If Freddie ever dumped her she would be finished. She knew it and *they* all knew it, and if it did happen no one would be more thrilled than her 'best mates'.

Jackie was the main wife, and she told her friends how her sister Maggie was stuck up her own arse, and, because she had a few quid, acted like she was some kind of fucking celebrity. She also pointed out that her Freddie earned good wedge, but unlike her little sister she knew where she came from and did not feel the need to rub her good fortune in everyone's faces. Or leave her roots.

She felt awful at times because of what she said, but she still said it. Especially when her husband was in earshot, though never when her mother was in the vicinity. Lena would scalp her for it.

Her girls held it against her and all. They loved Mags, they thought she was the dog's knob, and this just made Jackie feel more angry and more resolute about putting her in her place. *She* was the one who should be looked up to, and *Maggie* had looked up to her once. And she still should, *she* was the elder sister, *she* should have her sister's respect for that alone.

Every now and again the total disloyalty she showed towards the woman who made sure she had money, who made sure she was OK, who made sure her hair was done and her clothes were half decent, overwhelmed her.

Maggie, she knew, had actually fought with people

who had even remotely criticised her. Maggie never slagged her off, she just tried talking to her about her so-called drink problem, and about Little Freddie's carrying on. Unlike everyone else she had always tried to defend her on the one hand, while helping her in a positive way on the other. And Maggie, as little as she was, could have a row, a real row, a punch up if it was called for. Jackie knew that she was a fighter because of her personality while Maggie only ever fought because of a principle or because it was a last resort. And when Maggie did have a row, she was like a fucking maniac. And Maggie had fronted up enough people over her through the years, that Jackie knew she should do the same for her.

But Maggie was also the thorn in her side. Every time she looked at her she saw her own wasted life, saw her own youth that she had stupidly let pass her by with pregnancy and a penchant for self-destruction. More to the point, she now saw her only chance of happiness with her husband slipping away from her.

Because if Freddie *wanted* her little sister she could not compete, and whether Maggie wanted him back did not really matter any more. He wanted her, and that was enough for Jackie.

When she looked at Mags, she saw a young woman with a good job, a business head, a good marriage to a man who adored her and worst of all, someone her own children as well as her husband thought was far superior to her.

Maggie was everything she wanted to be, and for that alone, she could never forgive her.

'Let it go, Glenford. I am just tired, that's all. The bloke we hired from Amsterdam is turning out gear like he is a fucking limited company. And we have sewn up the market, and, you know what, we stand to make a fucking fortune.'

Glenford grinned, but he wasn't happy. He knew all this, he didn't need his friend to keep on repeating it.

He skinned up again. This time he made a twist, the Jamaican joint. This was when the papers were wrapped around a piece of conical wood and then, once the papers were removed, filled with just grass or in this case skunk. Once lit, it went up like a bonfire and then it burned lazily, and a few tokes could lay out Mike Tyson.

When it was offered to him Jimmy shook his head and said gently, 'Oh no, mate, I have to get home soon.'

He knew he was stoned out of his box, and there was no way he was driving anywhere. He would have to cab it and then pick his car up the next day.

'How's Maggie?'

Glenford had the throaty, deep rasp of a stoned Rasta, and this made Jimmy laugh. Beenie Man came on the sound system, and he lay back and listened to him intently. 'She's all right.'

Glenford shrugged and toked deeply once more. 'She looks troubled, and so do you. If you want to tell me what is the problem, you know that I will keep it quiet and within these four walls.'

Jimmy already knew that and he smiled his thanks but he didn't say anything.

Eventually, Glenford spoke again. 'You are a damn fool, boy. When me and Clarice were waging war, I keep it to meself. She living now with a white boy with a proper job, and me kids talk like fucking bankers. And now there's me with me little girl, and she lovely, but me Clarice, she the one, the only one me really interested in. But I fucked it big time, and I accepted that in the end. They go peculiar you know, it's the life we live, the uncertainty, the whole concept of the criminal lifestyle. It wear the decent women down, they want serious security, and them want the arms they loving around them every night. Well, she got that now, she got what she wanted, but I know deep in here –' he banged his fist against his chest – 'she would rather my arms than the blue-eyed fucker she got now. But you see, with decent women, they do what's best for them in the end, or in her case what was best for the kids. My kids, and I respect that, and him a good man, she whiter than him, she a natural blonde, collar and cuffs, if you know what me saying. But he love my kids and they got one of they own now, but I know one day, she will come back, when I am out of this life and retired.'

He took another deep toke on his newly lit twist and then he laughed even as he said seriously, 'You see, Jimmy boy, if me don't believe that, me life not worth it, is it?'

Jimmy looked at his friend and smiled, and they both knew that this was the final piece of their friendship falling into place. Neither had ever really trusted anyone with their deepest feelings before, but now they were willing to do just that.

'She ain't right, Glenford. She has become like a different person. Her nerves are so bad, every knock at the door she jumps, it's like she is waiting for something, but she won't tell me what.'

Glenford shook his head as if he understood perfectly. 'That's what me trying to tell you, it's the life, boy. They get to an age and a state of mind, and they frightened of the consequences of our chosen professions.'

Jimmy pondered his words for a while, then said sadly, 'Nah, it ain't that, Glenford. We are legal, mate, and if I get a capture it's through a grass. This goes deeper.

Something's happened to her and I can't get to the bottom of it. I don't know what to do, and I try and make her talk to me and she goes into one.'

Glenford was suddenly alert. Unlike Jimmy he had the knack of shaking off even the most severe of stoneds. Not an easy feat by anyone's standard. 'What could have happened to her?'

Jimmy sighed. 'I don't know, but I'll find out. It started when I went to Glasgow, and she ain't been the same since.'

Glenford was silent, but his mind was now working fifty to the dozen. He was a great believer in never saying anything to anyone until you had all the facts. He was annoyed now for getting so stoned, because something Jimmy just said had struck a chord with him. But he was gone and he knew this was too important to try and suss out now. So he got up from his chair unsteadily and did what he always did when he was rocking and he needed to remember something.

He went to his kitchen and he wrote it down in his notebook.

Then he got two more cans of Red Stripe, returned to the lounge and sat with his friend and buzzed happily.

'Come on, Maggie, we're all waiting for you!'

Dianna's voice was loud in the salon and everyone automatically turned towards it. Dianna knew that would be the case and she winked at Kimberley as Maggie finally emerged from her office.

This salon in Chingford, Essex, was the biggest of them all, and it was Maggie's baby. The girls, like Maggie, knew that this was the forerunner to the others now. It had worked so well that she was now investing a lot of money to bring the others up to spec. It not only had the hairdressing salon, it had sun beds, a nail parlour, and they were also offering waxing – legs, eyebrows and bikini, anything that was required. It offered facials, Reiki, massage and even a slimming clinic once a month where a doctor prescribed anything the clients needed.

It was a goldmine.

Maggie offered wine, spritzers, frappés and cappuccinos. She also let her customers snort to their hearts' content in her toilets, as long as they did it discreetly.

It was, to all intents and purposes, the place to be.

Dianna and Kimberley were now there all the time, Kim as a hairdresser, along with her college course in beauty, and Dianna as a trainee.

But Maggie was not her usual self, and they were determined to get her out of her shell today if it killed them.

Maggie wanted them there not just because she loved them, which she did, but also because they kept Freddie away. He was nervous of his girls, who had sussed him out at a very young age. They loved him in a haphazard, 'Oh, he is me dad, and what can I do about it?' kind of way. But Maggie knew that he loved them, and like he loved any woman in his orbit, he owned them. She also believed that he would be frightened of them knowing about what had happened. Unlike their mother, they would be inclined to believe her side of the story.

She had been a big part of their lives for so long. They knew her so well and they trusted her. They respected her, and their father had destroyed her.

Now as she looked around her, saw the busy salon bustling with people, pumping out loud music and coining in money, she felt the urge to scream.

'Come on, Maggie. Everyone keeps asking where you are lately, we can't keep telling them you're doing the books, can we?'

She looked into Kimberley's face, and, as had been the case since the girl had hit her teens, she saw herself. Kimberley looked like her, she could see it plain as anything and people remarked about it. She had her father's darkness, his dark hair and his sallow skin, but she had Maggie's fine bone structure that was at odds with Jackie's heaviness.

The thought of Jackie sent her heart racing.

'All right, Mags, long time no see. You sick or something, girl? You look dog rough!'

Maggie smiled widely at the woman who'd spoken. She was sitting there all tanned skin and streaked hair, having a manicure and a pedicure in the new and expensive black leather pedicure chair, with its own heated little foot bath, and its own drink holder, and once more Maggie wanted to scream. To tell this woman what a vacuous prat she was, how she loathed her selfish existence like she loathed the men like Freddie, because a lot of these women were with Freddie wannabes. Were with men who would shag a table leg if it was available, and who would not even have the decency or the sense to wear a condom. She knew women in this salon who had been given everything from a dose of clap to herpes from a foray their men had made to Thailand. Suddenly, all the gossip was like the Old Testament to her, like some kind of revelation. It showed her life and what it had become because she had once tried to save her sister's sanity, and tried to make her marriage whole. Look what it had got her.

She felt an urge to tell everyone to fuck off, but she didn't, she had taken to doing all her swearing in her head lately. It eased her somehow, but she was not sure for how long it would work.

Instead, she said as gaily as she could to the bleached-blond no neck who was apparently waiting for her answer, 'You only want me because I do the strongest drinks!'

All the women in the salon laughed. Maggie looked around at the perfect teeth and the perfectly toned bodies, and she broke down and cried.

Kimberley, who had a very good shit detector inherited from her grandmother, walked her back in the office before too many people saw what had happened.

Maggie held on to her young niece for dear life, and she sobbed her heart out. She was talking incoherently, and all Kimberley could make out was her saying over and over again, 'I am so sorry, sweetheart, so very sorry.'

When she finally calmed down, she still would not let on what the hell was wrong with her.

Freddie and Jimmy were at a house in North London. It was a large property in a nice tree-lined avenue. It had his and hers BMWs in the drive, and it had the air of an expensive and extended family.

Also in the drive were mountain bikes, slung down on to the concrete with no regard whatsoever, and a child's electric car. Judging by the state of its paintwork and the fact that it was full of leaves, it had obviously been dumped there a good while ago and left out in the recent rainy spell. Jimmy, who still knew the value of a pound, could not for the life of him comprehend how anyone with half a brain could have left over five hundred quid's worth of children's toy out unless they were either stupid, or, as seemed to be the case here, they thought they were always going to earn a serious crust.

There was also a double garage that had a door that was open halfway. That again was a mug's game – why would you invite thieves into your yard? Jimmy knew that the electric door was fucked, but even in the twilight he could see freezers, and he also counted three different lawn mowers, one a ride as you cut, and other expensive gardening equipment. Even he didn't have all that in his sheds, and his garden was like the fucking Serengeti in comparison to this fucking mong's.

Jimmy was angry, angrier than he had been for years. Well, he had some news for this ice cream, and he hoped that he took it on board sooner rather than later, and did not attempt to talk his way out of it. Because he was not a happy bunny at all, and this little reprimand was just what he needed to let off a bit of steam.

Freddie tapped on the front door lightly with his keeper ring. He always wore the ring, even though he knew that Jimmy thought it was dreck. Jimmy hated the way he wore so much gold. It was as if Freddie was advertising his wealth to the world, and it aggravated him. Keeper rings were for bully boys and fucking pub fighters. They were for teenagers who thought they were hard nuts, they were not for grown-ups and serious businessmen. But they did a lot of damage and so tonight Jimmy was willing to let the matter go, but he still thought that it made Freddie look cheap.

The porch on the house was a recent addition. It had leaded light windows, roses and green leaves, which matched the rest of the house. All the windows were recent by the look of it, as were the doors. The house was like a fucking new NHBC home, except it was a good twenty-five years into its life expectancy. The man who owned it had gone mad with his renovations, and at any other time Jimmy would have spent a good couple of hours, and a few beers, happily discussing all that with him. Unfortunately the man had gone a bit too mad, and had eaten into their profit to fund this marvellous but, in all honesty, overdone, pile of fucking stones.

Now Lenny Brewster was about to find out that he had been well and truly sussed, and that Jimmy and Freddie were not about to swallow it.

Lenny had seen the two men come up his drive. His wife, who was making a cup of tea and a bacon sandwich when the knock came on the door, noticed his unusual demeanour. He looked nervous. He looked positively *gutted*, as they said in her world, absolutely terrified and guilty as if he had just had the biggest capture of his life.

He was a spinner, a storyteller, and she accepted that, but in fairness he was earning like a drug dealer in a maximum security jail. The poke was constant and it was in large amounts. She knew he worked for the Jacksons, but until now she had never had any dealings with them. Lenny had given her the impression that they needed *him*, that he was a key player in their nefarious businesses.

Now though, like many a woman before her, she was seeing her old man as he really was and it frightened her. More so because she had, that very day, put a down payment on a Caribbean cruise and told everyone she had ever known in her life that they were going on it, first class, in a luxury suite with portholes and a large sitting room.

'Shall I get that, Lenny?'

He nodded and attempted to smile at her.

As she opened the door Freddie said, with all the considerable charm he possessed, 'Is that bacon I can smell wafting out of your gaff?'

She smiled at him happily. He was just her cup of tea, was Freddie. She was always up for a night out, since her old man was not the most exciting shag in Christendom, so within seconds they understood each other perfectly.

Jimmy watched the little display with his usual half

smile of disbelief. Freddie could pull in a mosque, he would lay money on that.

He saw Lenny come slowly into the hall. 'All right, Len?'

Jimmy's voice was friendly, but there was an underlying warning and Lenny was trying to decide what to do about it all. So he smiled, and said to his wife, 'Come on, June, make a fucking brew. Anyone want a sandwich?'

Freddie grinned. 'I'll have whatever is going, mate. Got a beer?'

June smiled and she looked at Jimmy who shook his head. Then Lenny walked them through the newly decorated hallway and sitting room into the large conservatory at the back of the house.

Jimmy and Freddie looked round them in a pleasant but distinct way. They made eye contact and raised their eyebrows theatrically to let Lenny know that they were surprised at this outlay on the wages he was pulling in. Even though they were paying him a good wedge, he could see they both felt that this house was far in excess of what he should be living in. And he knew they were right.

'So what can I do for you, then?'

'Come on, Lenny, play the white man. You know why we are here. Why would we bother to come and see a low-life like you unless we knew you were having us over, eh?'

Jimmy's voice was low, but it was reasonable.

Lenny decided to front it out, he had no other choice as far as he was concerned. He had an expensive wife, six kids and he also had his rep. He had worked for Ozzy when he had still been on the outside and surely that should count for something.

'I had a dip. So what? I needed the money.' He looked at Freddie as he said this in as reasonable a voice as he could manage. 'I am shifting three times the gear I was this time last year. I have asked you over and over for a bigger cut, and you just blah blah me.'

He waited for a reply and when none was forthcoming he said, with what he felt was justifiable anger, 'I have brought in fortunes for you lot, and you know that.'

Still there was no answer. Freddie and Jimmy just looked at him without any kind of expression on their faces, and it was this that made him lose his temper.

'I was on the streets working for Ozzy when you were still nicking cars and drinking pints of fucking Coca-Cola in the pub. I have earned my place in this firm. You should have given me my due, and then I would not have felt the need to take it.' Lenny was smiling at them now, he looked relieved to have said his piece, almost relaxed, and Jimmy saw for the first time a look of defiance. It was as if he was standing there thinking, well, it's done now, what can they do about it? He would swallow a hiding, and he thought that would be that, it would all be over and they would be quits. Lenny was a bigger mug than he had first thought if he believed that.

But before Jimmy could say a word, Freddie attacked him, and when Lenny hit the deck heavily on his hands and knees, he saw that Freddie had more or less gutted him with a boning knife.

Lenny was trying to keep his insides from popping out, and the blood was thick and pumping fast, streaming through his fingers, and making a terrible mess on the newly tiled floor of the conservatory.

Jimmy could not believe what Freddie had done. This was all they needed.

Freddie was grinning, that mad, lopsided grin that had always got him out of everything since he had been a kid. He was like a small child who had been caught pinching from his mother's purse.

But he wasn't a kid and he had just murdered Lenny, in his own home, in cold blood. And just because Lenny had fronted them. This was like a nightmare. This was what life sentences were caused by – acting first and thinking later. In many cases, ten or fifteen fucking years later, the person concerned was *still* thinking of that one moment of fucking madness.

Jimmy grabbed Freddie by his jacket and shirt, and he slammed him into the wall of the house with all the strength he could muster. The noise echoed around the conservatory, the glass was steamed up now, and the floor was covered in the deep red blood of Lenny, who had now dropped forward on to his face.

He was brown bread all right, and his wife was in her kitchen waiting to feed them bacon sandwiches and cups of bastard tea.

Freddie was giggling, he was laughing as if this was some kind of joke. Jimmy held him hard and fast as he tried to push Jimmy's hands away from him, trying to get clear of the wall. But Jimmy was not having any of it. Freddie could not move and he was using all his strength to try to change that fact.

It was only now that Freddie finally understood just how strong and how tall Jimmy actually was. He was as strong as an ox, and Freddie, who had always been the strong arm of the duo, realised that Jimmy was not only younger, but also he was bigger, healthier and faster than him.

The difference between them, Freddie finally acknowledged to himself, was that Jimmy had a controlled strength, a strength that went deeper than the physical. He was strong in his mind as well as his body. Jimmy used his nous, and he used it wisely, whereas Freddie used just his strength all day every day, to get what he wanted. No matter how trivial it might be.

Jimmy slammed his cousin's head into the brick wall over and over again. He knew he had drawn blood but he was past caring. This was the one thing he had always dreaded, this was a long time in stir if it all came on top, and it was a pointless nicking, devoid of any kind of principle or reasoning. A completely unnecessary death that could destroy the rest of their lives.

He chinned Freddie then with all the force he could muster. He hit him so hard that he had to hold him up to stop him toppling into the blood that had spread over the floor.

'You fucking cunt, Freddie, you stupid fucking cunt!'

Then June walked into the carnage and all hell broke loose.

Chapter Sixteen

Jackie could hear the girls talking, and she listened as she always did to their gossip about the salons and her sister Maggie. They were in the kitchen, chatting and eating a late supper.

Jackie was in her lounge as usual, with a large drink, her cigarettes, a bag full of sweets and her prescription medication on the small glass table by her chair. Her other medication, her real medication was in her purse, but she liked people to see her antidepressants because she felt it spoke volumes about her life and the way she lived it.

Maggie had once pointed out that her world was so small, it was peopled by her and her alone. Well, by the sounds of it Maggie was finally learning the facts of life.

'She was crying her eyes out, and I didn't know what to do!'

Roxanna, who was looking more like Maggie every day, was listening to her sister with wide-open eyes, and pulling on her cigarette in short nervous little puffs as she heard this terrible news about her lovely auntie.

Little Freddie was watching a video as usual. The sound of the gunfire was loud, and, seeing his mother listening to the girls, he turned the sound up even more.

When Jackie snatched the remote from him and turned the volume down, he kicked her hard in the chest. The pain was excruciating and she also lost the majority of the drink in her glass.

Jackie hit him with the flat of her hand and put all her considerable strength into it. Any other child would have screamed, but he laughed at her and let rip with a string of expletives even she was shocked to hear.

'You little fucker!'

He was still laughing at her, and his eyes told her exactly what he thought of her.

She stood up unsteadily and caught sight of herself in the mirror above the fireplace. Her nightdress was grubby, her hair was like rats' tails and she was bloated, her face and her body suddenly looking huge.

She walked to the mirror and stared at herself. She saw the thinness of her hair, which had once been luxuriant, and the sallow tint to her skin. Her back ached constantly, and she had trouble even eating her sweets, which for years had been her staple diet.

On the mantelpiece was an old photo of her and Freddie from when they were courting and she picked it up and looked at it properly, for the first time in years. She had been a beauty, and she had never really known that. But now, seeing herself in her little dress, with her happy smiling face, it was as if she was looking at a stranger.

She could hear Little Freddie cussing with the men on the video, word for word. As she walked out into the hallway, the girls were still in the kitchen and she went in and smiled at them. 'Had a good day, babes?'

It was forced and they knew it. She could not give a toss what they had done, but as always they humoured her.

'Great, Mum, and you?'

This from Kimberley who had sarcasm down to a fine art.

She overlooked the insult and said in a friendly way, 'What's all this about Maggie crying in the salon, then?' She sounded worried and interested and Dianna shook her head in disbelief. They knew what was going on with her mum and Maggie, they could hear everything that went on in this house and it amazed them that their mother didn't realise that.

Kimberley shrugged. 'Dunno, Mum, she wouldn't say.'

It was said with loyalty and also in such a way as to make her mother aware that they would not discuss it any further with her.

Jackie felt the anger that was always boiling away beneath the surface start to rise, but she kept it down and said in a quiet voice, 'She ain't right, and she is my little sister. Maybe I should go round and see her, what do you think? Woman to woman, like.'

The three girls just stared at her with expressionless faces, and she saw how good looking they were, how nice and tidy they were, and how they had no interest whatsoever in what she was saying.

She felt like an outsider in her own home, and it hurt. 'You fucking lairy little mares. I fucking do everything for you lot and you treat me like a fucking ear hole, like a no neck.'

Kimberley picked up her handbag and the others followed suit. Leaving their sandwiches and their teas, they tried to troop past her to go to bed.

She pushed them all back into the kitchen and stood in the doorway. 'You will answer me, or I will fucking deck you one by one.'

Kimberley sighed and said quietly, 'You're drunk, Mum. Go to bed and let us be, eh?'

It was said in such a reasonable way that for a few seconds Jackie actually considered doing just that. But then her temper and her paranoia kicked in as usual.

'Bollocks, I want to know what the fucking drama was in that salon. Was your father there? Does he ever go in there?' She could hear herself and she knew she sounded like a fool, but she couldn't stop.

'Why would he go in there, Mum?'

This from Roxanna, who was sick and tired of this woman and her histrionics.

Jackie laughed then. 'You don't want to know, babe, but listen to me and listen good. She is getting what she fucking deserves. You think she is so fucking great—'

'Oh, Mum, will you stop it!' Dianna's voice was so loud and so determined that Jackie was speechless. 'Maggie loves you, she never says a bad thing about you, and all you can do is fucking try and slag her off.'

Jackie looked at the three faces that were turned to her and saw the confusion, the hurt and the disgust in them. Then, with her voice full of self-pity and tears, she said, 'She has turned you against me, ain't she?'

Kimberley shook her head in utter despair. 'Oh, Mum, you've done that all on your own. Now go to bed, *please*. Will you stop this and leave us alone?'

'You think Maggie is so great, and that I am such a bad person. Oh, I know what's going on with you lot.'

Once more they looked at her with pity and irritation, and it was this that made her scream at them, 'She is a cunt, and she is trying to fucking ruin me and my life.'

She knew she should shut up but her hurt was so bad that she wanted to make them hurt too, make them feel how she was feeling.

'Stop it, Mum! Listen to yourself, you're drunk. Go to bed and sleep it off, will you.' Roxanna, her little girl, her baby daughter, was looking at her and she could see the contempt in her face, had just heard it in her words.

'What about me, girls? Can't you see what I am going through? Can't you try and spare a bit of your sympathy for your own mother?'

Jackie was nearly crying now with fury, shame and alcohol. She had been drinking all day and all night.

Kimberley pushed her sisters behind her protectively, she knew her mother was capable of violence when she was like this, but she couldn't stop herself from saying loudly, and with utter disregard for Jackie's feelings, real and imagined, 'Not everything is about you, Mum. If you could only see that then your life would be so much easier. Maggie is *lovely*, she has never said *anything* about you that we couldn't repeat to your face. She sticks up for you, she won't let us say a fucking dicky bird about you or your drinking or your bloody hatefulness. She is the only person who really cares about you and as usual, you can't see it. You eat her food and you drink her drink and you use her like you do everyone. But she is the only person who has ever been there for us, and you had better start to understand that and accept it. So, for the last time, Mum, go to bed.'

They left the kitchen then and she didn't attempt to stop them. Instead, she opened the fridge and took out another bottle of wine.

Her husband and her girls – Maggie had taken them all.

June Brewster was in a state of shock, but she was still sensible enough to know that Jimmy Jackson was not the main culprit here, and that he was the one she needed to sort this out with. Freddie Jackson was a murdering ponce, but she had already heard that expression in connection with him, many times before. She knew the score, she knew the life they were involved in. She had lived it long enough and she was a realist like many a blagger's wife before her.

When she had walked into the conservatory, she had screamed once, then she had contained herself as best she could. She had not phoned the filth, which she knew had endeared her to Jimmy Jackson.

He was also much calmer now, though when she had entered the conservatory she had seen the utter contempt he had for Freddie Jackson on his face.

Freddie had fucked up, and it was only her rep as a close-talking wife that had kept her on their good side. Married to Lenny, she had more secrets than the Dalai Lama, but they knew she had always kept them close to her chest.

Lenny had said once that it was young Jimmy Jackson who was the real brains of the outfit, and after tonight's debacle she was inclined to agree with him. Jimmy was already on the blower trying to salvage something for all of them. She knew she would get her comp, which had better be huge, but she wanted the life-insurance money on top, so now they had to make poor Lenny look like he had died in far less suspicious circumstances.

Jimmy was talking sixteen to the dozen, and in between his talking and scheming he was pouring her brandies, trying in his own way to lighten her burden.

But how could he?

Lenny was a ponce, she knew that better than anyone, but he was her old man and they had been together for the duration, over twenty years. Even though the last child was suspiciously dark in comparison to the other five, he had swallowed, he had given her the benefit of the doubt. So she had never gone on holiday to Tunisia again with her sisters, big deal. Lenny had neglected her shamefully and he knew it. In fact, it seemed that her ducking and diving with a young waiter with a six-pack stomach, a large cock and hardly any English had made Lenny realise what he had in her. So they had got over it somehow. In fact, the child, a daughter, had been the apple of Lenny's eye. They already had the five boys, and she was a very beautiful little girl who worshipped her dad.

Now she was on her Jack Jones with six kids and a house that they had only been doing up because she had insisted on it. Lenny, being a thieving toerag, had skanked off these two fucking Faces, and now he was dead, and all she could think about was Tunisia and the young fellow who had given her back her confidence and her sex drive.

She was seeing him in her mind's eye, with his tight little arse and his muscle-bound arms, a smile that was whiter than a Colgate advert, and his soft dark hair that was long, thick and tied back in a ponytail. She had thought about him every time she had slept with Lenny, because Lenny had stopped ringing her bells many years before. He had slept around and he had left her to basically bring the kids up alone, and it had hurt her. It had made her resent him, and she had often had a flier with a bloke on the quiet.

All the time she had been cooking the bacon sandwiches she had been thinking about Freddie Jackson, and pondering his prowess in the kip, and now he had killed her husband, the father of nearly all her kids. The man who, even though she was getting battered around the edges, and so her chances for romance were getting less and less, had pledged his undying love for her, had taken in a child that was not his, and who had ripped these two fucking lunatics off to give her the house of her dreams.

How many times had she imagined him popping off

over the years, and her being her own boss, being in a position to go away on holiday and shag herself stupid with men she would never see again? How many times had she wished for Lenny's demise? Now she had got it, and what she really wanted at this moment in time was for her Tunisian waiter to take her in his arms and give her the rogering of a lifetime.

She had actually been contemplating shagging Freddie Jackson, and now she was contemplating shagging someone else. Her head was going *mad*, she was thinking of all the wrong things, but with six kids hanging around her neck, she needed money, and she needed the insurance. She needed the house paid off and the loans off her back, not only for the cars, but also for the building work and the new furniture. She needed to focus on that now, and then when it was all over, she could fall apart in peace. Maybe in Tunisia, where the sun shone every day and where her mother phoned her and told her that the kids were fine, and where she could pretend to be footloose and fancy free, and where maybe she might forget about this night and what it entailed.

Every time she thought of Lenny on the floor in all that blood, she felt ill with the worry and the fear of what was going to be the upshot.

Freddie Jackson was eating the bacon sandwiches she had made earlier, and it freaked her out. He was drinking his tea and acting as if this was a normal evening. He had even winked at her. She had four kids in bed, and her eldest two were due round the next day and her husband, the stupid thieving fucker, was dead as a doornail in her new conservatory.

It was surreal, and yet she knew it was really happening because her brain had acknowledged it and was now helping her to try to make some kind of sense out of it.

She knew to an outsider she would seem mercenary, cold-blooded, and even hard and uncaring. But she had no intention of falling out with the Jacksons or with Ozzy himself. She had already seen what they were capable of if provoked.

She had *six* kids aged three to nineteen, and she had to keep her head above water. Get your priorities right had been Lenny's mantra, and that was exactly what she was attempting to do.

Maggie lay in the big bed alone, and wondered what time Jimmy would finally get home. It was three in the morning, and he had left a message saying that he had a bit of business to attend to, that she was not to worry and he would be home as soon as he could.

He was so thoughtful, and she knew he was worried about her and the way she was acting, but she couldn't do anything to allay his fears.

She was wide awake as was usual these days, but she had listened to his message without picking up the phone and talking to him since he would have guessed she hadn't slept yet. She didn't want him home yet, not really. He wanted to hug her, and kiss her, and try to make her happy. He wanted to love her, and she wasn't ready for that. Didn't want any of that, because with Jimmy a cuddle always had to end in sex. Now she just allowed him to take her, and she knew he was aware she was just letting him, that she was not joining in any more.

From the first time they had made love, she had enjoyed it. She had not climaxed then, but she had loved the feeling of him inside her, even though it had hurt. She mirrored his own excitement, and had felt a natural reaction as he had reached his orgasm. He had known that, and she knew he had loved her for it.

At fourteen she had been made aware of what sex was really all about, that it was not just for procreation, not just a quick release, but was the joining of two people who could not get close enough to each other, but who tried to with each encounter they had together. For every deep thrust that Jimmy had penetrated her with, she had arched her back up to meet him with the same fervour and excitement as he felt for her.

Now he kissed her and it felt wrong. His hands on her body no longer felt gentle, his tongue between her legs made her want to gag, because it felt thick and harsh, and coated with white scum like Freddie's had been that night. And even though she knew it wasn't Freddie, that it was her husband, who she loved, the feeling would not go away.

She could still smell *him*, and she could still feel *him*, and because of that night she had to live with the knowledge that Jimmy was no longer the only person to have had access to her. She had been proud of that, and she knew he was still proud of it. Only it wasn't true any more.

In the bathroom, where they had lain in the bath and laughed and joked and loved together, she saw only herself on her knees, with Freddie's hands in her hair as he painfully forced her to take him into her mouth. The floor was clean and tidy, but she still saw the long blond hairs that he had ripped from her scalp as she attempted to stop him.

It was ruined, and she could not make it better, not now, nor at any time in the future. Everything that they had worked for together was destroyed and Freddie had deliberately set out to cause that heartbreak. Jimmy's lovemaking was nothing to her any more. She loathed it, and she knew he had realised that, but he was also trying to make it all better somehow, and she knew it could never be fixed.

The deceit was killing her, and Freddie used every opportunity to bait her, to taunt her, like the bed. Taking the bed. Jackie was not thrilled about it, she could tell that much, and she had a feeling that her sister was going to work it all out.

She felt the burn of tears once more and fought to keep them at bay. If Jimmy came in and saw her crying it would start him off again with the questions and the kindness. It was the kindness she couldn't bear.

Maggie didn't sleep any more. She was tired out physically and mentally, but as soon as she got into bed she was wide awake. This new bed was not as comfortable as the old one. Jimmy hated it, but she had insisted that she wanted this one, and as usual he had relented.

When Freddie had asked for the old bed, and Jimmy had given it to him without thinking, she had nearly gone mad with grief. She knew he was lying there night after night remembering what had taken place on it. He had told her over and over that he had never had such a good night's rest, and she had sat at the dining-room table and nodded at him, all the while wanting to vomit up her dinner, and scream with frustration and anger.

Maggie felt the familiar crashing of her heart, and she forced herself to breathe deeply. Panic attacks, the doctor called them, guilt attacks was what she called them. And the guilt weighed on her heavily, because she had brought this on herself and that was so hard to accept. If she had not confronted him, spat at him, maybe this would not have happened. She was OK for days at a time, then it came on top once more. A word, a sentence, a TV programme, or Freddie staring at her with that smirk he had, brought it all back. She didn't know how much longer she could keep herself together.

She had taken to swearing out loud when she was by herself. She broke things, smashed them against the wall, and for a few minutes her pain would subside.

But it always came back.

'You have got to be some kind of fucking twat. What on earth were you thinking of?' They were sitting in the car. Jimmy was trying to get some sense out of Freddie, but it was a waste of time.

Freddie was on one of his quiet times. He had them after he had fucked up big time and normally Jimmy left him to it, but this time it had been too close for comfort and he wanted an explanation.

'Lenny was a fucking twonk, but he did not deserve that, and you know it. And if he had asked you for a ruffle, why didn't you give it to him? I was under the impression he had been weighed out, given a rise for his services. I didn't know he was still on the same *earn*. That means you were fucking having *me* over then, don't it? Because if he was still on the same poke then you had to be fucking pocketing the difference, didn't you? Pennies and fucking halfpennies to what we fucking rake in, and now you have killed him over your own petty greed.'

Freddie was still quiet. He lit another cigarette and smoked it calmly while watching Jimmy. He had a wary look in his eye but apart from that, he didn't seem to have a care in the world.

Jimmy was bewildered with it all. 'His wife and kids were in that house. Suppose his wife had fucking monged out, what would you have done, eh? Killed the whole family? Come on, Freddie, I am genuinely interested in what you have to say for yourself.'

Freddie shrugged nonchalantly. 'I lost me temper, that's all.'

Jimmy looked at him. The respect was finally gone, and they both knew it this time.

'You lost it because he had you bang to fucking rights. We should never have been there. He was earning us a fucking good crust, and you were taking his fucking poke. He was a good earner, *and* he was a friend of Ozzy's. What am I supposed to tell him?'

The mention of Ozzy brought Freddie's full attention, as Jimmy knew it would. He hated using Ozzy like that, but it seemed it was the only way he was going to get this sorted out. Because Freddie had to understand that this could never happen again. It was so fucking dangerous. They could get a life sentence for something that was completely senseless.

'You telling Ozzy, then?'

It was a threat and a statement in one.

Jimmy laughed then, a tired, annoyed laugh. 'Well, he'll have to fucking know. One of his oldest mates and biggest earners is dead, his wife is widowed with six fucking chavvies, and we will have to explain what happened. That is how it works, Freddie, you ain't a law unto yourself, see. We have to *explain* away things, especially dead fucking blokes who we are getting a good living from, and who are mysteriously gutted like a fish in their fucking own house.'

Freddie had heard enough. His anger was evident. 'Are you having a fucking laugh, mate?' He was stretching his eyes to their utmost. 'Are you telling me that you are going to tell Ozzy the score? Is that what you are trying to say?'

Jimmy was getting angry himself now, and Freddie was reminded of just how strong and fit he actually was.

'I would never do that to you, but I should! You need a fucking lesson, Freddie, you are an accident waiting to happen. Do you want another fucking lump, because I certainly don't want even a remand, let alone a ten or an eighteen.'

Freddie snorted in derision. 'You wouldn't last five fucking minutes in nick, mate . . .'

He had gone too far. He stopped talking and Jimmy stared at him for long moments before he started up the car.

As he drove along a Sussex country lane, Jimmy could feel the anger welling up inside him again. He stopped the car once more, and he said quietly, 'This has got to stop, Freddie, because I can't be around you any more. You killed that girl and she had your baby. I weighed her mother out for the funeral and the kid and *you* should have done that, it was *your* mess, *your* fucking balls-up. You're a fucking liability, mate. You seem to think you can do what you like, but I tell you now, one day, Freddie, your luck will run out and you will get sent down. And I for one won't give a flying fuck.'

Freddie had listened to him with half an ear but he was thinking about other things. He had a knack of doing that. When he'd made a big fuck-up, he had a clever way of forgetting about it by concentrating on something else he had done, something less important. But even he knew that Jimmy was just about finished with him, and that if that happened, he would not last long on his own.

Jimmy was Ozzy's boy now, and Freddie had been rowed out over the years. It was like he had never existed for Ozzy, like he was the younger man, the kid who had been taken under the wing, except this kid had cut his teeth under his wing and had since bitten it off and spat it out.

He was Freddie Jackson, he was the one who had started this off, and he was now like the fucking gofer.

But for all his anger, and his jealousy, Freddie was also aware that *he* could never run the different businesses. He had never bothered to listen to the ins and outs of them, he had no interest in minutiae, but Jimmy thrived on it. He should have made himself take more of an active part in the day-to-day running of everything, but he had never needed to. Jimmy had taken to it like a duck to water and he had been stupid enough to believe that he would never go against him. That Jimmy would run things in his own way, but that he, Freddie, the reason they had the fucking work in the first place, would be the key player. The main man, the overseer, the fucking plantation owner. But instead he had gradually been replaced.

He had expected *gratitude*, he had expected his little Jimmy to be *grateful* for their good fortune, he had expected his fucking *due*! Well, he knew different now and he would learn from that.

He had already started his revenge, but he could wait until he was back in the fold. He had plenty of practice at waiting. Plus, he now had something to use against Jimmy and, one day, when the time was right, he *would* use it. Jimmy would fuck up eventually, he would see to that personally, and when he did it would be of catastrophic proportions. He would see to that as well.

For now, though, he needed to stay in Ozzy's good books and get back on side with Jimmy. He had to help him dispose of Lenny, who was going to be crushed by a farm implement in, of all places, Guernsey. They owned a doctor there who was happy to write out a death certificate and who would make sure the body was cremated sooner rather than later. The main problem was getting the body over there, which is why they were in Sussex going to see a bloke with a boat and a penchant for doing literally anything for money and a decent bit of gear.

Right now, Freddie had to make like he was sorry for his little outburst. But Jimmy would regret taking what was his. Freddie was the taker, he was the one who'd given them the means to *take* in the first place.

Jimmy, sitting beside him silently, sighed heavily. Then he got out a small packet and cut a couple of lines on the dashboard. He snorted his quickly, aware that Freddie was trying to hide his amazement at what he was witnessing.

'I need this. I am knackered, Fred, and I have to go and visit Ozzy tomorrow, remember.'

Freddie had forgotten that and now he knew it was imperative that he made some kind of peace.

'I am sorry, Jimmy, I could fucking cut me hands off. I lost it, mate, the gear, the drink and fucking Jackie, she's off her tree again . . .' He left the sentence unfinished, then continued after a few seconds, his voice all pain-filled and sorrowful. 'Little Freddie, well, he's off his fucking trolley, you know that. I have to deal with it on a daily basis. He's out of hand, Jimmy. I can't fucking cope with it all.'

He snorted the line quickly and watched as Jimmy started to cut them another two.

'Are things that bad then, Freddie?'

Jimmy was trying to understand, trying to think the best of him, trying to make some sense out of it all. He loved Freddie, but for a long time he had not liked him. Since Stephanie's death and Freddie's utter disregard for what he had done there had been a wall between them, and now everything they had achieved was at risk.

'Oh, Jimmy, you don't know the half of it. He is seeing a fucking shrink. My little boy is seeing a fucking Looney Tunes expert and the geezer reckons he is borderline fucking psychotic. Jackie is drunk all the time, the girls avoid her like the plague, and poor Little Freddie is on course for the nut house. I can't cope with it any more. I was telling your Maggie about it all the other day and she understood what I was going through because she ain't all that great herself, is she?'

Jimmy stopped cutting the coke and turned to look at Freddie. 'What do you mean? What did she say?'

Freddie could hear the want in his voice, could feel the man's need to know what was wrong with his wife, and he said quietly, 'I don't know, mate. She is down, depressed, but you know that yourself, don't you? I ain't said nothing out of respect like, but it makes you wonder, don't it?'

Jimmy frowned. 'Wonder what?'

Freddie lit another cigarette from the butt of the previous one and then he shrugged, looking all concerned and innocent. 'Well, you know, if it runs in the family. Jackie with her drinking and everything, your Maggie with everything a woman could want, the looks, the nous and the house of her dreams, yet she is still not happy. Then my Little Freddie—'

'What the fuck are you trying to say?'

Freddie had him now, and he knew it. 'Don't get annoyed. I am just saying, she ain't right and you know she ain't. Jackie was telling me a while ago that she had been off the pill for yonks and that you were trying for a kiddie, so maybe that's what is wrong with her.'

It was obvious to Freddie that Jimmy knew nothing about any of this.

'Fuck off, Freddie, you talk out of your arse. We have a fucking dead body in the boot and you are talking about things you know nothing about. Let's concentrate on the job in hand, eh?'

But the damage was done, the seed was planted.

Freddie was contrite now, embarrassed. He held up his

hands in supplication, his whole demeanour was now one of abject sorrow and remorse.

'I was only saying, mate, that was all. Just trying to let you know I understand what's going on. Women talk, they tell other birds what they would never dream of telling us. I'm sorry if I spoke out of turn, and you are right. I made a major fuck-up tonight and it has to be sorted, so let's snort this and get this show on the road.'

Jimmy nodded, but he was troubled. He was already worried out of his mind and this new revelation had not helped allay any of his fears.

Chapter Seventeen

Ozzy was frowning, and Jimmy was trying to make the news he had to impart as palatable as possible. This was not the easiest task he had ever undertaken but at the end of the day, Freddie was his closest male blood relative, and the person who had given him the opportunity to work and earn for Ozzy in the first place. Freddie had explained that much on the journey down to the Isle of Wight, and Jimmy had to agree with him.

Freddie was outside the nick asleep in the car. He had promised to drive them home so that Jimmy could get a few hours' shuteye himself.

'So Freddie has killed my mate, is that what you are fucking rambling on about?'

Jimmy nodded. For the first time in years he seemed nervous, and Ozzy was reminded of the young man who had walked in all those years ago. A young man who Ozzy had educated and then watched grow in stature and in confidence. He guessed, in fact he had no doubt, that the death of Lenny was not a lawful, or indeed a righteous act. If it had been, Jimmy would have reported it with the minimum of fuss and with the facts all in place, confident that it would be understood and forgotten about in minutes.

'Lenny Brewster was my old mucker. He was a wanker at times, but then we are all guilty of that as you know. But what I want to ascertain is why he was wiped out. If it was for a good cause then I am with you. If it was because that mad cunt Freddie lost that famous temper of his then I want to know that, Jimmy. The truth, so they say, is good for the soul. Now stop fucking about and tell me what actually happened.'

Jimmy really did not need this, but he had to sort it out or Freddie could be dead by the evening. Ozzy had a long arm, and he had a short fuse. He decided to tell him the truth, more or less.

'Look Oz, Lenny was having us over. He was taking his wedge and still ripping us off. We went round his gaff to sort it and he went mad. Said he was your mate, he knew you way back when, all the old shit, and then it went off and Freddie done him. Bosh, bosh, simple as that.'

'Well, if that was the case, why were you dithering? Why the fucking cloak and dagger?'

Jimmy shrugged, and Ozzy saw the sheer power of this young man and knew he had made a good choice.

'He was your mate. I think he felt he had a right to take what he wanted, and Freddie was only going to give him a dig. It just all got out of hand. He was a lairy old fucker.'

Ozzy nodded knowingly. 'Lenny was always a cunt to himself, but he was a good earner, you said yourself how good he was. So why was he feeling the need to cream anything off the top?'

Jimmy was impressed. He realised that Ozzy had sussed it out and he hated himself for lying to him. But what could he do?

Ozzy could see the confusion and the divided loyalty on the boy's face and he liked him even more for that. Freddie was on a death wish, of that he had no doubt.

Even in stir he had caused untold aggravation with people he should have left in peace. It was what people like Freddie did. Their whole life was a series of events, and they caused most of them because without the upset and the danger they didn't feel alive. It was this trait that had made Ozzy take Freddie on in the first place, had been the reason he had found him so useful, but this was also what had made him overlook Freddie in favour of this lad here when the opportunity had arisen.

Ozzy knew all about his antagonising the Blacks at every opportunity. He knew all about the dead girl, and he knew about the other little occasions that Freddie thought were secret and therefore unknown to the general population.

Ozzy had a network of people who, in one way or another, answered to him directly, and Jimmy had no real concept of just how intricate that network was. Even Jimmy himself was watched and observed by people he had no idea were on Ozzy's payroll. That was how it all worked.

Ozzy was away for the duration. He knew that now, and his brief had explained it to him in simple terms. They had no intention of letting him walk out without a fight and without him doing a complete turnaround. That meant either becoming a born-again Christian, or doing degrees in sociology or psychology and acting like one of the *Guardian*-reading lifers he loathed so much.

Because he refused to show any remorse for his crimes, he knew his parole was a long way off, but this suited him. He had been away so long he was now at ease with his environment. He was happy enough because that was what you had to do to survive a big lump. He was cutting his nose off really, because if he would only feign remorse and regret, and kiss the parole board's collective arses, he would be out sooner rather than later. But it was his pride and his standing that stopped him from doing that now. Plus he liked it in here.

'Look, Ozzy, it happened and I dealt with it, OK?'

Ozzy smiled then. 'Did you listen to yourself just now?' Jimmy shook his head, glad that Ozzy had a smile back in his voice.

'You said, "it happened and I dealt with it", right?'

Jimmy nodded, intrigued. He loved it when Ozzy gave him a lesson in life, and this was what he was going to get now.

'Those words tell me that *you* had to sort out a mess, a mess that was caused by Freddie Jackson having a mad half-hour and therefore killing poor Lenny for fuck all. Was Freddie doing him out of his few quid? Because Lenny would argue the toss with Man Mountain Dean over a fifty pence piece if he thought he was being had over. Also, Lenny would not take on Freddie or yourself unless he thought he had just cause, which brings us back to money and a fair wage for a good job. He was an earner, he was also my old mate, so he had a right to expect a bit of leeway. Now I ask you one last time, son. Did Freddie do a wrong one, or was it really just a tear-up that got out of hand?'

Jimmy sighed and, pushing his fingers through his thick dark hair, he said quietly, 'He asked for it, Oz. He asked for it and he got it. What more can I say?'

Ozzy shrugged, knowing he was lying, but understanding why. 'Subject closed, then. One last thing, though. Is his old woman after comp?'

'Yes.'

'Cheeky mare, but give it to her because she has always had the knack of keeping her trap shut. Do not give her reason to open it, OK?'

Jimmy knew he was being told that if he didn't want Ozzy to find out the truth for sure, then he should pay her a decent sum.

'Tell Freddie I will let this one go, but tell him one more casualty and he will regret it big time.'

Jimmy was nodding again, but he was quiet, and Ozzy admired his acumen. 'Look, Jimmy, remember when a friend of mine left stir and came to you and Freddie, and the two of them became bosom pals?'

Jimmy looked wary. Bobby Blaine had been on course for a lump from the day of his release.

'Well, he is back inside, not something I was surprised about, but he had a few little anecdotes about Freddie that troubled me. Now, while Freddie is of use to me and mine he is safe. You have given him the benefit of the doubt and I respect that, but if he oversteps the line again, or becomes a liability in any way, shape or form, then I will expect you to sort it out for me once and for all. Do you understand what I am saying?'

Jimmy nodded once more and Ozzy could see that he was capable of doing what was needed. That was all he'd been interested in, really, and now he had his answer.

'Come on, Maggie, cheer up.'

Roxanna was smiling and Maggie forced herself to smile back. Rox was a good Saturday girl, and she used her so she would never be alone.

'Have you been sick again?'

'I feel a bit off, that's all. Nothing to worry about.'

Roxanna looked at her aunt closely. The hair was perfect, the make-up was perfect, but she looked wrong somehow, looked dilapidated, looked all frayed around the edges.

They were in the salon in Leigh-on-Sea. It had just

been refurbished in chrome and glass and it was looking fantastic. It overlooked the sea and today, even though it was cloudy and dark outside, the salon, named 'Roxy's' in honour of Maggie's favourite niece, looked inviting, sophisticated and, as was important in Essex, expensive.

Although it wasn't cheap it wasn't actually that pricey, which was the secret to making money in Essex and East London. If it looked good, and if it looked high-priced then you were laughing all the way to the proverbial bank.

As she looked at her newest addition to her chain, Maggie felt nothing. Her usual pride was lost inside her. But she was getting to be such a good actress that no one really noticed. Even her mother had got off her case. She was smiling, she was talking, she was to all intents and purposes back to herself.

But Jimmy knew that despite their success, and the love they had, they couldn't talk any more.

He had stayed out all night again, and she had been pleased, relieved that he wasn't there. Because he was with Freddie, she had even managed to sleep a bit, relaxed in the knowledge that Freddie wasn't going to pop round, or ring her up to talk to her about nothing in particular, while all the time terrorising her.

Roxanna had put the kettle on and made them both coffee. As Maggie sipped hers the urge to vomit was so strong she retched over one of the brand-new glass basins. Her coffee went everywhere, and she dropped the mug on to the floor as she dry-retched over and over again.

Roxanna put her own coffee down gently and went out the back. When she returned with the cleaning equipment, she saw her aunt sitting on one of the new black leather barber's chairs and she said softly, 'Why don't you just do a test, eh? You must know you're pregnant, Auntie Mags?'

Roxy was always with her lately. And the poor girl thought it was because she loved her so much, but that was a lie. She did love her, but she was also her insurance against Freddie. All the time Roxanna was there, he had to keep himself at arm's length.

Now this closeness had been the cause of Rox guessing her condition.

Maggie looked at her niece, and the girl could see the fear in her eyes. Going to her, Roxanna hugged her tightly and said in utter bewilderment, 'What on earth is wrong with you? Please tell me, Mags, I swear I won't say a word. Are you scared of being pregnant? Is that it, mate?'

Maggie pulled herself together. What she had feared more than anything had just been spoken of out loud, and that had somehow made it true. She had forced herself not to think about it, she had pushed the very notion from her head, and she had concentrated on trying to act as normal as possible. Now Rox had made her face up to the one thing she had never wanted to acknowledge.

She was pregnant, and it had to be Freddie's. Even though Jimmy had loved her on the same night Freddie had raped her, he had also loved her over and over for more than a year since she'd stopped the pill, and nothing had happened. Now, the thing she had wanted more than life itself *had* happened. The thing she had prayed for, dreamed of and wanted so badly, had finally been given to her and she didn't want it.

She felt as if she was being invaded by an alien, and every thought of this child brought nothing but terror and despair.

She hated it already, and now her heart, her little Rox, was looking at her as if she was mad. Maybe, just maybe she was. But her secret was out now and all hell would break loose.

* * *

Lena looked at her husband as he spoke and stifled the urge to smash him over the head with the nearest blunt instrument she could lay her hands on.

'You silly little mare, is that what you had your mother nearly in bits over, eh? A bleeding baby! You women and your hormones. I told her it was something and nothing, didn't I, Lena?'

Lena gave Joseph such a look it would have floored a lesser man, and he finally took the hint and shut up. Opening his paper, he studied the racing form and not for the first time wondered at the antics of females. Maggie was having a baby, but anyone would think she had terminal cancer by the look on her boat race.

He sighed and concentrated on his horses. They at least were consistent. They ran, they lost and they didn't answer back.

Lena handed her daughter a cup of tea, and sat down next to her.

'You look like the girl who lost a fiver and found a penny. Please, my love, tell me what is so bad about having a baby. I thought it was what you wanted.'

'It is, Mum. I think I am just whacked out what with the new salon and everything.'

As Maggie had predicted, Rox had started to spread the news. It was now three in the afternoon and her mother and father had already been informed. Now she had to face Jimmy and Jackie and *him*. Oh, he would be round their house so fast, she knew he would. And so she had to pull herself together and make him believe it was Jimmy's, even though she was certain it must be Freddie's.

It felt like Freddie's baby, it felt evil and wrong to her. It felt like an interloper. It had been planted inside her with hate, and that was all she felt for it.

She wished it dead with all her being, but she couldn't say that. She was going to have to tell Jimmy she was over the moon about it, and watch him celebrate his fatherhood.

And she would do it, because if Freddie guessed the truth then her life really would be over.

Jimmy was holding his wife in his arms and telling her how much he loved her. All her moods and her funny behaviour should now be forgotten, because it could all be put down to her condition.

She was having their baby, and even though he was worried about why she had kept it to herself for so long, he was thrilled.

All the family was coming round later, and he had bought champagne to toast the happy event. The girls were there already making sandwiches, and his wife was sitting on their bed and not saying a word.

After the night he had experienced, and his visit with Ozzy, this news had been a godsend. He had needed this, had needed something good to happen. Yet she had told him over the phone, just blurted it out. He had been speechless with wonderment and happiness, but now he felt once more that there was something radically wrong with her. She was like a robot, smiling and chatting, except the smile did not reach her eyes and her chat was forced. This all felt off kilter. It was like he was part of a play or it was a game. He loved this woman with all his being, but he didn't know her any more. They were both pretending that nothing was wrong, and he hoped against hope that it was just her hormones, as Lena had told him earlier.

She knew he had been worried about Maggie, because he had gone to talk to her a while back, had asked her if she had said anything, if he had done something maybe that he hadn't realised, and upset her.

But Lena had assured him then that it was just a blip, that all marriages had them, that the romance couldn't last and Maggie was probably tired from the work in the salons. Jimmy had grabbed that excuse with both hands, believing she was right because he'd needed to believe it. But now, here she was, sitting on the bed he had not wanted but she had insisted on getting, carrying their child, the thing that they had wanted more than anything else in the world, and she looked like death warmed up.

He was frightened. Kneeling down, he took her hands in his, and he said gently, 'Are you all right, Mags? Are you happy we're having a baby?' She looked into his eyes. He was so good looking, and he had been all she had wanted. He needed her to tell him what he wanted to hear, and she knew that she had to be convincing.

Abortion was not an option because of her Catholic upbringing, but a plan formed in her mind as she forced a warm smile and said, ' 'Course I am, mate, but I have got morning, noon and night sickness. I just feel so bloody rough.'

He kissed her gently on the lips and for the first time in ages she didn't pull away.

'I love you, Maggie, you are everything to me. You know that, don't you?'

She felt her eyes fill with tears, and she nodded her head and said sadly, 'I know, mate, I know.'

Jackie was delighted. Now that Maggie was in the club she could relax a bit. She knew from bitter experience that Freddie didn't enjoy pregnant women, in fact she had been ignored to the point of fighting when she had been carrying Little Freddie.

She wanted this so much because now she could be friends again with Maggie, proper friends, like before. All her little sister's power was gone. She was now a pregnant woman and Jackie could again play the older sister, giving her advice, helping her understand what was happening, and being the know-all. This was what she craved, what she needed. This was something she had already done, and Maggie, for all her cleverness and her salons, had never experienced.

The girls were already at Maggie's. Jackie was in the car with her two Freddies and she wasn't even bothered by the fact that her husband was ignoring her. In fact, he looked annoyed, but then again Little Freddie had thrown his gold lighter out of the car window earlier.

Maggie, her lovely little Maggie, was out of bounds, and that was all that mattered.

'Light me a fag, Jack, and clump that fucker before he falls out the window, will you?'

She turned in her seat and punched Little Freddie in the arm. Any other child would have screamed in pain. It was a serious and heavy punch that had all her strength behind it since any other kind of punch would have been useless.

Little Freddie grabbed her hair and tried to drag her into the back seat, all the time effing and blinding at her.

Freddie watched his wife and son and wondered at a life where everything was shit. Complete and utter shit. He let go of the steering wheel with one hand and he hit his son with such force the child was knocked back against the leather upholstery and badly winded. Once more, the boy did not cry out or express anything that could indicate he had been hurt.

He had let go of his mother's hair, though, and Jackie sat back up in her seat and tried to tidy herself up. She had really made an effort tonight and she was pleased with how she looked.

'Light the fucking fag, Jack, and *you*, little boy, had better watch yourself because I ain't in the fucking mood for all this, right?' He looked at his son in the mirror on the dash. Little Freddie nodded, but his eyes were slits and his face was dark with anger.

Freddie was annoyed, and he was tired, but as they pulled up on the drive of Jimmy and Maggie's lovely detached residence and went inside, his mood lifted without the aid of narcotics.

Maddie was there as always, and she was thrilled for the young couple. As she said to Lena, it was a new life and a new era.

Lena hugged her. She actually liked Maddie these days. She was a long way from the woman she had been when her husband was alive.

Jimmy's mum and dad were there for once, and quiet as always. Deirdre was taking everything in but not saying a word unless asked a question directly. Lena had gone right off them a long time ago, but like everything else in life, you had to smile and be nice because they were always going to be around.

Lena noticed that Maggie was looking better. She seemed happier than she had for ages, her make-up was perfect and she had dressed in a lovely white dress. It was fitted, and in it her little bump was evident and this alone cheered her. Jimmy and Maggie would produce a beautiful child, she was sure of that. Unlike Freddie and Jackie, who had gorgeous children but didn't appreciate them, she knew that these two would make wonderful parents.

Especially her Maggie, because even though Jimmy

was a Face, and a ducker and diver, he had more than provided for his family. Even if he had a capture her daughter would be all right financially. Unlike that ponce, who had just walked in like he owned the place, and who had left her oldest child without a pot to piss in and a belly full of arms and legs.

Freddie had bought a magnum of champagne. He walked straight up to Maggie and, giving it to her, he said loudly, 'Congratulations. We were all beginning to think he was firing blanks!'

Maggie smiled her brightest smile and said gaily, 'Well, you were wrong, Freddie. My Jimmy is all man.'

Jimmy was beside her by then, and as he slipped his arm around his tiny wife's waist Freddie said in a jocular voice, 'Sure you didn't have any help with it, Jim?'

But he was looking at Maggie as he spoke and she couldn't meet his eyes. Instead she hugged her husband and buried her face in his sweet-smelling shirt.

'Fucking cheek, like I would need any help in that department.'

Anyone who knew them would not guess that they were both pretending that everything was all right. Jimmy wanted to throw Freddie from his home, but he couldn't.

'I thought she might have changed her man for the night, that's what the old biddies used to say, ain't it, Mum?'

Maddie nodded, happy he had noticed her and brought her into the conversation.

Freddie raised his voice as he continued, 'Remember the other old saying, Jimmy, it's a wise child that knows its mother, and a *very* wise child that knows its father!'

Everyone laughed. As Jackie watched the little tableau, she felt the jealousy rise inside her. He had never ever made a fuss like that of her, and she had been through it five times if she included the baby she had lost.

Maggie went over to her, and hugged her. 'All right, Jack?'

Jackie tried to ignore her anger, and hugged her little sister with all the warmth she could muster. 'I am so pleased for you, Mags. Kids are the best thing that can happen to you.'

As she said that, Little Freddie kicked Lena in the shins and the slap she gave him was loud in the room, and knocked him off his feet. He was battered on a regular basis and consequently he was as hard as nails.

'You little fucker! You try that again and I'll skin you alive.'

Little Freddie was laughing his head off at his grandmother and as Maggie looked around her at the smiling faces she felt she was going to go mad.

She was sitting on the toilet seat and gathering herself together when Freddie finally managed to catch her on her own. The lock on the bathroom door could be opened from the outside if necessary. He had watched her covertly, and waited patiently all night to get her alone. He walked in and saw the fear come into her eyes at his presence.

'Calm down. I didn't know you were in here, did I?'

Maggie stood up quickly, and he looked down at her and marvelled at how little she was. He was a big man, and she was tiny even to most people of average height. This was one of the things that attracted him to her.

He remembered the feel of her, remembered how tiny her waist was, how full her breasts and how small her hands were in his. She was lovely, and he had never enjoyed a woman so much in his life.

As he looked her over she felt a rage inside her that made her almost happy. She had felt nothing for so long that any feeling was welcome.

'Get out, Freddie, or I am going to scream the place down.'

He smiled at her, holding his arm out as if inviting her to leave. 'Feel free, scream away.'

She pushed past him then, and he grabbed her arm, hurting her. But he made sure he didn't mark her, and she knew then that he was frightened of Jimmy.

After the debacle at Lenny's, Jimmy was on the edge. He had smoothed it all over with Oz, but Freddie knew that there had been a lot said this day that he would never know about. Jimmy had to have been given the hard word, he was sure of that much. He wasn't silly, he knew Ozzy was genned up on everyone he had on his payroll. So he was dicing with death doing this, because if Jimmy caught them there would be murders.

But this was too good a chance to miss. 'You sure you ain't got anything to tell me?'

He was giving her that smile which made the object of his mirth feel like they were nothing, a nobody.

'I'm sure. What on earth would I have to tell a piece of shit like you, Freddie?' She sounded strong and she was grateful that at least the anger was working for her, it was making her want to fight him.

'Funny you are pregnant now though, don't you think? Jackie told me about when you came off the pill.'

She didn't answer him, just raised her eyebrows as if he was a complete idiot.

'I mean, you have to see it from *my* point of view, don't ya? This could be another little *Freddie*, couldn't it?'

He was goading her, but she swallowed her fear as she shrugged his hand off her arm. 'You *really* think you are something special, don't you? Well, I am well over three months, mate, so stop congratulating yourself. Now get out of my way or this time I will cause fucking ructions. I know all about Lenny, Jimmy tells me everything. Unlike you and my sister, we have a good marriage. You or fifty like you couldn't ruin it for us, Freddie. You are nothing but a thug, and you can't hurt me any more.'

She was staring into his eyes and she looked triumphant when she saw the shock on his face at her words. 'You are nothing to me, and this baby is a little *Jimmy*. It will be decent, and it will be educated, and it will be as far from the animal called Little Freddie that you two dragged into the world as is humanly possible. Now get out of my way.'

He stepped aside this time and she opened the door. Her head was splitting, but she walked away from him with her head held high and her back straight and she made her way down the stairs and back to the party with a smile on her face and a cheery word for whoever spoke to her.

It was what she had dreaded more than anything, and it had happened, and she was still there. Her world had not collapsed and the fear was lessening now she had faced him. This was how she was going to play it, and having started this deceit she had to see it through to the bitter end.

Freddie had already destroyed so much that she held dear, but he would not find out that he must have fathered the child her husband believed was his. And it would never occur to Jimmy that it wasn't his. He trusted her, and he had once had every reason to trust her.

This child had been forced on her, and she was going to have to pretend that she wanted it, loved it and cared for it. She had to front this out and she was determined to do just that.

If Freddie even had an inkling that she thought it was his he would never let her forget it, and Jimmy would be completely destroyed if the truth came out. And she now realised that was what all this was really about. Jimmy had climbed up the tree of success while Freddie was still on the lowest branches.

He was a vindictive and dangerous adversary, but she had to protect herself, her husband and her sanity.

She prayed that night and every night that the child inside her would die.

She was delivered of a son on the first of November 1996.

He was named James Jackson Junior, and his mother cried for three days after the birth.

Book Three

Even if we take matrimony at its lowest, even if we regard it as no more than a sort of friendship recognised by the police.

– Robert Louis Stevenson, 1850–1894
Virginibus Puerisque

The fathers have eaten sour grapes,
and the children's teeth are set on edge.

– Ezekiel, 18:2
The Bible

Chapter Eighteen

2000

'You ain't leaving him here again, surely?'

Maggie snapped at her mother, in a high angry voice, 'Well, if you don't want to have him, Mum, just say.'

Little James Junior was watching the scene before him with his usual nervous demeanour.

He spent half his life at his nana's and he liked it there. At three years old he had already sussed out that his mother was not like other mothers. She rarely hugged him, or touched him unless it was absolutely necessary. Yet she took very good care of him. He was clean and fed but he was looked after most of the time by his nana and this suited him right down to the ground.

His father was a different kettle of fish altogether. He loved his dada and his dada loved him. He hugged, kissed and played with him until his mum bathed him and put him into his bed. It was his dad who read to him, took him with him in his car and who made him feel safe.

His mother, on the other hand, made him feel worried. He had a nervous tic and he blinked his eyes constantly when he was with her for any length of time on his own. He knew he wasn't quick enough for her, that he irritated her, and yet he also knew that she didn't mean to hurt his feelings, that she felt bad about it. Then she would give him a hug, but it was more as an apology than an expression of love.

Nothing he did was right in her eyes, and he didn't know how to make her like him.

Now his nana was doing her crust, as his granddad called her tempers, and he knew that he would be staying there no matter what. At least he hoped so anyway. His granddad made him laugh and told him stories. His nana made him lovely food and cuddled him as much as she could. It was as if she was trying to make up for his mother's complete lack of affection.

But he didn't mind. If he could live at his nana's and see his daddy every day then life would be perfect.

'Give us another kiss, you!'

Rox was going out with a local boy called Dicky Harmon. He was a good-looking lad, and he was also an up-and-coming young scoundrel. He was working for Jimmy and he was loving it. Freddie frightened him, but he was sensible enough not to let him know that. Freddie would put the kibosh on their relationship if he could, but Rox had put him in his place a long time ago. He knew, though, that Freddie could not bear the thought of his daughters with boys, no matter who they were, so he did not take his animosity too personally. He was sensible like that, he knew that Freddie looked after his girls in all the wrong ways but he could not bear for them to be treated as Freddie treated all the females in his own life. Freddie would take it personally if one of his daughters was fucked and left. It wasn't about them, though, it was about him and how he was perceived.

Dicky had sussed him out a long time ago. He had a

father just like Freddie, and he was determined not to be like any of them. Rox was a star and he loved her. He didn't want anyone else just yet, but when he did he would take them discreetly and without fear of hurting the love of his life.

Rox was like a clone of Maggie at the same age. At twenty-one she was stunning, and she was also a qualified hairdresser and beautician. She ran Maggie's second-biggest salon in Chingford, and she had bought her own little flat and her own car. Maggie had helped her, though no one knew that, of course.

She thanked God every day for her aunt, and she worshipped her. Maggie had helped her get away from the dump she had grown up in and shown her a better way of life.

Now that she had Dicky and she was in love, her life was better than it had ever been. Her father had tried to stop them, but once Jimmy gave his blessing he had calmed down a bit. Plus, she thought that her father actually liked Dicky but just couldn't admit it.

It was a Friday night and the salon was packed out. The sun beds were all booked up and the smell of the tanning accelerator was heavy in the air, mingling with the perfumed smell of the hair products used by the stylists. Rox was tired, happy, and trying to make Dicky get out of her little office so she could get on with her work.

One of the juniors, a pretty girl with heavy hips and hair extensions, called through the door. 'Margaret's buzzer just went. Shall I wash her colour off, or do you want to check it first?'

'I'm coming, Renee. Pour her a glass of white wine, and pour me one and all. I'll be right there.'

She pushed Dicky towards the door. 'Come on, you, get a move on. I have work to do.'

He laughed. 'We still on for tonight?'

She nodded, amazed as always that this lovely man wanted her. 'Meet me at me flat about half eight, or would you rather meet me in the pub?'

'Better be the pub, eh? Your dad and that will be there, won't they?'

She sighed. They walked out together into the bustle of her little domain, and she felt the thrill she always felt knowing this was all under her control.

Dicky left just as two women came in, hoping for quick blow-dries, and she smiled professionally at Margaret Channing, checking her hair with an expert eye, even though her mind was on the night ahead.

'Where's me boy, then?'

Jimmy sounded annoyed and Maggie said, as nicely as she could, 'He is at me mum's. We have Jackie's birthday, don't we?'

He nodded, but she knew he was not happy and he would have preferred to drop the boy off on the way there. She had justified leaving Jimmy Junior there already because she had a lot of work to catch up on and she needed the time to herself. This was really a complete fabrication but she still tried to convince herself that it was true.

'Ain't your mum and dad going, then?'

Maggie turned to face him. As he looked into her lovely face, Jimmy wondered for the millionth time what was so wrong with his wife that she couldn't take to her own child.

'Maddie is going to me mum's and having him for a while. They won't stay long anyway, you know that. Me dad hates Freddie, and me mum only tolerates him. Once Jackie has a few and gets stroppy they'll bugger off.'

Jimmy nodded, but he was still upset that his little fella was not at home to greet him. He looked around his home, and knew that this was a home to be proud of. It was a six-bedroomed detached Georgian house in three acres. It had a pool, a sauna and was like something from a magazine.

Maggie had the knack of doing the places up, he could not deny that. Yet this house felt empty, devoid of any real life. It was crazy because he had wanted a home like this all his life, and now he had it, he couldn't enjoy it. He knew it was because of Maggie and her attitude towards the boy, and as much as he loved her, he adored his son. Jimmy Junior was a diamond, clever, funny and good natured. When he looked at the child, he saw himself, like looking in a mirror, and his mother and Maggie's mother loved him. If he had been a bugger, like Little Freddie, then he could have understood Maggie's attitude, but even though she did all that was supposed to be done for a child, he knew, and more importantly, little Jimmy knew, that she did it because it was expected, not out of any kind of love.

She had never seemed to really care for him. After his birth Maggie's attitude had been put down to postnatal depression, but although she had recovered from that eventually, she simply hadn't ever bonded with the child.

He walked up the large staircase, and as always marvelled at the beauty of this house, and he knew that he would move out in the morning to a little flat if it would bring back the happiness they had shared in the early days of their marriage.

Maggie came out of their bedroom suite and she looked stunning. He smiled at her and said sincerely, 'You look fucking gorgeous, Mags.'

She smiled back and he saw the professionally whitened

teeth and the immaculate make-up and knew the smile was there and reaching her eyes only because her son was not in the house. She relaxed when the boy was away from her, and he knew that was not fanciful thinking because he felt the change in her, saw the difference in her moods.

She moved sedately past him and he walked into his large bedroom with its twin bathrooms and dressing rooms and he felt completely empty inside.

Jackie looked lovely. The girls had done her hair and make-up, and had made sure she did not get pissed too quickly by rationing her drinking.

Little Freddie, who was now huge and cumbersome, was lying on the front-room floor as usual, watching Sky TV.

Dianna looked around the place and sighed. It was rotten again, and she knew that if she didn't give it a good go over then no one ever would. The way her parents lived amazed her even as it annoyed her. The money that was wasted on furniture and decorators was astronomical, yet nothing was ever looked after or respected. Her bedroom was perfect, but it had a sturdy lock on the door to keep Little Freddie out. That little sod would rob anything if it wasn't nailed down, and she hoped that this time when he went to court they sent him away somewhere.

He was already well known to the police and hated by nearly everyone in his orbit. Because he was Freddie Jackson's son and heir he was allowed to get away with murder and one day that would be what he was charged with. She had no doubt about that whatsoever!

Jackie burped, and the sound made Dianna's stomach churn. She was like an animal at times. She only hoped that her father turned up, because if he didn't there would be trouble. Her mother laid great store on her birthday, and on her husband being with her in the pub for all to see. It was a sham, and Dianna was sick to death of it all.

Jackie was dressed in a black trouser suit and she looked nice. She was pleased with how well she had scrubbed up, but the drink had bloated her and although the weight that had piled on a few years ago was now dropping off her at an alarming rate, her hands and face were still puffy. She should cut down on the booze, but knew that she wouldn't.

Anyway, it was her *birthday*. If you couldn't have a drink on your *birthday*, when could you?

Dianna looked great, Jackie thought. She was a beauty, and Kimberley was looking lovely too. Kim worried her, though. Unlike Rox, who had fucked off at the earliest opportunity, she looked like she was here for the duration. Kimberley, who had always been the mouthy one, had changed over the last few years. She rarely went out in the evenings to the pub, or to go clubbing. She was like the ghost of Christmas past, and now she didn't even seem to work that much. Jackie knew Maggie had tried to stick a firework up her arse on more than one occasion because she had let her down in the salons.

Kim always looked like she was sickening for something, as if she had the weight of the world on her shoulders. But she was all grown up now, so it was none of her business what went on in that girl's head. She had done her bit, and it was up to them to sort themselves out.

Jackie put her daughters out of her mind and wondered if her Freddie would turn up like he had promised. He had better. She didn't ask a lot of him, just that he came out with her on high days and holidays. Surely as his wife she was entitled to that much?

Little Freddie kicked out at Kimberley as she walked

past him and she ignored him. He started shouting and swearing at her as she walked up the stairs to go into her bedroom.

Dianna watched her go and sighed. There was trouble waiting to explode and it would happen sooner rather than later. If her mum or dad actually looked at Kim one day they would realise exactly what the score was. But they were not going to hear it from her. She had enough to contend with as it was.

Freddie was already in the pub, not because he was waiting for his wife, but because he was chasing a piece of skirt who worked behind the bar. She was young, only eighteen, but she had the knowing look he loved, and the slutty way of dressing that told him she was well up for it.

Well, so was he. He was now investing in his future sex life by buying her drinks and charming her with his stories and jokes. He was a Face, and as such was already halfway into her knickers. He was half pissed, too, but he was being a good boy because he wanted to impress this little hussy and hopefully bed her before the night was out.

He knew she had a baby, which was always a guarantee for a good time in his experience. Once they were lumbered with a kid and a council flat, the novelty of motherhood soon wore off. Then they were lonely, skint and, more to the point, looking for a bit of excitement to liven up what had turned out to be a very dull and boring existence.

Girls like this little barmaid amazed him. They wanted kids but when they arrived, very few actually enjoyed the experience, and then they wondered why the men in the equation fucked off out at the earliest opportunity. What man in his right mind would believe that the same girl who had dropped her drawers in nanoseconds for him had not done the same thing many times before with other mugs? So the girls quite rightly ended up on their Jack Jones, and then became the local shag for married men like himself.

Oh, he knew all the signs. They were dressed to kill – even just going up the local shops for a loaf of bread or their family allowance, they were half naked and plastered in make-up. Their lives revolved around a few mates in a similar position to them, their mums, and their mum's houses, and pulling a bloke, hopefully a live one.

They were accidents waiting to happen, and he liked to get them while they were still halfway decent. Within a few years, this girl would have produced another baby, maybe two and she would be relegated to being a booty call for the local no necks, giro blasters and tracksuit wearers. At the moment, though, he wanted her, and he was determined to have her.

He felt in his pockets and caressed his wad of cash. Every time he pulled it out to get a drink her eyes nearly popped out of her head. So far he knew her name was Charmaine, she had a baby girl of thirteen months and a flat within walking distance of the pub and the house where he lived with Jackie, and that her big dream was to go to Florida. She was already proving to be uncomplicated and without any kind of imagination at all, so there was no chance of her wanting long conversations or trying to impress him with her staggering intelligence.

He was on a roll when Jackie and the girls walked into the pub, and he sighed heavily as Charmaine took one look at Jackie, who was now standing beside him like his minder, and sensibly made her way to the other end of the bar in a state of extreme fright.

'Ain't you going to wish me happy birthday, then?'

Freddie smiled and said casually, as he tried to get the landlady's attention for a drink, 'No, Jackie, I ain't.'

* * *

Little Jimmy was watching a cartoon and eating a biscuit when Little Freddie finally rolled up at his nana's house. Jimmy Junior was terrified of his cousin because he was such a noisy and aggressive lad who seemed to take great delight in frightening him.

As soon as he came into the flat the atmosphere changed, and Maddie, who had hoped that Little Freddie wouldn't want to come and sit in with her and Jimmy Junior, was already feeling a nervous wreck.

Little Freddie was enjoying the effect he was creating. He loved the way people were scared of him and tried to get round him, to get in his good books. He was a handsome lad, though his features were marred by his surly and unhappy expression. He was also badly scarred since he had been stitched up many times, mainly over his refusal to feel any kind of danger, and because he had been in so many fights.

Now he looked at the little boy who he knew was hoping that he would not be nasty, and he smiled at him because his father had warned him that one more incident with Jimmy Junior and he would really take him in hand.

Little Freddie had realised that his father was wary of Big Jimmy, and that had been a learning curve. He had never imagined his father fearing anyone or anything. But he had realised a while back that it was Jimmy who ran everything and that even his father had to do what he was asked.

So he smiled at his little cousin and, giving his old nana a big hug, he sat down and watched the cartoons with a light heart and a calm exterior.

Like his father before him he was formulating a plan, and like his father before him, it needed serious plotting and serious intention. Unlike his father, though, he paid attention to the details.

* * *

Maggie looked around the pub and willed the clock to go faster. She hated this place now, though there had been a time when she had loved coming in here. It was still dirty, still had the same cloying smell of disinfectant and beer in the carpet and, more worrying, it still had the same people in the same seats as when she had first come in there all those years ago.

The place was like some kind of time warp.

Her mother and father were having the time of their lives, despite having sworn they'd leave early, and she envied them the carefree joviality they seemed to possess no matter what happened to them.

Jackie was pissed out of her brains, and Freddie was watching a skinny barmaid with too much make-up and greasy hair. The girls were all laughing and joking at the bar, and that young Dicky was looking at Rox as if he had just won the Rollover on the National Lottery.

Maggie felt a pang in her breast as she remembered that she had been like that once – carefree, young and madly in love. She sought out Jimmy with her eyes and saw him in earnest conversation with Dianna.

She was a beauty, was Dianna. As Maggie watched them talk, she heard Jackie's high-pitched voice as she started to abuse the young barmaid. She closed her eyes, and when she opened them again she saw Freddie being held back by Jimmy and her father, and the girls trying to help Jackie up off the filthy floor. Jackie had a bloody nose, and she felt an urge to cry at the complete abortion that constituted her life.

Instead she got up and walked to her sister and, taking her gently by the arm, she helped the drunken and bleeding woman into the toilets.

Freddie pushed Jimmy and Joseph away from him,

waving his arms to let them know he was calmer and then he said loudly, 'Cabaret's over, let's get another drink.'

Everyone in the pub went back to what they were doing. This kind of occurrence was the norm, and broke up the sheer boredom that most of them felt for the majority of the time.

Rox and Dianna watched their mother as she limped into the toilet with Maggie and then saw their elder sister sneak out to the other bar. Dicky looked at Rox and made a face that told her he wanted to go, and go sooner rather than later.

She nodded in complete agreement. They had done their bit, and now they were free to leave and enjoy themselves at last.

Maggie had a headache and she knew it was going to be a blinder. As she stripped off her clothes, she glanced at herself in the full-length mirror on the dressing-room wall. She didn't have a mark on her, no one would ever believe she had given birth to a child. She knew this fact annoyed her sister Jackie no end, but it didn't bother her either way. Any pleasure she had ever garnered from her body was long gone.

Freddie had seen to that.

In her salons, she was complimented all day by women who wanted perfection and thought that she possessed it. If only they knew the truth of it. She saw her body as something corrupt, something disgusting and something that had been the vessel that had brought her and her family to this point.

She slipped a white silk nightie over her head. Seeing her reflection again she knew she looked lovely, and that Jimmy would take her and she would let him. It was easier than trying to make excuses not to make love.

She walked back into the bedroom and sat on the chaise longue that was supposed to have been used for romance, but was used for her to watch TV. Jimmy was putting the boy to bed, and she knew he was making up for not seeing him earlier and, as well, trying to make up for her complete lack of interest in the child.

She placed a hand softly on to her belly and rubbed it unconsciously.

She had never taken any precautions since the boy's birth and there had been nothing. This had only strengthened her belief that Jimmy was besotted with Freddie's child. And Jimmy Junior was by some strange quirk of nature a *nice* child, he was a dear little soul. But she knew that one day he would change. He would turn into his true self, and then Freddie Jackson would be living under her roof.

Maggie knew he still believed that Jimmy Junior was his child, and that he was pleased about it. She heard him telling Jimmy how much he looked like his father, and he would be looking at her as he said it. The two men looked so alike it was uncanny.

She hated Freddie Jackson, and the boy had just been another stick to beat her with. If she had only had another child, she could have got away with her deceit, got Freddie off her back. But it had never happened, not even a threat of one.

Every time she allowed Jimmy to take her, she prayed that this time he would give her a proper child, a child of their own.

But inside herself, she felt that would never happen.

'Did you have a nice time at Nana's, mate?'

Jimmy Junior nodded. 'Freddie came and was nice to me.'

Jimmy could hear the relief and surprise in his voice, and he hugged the boy to him, feeling, as he always did when near to him, the sheer strength of his love for his child.

The boy's blue eyes had incredibly long lashes and his little nose was a perfect blob on his handsome little face. His thick dark hair was so like his, wavy and black, and the smell of his small, chubby body was distinct and wholly his own.

'Are you happy, my little soldier?'

The boy looked up at him with complete trust and said happily, 'Yes, I love you, Dad.'

'And I love you, son. Now, off to sleep, eh?'

He watched as he cuddled up to his teddy bear and closed his eyes, and knew it was not natural that this child had never once tried to get into bed with his mother and father.

Jimmy looked around the perfect bedroom. It was a real boy's room. Trains were hand-painted on the walls, and pennants were pinned up to show all the places he had visited in his little life. All his other toys were hidden away in the large toy store, as Maggie insisted on calling it, and the few toys lying around were jigsaws of Thomas the Tank Engine and colouring books and pencils that were all neatly put away in their cases.

This was not how a three year old's bedroom should look. Jimmy didn't know how he knew that, but he was convinced he was right. The jigsaws and colouring books signified solitude to him, and he knew that this child was alone far too much for his own good.

Kissing his little son's forehead, he walked quietly from the room.

Freddie was at the delectable Charmaine's house, and he was happily drinking a beer and watching a video while she made him something to eat.

At least her flat was clean, he would give her a few points for that much anyway, and the kid seemed a nice little thing from the photos that were all over the place. She was at her grandmother's house. Well, there was a novelty on this estate. He would bet not one child under the age of twelve had ever stayed in with their mothers on a Friday night in their life.

Char, as she liked to be called, came back into the small lounge and gave him a cheese sandwich and another beer. She was a nice little thing, well house-trained and with a cracking little arse on her.

'I didn't realise you were Kimberley's dad.'

Now this was a new concept to him. Surely she wasn't his daughter's mate!

'How do you know her, then?'

Charmaine laughed at his tone, and said with a smile, 'I just know her from around the estate, that's all. She pops in sometimes to see my mum for a cuppa, you know.'

Freddie nodded, not sure where this conversation was taking them. 'I see, now why don't you get your kit off while I eat this sandwich, eh?'

Charmaine nearly fainted, and he was surprised that she was so shy. He would have laid money on her being a right little raver.

'Leave it out!' She was genuinely embarrassed, and this endeared her to him for some reason.

'Well, sweetheart, you saw me wife tonight. I ain't come round here to read the fucking Bible with you, have I?'

She laughed, and then she said seriously, 'Do you fancy a joint?'

She opened a small tin, and he watched her in delight as she rolled a perfect little joint and then sparked it up and drew the smoke into her lungs like a true professional.

She passed it to him and he drew on it deeply.

'This is a nice bit of scran, where did you score it?'

She was sipping her own beer now, and he saw that she was very ladylike and dainty.

'I get it off Taffy Robin.'

He laughed then, a big booming laugh that made the girl jump in fright. 'Off fucking who?'

She started giggling as she repeated, 'Taffy Robin, you know, the Welsh bloke who lives in the flats over by the mini park. He always has a good stash on him, anything you want he's usually got it. Ask your Kimberley, she should know.'

He was alert now and sobering up faster than a high-court judge on a drink-driving charge. 'You what? How would my Kimberley know about him?'

Charmaine heard the subtle change in his voice and realised she had said the wrong thing. 'I don't know, Freddie, I thought she knew him, that's all. I was probably wrong, eh?'

She was trying to recover and she was doing a sterling job, but he knew a lying cunt when he saw one. His dad used to say, 'How do you know when a woman's lying? Her lips move,' and he was right about that.

He sat up and, putting down his plate, he said nicely, and with his most charming smile, 'Oh, no you don't, Char. You know something that I don't, see. Now, you can either tell me the truth, and I mean the truth, and me and you can remain friends or you can go to the nearest casualty department via the end of my boot. The choice, my little love, is yours.'

Charmaine was nervous. The dope she had smoked had just hit and she was not enjoying it at all. In fact, she was starting to sweat, she could feel it all over her body and she knew it was through fear.

'I don't know what to tell you, Freddie, I only know she goes round there sometimes—'

She was on her back with him holding her by the throat within seconds, and the force with which she hit the floor winded her. The pain was acute and she was suddenly reminded of just how dangerous this man might actually be.

She looked into those blue eyes that earlier had seemed so sexy and inviting, and now all she saw was anger and threats.

'I am warning you, Charmaine. You had better tell me what *my* daughter was doing in a Welsh fucking dealer's house, and you better tell me what she was scoring. Because if you lie and I find out you fucking lied to me twice, I will break your fucking neck. Now tell me what it was.'

The girl's eyes were bulging and he was so angry it was a few seconds before he realised that she literally couldn't answer him. He released his grip a little, and then he bellowed over her coughing and spluttering. 'Fucking answer me, you cunt!'

In minutes her life had gone from happy and carefree, with maybe even the promise of a romance, to violence and terror. She was shaking with fear and shock and she said through her tears, 'It's the brown, she's on the brown.'

The words took a few seconds to penetrate and when they did he could not for the life of him form in his mind the correct term for brown.

Then he heard the word heroin in his head like a screaming klaxon and he knew then, without a shadow of a doubt that it was true, it was all true.

And he slapped the girl on the ground around the face and head a few times, before he gravitated to punches and kicks. He was so angry he could kill someone, and he knew exactly who that was going to be.

Maggie lay awake and listened to Jimmy gently snoring. She liked to feel him beside her in the dark, and she liked to hear him breathing as he slept because it made her feel safe.

He had not touched her when he had got into bed, and she was disappointed because she had psyched herself up for it. And she wanted a child of their own, felt that this alone could cleanse her, make things right again.

As she lay there, he turned over and she felt his hand touch her thigh and she jumped as she always did when touched without any warning. Her stomach turned over and she felt the now-familiar sickness as she once again felt Freddie's hands, and smelled his breath and his body odour. She knew that as long as he lived those stenches would stay in her mind, and she would be able to smell them as acutely as she had then.

The phone started ringing and she answered it gingerly, nervous in case it was Freddie. He rang sometimes in the night and asked for Jimmy, though she knew it was part of his campaign against her. But instead of Freddie's voice she heard a practically incoherent Jackie screaming and crying down the line.

Chapter Nineteen

Robin Williams, a name he saw as a curse thanks to a certain movie star and now a singer from a boy band whose sexuality was questioned, was carefully burning up some skag. A couple of young friends, young female friends, were happily going like lambs to his slaughter-house as he showed them how to bubble it on the silver paper. Then he was going to explain the intricate mystery of how to load a syringe.

He was in his late thirties, but he looked younger. His hair had a ginger tinge and was long and straggly, as was his little goatee beard. He was tattooed everywhere, and these home-made drawings consisted mainly of skulls and other death-related objects. He only listened to Pink Floyd, Led Zeppelin or his idol Ozzy Osbourne, and his life revolved around his habit and/or the maintaining of his habit.

Like most heroin addicts, any kind of real life had been put on hold the day he had become addicted. He had no real friends, no real social life and no idea of conversation outside of the best high he had experienced or the death of people who were only friends now because they had overdosed and died and could not contradict anything that he said about them.

It was a lonely, depressing and seriously dangerous way of life. But to these two young people, who he saw as earners for himself in the future and nothing else, it seemed an exciting and fun-filled existence.

Robin, or Taffy Robin as he was known, had three children he never saw, a string of women he had destroyed and left, and a debt that was, in their world, the equivalent of a Third World country's which he could not pay back. Hence the new recruits.

He was also into crack when the fancy took him, and he smoked dope to mellow himself out. He sold his methadone but kept up the scripts, or prescriptions to give them their correct term for it, because that was his magic ticket to the dole office. He knew every scam going and he had never worked a day in his life.

He was an addict, and that meant that every agency the Labour Government funded was there expressly to help people like *him*. He had never had it so good, life had simply got better and better.

His addiction had helped keep him out of prison, had helped him get housed time and time again when the going had got a little too tough, and it had made sure he got his drugs whenever he needed them because he was, after all, big roll of drums, *addicted*.

Roll on Tony and his wonderful nanny state.

As he drew the brown into the syringe, his front door came off the hinges and his front-room door, which as usual was wide open because of the smell, brought into view his worst nightmare.

He had dealt with more than his fair share of irate fathers in his time, but this was not the usual angry dad. They were normally flabby, beer-drinking men who gave him a small dig that left him with a black eye, and gave them the prestige of their wives and friends.

This man was what he had been dreading all his life, this man was a lunatic and it was there in his eyes, in his demeanour and also in the crowbar he was holding with both hands and which Taffy knew was going to come down on to his skull in the very near future.

Like all addicts he tried to quickly put down the brown, to save it, so it wasn't wasted, because to him it was more important than his own life.

The two girls looked at the huge man with fear-filled eyes and when he bellowed, 'Out, you pair of useless junkie cunts!' they did not need to be told twice.

The two girls grabbed their belongings and made a run for the now-gaping hole that had once been the front door.

Freddie pointed at them with the crowbar to stop them leaving so quickly, and he said in a conversational tone, 'You phone the filth or anyone and I will come after *you*, understand?'

They stood stock still and nodded. He was talking like their dad, like a regular person and they nodded in unison again so hard they hurt their necks.

'Well, fuck off, then!'

They were running out the door now, and on the stairs they encountered neighbours who were all interested to see what was going down.

Taffy Robin was a thorn in their side. He had people in and out at all hours of the night and day, and they had to be careful of being robbed, because an addict would not go too far from his source to steal unless he had to. These people had come home from the shops to see their TV or a video recorder gone, just enough to get the thief a few quid until the next time. Get the thief a ten-pound bag.

The flats had gone downhill since they had been built just after the Second World War, and that meant that insurance was unheard of. No company would take on the responsibility. If something was stolen, it was *gone*, and that was that. It had to be replaced by the individual who had lost it. The police rarely came out if called for theft or burglary, and if by any miraculous chance they *did* bother to come, they told the victims what they had already sussed out for themselves. It was junkies. So, other than making a cup of tea for someone Taffy's neighbours instinctively saw as an enemy anyway, and everyone knew the filth could drink tea for England, they had to sort things out for themselves.

Now, it seemed that this was finally coming to pass.

An elderly man in pyjamas and a baseball cap shouted through the door, 'Fucking do him, Freddie, he's a cancer. Fucking do him, boy.'

Freddie did not need to be told twice.

The crowbar was brought down with all the force he could muster over and over again. When Taffy stopped moving, Freddie started on the front room and he trashed it, windows, TV and anything else that got in his way.

The whole thing took twenty minutes, and he walked from the flat a conquering hero.

'Who did this to your daughter, Mrs Jackson?'

The WPC was a kind girl with nicely cut blond hair and almond-shaped green eyes. Maggie looked her over with a professional eye and decided she could take five years off and make her look like a movie star.

Jackie was not talking, and Maggie sighed as she said seriously, 'She was attacked in the street, mugged. It was her mother's birthday party tonight, and she stayed at the pub. When she couldn't get a cab, she walked. It's only ten minutes away, you know. And from what we can gather she was jumped from behind.'

'But she managed to get home?'

Jackie and Maggie nodded.

'With a broken leg?'

Jackie shrugged then. 'We found her out the front. What can I say? Maybe someone helped her, we don't know. That's your job ain't it, at least it was last time I read a crime novel.'

'What about you, Mrs Jackson, how did you get the bloody nose?'

Maggie and Jackie could see what her questions were leading to now, and Jackie said with deliberate and calculated disrespect, 'Fuck off, sweetheart. We can see where you are going with this shit.'

Maggie winked at Jackie and she walked the WPC from the little family room. 'Look, love, my sister is an alcoholic, as I am sure you probably know. You spend enough time around there sorting out her different tantrums with the neighbours. She *always* has cuts and bruises, drunks tend to fall over a lot.'

She yawned delicately before continuing, but it was an insulting yawn, a bored yawn and the WPC knew without a shadow of a doubt that the person boring this well-turned-out and well-spoken woman was herself.

'Now you listen, and you listen good. That girl's father is Freddie Jackson, and you had better hope you find the culprit before he does. But don't you ever dare to insinuate anything like that about my sister again, not unless you want to deal with her and hers. All right?'

The girl nodded. She knew when she was beaten. This family was a law unto itself, which was, she realised, why she had been assigned to them. She saw that now with crystal clarity. No one else wanted the aggravation, or indeed wanted to get involved at all!

The Jacksons would sort this out and the local police would let them. It was how their worlds worked.

She heard later that night in the canteen that some bloke called Mr Thomas Halpin, who was part of the Serious Crime Squad, had apparently already warned the station to back off. It was not the first time that had happened and she was sure it would not be the last.

So she would do the same as everyone else. She had tried her best, done her job, and if she was honest she hoped that Freddie Jackson did take the fucker out. If there *was* a nutter on the streets and Jackson cleaned him up, it would save them all a job.

She wanted to be a plain clothes one day, and if that meant letting the Jacksons have a get-out-of-jail-free card, then so be it.

Ozzy was ill and he was feeling the pain in his chest acutely. He sat up in his cell and clutched his arm. It was like a big cold weight was crushing his chest. Like a block of ice had been dropped on him from a great height.

He was sweating heavily, and his breathing was getting shallower and shallower.

He wondered if he should ring the bell, get a screw in. But he had to lie down first, he had to try to lessen this pain a bit.

Finally he fell asleep, and the pain eased.

Jackie and Maggie came home from the hospital at six thirty in the morning. The girls had stayed behind, and were told the same story, that she had been attacked by a stranger. Though none of them believed it they would keep up the pretence, especially Kimberley, who was already remembering details of her mystery attacker.

Maggie put on the kettle in the kitchen while Jackie

took a bottle of vodka out of the fridge. She mixed it in a large water glass which already contained lukewarm white wine and gulped it down. Maggie watched as she poured out another drink with trembling hands, and her heart broke once more at the sorry excuse of a woman her sister had become.

'You have to make him go, Jack, you can't let him get away with that.'

Jackie looked at her in utter bewilderment. 'What you on about, you silly mare? He done a good thing, he was looking out for his own!'

The pride in Jackie's voice made her sound almost happy at her daughter's predicament. Freddie had come home, practically murdered the poor girl, caused ructions with everyone in the house, and to Jackie that was *love.*

Maggie wanted to laugh. 'Will you listen to yourself, Jackie? He didn't attack her because he *cared about her*, he attacked that girl because it's a taint on him if she's a fucking junkie. Use your loaf, wipe the shit from your eyes and see him for what he really is.'

Jackie looked at Maggie. Even in jeans and a shirt she looked lovely, perfect. She always looked perfect, always looked like an advert for healthy womanhood. But she wasn't anything, not really, she just thought she was better than everyone else.

'If his daughter is a junkie then he has to deal with other people knowing that. It's like admitting defeat, admitting he has failed as a father. It has nothing to do with you or the kids or love. It's not about *you*, you silly bitch, it's about *him.* It's always about *him.*'

'You are wrong, Maggie. For all his faults, he loves us.'

'He treats you like dirt, he laughs at your drinking, he takes what he wants from you and then he leaves you for weeks on end and you let him. You let him, Jackie, because for some unknown reason you think that he is a wonderful person, yet he has systematically destroyed you and those kids since day one.'

Jackie shook her head then. This was getting too near the mark, too near the truth and she could not take that, not tonight, not ever. 'You are wrong, Mags, he loves us, he loves his family.'

Maggie picked up Jackie's cigarettes and lit one before saying through a sarcastic smile, 'Look around you, look at your life, at how you live. Your daughter is an addict because *you* are an addict. Any one of those fucking, shite-talking, pop psychology daytime TV shit shows you watch would tell you that, Jack. Kimberley has had a good teacher and it was you. You've been *pissed* for years Jackie. You're a fucking *drunk*.'

Jackie was frightened by what was being said now, she didn't want this. She just wanted to drink in peace and get a few hours' kip.

'How dare you fucking lecture me—'

Maggie said through gritted teeth and with as much menace as she could muster, '*I* dare, Jackie, because someone has to tell you once and for all that this has all got to stop! The man you love *hates you* and you are too fucking *thick* to see it. Do you know that him and Jimmy earn the same money, more or less, and you are still in a council house? Love, think about it. What's he spending that dosh on, eh? It fucking ain't you and yours, is it?'

She looked around the ruin of her sister's home and then said sadly, 'It's a shit hole, Jackie. And look at fucking Little Freddie. He is off his trolley, and no one seems to care! Where is he now, eh? Still wandering the streets, I bet. And what about poor Kim? She has been on the brown for ages and *you* never noticed. I knew there was something wrong with her, and I tried to help her, but *you* never noticed! Those kids are invisible to you unless they are the reason that keeps Freddie by your side. Freddie has an eighty-grand car parked outside on the kerb, and your toilet has been broke for weeks. Don't you think that is a little bit odd? Does nothing penetrate that drink-sodden brain of yours?'

She lit another cigarette and watched as Jackie gulped at her vodka and wine once more.

'Stop it, Maggie, you say one more word and I'll fucking knock you out.'

Now Maggie did laugh. 'I ain't a kid any more, Jackie, frightened of my big sister. You raise your hand to me and I'll lay you out once and for all.'

Jackie knew what she said was true, and that was what stopped her from attacking Maggie physically. Jackie made a point of attacking only the people she knew would not fight her back. Unless she was drunk of course, when anyone was fair game, but even then she relied on the other people around her to stop the tear up at some point.

'I am trying to help you, Jackie, trying to make you see sense. Even Freddie can see you have a problem, so if he loves you so much why ain't he tried to get you any help? I know the girls have tried to talk to you, they tell me how worried they are about you, and I try and talk to you too but it's a fucking waste of time. But now you have to see the fucking big picture. Your life is a mess and you have to try and do something before it's too late.'

Jackie understood her sister genuinely wanted to help her, while the majority of the people in her immediate orbit were hangers-on who ignored her problems and just used her. But it was so hard for her to admit, because she knew no one else would want to be with her. If she let herself think about it, she would see exactly what she was, and exactly what to expect from her life.

'Go home, Mags, I can't handle this.'

Maggie sighed. 'Do you realise you ain't once mentioned the fact that your Kim is on drugs, or wondered where your son is? Do you *realise* that, Jack? You only mentioned it when you were telling me how your Freddie loves you. Are you going to get her any help at all? Are you going to sort out some kind of rehab, or will that be left to me as usual?'

Jackie didn't answer her.

'Look in the mirror, Jackie, smell the house you live in with your family. Look at the floor and the walls and the furniture, and then you tell me that you are all right with the way you live and I promise I will back off.'

Jackie sat down on a stool and finished her drink, and as she poured herself out another one she heard Maggie leave the house.

Jimmy and Freddie were sharing a beer in Jimmy's new snooker room. Maddie had been asked over to watch Jimmy Junior, and when Jimmy had finally picked up Freddie in the early hours he had no other option than to bring him back to his.

He knew Maggie would not be best pleased, but what else could he do? Freddie, as far as he was concerned, had done a good thing, had done what Jimmy would have done in a similar situation. Though he admitted he would not have harmed Kimberley, Freddie and his temper were legendary and he felt bad about it now.

'Fucking some drum this, Jimmy.'

Jimmy shrugged. 'It's all relative, ain't it? I like this house and so does Mags, in fact she loves it.'

'At least she looks after it for you. Not like Jackie, she wouldn't clean up if her life depended on it.'

Jimmy smiled. 'She never was one for the Hoover, old Jackie.'

They both laughed. It was the first time they had actually sat and talked properly since the night that Lenny had died. They made a great pretence of friendship, but the tension was always there between them. Tonight, though, they seemed to be back on track.

'She tried, a few times she really tried, you know. But the drink and Jackie . . .' For the first time ever, Freddie was talking about his wife without a joke, or a nasty remark. 'Now my Kimberley is on the skag. Ironic, ain't it? I fucking shifted enough over the years, and now my daughter is a slave to the brown.'

Jimmy refilled their brandy glasses. 'Come on, Freddie, it could happen to anyone, any family, it's part of society now.'

Freddie held up his cut-glass brandy snifter and said sarcastically, 'Thanks to us, and people like us!'

They both laughed once more.

'How's me little fella, then?'

Jimmy grinned. 'I love that little boy, Fred. He is so fucking clever, only three and he can write his name.'

Freddie nodded. 'His father's son him, eh?'

It was said with a laugh but Jimmy felt, as always, that there was an underlying current he could not put his finger on. 'What do you mean by that?'

Freddie feigned innocence. 'What on earth is wrong with you, Jim? I said he was his father's son and you are his father, right? So where is there anything to fucking mean?'

Jimmy relaxed. 'Sorry, Freddie, but sometimes I feel you are taking the piss, and you do take the piss, you know.'

Freddie sipped his brandy before saying, 'I don't, Jimmy, not with you, anyway.'

It was heartfelt and it was enough to placate Jimmy.

'He is a lovely kid, Jimmy, and I think the world of him. He is a real little Brahma, bless him. How is Maggie, by the way?'

Jimmy shrugged. 'All right, why?'

'Nothing, mate. It's just she seems very offish with everyone. Now she's always been like it with me, but Jackie thinks she is not coping that well with motherhood.'

Jimmy wanted to laugh out loud, and Freddie said in a jokey voice, 'Talk about the pot calling the kettle, eh?'

Jimmy smiled. 'She is just a perfectionist, that's all. If Maggie does a job she does it to the best of her ability.'

'Now, Jimmy, if you had a son like mine you would know what worry was. That little fucker is out all hours, roaming the streets, causing havoc. I reckon they'll take him away soon, and do you know what? I think it would be for the best.'

Jimmy was astonished. 'You'd let him go away, into a home?'

He spoke in disbelief, and Freddie answered him as honestly as he could. Needing to say the words out loud.

'Look, Jimmy, this is strictly between me and you, right?'

Jimmy nodded, intrigued.

'The other week he was accused of sexual assault. Now the little girl said it was him and his mates, but she withdrew the allegation. Jackie won't have it. She thinks the girl was up for it, it was just a kids' game, but I think that he has got something drastically wrong with him. He killed the neighbours' dog a few months back. He put a fucking plastic bag over its head and suffocated it. I know it was him. They were too frightened to accuse him outright, obviously, but I knew it was him when Jackie told me, because he killed Bugsy's boy's rabbit the same way.'

Jimmy was in utter shock at these words.

'How do you know he killed the rabbit?'

Freddie shook his head in dismay. 'I caught him. He was supposed to be caring for it while they went on holiday. I went into his room and it was on his lap, dead, and the bag was stuck to its face.'

'What did you do?'

Freddie wiped his mouth nervously before saying in a quiet voice, 'I mullered him, and then I told him that he had to keep stumm. But I tell you I was sickened, and you know me, there ain't much that can bother me. But he is a kid, and he is mad as a cunt. As soon as they said about the dog I knew it wasn't the first time.'

Jimmy nodded, but he wondered if, in all his grief, Freddie remembered his own need to hurt and his own loss of control that had caused two deaths, to his knowledge. But then Freddie lived by a different set of rules to everyone else.

'Remember we were all laughing in the pub because I said the rabbit had died and we'd put out an APB on a white fluffy rabbit with a black tail? Well, I got a new rabbit and gave it to Bugsy's boy, and he never knew the difference. I told Bugsy the other rabbit had dropped dead, but I know he wondered, could see it in his eyes.'

Freddie swallowed down a big gulp of brandy before saying angrily, 'I blame her. She was drunk all through her pregnancy, you know that. I think that affected him. I love him, he's my son, but unless something is done about him he will end up on a psych wing somewhere on a fucking no-parole life sentence.'

Freddie had seen people in prison like his son, and he had experienced them first-hand. 'He is a big fucker for his age and all. What happens when he's a six footer? Even I won't be able to handle him then, do you see what I mean now? He has got to go, and fucking Jackie, well, she won't believe there's anything amiss. He could kill everyone in the house and she'd still give him an alibi.'

'Fucking hell, Freddie, that's outrageous. Can't you get him seen to privately?'

Freddie laughed then, a tired, sad little laugh. 'Do you think spending money will change the diagnosis? Only, according to his social worker he exhibits "classic signs" – her expression, not mine – of a sociopathic personality. In short, he has no morals, no remorse, no feelings for anyone or anything, no emotions whatsoever. So what he does, right, to *hide* his fucking nut nut status, is he *mimics* them. Pretends to feel things he cannot feel. At least that is what the book said in the library.'

Jimmy knew he spoke the truth, and he felt sorry for him because he knew that Freddie, for all his faults, did in his own way care for his kids. Little Freddie had kept this man tied to a drunken woman he loathed. Though, of course she also suited Freddie at times because she put up with anything he could throw at her.

He found it hard to believe this was his blood relative, the man he had once looked up to, loved and admired. Now he was often hard put to even talk with him, and if Freddie knew just how much Ozzy had given over to his cousin in the last few years, he knew that Freddie would not be able to cope with it. He knew Freddie saw himself as the instigator of their empire, and he accepted the truth of this. But Freddie also conveniently forgot that if it had been left to him, they would have both been back on the pavement hustling within a year. He had wiped out Clancy and that act had given them the opportunity, but it was *him*, Jimmy, who had brought them to where they were now. Freddie needed to accept and understand that, but instead he saw himself as having *been done down*, the street expression for his situation. If he only looked at how he lived, not a penny to call his own, expensive things bought for cash and then left to go to wrack and ruin. And Jimmy knew he had never once put a few quid away for a rainy day.

Yet this was the man who honestly believed he should be running what in effect, if legit, would be the equivalent of a big corporate company. They dealt with Europe, Africa, the Far East. Anywhere there was drugs or contraband to be exploited. Freddie did not know the half of it, and never would if it was left to him.

'So what are you going to do about him, Freddie?'

He shrugged. 'Only fuck himself knows the answer to that one, mate, and he ain't talking.'

Ozzy was glad when the cell was opened by a screw he trusted and owned. He motioned for him to come to where he sat on the bed and then he asked him to get two other inmates as he wanted to see them.

The man nodded.

Five minutes later, a young Irishman called Derry and a large black man called David bowled into the cell.

'What you want, Oz?'

He smiled. 'Get me to the wing doctor. Last night I was doing press ups when I cracked me fucking ribs.'

They laughed, as he knew they would but they did what they were asked.

Ozzy knew, one sniff of weakness and he might as well lie down and wait for the chiv to arrive. This way he had a valid reason to see the quack, and he knew the doctor well. He had been dealing out fucking contraband to the cons for years.

* * *

Maggie walked into the snooker room with young Jimmy in her arms, and smiled tightly at the two men.

'Shouldn't you be at home with your wife?'

Freddie had noticed that over the years she had become more and more cocky towards him and he also knew that the more she pushed him, the more he would make her life a misery. Sometimes he left her alone for months, then out of the blue, when Jimmy had overlooked him, or he heard a whisper that Jimmy was involved with something he knew nothing about, he would remember this little piece before him and it would all start again.

'Come on, Mags, would you want to go home to Jackie?' Then, holding out his arms, he said to the child, 'Come to me, my little darling. He's his daddy's boy all right, like the spit out of his mouth.'

Maggie snorted in derision. Placing the boy carefully on the carpet, she said nicely, 'Go to Nana, sweetheart, while Mummy talks to Daddy.'

Even her voice was wrong when she spoke to the child, even her endearments sounded forced, but Jimmy Junior did as he was bidden.

'You stop trying to be nice to my boy, and try being nice to your own fucking kids. How about Kim, then? You going to see her? Only, you know you broke her leg, don't you?'

Freddie didn't know this, and Freddie didn't much care.

Jimmy said calmly, 'Come on, Maggie, this is not the time or the place.'

She snapped her head towards her husband and said angrily, 'Well, I am sorry, Jimmy, but I think it is.'

Freddie laughed then. 'Careful, you don't want to be in the doghouse now, do you?'

Maggie walked towards where he was sitting. It was a big room, with a snooker table and a pool table. It had a large and well-stocked bar and it was wood panelled. One of these men was the love of her life and the other was the canker that had grown inside her for so long she felt that she would explode with hatred. Yet she had to tolerate him no matter what. Because if the truth ever came out she would lose everything, and so would everyone she held dear.

The huge fireplace had a large leather wing chair on each side, and the men were sitting there as if they did not have a worry in the world. This made her so angry she felt she could physically attack them.

'Don't you try and cause a fucking row with me and him. Unlike *you*, Freddie, my husband respects me, and I respect him. But I would not expect you to understand that concept because you treat everyone in your family like shit. By the way, Kim is going into rehab. I sorted that out today, so you needn't worry about her. Not that you would.'

She was poking her finger into his face now and he could see the hate inside her.

'But I tell you now, Freddie, my sister is in bits and you need to talk to her about her drinking because for some unknown reason she thinks you care about her. So put your drink down, and get a cab, and fuck off out of my home.'

'You going to let her talk to me like that, Jimmy?'

Jimmy got up and stretched before saying, 'She has got a point, Freddie. It's time I got ready for work, anyway.'

Freddie couldn't believe what he was hearing. In his book Maggie should be getting the clump of a lifetime for that little outburst. Instead, she was still in his face.

'If you have anything else to say to my husband about

me, say it *now*. *Now*, do you hear me? I dare you to say it to him now.' Her eyes told Freddie that he had lost this game, that she was angry enough to let the cat out of the bag.

Better to retreat on this occasion, and gather his ammunition for the future. Freddie put his drink down and walked silently from the room.

When the front door slammed Maggie turned to Jimmy and said sadly, 'Thanks, Jimmy.'

'I liked the way you fronted him. In his book I should have slapped you one upside your head. But he's a Neanderthal, he don't mean the half of it.'

'I can't have him here any more, Jimmy, not after this little lot. Poor Kim, and fucking Jackie, well . . .'

'I understand. I'll keep his visits to the minimum, all right?'

She smiled her thanks and he hugged her to him. For once she let him, relaxed against him.

At the breakfast table she was even relaxed with Jimmy Junior, even hugged him with real care and attention. He felt as if they had crossed over some invisible line, but why he should think that he had no idea.

Maddie, who had stayed for breakfast, winked at Jimmy from across the table, and it occurred to him that Freddie had left without even acknowledging his own mother's existence.

Chapter Twenty

Maggie and Rox were laughing as they chose the material for Rox's bedroom curtains. She was finally getting married to Dicky, and her happiness was complete.

'Oh, Maggie, that is lovely. You have such good taste.'

Maggie smiled. She had chosen a soft grey silk that she knew would look stunning against the pale pink paint that Rox was determined to have on her walls.

'Once you get married you have to live with this for a long time, so make sure you choose something that is not only good quality, but also durable.' She could hear herself giving this child advice, and all she wanted to do was go back and drag that lazy drunken sister of hers out with them.

Not that Jackie would be any use, but it was terrible that everything to do with this wedding and their new home was left to her to sort out. Maggie didn't mind, it was just that she knew Rox really wanted her parents to be involved. Her mother at least – Rox had never been her father's biggest fan.

Jimmy Junior ran up to her and Maggie picked him up with difficulty. At four he was getting a large lad, and she kissed him on his cheek as he said in excitement, 'I saw a clown, Mummy.'

The clown was a poster on the wall, and she knew he would ask to go to the circus, and she knew she would take him.

'It's the circus, Mummy.'

'And you are going, honey!'

He laughed out loud and she kissed him once more.

Rox watched them and sighed happily. Maggie was all right now, and had been for some time. It was as if she had changed overnight, she was happier, more carefree. And Rox loved her more than anyone in her life except her Dicky boy.

But Maggie went off at the drop of a hat these days, and everyone knew it. One word out of place and she was up for a fight. It was so out of character, yet so much a part of her now, part of this new and improved Maggie, that everyone just accepted it.

'You know you have to sort me out first, before you take any kind of a cut. That is what happens in this place no matter who you are.'

Ozzy's voice was heavy with anger and the man he was talking to was wondering if he was in with a chance of retribution. He looked around him, and wisely decided he wasn't.

Ozzy was impressed, though, that the young chap had actually *considered* trying to fight his way out of this reprimand, and this endeared the boy to him.

'Look, Ozzy, I didn't think you would be interested, mate.'

Ozzy laughed and shook his head slowly as if in the presence of the stupidest man in history. And he wondered if Carl Waters *was* the stupidest man in history.

He spoke loudly in his deep, serious voice, because unfortunately he had no other. 'Do not take me for a cunt. I know you run with a good crowd, but remember, son, *they* are out there, and *you* are in here. Any more cuntish behaviour and you will be on the hospital wing, see.'

Carl nodded, but he knew instinctively that Ozzy wasn't going to hold this against him. Ozzy was a realist and he would probably have tried it on just the same if he had been in his place.

'I am sorry, Ozzy. I am a mug, you are right. I just wanted a bit of dosh, that's all, and I have a little bloke who is willing to weigh me out.'

Ozzy grinned. 'You *will* ply your trade, son, I've no dispute with that. You will just trade in *my* name and give me a good drink, see. We ain't fucking that behind the times, though it seems like we are still in a feudal society to newcomers.'

It was more than the lad had expected, and he left the cell with a cheery demeanour a few minutes later.

Ozzy slipped a tablet under his tongue, and marvelled at a young man who had so much going for him, yet was happily taking the fall for a couple of complete fucking tossers. Carl had been on a robbery with two so-called Faces. The filth had jumped them on the chop, where they would change cars, clothes and if necessary divvy up the money before going their separate ways, which meant they must have been grassed up. How else would filth know where the chop was going to take place? This was a calculated fucking event, and this poor boy had been the fall guy.

So he had been caught, had kept stumm about who his accomplices were, and got himself an eighteen stretch. All his youth would be spent in this dump, while the older, wiser 'Faces' would still be on the outside plying their trades.

It was a fucking crying shame really, but the boy could be of use to him. He was young, he was willing and he could keep his trap shut.

Ozzy was ill. For a while now he had been on heart medication and he wasn't sure if he could do this any more. He needed to talk to Jimmy properly, and he decided it would be on the next visit. He was losing the urge for it all, and once that happened in their environment, you were living on borrowed time.

His sister Patricia was still trumping anything with a nice smile and a big cock, Freddie Jackson included, and he didn't entirely trust her any longer. As she was getting older she was getting less choosy about who she knocked about with, and this was becoming a worry to him.

He had serious poke and serious business to sort out, and now he was ill he had to do it. He had worked hard for his wedge and he had enjoyed the making of his money. So many people lost sight of that buzz when they made it to the big time, lost the want, and lost the respect for money that was actually a requisite for being rich. The spending of it had never been his forte, but the *gathering* of it was something he had lain awake at nights planning. He wanted to give his wealth to someone like him, someone who would use it wisely, someone who would understand just what it had taken to gather it in the first place.

He had to get his house in order, and he had to do it sooner rather than later.

He snapped his head around to look at his portable TV. *Emmerdale* was just starting and he loved to see the wide open spaces it showed. He was sorry now he had never bothered with the Dales when he had been on the out.

They looked lovely, stunning. So he enjoyed watching them by proxy, on Emmerdale Farm.

The birds were fit as well, so it was not a completely wasted half hour.

But he wished he could explain to the general population that even though they might go to Spain or America and travel all over the world, they did not know their own country. This annoyed him now, because he had realised over the years just what a green and pleasant land it actually was. If he had a chance to do anything different, it would be to make sure he travelled around England. People came from far and wide to live here. They saw it as a haven and as a place to make something of themselves, and it took all this time in stir for him to understand just where those people were coming from. Like the old adage, you never knew what you had till it was gone.

Well, that could be said of the people he had been dealing with all these years.

He was finally going to make his last will and testament, and he knew it would cause fucking ructions. So be it.

'Where is he, Jackie?'

She was panicking and this was annoying her husband.

'I don't know, Freddie.'

'Then you fucking well should! What the fuck are you getting my wedge for, eh? You can't even look out for little Fred. You know he is on a curfew, so where the fuck is he?'

Jackie could have skinned her son alive at this moment because his fuck-up had caused them to have a row. Freddie had put him on a curfew and, unlike every other time he had tried to rein his son in, this had been adhered to because Freddie had made a point of checking his son was at home. She was happy about this in one way, because it meant he spent more time with them, and not with his other women. But it was also nerve-wracking because Little Freddie didn't think he should be timed, thought he was too old and experienced to be treated like a child.

His father was not a man to be mugged off but although she had tried to explain this to her son many times, he wouldn't listen to her. He had never listened to her, that was the trouble.

As they stood in the front room like adversaries in a boxing match, the front door opened and Little Freddie strolled in with all the arrogance he possessed. He was enormous, and he was Freddie's double, but unlike his father, who had been a tearaway at his age, this boy was in deep trouble. It was only Freddie who could keep him in check. Jackie knew this, and she was glad someone could keep him in line, but she still could not bear to see him told off, in trouble or accused of anything.

Little Freddie stood in front of his mother and father and cleared his throat noisily. It was a calculated insult.

Freddie looked at his son and wondered for the hundredth time why he bothered with him. But he was not the usual little fuck, he was a *dangerous* little fuck. Well, the buck stopped here. He pointed his finger at him and said loudly, 'Where you fucking been, then?'

Jackie tried to lighten the situation by saying cheerfully, 'Here he is! I told you he would be here, didn't I?'

Freddie pushed her away from him and, looking at his son, said in a deep and angry voice, 'You telling me you can't tell the time?'

Little Freddie was staring at his father, and there was not one iota of fear in him despite his father's anger. Freddie knew this boy was out of order, that he was off the fucking scale and he was determined to bring him back to the fold, whatever it took.

The questions and answers then came thick and fast and without any kind of hesitation on either side.

'I said, where have you fucking been?'

'Out.'

'Out where?'

The boy shrugged. 'Just out with me mates.'

'What mates?'

'Just mates.'

'Do they have names?'

'Do yours?'

Freddie's fist connected with his son's chin so fast that the boy didn't have time to move away and protect himself. He was not expecting it, and he was even more surprised when his father followed through with another punch and then began beating him viciously.

Jackie watched her son as he was punched across the room, landing in a crumpled heap on the sofa, and she saw his father descend on him with that look on his face she deplored. She was screaming now, she was like a mad woman. No one hurt her baby, *no one.*

'*Leave him alone!*'

Freddie grabbed her arms and forcefully threw her from the living room, shutting the door behind her. Then he carried on the interrogation as if they had never been interrupted.

'What mates?'

His son was looking at him with open hatred and Freddie didn't care. He needed to know where he had been.

'Were you in the subway today?'

He saw Little Freddie's eyes widen and knew that what he had suspected was true, and no one was more sorry than him.

'So you were, then?'

Little Freddie shook his head in denial, with tears in his eyes. 'No, Dad, please, it wasn't me, it was them . . .'

Freddie looked at his son and wondered if he should do the world a favour and wipe him off the face of the earth now.

'Where the fuck is he, Jimmy?'

Jimmy held his arms out in supplication. 'How the fuck am I supposed to know that? What am I all of a sudden, Freddie's fucking dad?'

The anger in his voice did not go unnoticed by the other men in the pub's back room. Glenford, ever the peacemaker, said in a reasonable way, 'Relax, this is only a meet.'

Amos Beardsley knew he had overstepped the mark and was contrite. Everyone knew Freddie was a nutter, but Jimmy was the one to be seriously frightened of. Jimmy didn't need anger to hurt people, Jimmy needed *just cause*. A different thing altogether. With Jimmy, violence was always the last resort, and that meant whoever was in the frame was in deep shit.

He might have started out as Ozzy's front man but he was a main man now in his own right and, like all the big money makers, no one heard about him until it was too late. He surrounded himself with names, and yet he had never personally even had a parking ticket.

'Any chance of a drink?'

Glenford's voice was jovial. They all breathed a sigh of relief, including Jimmy, who knew what his friend was doing. 'Come with me, Glen, and we'll bring in a few bottles.'

They left the room. Once outside and in the bar area, Jimmy said quietly, 'I could fucking stomp that cunt, I really could.'

Glenford ordered the drinks and then pulled Jimmy to the main door and out into the cold night air. 'Stop it, Jim, you need to do damage limitation now. Freddie has had them over. You know that, I know it, he knows it, but more importantly, *they* know it. Now, boy, you have to give them their due. Do it with a bit of respect and they will let it go. Then you *have* to collar Freddie and read him the riot act once and for all.'

Jimmy didn't answer, but Glenford's easy-going, slowly spoken but serious-sounding West Indian accent was penetrating his brain.

'*Me* mean it, Jimmy. This have affected *my* earn as well, you know, and my boys are fit to be tied. Blood is blood, we accept that, but this is not the first time. They have only come to you now because Freddie won't listen to any kind of reason. Now he has disrespected them by not even bothering to turn up here tonight. These are *Africans*, and they won't care who he is, or *who* he working for. They will not forget this. And they are earners, boy, good earners. Not a fucking liability like some I could mention.'

Jimmy looked at his friend, and he *was* a friend. He loved this man and he knew Glenford loved him. In their world, real friends were few and far between.

'What am I going to do about him, Glen? It's like he thinks he is a separate entity, like he believes he is a law unto himself.'

Glenford smiled then, that friendly gap-toothed smile that had guaranteed him women and sexual favours all his life, and he answered his friend now with absolute truthfulness. 'But he is his own law, Jimmy. *You* have seen to that. No matter what he does, you protect him, and now I am going to tell you something that you won't want to hear. He *cunts* you, he has even tried to cunt you to *me*. Many times, and he knows we are *close*. In drink he is a fucking treacherous bastard, and you got to rein him in, *sooner* rather than *later*, because if you don't, you will lose your self-respect as well as everyone else's.'

Glenford was telling Jimmy something he had known for a long time but had not allowed himself to accept. He had let himself believe that Freddie lived by the same rules as he did, but he knew in his heart that Freddie was not capable of that. Freddie saw himself as above them all, himself included.

He had to put the hard word on him, and he had to do it soon, but he was dreading it. Not because he was frightened of him, but because he knew it would be the end of them.

'Leave him alone, Freddie, you'll fucking kill him.' Jackie had run back into the room and was trying to drag her husband off her son and stop the beating that was starting to look like a murder.

'You little bastard, you fucking little cunt!'

Freddie was so angry he was spitting, and Jackie knew in her heart that this was serious because he wouldn't bother unless it was for a good reason.

She pushed herself in between them. 'Tell me what he's supposed to have done.'

She sounded like she knew he was going to give her a load of old fanny. As if *he* would *cunt* his own son unless he had to! This was not getting them anywhere. All the time his mother was there Little Freddie felt that he would be in with a chance.

So Freddie pushed his wife away roughly, but even he felt sorry for the woman who was still trying to hang on to a child, to a dream, that had never been there.

Little Freddie *hated* her. He hated everyone.

Jackie, the drunken fucking prat, really seemed to think

that Little Freddie was just a *tearaway*, that everything he did was just kids playing. She had to know by now that was not true, she had to have realised by now that he was not *normal*, that he was lacking something, was not the full ten shillings.

'Well, come on, tell me what you think he's done now.'

She was actually fronting him up, yet he could hear the fear in her voice. She suspected her son of being the perpetrator of something terrible, but she was more scared of hearing about it than of the actual deed. So, as usual, she would try to pretend that it was everyone else's fault but his.

She was yelling at the top of her voice. 'You never give him a chance, do you, Freddie? You always try and make out that he is doing something wrong. Well, he was with *me* all day. What have you got to say about that, then?'

Freddie shook his head, as was his usual habit when faced with Jackie and her ramblings. 'Go and have a drink, Jack. I brought you in a bottle of good vodka to keep you out of my fucking face while I sorted this ponce out once and for all.'

'But what is he supposed to have done?'

Freddie decided to tell her the score. He dropped his son on to the floor without even looking at him. He then walked his wife out to their kitchen, or what passed as a kitchen anyway, and he said in total seriousness, 'Pour yourself a large one, Jack, you are going to need it.'

She sat on the stool nearest to her and started to cry. Pouring her a neat vodka, Freddie said, 'Sexual assault and mugging, Jackie. That is just for starters, love. We bred a fucking right good one, us.'

Jackie was shaking her head vigorously, she was denying that anything like that could ever happen in their family. She was really sobbing now, a noisy, frightened crying that told her husband that despite this denial, on one level she believed everything he was going to say without even hearing the facts.

'No, Freddie, you are wrong, not our boy, not my baby . . .'

Freddie dragged his wife up off the stool and whispered into her face with such hate and anger she was terrified all over again. 'She was eighty years old, Jack, and she was robbed and assaulted. And it ain't the first time he has done something like this either. I was guilty of letting it go the last time. I sorted it for him because that's what we do, ain't it, for our kids? But not this time, I ain't going to do it, he is a fucking nonce, a *nonce*, and I ain't fucking turning a blind eye. You had better shut your fucking trap, before I fucking shut it for you once and for all. He is a fucking *beast* and we have to sort this cunt out now!'

Jackie was bawling now. She was in bits, and she was also petrified that what Freddie was saying was true.

'You are wrong, Freddie, he is a little boy!'

For the first time in years Freddie felt something for his wife, he was so impressed with her loyalty towards their son. If Little Freddie had robbed a bank or even murdered someone he would have stood beside her and lied with her. But this was different, this was wrong. This was beasting, this was about the fucking nonces on the VPU units. This was so far out of his sphere it frightened him. Supposing this boy did something and people *heard* about it, knew that this fucking sex offender was *his* flesh and blood.

'It was Mrs Caldwell, your old granny's mate! They robbed her, *assaulted* her and then, how is this for a fucking party piece, Jackie, they set fire to a fucking tramp who had tried to help the poor old cow!'

Jackie was now on the edge, she was hysterical. 'He *wouldn't* do anything like that, Freddie, he ain't like that. My baby ain't like that . . . Why ain't they come for him, then? Why ain't Old Bill come here, eh?'

Freddie sighed. 'I was told about Mrs Caldwell by the attending officer. As luck would have it, we pay him off. He alerted me to what was going on, Jackie, and I have had to lay out serious wedge to keep this fucking ponce out of the nick. Now will you fucking believe me, Jackie? I only gave this cunt a pass because I can't live with what he's done. Or with people knowing what he's done. Can't you fucking understand that much at least?'

Little Freddie lay on the sofa in the living room and listened to his parents arguing. He knew from experience that eventually they would forget about him. He had fucked up, but for all his father's threats he wouldn't really put him away. He would ground him, watch him, and give him another curfew.

Then it would die down. The man who had sired him would find other things to do, and his mother would let him out and lie for him as always.

All in all, he had got off lightly.

Jackie came into the living room and gave her baby a gentle hug. She had finally understood where her husband was coming from, but no matter what he said or what he threatened, her son was going nowhere. He was not *bad*. If only Freddie could see him like she saw him. He was only a kid. Because he was a big boy for his age people thought that he was older than he was and tried to treat him like an adult. But he was only a kid and Freddie was too hard on him.

Everyone was against them, since day one she had fought against getting any kind of help. He was just a child and because his last name was Jackson he was ostracised and picked on by everyone. The filth hated him, the courts hated him, the social workers looked at her as if she was dirt! They had it in for him and all. He was her baby, her last-born, and she was not about to let anyone tell her that he was bad.

He was in with the wrong crowd, and because he was such a big fucker people remembered him more than the others. He was easily led, and that was all that was wrong with him. They wanted him to be put away, put in care, or stuck in some fucking home, some fucking institution. Well, not while she still had a breath in her body. She would fight for her baby, she would keep him home with her. No one was going to take him anywhere.

She knew inside that none of this was true, that the name Jackson actually stopped anything even remotely like that happening, but it was the only way she could cope with her son's problems.

She was grateful for the vodka Freddie had brought in for her, although it also told her how bad this had become. But as ever she pushed all the terrible things from her mind, drank herself stupid and made a point of forgetting anything detrimental to her own peace of mind or wellbeing.

Freddie had fucked off and for once she was glad he had gone out. Over the years she had wanted him home so badly, but now she didn't care either way. Her Little Freddie was sitting with her, cuddling her, and she didn't need anyone else. He was her life, and no one would take him from her.

Now she was drunk as a skunk, she told Little Freddie that over and over again.

Maggie was lying on the bed with her son. He was asleep in her arms and she marvelled at the love she had for him.

When she looked at him she wondered how she had ever let Freddie dictate her feelings for someone so precious, someone who had come from *her* own body. He was half hers, half of him was made up of her and she had let her hate for Freddie come between her and her child.

Her child.

Since the day she had fronted Freddie up, she had felt so much better. She felt she had taken the power back, even though that expression irritated her, especially when she heard it from complete drongos on daytime talk shows, who had no concept of real women's problems. She *knew* what having real power over someone meant. She had lived with it day in and day out for so long.

Freddie had possessed the power over her because she had been terrified he would tell his wife what had happened and Jackie would blame her because she could never admit that her husband was capable of raping her sister.

It was Jackie's reaction she had been most afraid of.

She had also been so scared that Freddie would tell her husband, tell everyone they knew that he had *slept* with her, and she had believed that *everyone* would think it had been by choice. Now, all this time later, she knew no one would think that she would even contemplate touching him.

Now, she was happy, happier anyway, than she had been in years.

Seeing Kimberley in the hospital that night, and seeing Jackie for what she really was, a fucking coward and a drunk, had made her understand her own fears and her own problems.

Telling Jackie that she would lay her out had been such a big step for her. All her life her elder sister had dictated to her, told her what to do, given her advice, slagged her off, insulted her. She had treated Jackie like some kind of fucking goddess when, in reality, she was a drunk. A manipulating, vicious, drunken bitch who for some reason she had always felt a strong and genuine love towards. And she had always assumed that the feeling had been reciprocated. Now Maggie wasn't so sure. She knew Jackie ran her down to her mates and talked badly about her within the family.

Maggie had also realised that, whatever happened between her and Jackie, she wouldn't lose the girls' love. She had taken them over many years before and they loved and needed her. The girls would still be there, whether she was talking to Jackie or not.

So she had told her sister what she thought of her, and gone home to find Freddie trying once more to inveigle his way into her confidence, into her mind and, worst of all, into her real life with her husband.

He had sat in her house with her man, and she had finally had enough. She had wanted him to tell Jimmy what had happened so badly. She was sick of keeping it secret, protecting people who did not deserve her care or her protection.

If she had never seen Jackie again she wouldn't give a fuck. She felt, for the first time in years, free, unencumbered, light-hearted and indifferent about who she might hurt if anything did come out.

Fuck them all, her Jimmy included. It was knowing that she didn't now care about how he would react that had actually made it all so much easier. Jimmy had become the one she had been trying to protect, and Jimmy was the strongest of them all.

She had dared Freddie to spill the beans and he had walked away. She had taken back the power.

Now, she was happy. She loved her boy, had *always*

loved her boy – the half that was hers anyway – but thanks to Freddie she felt so guilty about the circumstances of his conception she had found it hard to watch her Jimmy being his father. And loving Jimmy so much, she had been terrified that Freddie would let the secret out, just to prove a point, just to make trouble. Just to *teach* her a lesson.

But that night she had discovered that he was *wary* of Jimmy, scared of him in fact. And she had finally sussed out that Jimmy was the reason it had started in the first place.

Things weren't *all* back to normal, but she was trying to make things right, and if Freddie would only leave them in peace, their lives would be so much better.

And look at his kids. Without her, what the fuck would the girls do? He was not even interested in Rox getting married. She had made a fucking good match in their world, and he had no interest.

Jackie had no interest in any of them either. Kimberley was off the gear, and Maggie had helped her get a flat, but neither Jackie nor Freddie had bothered to go and see her, which had hurt the girl. Maggie knew how she felt, knew how it was when you had let people down, but these were people who let *themselves* down and Kimberley was better off without them. All the girls were better off without them. Even Dianna was seeing a little fucker, and would be gone before they knew it. Neither of them gave a shit, yet when Freddie finally found out who the bloke was, Maggie knew the Third World War would erupt.

Why was one person allowed to have so much power? Why did everyone feel the need to make *his* life easier when all *he* did was use people? And Jackie was just the same, full of her own self-importance.

Maggie had pointed out to Jimmy that he paid the

wages, not Freddie, and yet he still fucking pandered to him. She knew it had hurt Jimmy, she knew it was a provocative statement, but as she had said it time and time again, who the fuck did Freddie Jackson think he was? What gave him the right to treat people like he did, including her Jimmy, her husband?

She had argued that with Jimmy the night before. He had been telling her how Freddie was still conning money off people. Big news on the grapevine that was. All these years later, he was still nicking pennies and halfpennies off fucking no necks. And she had told Jimmy, '*You* give *him* his power, and until you take it away from him he will always be trouble.'

Now she had his daughters' lives in her hand, and she wanted to help them out because she loved them. Like her little son, she knew he was only half of them, and the other half was nothing to do with him and his life.

For all that, though, Little Freddie was scary, and she knew that he was on borrowed time. She made sure her little man was never in his orbit for any length of time, and that he was never alone with him.

If it was left with her now, she would blank Freddie and Jackie without a second's thought. They were just not worth the aggravation.

Jimmy Junior opened his eyes and she smiled at him. He sat up and she kissed his handsome face and she tickled him until he was screeching with laughter.

This was her life now, this boy, her baby, and she was determined to make his life everything it could possibly be.

Chapter Twenty-One

'Look, Jimmy, I had a lot on my fucking plate.'

It was obvious that Jimmy thought that Freddie was taking the piss. He laughed in derision and annoyance. '*You* had a lot on *your* plate? I had Amos here, Glenford, the whole fucking shebang. It was like the *Black and White Minstrel Show* – your term for the meet if I remember rightly, not mine. Remember now, do you? The meet where you should have talked your way out of the shit? Ring any fucking bells, does it?'

Jimmy's sarcasm and open animosity were so unusual that Freddie was for once speechless. Jimmy never goaded him, Jimmy never lost his rag, that was Freddie's department, not Jimmy's. Freddie was the wild card, he was the one no one knew how to deal with. Not Jimmy. Jimmy was the placid one, the thinker, the fucking brains of the outfit, according to the gossip.

'You made me look a right fucking knob. Well, not any more, Freddie. You can go and fuck yourself from now on, and I mean that.'

Jimmy lit a cigarette and pulled on it deeply before saying, 'These are shit, how can people buy them!' He put the cigarette out and rummaged through his desk until he found another pack. The cigarette he had lit the first time was Chinese contraband. They looked like Benson & Hedges, they were in the same packaging, and they had the same health warnings. However, they were made and rolled in China and sold off here for a fraction of the original cigarettes' asking price. The tobacco was cheap, they were easy to manufacture and they were selling like hot cakes thanks to Gordon Brown and his determination to make smokers into the elite. Jimmy, however, always knew a snide fag, and he hated them.

He lit up again, his fury still evident. 'I tell you, Fred, I looked at Amos and all the others and I could see their point. Why should they have you ripping them off, eh? Who are you to do that to them? What gives you the fucking right to have them over when they are only grafting a living the same as us?'

Freddie was astonished. Jimmy had always tried to be respectful of him and his feelings, and he knew he had not always given young Jimmy the same respect back.

'It was Little Freddie, he is in big trouble . . .'

Jimmy waved his hands in dismissal. 'Oh, fuck off, Freddie. His whole life will be trouble, he is his father's son. You left me standing on my Jacksy like a fucking cunt, and I had some serious people here because of *you*. And I have had enough. Do you hear me? You and me are that far –' he held up the thumb and forefinger of his right hand about an inch apart – 'from fucking falling out altogether. You fucking cheap *ponce*. I had to kiss their arses over fucking twenty grand! *Twenty fucking grand* they were light, and it wasn't the first time, was it? Jesus Christ, but fucking Ozzy had you fucking taped from the off.'

Freddie had never seen Jimmy like this, he had never seen him so angry or so uncontrolled in what he was saying. Jimmy always thought before he spoke, even in anger, and Freddie knew this could mean he was on his way out.

He watched Jimmy as he walked around the office. His huge shoulders and his taut body denoted a man who looked after himself, and Jimmy did just that. He took care of himself inside and out. He also took care of everyone around him, and that was the bugbear.

Now Freddie was finally accepting that Jimmy was the better man and it was too late. Jimmy had reached the end of his tether and Freddie was wise enough to know when it was best to keep quiet. Let him get it out of his system.

'Don't worry, I weighed them out, Fred, don't *you* fucking worry about that. I weighed them out and gave them a drink on top for their trouble. You cost me a fucking fortune, but what I can't understand is where your poke goes! You don't even possess a decent bit of clobber. You must spunk it up like no one's business. You earn a serious fucking wage and you got fuck all to show for it. You are thieving off *my* workers and they are not earning anything near your fucking wages, and so I want to know, where the fuck is it all going?'

Freddie didn't answer him, but just shrugged nonchalantly.

Jimmy sighed. This was the older cousin he had always loved, and who he had once revered. All he saw now was a large man with a beer gut and a bad attitude who was ageing fast. He could not for the life of him understand what was going on in Freddie's head, what was making him tick, and the worst thing of all was, he had stopped caring.

Maggie was right. He had carried Freddie all these years out of guilt, but as she had pointed out so many times, if Ozzy had wanted Freddie to run the businesses he would have given them to Freddie. But he hadn't, he had given them over to Jimmy, and now he had to finally and irrevocably make that point. Freddie seemed to think that he had been done over, but *Ozzy* had decided that Jimmy was to be the main player and so anything that Freddie thought was now moot.

It was *Ozzy's* world they lived in. Ozzy still pulled the strings and called the shots as he always had done, and it was Ozzy who had given Jimmy the main shots. Ozzy was the number one and the sooner Freddie understood that, the sooner they could all get on with their lives.

He was a fucking albatross hanging round their necks and, as Maggie also said, although she was related to him by marriage and Jimmy was related to him by blood, that did not give him any Brownie points where Ozzy was concerned.

Jimmy knew she was right, and the last few days had just proved her point. He just wished that he had brought this out into the open years ago.

'You are out, Freddie, out of the main drag. You will be on an earner now and you will be nothing but a collector. You can kiss goodbye to anything else until you show me you can be fucking trusted.'

Freddie was convinced he was hearing things. 'You what? A collector, me?'

Jimmy nodded, and Freddie was reminded of just how far his little cousin had come. Jimmy was a man's man. He had the presence of a leader, and he also had the backing of Ozzy and all his counterparts. Freddie knew that Jimmy deserved everything he had accomplished, but that knowledge did not make it any easier for him. Now, this boy was seriously considering putting him on to the collecting, like he was a fucking no one, a fucking no neck.

It was outrageous, it was unbelievable, and it was also long overdue. If the boot had been on the other foot he would have aimed Jimmy out long ago.

'Don't do this, Jimmy. I mean it, you do this to me, humiliate me in front of everyone, and that is me and you finished.'

Jimmy looked into Freddie's face. He saw the worry there, and the hate, and he suddenly saw again the man he had looked up to all those years before.

He couldn't do it to him.

He knew he should row him out, because Freddie's penchant for trouble would one day be their downfall. But he could not take away from Freddie the only thing that gave him real pleasure. His job with Ozzy and his belief that they were equals was what made his life bearable, but it was also the thing that made him so unhappy. He knew he was not a real partner, he must know. But even after all this, he could not bring himself to destroy his Freddie. He loved him, even though he had not liked him for years.

'You listen to me, Freddie, and you listen good. I'll give you one more fucking chance, and if you even think about mugging off anyone, me included, you will be out on your fucking arse. Do you hear me? I mean it, you have caused me untold fucking trouble over the years. I have had to talk Ozzy down, lie to him, and fucking argue with him about you. I know you see me as your *usurper*, but Ozzy chose me to be the go-between, you lost any chance of being his number one years ago.'

Freddie was quiet, he was listening for once, and Jimmy knew that this had to be said now, while Freddie was *willing* to listen to him.

'Ozzy hears everything in there. I tell you, he has a better fucking network than Bill Gates and the Pope put together, and he hears *everything*. He knew about the brass you topped. He even knew she had your kid, and I have never ever discussed that with him. You think that I have deliberately set out to do you down and take what's yours. I know what you say about me in the pubs and the clubs, Freddie, people can't *wait* to tell me when you bad-mouth me. But I swallowed because you are my blood, and you are my family. But it has got to stop.'

Freddie sighed heavily, puffing out his cheeks like a kid, and making a loud noise. 'Well, that has told me, ain't it?'

Jimmy had to stifle the urge to smack the man before him in the mouth. He shook his head slowly and said with quiet desperation, 'I can't do this no more, Freddie. I have been carrying you for years. You might not think I have, but I can assure you that is the truth. Now I have tried my hardest to keep us on an even keel, keep us together, like partners, but that has become impossible. You can't be trusted any more. Since Lenny you have been too unreliable for me, Fred. Your temper and your carrying on will get us all a capture if you ain't careful. You have been lucky up till now, and I have stepped in a few times to see you all right, but this last lot has finished me. You stood me up in public like I was a cunt. Not a phone call, not a fucking message, nothing. Well, you try and take a fucking bean in future, one fucking quid goes on the missing list, and I tell you now, Freddie, I swear on my boy's life, I will fucking finish you off meself.'

Freddie stood and watched Jimmy. One thing he had going for him was that he knew when he was beaten. Well, he would wait and he would watch, and when the time was right he would strike. He knew Jimmy had every right to say what he had said. He was aware he was just a fucking ornament, that point had been rammed down his throat. He was just a fucking heavy who had believed he was in a partnership, and now he knew the score. He would keep his head down and his arse up, as the old boys in the docks used to say, meaning they would do their collar and that was all, no overtime, no nothing. Well, as his old mum was always saying, God paid back debts without money.

Dianna was dressed to kill. She was a small girl, with high breasts and a very slim frame. Her thick brown hair was her crowning glory. It was beautiful and she knew it was the envy of every woman who came into contact with her.

In her short black dress she looked older and sophisticated, which was exactly what she was aiming for.

Dianna was also very pretty, and she knew how to make the best of herself, thanks to Maggie who had let the girls work for her as soon as they were old enough, or expelled from school, whatever came first. She wondered what they would have done without their Mags sometimes. She had always made sure they had things, little things, like Tampax and deodorants, things that their mother wouldn't dream of wasting money on. Yet Maggie had known how important those things were to young girls when even toothpaste had not been seen as a necessity by Jackie. And Maggie would bring it round their house by the carrier bag, along with all the other little things that made them feel good about themselves.

Now Dianna was sitting in a pub in Bow dressed to kill, or thrill as Maggie had said to make her laugh. She was waiting for a man she was so besotted with she couldn't eat, sleep or concentrate, because he had taken over every aspect of her life. She thought about him constantly. It was as if her life had been on hold until he had arrived, and she suddenly knew the reason why she had been put on this earth.

They were all brought up Catholic. One thing her

mother had done was to make sure they had been baptised, made their communions and been confirmed. She knew a lot of that had been because of her grandparents, but she still went to Mass and she still believed in God. But since she had met Terry Baker, she had finally understood the sacraments, and that sacraments were important.

And love. She finally understood how it could be so important. All her life she had seen her parents' marriage and her mother would tell them all, when she was pissed out of her brains, how she loved her husband and that they were married in the eyes of God. But she had always believed that God would not be interested in them, that they were beneath his notice. Now though she wasn't so sure. She knew that, if she married Terry Baker in a Catholic church, she would be like her mother. Nothing would ever make her leave him.

Just as she was starting to wonder if she had been stood up, Terry breezed into the pub all testosterone and expensive aftershave. One glimpse of his killer smile, and she was finished.

Jackie was trying to get up some enthusiasm for her daughter's wedding, but it was hard. Rox kept going over the same things, and she felt like screaming at her to get to the fucking point. But she didn't. Instead, she watched as Maggie discussed everything in minute detail and marvelled at how her little sister could even be interested.

Rox really had no idea about life. Anyone in their right mind, seeing Jackie's marriage to Freddie, would run a fucking mile. Not her girls though. They thought it was all going to be wine and roses like Maggie's and Jimmy's.

What really pissed her off, though, was that thanks to Maggie she would have to get gussied up and go to the fucking wedding whether she liked it or not. She did want to see her daughter wed, but it was her Little Freddie she was worried about. Rox had banned him, said that no kids were allowed, even her brother. She meant, of course, *especially* her brother.

They were a crowd of treacherous bitches. She had given birth to a crowd of bastards, even Kimberley. The little mare never even popped her head around the door to see how any of them were. If it wasn't for Rox and Maggie, she wouldn't know anything about her at all. When she had rung, all she had talked about was her *rehab*, and her new life.

What was that all about?

Now Rox was nearly off her hands, and Dianna was going to fly the nest, she was sure of that. So for the first time in years, her life would be her *own*.

She was relishing the prospect of being alone with her son. Little Freddie was like his dad and if she couldn't have him full time, then she was determined to have the next best thing. No matter what they said about him, she was his mother and she knew him better than anyone. Once the girls left home, she would devote all her time to him, that was what he needed, someone to dedicate their life to him.

Freddie Senior was trying to help him, and so would she. Together they could make him into a regular, happy boy.

Freddie was drunk, really drunk, and he was still reeling from the events from earlier in the day. Jimmy was with him but he knew that was only because he felt he needed to be there, not because he *wanted* to be there. This was their public show of strength, their way of clearing the air, not only with each other but with the people they dealt with on a daily basis. This was an exercise in damage limitation, and it was also a way for Jimmy to tell him he was forgiven, and that he was still a part of it all.

Like he gave a fuck now. He held all the fucking cards, and he could destroy Jimmy in an instant.

Freddie was very drunk, but he was also aware that he must not, at any time, say anything that might bring the wrath of this young man down on his head. After all these years he was finally having to admit to himself that Jimmy had it all sewn up. But for all Jimmy's being the big man, he knew something Jimmy didn't.

The thought made him smile now. If Jimmy knew, there would be fucking ructions, and those ructions would reverberate down the years. Freddie felt much better reminding himself of just how much trouble he was capable of causing if the fancy took him.

It was very tempting, so tempting. But he wouldn't. Not tonight. This was something to be kept on ice until a future date. He *needed* to have this secret inside him, because just knowing he had something that could blast Jimmy's world apart was making it all so much easier to cope with.

Worst of all, although Jimmy was playing fair, for once in his life, he had let Jimmy down for all the right reasons. He had stood him up, because of his son, not because he didn't want to or couldn't be bothered.

But he knew it was not the time to tell Jimmy about his boy. He was sorry that he had not let him be taken, but he knew Jackie would die if her son was charged with something like that and, truth be told, so would he.

He had been worried, though, because at one point he had not believed that he could smooth this one over. He had not *intended* to smooth it over, but blood will out, as Jimmy had proved to him today.

'Come on, Freddie, let's have another drink, eh?'

Jimmy was so happy, so boring, and so fucking smug, he wanted to smash the nearest pint pot into his handsome fucking face. Instead he smiled back and said happily, 'I'll get this one, Jim. It's my round, mate.'

'Go home will you, please.'

Little Freddie smiled at his nana with all the charm of his father, but Maddie wasn't fooled.

'I just want to talk to you, Nana. I want you to tell me about me granddad that's all.'

Maddie looked at the boy she had adored as a baby, but who she had quickly realised was not quite right. He was like her Freddie, like his father, and whereas once that would have been the icing on her cake, now she saw it as a fault. Saw this child as an accident waiting to happen. His father had been the light of her life, but not any more. She knew too much about him and one day she would tell him.

Until then, she would try to make life bearable for herself and most of the people around her, but this boy, this big handsome child, frightened her. He was just like her Freddie at the same age and she had cosseted him just as Jackie had cosseted this one. She had seen in her Freddie something that had never been there. She had invented her son, had built him up in her head, made him into the person she had wanted him to be. Now she had to pay for that.

'Please, Nana, let me stay a while.'

She saw the way he looked at her. He would fool a lot of people one day, and now he was playing her, using his good looks to get what he wanted.

'Go home, I said.'

'Please, Nana. I just want to sit with you that's all.'

'I want you to go.'

Her words were said with a finality that alerted Freddie to the fact he would get nothing from her. He was in a bind, he was being watched like a hawk and this old cow could have been a bit of light relief, and he was interested in his granddad. He wanted to hear about his suicide, wanted to hear about his life and his reputation for fighting. He had heard it all second-hand from other people, but she was the horse's mouth. She could tell him everything he wanted to know.

'Will you go, child, and leave me in peace.'

He punched her in the chest then, as his temper got the better of him. 'You fucking old bitch, you're an old woman, who would fucking want to sit with you anyway?'

She sighed, and said, without raising her voice, 'Go, and leave me alone, or I will ring my son.'

He finally left her then. The threat of his father had done the trick, and she bolted her door behind him.

Lena and Joe laughed at the antics of little Jimmy. Maggie had dropped him off earlier because she had a late night at her Leigh-on-Sea salon.

Lena loved this child, they all did, because he was such a dear little thing.

'Oh, Joe, I was so worried about my girl. Now when I watch her with him I feel like I have won the lottery.'

'I know, love. Like I always say, things work out in their own time.'

Lena nodded. 'Want a cuppa?'

Joe smiled. 'Why not, and make me little bloke a hot chocolate, he loves that.'

As she watched her husband sit the child on his lap, Lena breathed a heartfelt sigh of relief.

She put the kettle on and quickly prepared the mugs,

and made Jimmy Junior's drink. He loved his hot chocolate and she should know, he had spent half his life here. With Maggie having been so offish and leaving him with them at the drop of a hat she knew her grandson better than anyone.

There had been times when she had thought her Maggie's behaviour was unnatural. For years she had not treated that boy properly. Oh, she had done everything that was expected, but it was as if he wasn't really hers, that he was someone else's and she had to take care of him. It was as if she was his mother once removed. That was the only way Lena could explain it.

Now, though, her Maggie was back to her old self and she thanked God for that every day of her life. She had finally turned into a proper mother and that child was all the better for it.

There was a knock at the door and she opened it to see Little Freddie.

'Hello, mate, what you doing here?'

He gave Lena that charming, handsome smile he could command at the drop of a hat. 'I just wanted to see you, Nana. Can I come in?'

She opened the door wide then, and he slipped past her happily.

Lena grabbed his jacket and pulled him round to face her. 'Any of your antics and I'll fucking brain you, right?'

He looked into her eyes and said seriously, 'Fair enough.'

These were two people who understood each other perfectly.

'So, do you think Freddie took it well?'

Jimmy shrugged. 'I really don't know, Glen, but what I do know is, I let him off with a fucking caution.

However, he is on fucking trial and even he has to comprehend that much.'

Glenford nodded. 'He is a dangerous fuck, Jimmy.'

'I know that, mate, you are preaching to the converted, but I ain't scared of him. I was, many years ago when I was a kid. But not any more, and he knows that. What I couldn't get through to him, though, was why what he had done was so outrageous, he still doesn't think he's done anything wrong.'

Glenford looked concerned. 'You will regret this. You have taken a viper to your chest, boy, and the fucker will bite you at the first available opportunity. Freddie ain't like other people, Jimmy, he sees the world through his eyes only. You will become the target for his next bout of hatred and violence. But I think you have already worked that one out for yourself, eh?'

Jimmy sighed. 'What could I do, though? If I had aimed him out of it, he would never have let it go. I just couldn't do it to him. I don't *want* to do that to him. But I had to make him aware of what was going down.'

Glenford grabbed Jimmy's hand and said seriously, 'He is your nemesis, Jimmy. Everybody have one, you're a lucky man because you have your one's address.'

They laughed together, but neither of them thought that it was funny really.

Jackie had her dream. Her husband was coming home every night, and instead of loving it she was hating it. In he came like the big 'I am', expecting all sorts. And if Little Freddie wasn't there he went looking for him.

This was worse than being under house arrest. He mentioned every drink she poured and watched what he wanted to watch on TV. She had always had her viewing down pat, but now she had to make him sandwiches, run up the chippy or the Chinese, and get him beers from the fridge.

Little Freddie had to be on his best behaviour, and she had to sit there and make excuses to nip over the off-licence to get herself a drink. The way Freddie carried on anyone would think they were hard up or something. He was well wedged up, and she even wished he would fuck off round one of his birds' houses. Anything was better than this.

He watched her and all, she could feel his eyes on her.

She had taken to bathing every day just to stop his fucking harping on about the state of her and the house. Anyone listening in would think he had been brought up in Buckingham Palace, but she knew who the real culprit was: Maggie. Maggie was too clean, she was fucking demented with it. The housework would still be there when she was gone, so why devote your life to it?

'Where have you been today, then?'

Little Freddie looked at his father and said quietly, 'I was round Nanny Lena's and Granddad Joe's.'

Freddie drank half his can of Tennents before saying quietly, 'I never said you could go out.'

Jackie was on the edge of her seat. 'I said he could go. What are you saying now, then? He can't leave the fucking house?'

Freddie looked at his wife. She was a mess, a bigger mess than he had first suspected. 'Shut the fuck up, Jackie, I am talking to the organ grinder, not the monkey.'

Little Freddie started to laugh, and he had to hold his hand over his mouth to stifle the sound.

Jackie was drunk and she was fed up with her husband and his constant presence. 'You make me laugh, Freddie Jackson. You come in here and you throw your weight around, and expect everyone to jump to your fucking tune.'

Freddie sighed. This was the woman he knew and loved.

'What's happened, eh? What brings you home here really? Why are you suddenly father of the year? You in trouble of some kind?'

Jackie had inadvertently hit the nail right on the head. She had sensed that the only thing that would get him home early was trouble.

'You haven't listened to a word I've said, have you, Jack? This fucking child of ours is in deep shit. You think he is a fucking choir boy, you think he is being led on by other, more sophisticated boys. Well he ain't, anything he has done he has done on his lonesome. This cunt has all his faculties, don't you worry about that. As for me being in trouble, I might point out that you have spent your whole married life trying to keep me in this house and now I am trying to make something of my son, trying to help him, you want shot. It's a fucking joke, except I ain't laughing. Now you had better calm yourself down, woman, button your fucking mutton and show me a bit of respect, because in a minute I am going to fucking muller you.'

Little Freddie watched them both and decided his mother was right, his father was in it right up to his neck.

Why else would he want to be in this shit hole?

Chapter Twenty-Two

Ozzy watched as Jimmy walked into the visitors' room. As he turned out his pockets once more and waited to be searched again, Ozzy observed him with pride.

He was a handsome man, and he also had a real presence. Jimmy had the air about him that most men dreamed of and the walk of a man completely at ease with himself and his surroundings, no mean feat on a unit that was peopled with serious criminals.

Ozzy knew that he had given this man his confidence, and he was proud of that. Jimmy was the son he had never had, and he did think of him as a son. He was a good man, he was a decent man, but most of all he was one hundred per cent trustworthy.

As Ozzy watched Jimmy, he observed the other people around him, noticing that they unconsciously acknowledged him as one of their own, even though he had never served a second's time anywhere. His years of coming here had given him that prison swagger, he was as relaxed here as he was in his own home.

Ozzy's big prayer was that this boy never ever had to experience prison other than as a visitor. It was not an existence that Jimmy would ever accept. Freddie, on the other hand, would relish another stint, he was that fucking stupid, and it was only Jimmy's nous that had kept Freddie on the outside for so long.

Freddie Jackson was an ungrateful cunt and he knew Jimmy was having trouble with him, but Ozzy was sure Jimmy could handle it. It had grieved Ozzy though that once on the outside Freddie had reverted to type. He had been well treated in stir and, in fairness, Freddie had his creds. He could handle himself, and he was not frightened of anyone or anything.

So why he let it all go to the wayside Ozzy didn't understand. But he did know that Freddie was cunting Jimmy up hill and down dale, to all and sundry, and he was not going to let that happen for much longer. If he cunted Jimmy, he was cunting *him*, Ozzy, because Jimmy was his front to the world. He was also aware of Freddie's light-fingered forays, and he was not impressed. He was nicking off his own, and that was a definite fucking no no.

As Jimmy walked over to him, Ozzy was smiling, that easy, friendly smile that denoted a man without anything bad on his mind.

Ozzy stood up and they hugged for long moments. Ozzy had never hugged anyone in his life until Jimmy and he felt like he knew this boy better than he knew himself.

'All right, Oz?'

Ozzy smiled again as they sat down together. 'Fine, Jim, yourself?'

This was always how they started the visit, it was mundane and it was boring but it was heartfelt.

'Fucking kicking, Oz, everything is lovely jubbly!'

They both laughed.

As always, another inmate brought them over their teas and their Kit Kats. Once that was out of the way, the serious business of the day began.

* * *

'What the fuck has happened to your Little Freddie, Jackie?'

Lena's voice was harsh but jovial as she made one of her endless cups of tea. She watched her daughter drinking what was supposed to be a can of Coca-Cola but what was actually a vodka and Coke. She was drinking all day now and it was taking its toll on her.

Jackie was thrilled at her mother's words and she gulped at her can before saying loudly, and not a little drunkenly, 'He is my baby, Mum. I fucking love him.'

She was slurring her words and Lena closed her eyes in distress. When pissed, Jackie started off loving everyone, but by lunchtime they would all be arseholes and wankers, her son included.

'Since my Freddie has taken him in hand he is a changed boy!'

Lena smiled as best she could and said as happily as she could manage, given the circumstances, 'You're telling me! He has been round a lot lately and if Jimmy Junior's here he plays with him, helps him do things. Fuck me, Jack, I thought he'd had a personality transplant.'

Jackie was almost bursting with drunken pride. 'Now the girls are gone, more or less, he is getting a lot of one-to-one attention. He is also coming to terms with any feelings he has, feelings that he needs to express more—'

'Oh, that's lovely.' Lena was regretting asking her daughter anything now, she sounded like a fucking social worker when she spouted that crap. She knew from experience that this kind of talk could go on for hours and she wasn't in the mood today. 'How are you, anyway?'

Jackie knew she had been cut off mid-sentence and she swallowed down her annoyance. If *Maggie* had been sitting here talking intelligently they would all be hanging on her every word. Freddie was right in what he said, they mugged her off.

'How's the wedding plans going?' Lena asked, trying to start a different conversation.

'All right. It's not till next year, so why they have to fucking keep on about it I don't know.'

Lena swallowed down the retort that had sprung to her lips, and changed the subject once again. 'How's Big Freddie?'

'He's fine. Why are you asking about him?' Jackie's voice was now full of suspicion and the underlying anger that was always close to the surface.

'Oh, for fuck's sake, Jack, I am making what is commonly known as conversation. But with you that's a fucking impossibility. Relax and have a natter, will you, girl?'

Jackie was mortally offended and it showed, which made Lena so angry she bellowed, 'You are such hard work, Jackie, do you know that? You are always on your fucking dignity, always looking for an insult or a slight. I am fucked if I know why you even bother to come round here.'

Jackie felt like crying. It was always the same, she did her best to chat and she *tried* her hardest to be nice, and her mum always ended up having a go at her. Maggie was the golden girl, she was the fucking queen of this house, and her little boy was the little darling, the prince, which meant her and her kids were relegated to second position. It hurt, it really hurt her at times.

Lena saw the tears in her daughter's eyes and felt awful for shouting at her as per usual, but talking to Jackie was like trying to make conversation with a Pakistani Dutchman. Nigh on fucking impossible. If her daughter wasn't always half pissed she might get a decent chat out of her, and she might also relax long enough to let the self-pity go for a few minutes, Jackie's drinking and her fucking stupid way of carrying on worried Lena. She could see the toll the drink was taking on her eldest daughter, and she didn't know what to do to make it all right, to make it better.

Patricia was seriously worried, and Freddie was not making her feel any easier. In fact, he was starting to annoy her. If he didn't stop going on about Jimmy and how he was mugging him off, she was going to scream.

'Have you listened to one word I've said, Freddie?'

He nodded. ''Course I have.'

'Well, then, what do you think I should do?'

Freddie was fucked now because he had not been listening to her for ages. Instead, he had been watching one of the new girls through the doorway and she was just his cup of Rosie Lee.

'What do *you* think you should do?' He was pleased that he had years of experience with Jackie to fall back on, because he had not listened to her since before their honeymoon.

Patricia said, softly, and with an underlying malice, 'My brother has requested that I bring all the books up to date and then give them to Jimmy, and you ask me what I think I should do?'

Freddie was quiet.

'Funny how you can fucking go on about Jimmy for hours and when I mention him you don't even take it on board. Yet I am expected to take the books that denote my livelihood and pass them to him without a fucking murmur.'

She closed the door because she had also caught sight of the new girl. If she wanted some serious answers from Freddie, that meant no distractions whatsoever. She knew him too well, and if he wasn't such a good fuck she would have crowned him.

'Has Jimmy said anything to you? Why would my brother suddenly ask me to do that, give the books over to what is in effect a fucking stranger, when I have run his houses single-handedly for years?'

Freddie felt as if his head was going to explode. 'Did he say anything to you about it the last time you saw him, Pat?'

She shook her head, glad that she finally had his full attention. 'Not a fucking dicky bird. It was the usual. I told him what we were making and he seemed happy enough, and then we chatted as we always do.'

She didn't let on that she grassed up everyone and anyone she could, Freddie included. It was through her that Ozzy knew Freddie had lightened more than a few money bags. Jimmy was so close with things like that he was like a fucking statue, and she knew how to earn her Brownie points.

Freddie looked her in the eyes and said carefully, 'Are you creaming anything off, Pat?'

'How dare you? You can fucking talk! You're the one who keeps taking dips out of everyone's fucking bunce, not me.'

Freddie waved his arms to shut her up. She was so livid at his words, that alone told him he was on the right track. 'I don't give a fuck what you do, you silly mare. I am trying to help you out here. If you are scamming him, sister or no sister, he won't put up with it. He hates anyone trying to take what he sees as his. That is why him and Jimmy get on so well; Jimmy would haunt you over a fucking pound.'

Freddie looked at Pat to make sure she was listening. 'When I was banged up with Oz, I remember we had a lag in there who managed to get his hands on some LSD. Now the northerners love a bit of brown or a bit of acid to make their sentence go faster. They do their lumps out of their nut as is their prerogative, any way you can find to do your bird in peace is your business.

'This fella had a lot more than he let on – he wanted a few quid for some luxuries. To Ozzy, right, this was pennies, fucking nothing. But he sussed him out, made a point of counting down each tab that was sold. On the quiet, of course. Well, when Ozzy realised the fella had held some back he went fucking ballistic. He even frightened me, and I was supposed to be his minder. But he got that money. It was only about forty quid, if that.'

Freddie shook his head as if bewildered. 'And I remember saying to him, "All that for forty quid," and he turned on me, Pat, and he said, all serious-like, "Forty quid is forty quid, Freddie, and it's forty quid I never had." It was fucking mad. All the other lags understood him, *agreed* with him, but I just felt that forty quid was not worth the hag. He nearly killed that fella, we all ended up on a lockdown, and I know it annoyed him that I couldn't see the principle that he assured me over and over again had been at stake.'

Freddie held out his arms in wonderment. 'It was forty quid, for fuck's sake, but to him it was like forty grand. So now you know why I am asking you if you have not been completely honest with him about the takings here. I know he loves you, Pat, but I also know he won't be mugged off, not by you, not by anyone. I know Jimmy would never have told him that I had a touch, but I also know that Ozzy will never forgive me because of it.'

Pat listened to Freddie with increasing fear. She knew Ozzy better than anyone, but she had still been buncing the last few years. Why not? He was never coming out, he didn't want to, so what the fuck did he want all this money for anyway?

He was gathering it up in shedloads and he was never going to be able to fucking spend any of it. She had started paying herself over the odds because she had felt that she deserved it, and after a couple of bonuses she had made it a regular thing.

She was terrified now. She knew Ozzy wouldn't hurt her physically, but she also knew he was capable of cutting her off without a backward glance, and, money or no money, she loved Oz, always had and always would.

She sat down at her desk and for the first time ever Freddie saw her looking vulnerable. It reminded him that Ozzy might be banged up but he was running the show. Had always run the show. He had dipped himself, on more than one occasion, and Jimmy must have smoothed it all over with Ozzy. It suddenly occurred to him just how fucking lucky he had been. Like Pat he had thought no further than that Ozzy was away for the long haul, and he had not allowed for the mind-set of a man who was marking his prison time by still making money.

'Can I leave Jimmy Junior with you tonight, Mum?'

Lena smiled. ' 'Course you can. You off out, love?'

Maggie grinned. 'Jimmy wants to take me out to dinner, he just rang. He is on his way home from the Isle of Wight, and he is in a really good mood.'

'You leave my little babes here, and you go and have a good time. Let him sleep over, he ain't done that for ages.'

'Okey doke. I'll drop him off later then.'

'You want a sandwich or something?'

'No thanks. Has Jackie been round?'

Lena sighed. 'Don't start me off about her, for fuck's sake. She was pissed out of her brains this morning and I tell you now, Mags, I love her, she's me daughter, but she is such hard work.'

She sat down at the small kitchen table and said conspiratorially, her voice a whisper even though there was no one else within earshot, 'She walks around with a can now, a Coke can that is full of vodka and she honestly thinks that no one knows, that no one's sussed it out, and that we think she is drinking fucking Coke. I am really worried about her, Mags, but what can I do?'

Maggie was always sad when she thought of her sister and her way of life. 'We've all tried, Mum, but until she decides to get help, it's a waste of time, ain't it.'

'At least Freddie is at home more these days. He is doing a marvellous job with that little fucker of his. He has been round here, and you wouldn't know him, girl. I still think he has a screw loose though. You could never trust that child. I don't think so, anyway.'

Maggie looked at her mother and she saw how much she had aged over the last few years. She was sorry to see her getting so old, even though she knew it had to happen. But her mother had always seemed so strong, had always made her feel safe and loved and cared for. Now Lena was starting to look old it was frightening, because one day that was going to be her.

She was into her thirties now, and even though she looked good, you couldn't fight age, not really. If you had ten face-lifts and your whole body remodelled, you might look younger but you would still be fifty or sixty or whatever. *Looking* younger did not *make* you younger. Time passed, and the older you got the quicker it seemed to go.

'Do you think it might be worth talking to Freddie about Jackie?'

Maggie shrugged. 'I never talk to him unless I have to. He is the reason she bloody drinks anyway.'

'True, but I worry that one day I will get a phone call, or a message telling me she's dead. She is going yellow, Mags, and it's her liver, I know it is.'

Maggie could see the worry and fear etched on her mother's face, and she felt the sting of tears.

'I love you, Mum.'

Lena flapped her hand at her daughter and laughed. But Maggie knew she was pleased she had said it. They were not really that kind of family, they didn't hug or touch too much. But she wanted her mother to know that she did love her.

All day, every day, she loved her.

Freddie had decided to actually do the work he was supposed to be getting on with. He needed time to think, and seeing Pat like that had thrown him because he had a feeling that Jimmy would be in the know about everything. He also had a feeling that Jimmy was about to inherit the houses along with everything else.

He was so fucking angry. Jimmy was walking off with everything and, without him, he would not have even known Ozzy existed. That meant Jimmy owed him a slice of the very lucrative pie he was going to inherit from Ozzy.

Freddie felt hard done by. Here he was running all over the Smoke picking up money and sorting out problems in clubs, pubs and eateries, and where was Jimmy? Sitting on his ring, doing fuck all.

He stormed into a drinking club in Brixton that owed them a weekly take, and saw Glenford Prentiss standing at the bar. Glenford waved him over and Freddie forced a smile on to his face as he said happily, 'All right, all's well then, I take it?'

Glenford grinned. 'Always good me, and you?'

Freddie shrugged nonchalantly. 'All the better for seeing you. Want a drink?'

They were served immediately, and Glenford watched as Freddie downed the large whisky he had ordered in one large gulp. He was given another one straightaway.

'You needed that, eh?' Glenford was sipping his own drink, a pint of Draught Guinness, and savouring it.

'Wouldn't you if you were me?' Freddie looked annoyed.

Glenford didn't answer him, he was not getting involved in any kind of conversation that revolved around slagging off Jimmy, work, or anything else, other than the mundane and the fucking boring.

'Seen anything of Jimmy?'

Glenford nodded. ' 'Course, he is my friend.' He could see that the answer was not what Freddie had wanted to hear.

Freddie didn't respond to him. He sipped at his Scotch and his scowl was once more back in evidence.

Freddie and Jimmy were so alike, and yet so different. Freddie, he noticed, looked good for his age, but he had that petulant look about him that was peculiar to white men. It was odd, but there were a lot of disappointed-looking white men walking around. It was mad, but it was a fact.

Freddie had that look. He was a big man, with a big, powerful physique, and that was what made him look so disaffected. He was still handsome, still had the look that women loved. Glenford had seen the man in action and he had to take his hat off to him. But Freddie's disposition meant that no matter what he got, he would never be happy.

It was a shame, because he had been given more opportunities than most men could even hope for.

Freddie was now eyeing up a girl at the end of the bar. She was mixed race, in her early twenties and Glenford had considered giving her the old Prentiss charm. But he watched in admiration as Freddie turned from morose and scowling to cheerful and carefree. Skirt could do that to a man, and Freddie was only happy when he was conquering someone or something.

Seeing him now, with his smiling face and his jokey voice, he knew no one would believe that this was the same man who had walked in not ten minutes ago looking fit to be tied and up for a fight. It was like a miracle, and the girl was thrilled with herself.

Glenford toyed with the idea of telling the girl what to expect, how Freddie would romance her, bed her and then own her until he got fed up. But she was already walking towards them with a huge grin and a sultry swagger, and he decided to let her find all that out for herself.

So he drank his beer and listened with half an ear until Freddie finally went in for the kill.

'Oh Jimmy, it's beautiful.'

Maggie stared in awe at the watch her husband had presented her with. It was a gold Rolex, and she loved it. She had wanted one for a while, and now she had it and she was absolutely delighted with it.

She snapped open her Cartier and dropped it on to the dressing table, and she allowed Jimmy to place her new timepiece on to her wrist.

'Oh my God, what is this for?'

He shrugged, then kissed her tenderly, and once more he marvelled because she wasn't trying to move away from him. 'It's because I love you, Mags, and I always will.'

He was so earnest she wanted to cry.

Jimmy Junior ran into the room and he was laughing loudly. 'I saw you kissing!' He was all embarrassed and they both laughed with him.

Jimmy picked him up effortlessly and placed him on his shoulders. 'Come on, my little man, let's get you to Nana's, eh?'

They all walked down the stairs together and their laughing and chattering echoed around the house. Jimmy was so happy to hear it and that his family was mended and healed that he felt the urge to cry. Instead, he grabbed his wife's hand and, still holding on to his little son, he started them all off singing.

'One man went to mow . . .'

It was his son's favourite song, and as they walked from the house the sound was ringing in his ears. Especially Jimmy Junior's laughter. He had a dear little giggle that was so cute, and it proved he had a real good sense of humour too.

He was blessed. His life was perfect, and his family were perfect. What more could any man want?

'Will you be all right with these two, Joe, if I pop over Sylvie's?'

He nodded, his eyes glued to the TV, just like his elder grandson's. Little Freddie had joined them after tea, and played nicely with his cousin until bedtime.

'You go, Lena, and leave them with me, girl.'

She slipped on a cardigan and crept from the flat. Sylvie was always up for a laugh and she was fed up with Joe and his bloody telly programmes. Jimmy Junior was dead to the world, and now Little Freddie was sitting with his granddad like a little angel – not a phrase she had ever thought she would use about him – and she was going to have a nice cuppa and a good old gossip.

At the next ad break, Little Freddie stood up. 'Can I use the loo, Granddad?'

''Course you can, you silly little sod.' Joe smiled at the change in the boy. Imagine asking to use the loo.

He was still glued to the TV an hour later when Jackie came by to pick her son up. She was drunk, and she was also belligerent.

Lena arrived just after her daughter. She could hear her strident voice through the front door, and she hoped she didn't wake that little child with her noisy carrying on.

Jackie was stoned out of her mind, and on one level she knew that she should not be in her mother's shouting the odds, but she could not stop herself. Freddie had told her in no uncertain terms that Jimmy and Maggie had walked away with his job, that her sister and her family had all conspired against him, and that she was nothing but a drunken whore and she could expect him when she finally saw him.

She knew he was annoyed with her for being so drunk and he was taking his anger out on her, but she was determined to make *someone* listen to what she had to say.

'Will you keep your fucking voice down, Jackie. That little boy is asleep.'

Jackie looked at her mother through unfocused eyes and she said in a stage whisper, 'Oh, fucking hell, mustn't wake Maggie's baby, eh? You never fucking had mine round here, did you?'

Lena sighed. 'I had your girls all the time, Jackie, remember? They practically lived here at one point. Now either calm down or fuck off home. I ain't in the mood for you tonight.'

Jackie looked awful. Her hair was matted where she had slept on it all afternoon, and her make-up was streaked over her face. She was dressed like a refugee, and she was up for a fight.

Well, Lena and Joe were determined to see that she did not get one.

Joe motioned with his head and Lena nodded. He was getting his coat to walk Jackie home. This was a running joke now. Tomorrow she would have no memory of this whatsoever, but for now Lena had to try to calm her down.

Little Freddie was standing there watching her, and for the first time ever Lena felt a twinge of pity for him. No wonder he was like he was, with this sorry excuse for a mother and that ponce Freddie as a father.

'You are wankers, you and my dad. Nothing but fucking wankers.' Jackie was pointing at her mother now, poking a grubby finger into her face.

'Stop this, Jackie, stop it. Why do you do this?' She was trying to walk her towards the front door, but Jackie was so unsteady on her feet Lena was convinced her daughter was going to fall over and hurt herself.

Little Freddie was attempting to help his mother stand upright when she pushed him away from her and shouted, 'You are trying to send me away again, ain't you? You don't want me or mine here, you don't care about us. It's all about Maggie, ain't it? I can count on one hand the amount of times you've been round my house, but I come here every day, every day I come to see you. Well, not any more, you can all fuck off now. My Freddie was right all along, none of you care about me. None of you.'

She was on a roll now, gesturing madly with her arms, and Lena watched her eldest child in abject sorrow. No wonder the girls were never home, no wonder they avoided her like the plague. At this moment she could even find it in her heart to sympathise with Freddie, because Jackie couldn't be the easiest of people to live with.

Jackie screwed her face up in hate, and spewed out her vitriol and her anger while all the time being led out of the flat. Joseph had the front door open and he was dressed for the outdoors. When Jackie saw him standing there, she laughed out loud.

'Oh, here we go, the big guns are out, are they? Walking me home, are you, Dad? Making sure I don't stay here with you pair of fucking tossers.'

Little Freddie helped his mother out of the door. He was holding her up now, and Lena watched them go down the stairs until finally she could shut her front door. She knew that her neighbours had heard Jackie's ranting and raving, and she felt angry and upset.

She sat at her little kitchen table and put her head into her hands in utter despair. This was happening more and more, and she knew that something would have to be done before that girl drank herself into an early grave.

No wonder that boy was a mad bastard. What had he ever had in his life that was constant, that was good? She had a memory, suddenly, of Little Freddie as a baby, only about eighteen months old. Jackie was half cut as usual and she was saying to the boy, 'Here, Freds, phone Daddy.'

And the child had picked up the phone and said over and over again, 'Tunt, tunt.'

He could not say 'cunt' yet, but Jackie had rolled up.

Joseph had said to her then, all those years ago, 'God help that child, Lena. Between the two of them he has no fucking chance.'

And he had been right.

Chapter Twenty-Three

'I have never felt more happy in my life, Jimmy.'

His wife was relaxed, so liquid in his arms, that he felt as if he had been given a second chance at happiness. In the last couple of years she had gradually become again the girl he had known, the woman he had always needed.

Last night had been one of the most fulfilling nights of his life. His Mags had given herself to him with such forcefulness he had been amazed. All the hurt, all the distance was gone, and this was a new beginning for them, a new start to a marriage that even at its worst was better than anything else he could imagine.

He kissed her gently on the lips and she snuggled closer to him.

It was so long since Maggie had felt this calm, this happy, and she wanted the feeling to last as long as possible.

Jimmy held his tiny wife in his arms and marvelled at the change in her. Whatever had ailed her after Jimmy Junior was born, it seemed it was finally gone, and the laughing, happy girl he had married was back for good. Just to hold her like this was wonderful, to feel her soft skin next to his, to smell her perfume.

Unlike Freddie, and even Glenford, birds had never been a top priority with him and he had never really wanted anyone other than Maggie. He had taken a few fliers over the years but they were few and far between and he had regretted them immediately. No other woman had ever made him feel like his Mags did. And Little Jimmy was like the icing on the cake. He was their world, and they would see that he had everything that they had never had.

'So is Ozzy giving all his businesses over you, then?'

Jimmy kissed her again. 'It seems like it, but he ain't *giving* them to me as such, though Freddie won't believe that. I am just going to run them all for him. Like I do with all the other businesses.'

'He must really trust you, Jim.'

He smiled then. 'I hope so, babe, he ain't never had any reason not to.'

He was so dependable, her Jim, no one would ever say a bad thing about him because he was as right as the mail, as her mum always pointed out.

'What's he like?'

'Who, Ozzy?'

'Well, who else, you twonk!'

He shrugged, and hugged her even tighter, laughing at her as she knew he would.

'I told you, he's . . . different. He's sort of very much his own person, and when you are in his company you know he is someone of repute, someone important.'

Maggie could hear the pride in her husband's voice and she thought it was probably this self-effacing way he had that made Ozzy think so much of him.

'He sees you like I do, Jimmy, as a handsome, clever and kind man.'

Jimmy laughed. 'I think he sees a different side to me actually, but I will take your word for it.'

They laughed together. The hard-nosed Jimmy she rarely saw, and she was glad of that. But she knew it existed, and she had heard about his escapades, knew he was capable of violence if necessary. She knew he would use his considerable strength but only when all else failed. He was not a vindictive man, and she was lucky in that respect. But he was a serious Face in their community and she must bask in his reflected glory whether she wanted to or not. Jimmy had taken out enemies on more than one occasion, she accepted that. But he had to do it, that was what Ozzy expected from him and what he paid him for.

Brought up as she had been on the periphery of that world, she understood it was nothing more than a means to an end. It paid for their life, made sure they were taken care of. It was, after all, his chosen profession and his prerogative.

When he came home, though, he was just Jimmy, her Jimmy, and he was a husband and father. And she loved this man so deeply, nothing could change her feelings for him, no matter what he did.

He was also popular, not just with their close friends, but with everyone they mixed with, except, of course, Freddie. She forced Freddie from her mind, he had no place here, not any longer. He had spent too much time like a spectre between them. She would not allow him to hurt her or her family ever again.

It had taken her far too long to realise that her mother's old saying was true: 'People only do to you what you let them.' How many times had she heard that over the years?

As long as she let Freddie dictate her happiness, she was never going to experience any. Now she had fronted him, made *him* frightened of the truth coming out, and she felt almost euphoric in her happiness.

Jimmy Junior was, when all was said and done, *her* child. Hers, and her Jimmy's. They adored him, and no matter what anyone said, or anyone did, they could not take that away from them.

She glanced at the clock and saw it was eight thirty. They had slept in for the first time in years, and she had enjoyed it as well. She missed her baby, though. He had taken to coming in to them first thing and getting a few cuddles before they all got up and ate breakfast together.

It seemed strange without him, but she yawned happily. She had better get her arse in gear and go and pick him up. But Jimmy's hand on her breast told her that she might be longer than she had first thought.

'You what?'

Rox sighed, and said again, 'I am pregnant, Mum.'

Jackie was bleary-eyed as usual, and Rox wondered why she had come round to this house on her way to work when the woman she called her mother didn't even function until after three o'clock.

'The wedding is being brought forward, that is what I am trying to tell you.'

Jackie yawned and searched through the legion of empty fag packets on the kitchen worktops until she found a cigarette. Lighting one she said sarcastically, 'Oh, well. I'll sleep better for knowing that, Rox.'

Roxanna closed her eyes in annoyance. No congratulations, nothing.

Freddie padded down the stairs and Roxanna smiled at him. It was a forced smile as always and he said tiredly, 'So, Dicky boy has been rogering my baby, eh?'

Rox was hurt by her father's words. And her own mother had no interest in what was going on in her life, but then, when had she ever been interested in anything other than drinking and this big twit who was allegedly her father?

'So, and?'

Freddie took the cigarette from his wife and pulled on it deeply before saying, 'Always got a fucking answer, ain't you? Suppose I decide to take umbrage, eh? Give him a fucking kicking, what would you do then?'

Rox shook her head sadly and he was reminded of just how good looking his daughter was. She was so like Maggie, thank fuck, and not the fat whore who was now eating a slice of day-old pizza. In his own way he was proud of his Rox. Considering the way she had been dragged up she was a fucking diamond, really.

'Here, Fred, I just realised you'll be a fucking granddad!'

Jackie's laughter turned to a hacking cough and she spat into the sink. The scene made Rox, with her morning sickness, feel like heaving.

She flapped her hand at her mother. 'You are like a fucking animal, Mum.'

'Yeah, look around you, Rox, you were all dragged up in her den of shit!' Freddie was laughing now, but he shocked them as he hugged his daughter briefly, pleased she was going to have a child, pleased that she had turned out so well. Suddenly that was important to him.

He was proud of her. People talked about her in glowing terms, and he was impressed that she had made such a success of her young life. Considering how she had been brought up it was amazing she wasn't on to her second or even third baby by now, he knew a lot of her mates were. He should know, he had fucked half of them.

She could do a lot worse than young Dicky and all. The boy always gave him his due and was respectful and polite.

But if he ever mugged her off he would put the little fucker in his place, no danger.

Freddie went into the lounge and, picking up his coat, he took out a wad of money and peeled off five hundred pounds. He walked back to the kitchen and said almost shyly, 'Open an account up for it, babe, so it'll have a start in life. That is what Mags and Jimmy did and that kid's worth a fucking fortune now.'

Jackie and Roxanna looked at the man who had been the thorn in their sides for so long that they had forgotten how to like him, and their mouths were open and their eyes were round.

Rox saw the confusion in his eyes, and she knew it was mirrored in her own. Of all the things she had expected this morning, this was not one of them.

'Fucking hell, thanks, Dad.'

She was on the verge of tears, and for the first time in years Freddie understood what a small act of kindness could accomplish.

Rox hugged him back then, and he smelled the cleanliness of her, smelled her happiness and he also felt the love of a child he had never really taken any notice of.

She was a good girl, his Roxanna. He suddenly knew that they were *all* good girls really. Even his Kimberley, and especially his Dianna.

Why did he never appreciate that fact before?

'He must still be dead to the world, him, it's nearly nine o'clock!'

Joe's voice was high and Lena grinned. Joe loved that little child and she knew the feeling was reciprocated, since Jimmy Junior would listen to his old crap for hours.

'Go and wake him up, then, you rotten old sod. You know how much he likes his kip.'

'Have you done him his boiled egg and soldiers?'

She turned from the draining board where she was cutting the bread and butter into thin strips.

''Course I have. He would do 'is crust if they weren't waiting for him!'

Joe laughed with her. They were happy these days and it was mostly because of that little child. Maggie's postnatal depression had meant they had been privileged to be a very big part of his little life, and they were grateful for that.

'Go and get him, Joe, and I'll make him his cup of tea. He loves his cuppa in the morning does our little man.'

Lena watched as her husband raced off to wake their grandson. She would have let him sleep, he loved his Sooty and Sweep, bless him.

Little Freddie sat with his father and ate his cereal. Freddie watched as his son shoved the Coco Pops into his mouth with no manners whatsoever. He was too busy watching *Mighty Morphin Power Rangers* on Sky. Jackie was pretending to drink black tea, which he knew was sherry, because the smell was overpowering, and the house reminded him of a fucking rubbish tip. There were overflowing ashtrays, the curtains were half drawn as they were most of the time, and the feel of decay was everywhere. He had spent fortunes on this drum and it was still like a fucking squat.

An advert came on the TV and there was a lovely family, with lovely kids. They were being urged to borrow money, but as they sat there, eating toast and jam and being nice to each other, he knew that other than the poncing to pay off debts they shouldn't have had anyway, that was probably how Maggie and Jimmy acted first thing in the morning.

Jimmy Junior probably had egg on toast, or fresh fruit, they drank tea from a teapot and Jimmy probably read a paper that had been delivered by a smiling paper boy.

As he looked around his own home, he was suddenly pleased his Rox had got out of it all. He had seen her drum, it was clean and tidy and decorated to death.

She would pore over catalogues for hours just to find the right cushion, or the right blind. And he knew that if Maggie had not been in her life she would not have known about anything like that. Would never have realised that people like them were just as entitled as everyone else to have a nice home, a nice life.

Jackie cared about nothing, except maybe the drink and then him, and then Little Freddie, in that order. But Maggie and her fussy ways also angered him, and his daughters' utter adoration of her irritated him. He felt that she and Jimmy were living *his* life and it was this which made him so bitter.

'Eat properly, shut your fucking mouth!'

Little Freddie stared for long seconds at his father and then did as he was asked.

Jackie was still sitting on the sofa in her grubby dressing gown. She was smoking a cigarette and drinking her sherry out of a chipped white cup.

It took all his willpower not to kick off there and then, and smash her face in.

Joe was staring down at his grandchild and the tears were running down his face. This could not be happening, this could not he true, he had to be in a nightmare. His heart was pounding in his breast, and he was sure it would stop at any second. Wanted it to stop completely, so he would die and this scene would be wiped from his memory.

He was panting. He had wondered, briefly, if it was the

child breathing so heavily, wondered if it was the child making this awful wheezing noise but he knew that this child had not taken a breath for a long time.

His little face, when he had pulled the quilt back and seen it, had been the single most terrifying thing he had ever experienced.

He was so small, so small and so stiff and he was all wrong. He was lying all wrong, and they had slept in the room next door all night, and this little child had been dead. They had not gone in to tuck him in because he was such a light sleeper and as Jackie had been round causing ructions, they had left him. Left him alone, and he was dead.

He had tiptoed in and seen the little lump in the bed and then closed the door on him, his little grandson, the light of his life, and the reason his Lena got up in the morning.

Why hadn't he gone to him then? Looked at him properly and made sure the child was all right?

He was clutching his chest, and he felt the pain in his fingers.

'Hurry up, your egg's getting cold! What are you two doing?'

It was Lena's voice that finally made him move. Lena's happy voice, Lena, the woman he had hurt so much over the years and who he knew he could never be without. It was her, and the thought of her seeing this, that made him move at last.

Joe left the room and shut the door behind him.

She was in the hallway when he walked outside and she saw the tears on his face. 'What's going on, where's me boy?' Her voice was harsh, high and she was looking concerned, frightened.

He was shaking his head.

'What's wrong, you stupid old fucker, where is me little man, me little fella?'

He could feel the fear coming off her in waves, hear it in her voice.

'Let me see him, get out of my way . . .'

He was holding her now, struggling with her, making her stay outside, stopping her seeing what he had seen. The sight would kill her, he knew it would.

She was staring into his eyes now, and he was holding her by the forearms, afraid to let her go in case she went into the room, the mausoleum that was now holding the body of their dead grandchild.

'You're frightening me, Joe, *stop* it. Let me see me boy, please, Joe . . . *Please* . . .'

She was crying now, she was almost hysterical, and still he could not answer her. She was begging him, begging him to tell her everything was OK, and he couldn't.

How did you tell someone you loved about something like this?

Where the fuck did you even start?

Freddie sat beside Jimmy and watched his cousin's grief. It was so awful to witness another man's complete desolation. And he was feeling the same way. He was feeling the loss as acutely as Jimmy but he couldn't tell him that.

They had been together in the car and he was taking stick about being a granddad and they were laughing together, like they used to before. Then the call had come, and he had watched in amazement as Jimmy had swerved the car across the road before dropping the mobile, parking, and then starting to cry.

'What on earth has happened?'

He had for a few moments hoped that Ozzy was dead, that Ozzy had been wiped out but he also knew that that happening would not cause this kind of grief. It had to be Maggie, and he thought that she might have crashed her car, that fucking flash Merc she swanned around in. Or, at the least, that she had experienced an accident of some sort.

Freddie had nearly passed out, when after what seemed an age, Jimmy had turned to him and said brokenly, 'It's Jimmy, my little Jimmy. He *died*, Freddie, he died last night.'

Then he had cried, loudly and painfully and he had punched the steering wheel, and then he had cried again and Freddie had sat beside him in shock and wondered what on earth could have killed a dear little boy like that.

And he was a dear little child, and he had used that child to destroy his mother and now he was dead. That dear little Jimmy, with the bright smile and the funny little ways, was dead.

The world had gone fucking mad.

Lena and Joe felt guilty, and as the hospital room filled up with the family they felt even worse. He had died in their care, he had died while they had slept in the room next door. How were they ever going to get over that, how would they ever sleep again? Know another happy day without that little boy beside them?

Maybe they could have helped him, maybe they could have avoided it happening if they had only checked on him.

Maggie was sitting there, and she had not said a word. Rox was holding her hand and trying to comfort her as best she could.

Dianna was crying with Kimberley, all the time shaking their heads in disbelief.

Jackie was smoking outside. The hospital was all no

smoking, and as always, she put her own needs first. She was watching the world go by, and every now and then she took a nip from the bottle of vodka she had placed in her large shopping bag.

A nurse walked into the visitors room and said quietly, 'Can I get you some more tea?'

Lena nodded. Tea gave you something to do, it made you move, made you respond, and she knew that as they were sitting there, Jimmy was on his way and she didn't want to face him, or his parents.

Jimmy's *parents*. As usual they had forgotten about them. Jimmy was more their family than his own. Since Freddie Senior's death, no one really saw them any more, least of all Jimmy.

'Has anyone phoned Jimmy's family?'

No one answered.

She sighed. They would know soon enough, why break their hearts before you had to?

Freddie and Jimmy were walking into the hospital when Jackie called out to her husband. He squeezed Jimmy's arm and walked over to his wife.

She walked him away from the busy doorway of the A and E and lit a cigarette. He saw she was pissed, but for once this didn't bother him. He was still in shock about the child dying.

This was *his* child, his boy, not Jimmy's, his, and he was dead. The thought had been careering around his head for what seemed like years and was in reality only minutes.

Jackie was really crying, sobbing, and he couldn't be angry with her. 'Ain't it terrible, Fred? How lucky are we, eh? Our Little Freddie might be a fucker, but imagine if he died.'

She was crying loudly, and she was in pain and he knew

how she felt, so he instinctively held her to him. Even Freddie knew she was crying this time with just cause. They clung together for the first time in years.

'My poor Maggie, she looks like a fucking corpse herself. What a thing to have to go through! What a thing to have to *live* with!'

'What happened, Jack, do they know yet?'

Jackie looked up at her husband and said, her voice cracking, 'Don't you know, Freddie?'

He shook his head. 'No, what happened?'

'He put a plastic bag over his head, and he suffocated.'

Glenford arrived at the hospital and went straight to Jimmy. He pulled him into his embrace and Jimmy broke down crying. It was strange watching the little man holding on to Jimmy. Jimmy was huge, and his shaking shoulders just made it look all the more outrageous.

Glenford was crying with him and as Maggie watched she envied them that closeness, because Jimmy deserved that comfort. Unlike her, Jimmy had nothing on his conscience where that little boy was concerned.

Nobody else in the room did. But she was eaten up with guilt, seeing him, seeing him so small and so vulnerable and knowing he was never going to open his eyes and smile and laugh, never going to hug her again. The guilt was too much for her to bear.

All the time she had tolerated him, because she had kept a secret that she had felt was like a lead weight inside her chest. And now it was all over, and instead of relief, which is what she had yearned for all those years, she felt a deep and agonising hatred for herself.

Her poor mother and father had aged in hours. She saw the way her mother kept picking at her sodden tissues, how her eyes kept darting around the room as she waited for someone to accuse her over what had happened, and she knew that the poor woman blamed herself.

The same woman who had loved Jimmy Junior when his own mother had been incapable of it, who had shouted and argued with her, called her unnatural, and who had tried to make his short little life as bearable as she could, knowing that his own mother found it impossible to care for him.

And Jackie, Jackie kept on and on about her Rox having a baby, and how when God closed one door another one opened. The stupid drunken bitch had four kids and she cared for none of them, not really. She was like all drunks, she only cared about herself and how she felt and what she wanted. Her life was about her and Freddie, and she had spent years trying to gain the love of a man who despised her.

Freddie had destroyed her and he had destroyed her sister and she knew he had enjoyed every second of it.

She wondered, then, if he was feeling the loss of the little boy he had used as a weapon against her. Wondered if he was feeling remorse about all the years he had caused her so much heartache. She hoped that bastard never knew another happy day, she hoped all his kids died and he had to sit in a hospital knowing their lifeless bodies were feet away and he could never again touch them or love them.

But where was Freddie now, anyway? He had not been in this place and why would she expect any different? She wanted to kill him, scratch his eyes out, make him pay for the way he had caused her to feel about a child of her own body.

A child who was now dead and gone to her. Now she would never be able to make up to him for the first years of his life, when even feeding him had been anathema to her. But she had loved him, she had just been frightened of him and what he could cause if the truth of his conception had ever come out.

Now she would shout it from the roof tops and take the consequences with a light heart if he was only still with her.

Jimmy knelt in front of her and she put her head on his shoulder and finally cried, really cried. And once it started she couldn't make it stop. She could hear herself screaming but it sounded like someone else, as if someone else had taken over her body because that shrieking couldn't be coming from her, surely?

And when the doctor finally slipped the needle into her arm, she was so thankful for the oblivion she knew would come that she hoped to God she never woke up again.

Why would her little son put a bag over his head? Why would he do something like that and what on earth would possess him to want to do something like that?

Those were her last conscious thoughts.

Jimmy and Glenford sat in the darkened room and watched as Maggie's chest rose and fell softly. She looked so peaceful that he envied her.

He had held his little boy in his arms for long minutes and kissed his little forehead, and Glenford had cried with him, and they had both sat there in absolute shock and horror at what had befallen him and his family.

Glenford had not tried to talk, he had sat beside Jimmy and he had just been there. It was all he could do now, be there for the man he had come to love and respect as a friend and as a brother over the last fifteen years. But he had wondered over and over again why Freddie wasn't here with them, why Freddie had left the hospital and not come back?

The one time in his life he would have laid money on Freddie Jackson doing the right thing, and he had been wrong.

Jimmy needed him now, more than he had ever needed anyone in his life. Even a selfish shite like Freddie had to at least understand that much. And Jimmy had not even asked for him, it was as if he knew that Freddie would not be there. It was weird, as if Freddie not showing up was *expected*, even.

This was a sad and deeply odd day and Glenford prayed to God that he never had to experience anything even remotely like it in his own lifetime.

Little Freddie was on his game console when the front door opened. He didn't hear it, he was too busy killing the characters on the TV screen.

He was enjoying having the house to himself. He had not bothered to go to school as was usual. He was suspended again anyway, so he had popped round to his mates, who were also suspended, and relished telling them his news, and then he had come back and gone straight on his new game.

He hated the smell of the carpet, but he was used to it, though every now and again the stink of cigarettes from the overflowing ashtray near him made him wrinkle up his nose. He had a bowl of treats, and a large glass of orange juice that he had laced liberally with his mother's stash of vodka. She was buying it by the case these days off a geezer who lived nearby, and who did the Frog run to Calais once a month for drink and fags.

He was happy, relaxed and he was pleased with himself.

On his way home from his friends' he had pinched a few goodies from the local Indian shop. The man there was new and Little Freddie was always nice and polite to him. He had no idea the lad was smiling away while robbing him blind.

People were such fucking *marks.* His dad had always said that and it was true. People never expected you to be bad, they expected you to be like them. Nice and friendly and talkative, they wanted you to *care* about them, *care* about their feelings and their fucking boring lives.

But who wanted to be like them?

Who wanted to be fucking no necks all their lives?

Fear was a useful tool, and he had seen that over and over again in his young life. His father ruled everyone around him through fear, and it was a dangerous weapon. Kids at school had learned about fear sooner rather than later, he had seen to that, and it had taken him a long way in his little life.

He took anything he wanted from them, and they gave it gladly.

He was his father's son, and he was proud of that, but only because he admired the way his father used everyone around him. How his name had guaranteed this boy a pass from almost everything he had ever done.

He looked up then and saw his father in the doorway. As they looked into each other's eyes, Freddie Junior knew that he was in deep shit.

Chapter Twenty-Four

Jimmy had told Glenford to go home, but Glenford was going nowhere. He was staying outside the room where Jimmy was sitting with his wife, trying to make sense of the day's events.

He felt as if he was on guard, was looking out for Jimmy, but he didn't know why he should feel that, or even what he was supposed to be looking out *for*. He had this mission come over him, and it was to take care of Jimmy.

There was something he was not telling anyone, and Glenford could feel that inside himself. Glenford felt sure that whatever Jimmy was holding back was so explosive that, if he let it go, it would reverberate through the whole of their world. But if he needed to let it go, then he would be waiting here for his friend.

It was respect, it was friendship, and it was all he knew to do that would be useful at this terrible time. If Jimmy needed someone, he would be there, on hand. That was what he wanted to do.

He could feel his pain and he wished he could take it from him even if only for a while.

He had popped out to his car and made a few calls,

alerting everyone to the tragedy that had befallen Jimmy and his family, and then after a quick toot on his pipe he had come straight back inside.

He loved Jimmy, but he had never realised just how much until this had happened. It was like some kind of revelation he had experienced. He knew now that he loved Jimmy Jackson more than his own kin, more than his own family. Jimmy had been more to him, after all was said and done, than anyone else in his world.

He *loved* the man, and why shouldn't he? Jimmy had always been there for him. In fact they had always been there for each other.

And Glenford could not leave him. He didn't know why, but he could not leave him alone this night. That would have been far too *cold*, almost *unreasonable*, and if Jimmy went off at any point, then he would be sitting nearby, waiting to stop him going overboard. He knew that at some point Jimmy was going to lose his mind, and when that happened, he would be there for him.

It was dark when Freddie finally walked into the hospital, and Glenford, who had never been his biggest fan, was shocked at the look of him. He was bedraggled, he was grey-faced and he was obviously in great pain, not so much physical as emotional.

He had been crying, that much was evident. In fact he looked devastated, and that was something Glenford had not been expecting.

So he found himself standing up and saying gently, 'You all right, man?'

Freddie sat down beside him, and putting his head in his hands he said, 'No, no, I'm not, Glenford. How is he?'

Glenford rubbed a hand over his face. 'How would

you be if it was you? The man is completely and utterly disrupted. His life is finished. I never seen him look so bad before. He is on the edge.'

Freddie knew he was speaking the truth, knew he was telling him the score.

'Has he said anything?'

'About the boy? Nothing, really. I think he's in shock . . .' He sighed. 'I feel like he's keeping something back. It's weird but he's all off kilter. You know what I mean?'

'I know exactly what you mean, Glenford.'

It was a strange answer. Something was seriously wrong and Glenford Prentiss could not shake off the feeling that both Freddie and Jimmy had another completely separate agenda.

'How's Maggie?'

Glenford smiled sadly. 'She been sedated, she be out for the night, and me envy her, Fred, because that child dying has been like a bomb going off among them all. And you know something? I wouldn't be any of they, for all the money in the world. Maggie's mum and dad can't believe him would do something like that, you know. The police were called in of course, but I think they see a tragic accident. What else could it be?'

Glenford sighed heavily once more. 'Why would a little child *want* to do that to himself? Him just playing, kids so fucking dangerous, you know. It make no sense what they doing, they just kids.' He could hear the upset in his own voice and coughed harshly. 'The bag was stuck to his little face. What a fucking thing to have to live with, that sight, what a fucking sad and terrible situation for any parents.'

'What did the filth do?' Freddie made his voice as neutral as he could.

Glenford shrugged. 'Who know what they thinking,

fucking scum they are? But they look at everyone and you could see they sorry as anyone else. It was an accident, a tragic accident.'

Freddie didn't answer him. He didn't know what to say.

Instead he walked into the room where Jimmy sat beside his silent, shattered wife, and quietly shut the door behind him.

Jackie was drunk, drunker than she had been in years. But she didn't want to be sober, and as she watched her daughters drinking with her, drowning out the awful knowledge of that child and the way he died, she knew that they finally understood her attitude on life.

Paul and Liselle were serving up the drinks. It was very rare that this lot drank in their pub, but tonight, they knew, was not the usual. Freddie had rarely allowed Jackie inside what he saw as his bastion of maleness, and when he had, it was always a quick visit. But tonight, they were in for the long haul, they were not going anywhere.

Poor Jimmy and Mags, what a thing to happen to them. Liselle and Paul were both devastated at the news, and that was why they were serving this lot up free gratis.

Liselle remembered all the times Jimmy had brought the boy in for a few minutes. He had been showing him off really, and Liselle understood that. He had been such a proud father, and he had taken that boy out with him as often as he could.

He doted on him, and everyone knew about poor Maggie. She had been rough after his birth and it had taken her a long time to get back on her feet. Jimmy had taken on the burden of the child without a second's thought. They had finally got back to normal, were a happy little family and then this had to come on top. What a fucking thing to happen to anyone. She was so sorry for them, they were a lovely couple.

The thought of that poor child being dead was more than anybody could bear. The whole place was in silent mourning, except when Jackie Jackson's big trap was flapping of course.

Liselle and Jackie had never got on. Liselle loathed her, whereas she loved Mags. And Jackie had been convinced for years that Liselle had something going with Freddie. Poor Jackie thought that about most women at some time or another, but this knowledge did not stop Jackie getting on Liselle's tits.

Paul thought it was hilarious. Well, good for him, but she was just about on the verge of giving Jackie Jackson a slap. That child was on his way to the grave and she was using him as an excuse to cause aggravation.

For once she was not putting up with it.

The girls, though, were lovely. They were doing their best to keep their mother on an even keel, but one more remark and she was going to start the Third World War.

This place was a private drinking hole, a members' only pub if you like. It was used by specific people and that was its main attraction. Liselle felt now, looking at Jackie and hearing her bloody miserable voice, that Freddie for all his faults needed a bolt hole from this fucking drunken pig who was still trying to cause a row with her after twenty years. Like she would touch Freddie Jackson with a barge pole!

Jackie and her company were not paying for their drinks and she was all right with that, why wouldn't she be? But Jackie was acting like this was her due, like this was her manor and this was her local. Well, Liselle was drinking as well, an unusual occurrence for her, and she was up for a fight herself tonight. She needed to get a few things out of her system, off her chest.

Watching his Liselle eyeing Jackie, Paul could feel the tension rising in the room. Then Patricia O'Malley walked in and he sighed and relaxed.

If there was going to be a tear up, he hoped it would be with Pat and Jackie, and not his old woman, because Jackie was going to have a *fight*. It was not about *when* or even *if*, it was more a case of with *whom*.

Roxanna watched as Pat came in the pub, and she hoped her mother was going to keep a lid on it. She knew about her dad and Pat, everyone did. And Pat, in fairness, was a nice woman who had always been friendly towards her and her sisters.

And Rox understood her father's attraction for this woman, as she understood his attraction for her. Pat was so in your face, so strong-minded, and so independent she knew that she must do her dad's head in.

Rox was shrewd enough to know that it was also what made him want her. Pat was like a man in some respects, she used men like most men used women.

Good luck to her and all, she had the right idea.

Rox admired Pat and her way of life. Even though she knew her mother would muller her for thinking it, when she saw Pat, which she did a lot because of Dicky and the fact they drank here weekends, she thought she looked great. And when she talked to her, which she had been really wary about doing at first, she had found Pat was so with it, so on the ball and so funny that she had forgotten about her mother's very genuine grievance. And she also knew that Pat gave her father something her mother never would or even could. And that something was plain and simple. She gave him normality.

She was the only woman who could treat him like he treated every woman he had ever come across and get away with it. Consequently, he respected her. She took no shit from anyone and she looked fantastic for her age.

Roxanna actually looked up to her.

Now she was interested to see how her mother coped with being in the same room with her biggest rival. But then, her mother was gone as always, she was completely out of her brains and as Rox watched her she understood for the first time both why her father stayed around, *and* more to the point, why he played away from home.

Sipping her tonic water, she watched the different little plays that were being acted out in front of her. Jackie had all but forgotten about poor little Jimmy. She was just drinking now because it was *there*, and she had taken some coke, because it was *there*. Her mother was nutting it now, she was rocking. She had seen her like this so many times as a kid, and now she didn't even get annoyed any more.

Her own child would have so much more than that from its mother, she was sure. She was going to be there for it, like Mags and Jimmy had been there for their little man. She rubbed her belly, and imagined giving birth to a child and then losing it. As her granny had said in the hospital, it was the wrong order. You should never have to bury a child. They should be the ones to bury you.

Pat had said her hellos. She had hoped to see Freddie but he wasn't here and his wife was, as always on their occasional meetings, giving her the long look.

Like she gave a flying fuck.

But she liked the girls. They were good kids, despite being spawned by the dirty bitch with the grubby feet and the bloated body. She knew her place, though, so she said, in as friendly a manner as she could, 'All right, Jackie. What a terrible thing to happen. My heart goes out to them.' Pat really meant it. 'Poor Mags, she must be in bits.'

Jackie watched her rival, saw her girls as they smiled and said hello to her and noticed how Paul and Liselle were all over her. Then she remembered this was Ozzy's sister, and in fairness, Pat was always nice to her, never rubbed her nose in it like some of his whores had tried over the years. She quite wanted to start a fight anyway, though she knew any trouble with Pat and she would be the one aimed out the door. She was enjoying being with her girls for once and Rox had just brought her another large vodka, so she said sadly, 'She is heartbroken, Pat, as you can imagine.'

Jackie was going to play this one nicely. After all, what would she gain this night from having a tear up? Freddie wasn't here and in her heart she actually liked old Pat.

Pat and the entire bar staff gave a collective sigh of relief.

'Do they know how it happened?'

Rox shrugged. 'It's kids, ain't it, but why he put that fucking plastic bag over his head we'll never know.'

Jackie agreed. 'They think everything's a game, don't they? They never understand at that age the dangers of life. But what a terrible thing to happen to any family.'

They were all nodding their heads sagely, and the girls caught each other's eyes, thankful Jackie was not on one of her mad benders. Yet.

'All right, Jim?' Freddie knew that nothing would ever be all right again, but it was just an expression. Something to say, an opening for conversation.

Jimmy nodded. He had aged in the last few hours and Freddie would lay money that his hair was greyer than it had been this morning. Being so dark they had both gone grey early, and their hair was so thick it looked good on them. They could carry it off, it made them look more manly, somehow.

Right now they looked more alike than ever, but that was mainly because they both looked deeply sad, both looked devastated. They had a secret, and this was the moment that they had to decide what they were going to do about it.

'I am so sorry, Jimmy. I swear that to you, mate.'

Jimmy didn't answer him.

'Please, Jimmy, say something. Please say something.' Freddie was begging, a first for him as Jimmy knew better than anyone.

Jimmy sighed and turned to face him, and when he finally spoke his voice was flat. 'I can't tell you what you want to hear, Fred. I am sorry, but I can't. You told me about him a long time ago, and I was sorry for you, really sorry. But this ain't a fucking rabbit or a neighbour's dog, bad as that was. This was my baby and I can't let this go. I am sorry, mate, but I can't.'

'I am sorting it, Jim, I swear.'

It was the word 'sorting' that did it. They were always sorting things. It was their job, what they did for a living. But you couldn't sort out the death of a child, a death that had been caused by another child.

Except Little Freddie wasn't a child, he never had been. He was an animal, a mad bastard. Until now Jimmy had not really cared about that, but then why should he? He was Freddie's son. Why would Jimmy have ever thought he could encroach on his own life and family like this?

That boy had been an accident waiting to happen, and now it was too late.

'What you going to do then, Freddie?'

Freddie was quiet. He was so quiet, it was as if he were a different person, as if all his life had been leading up to this moment. And who knew, thought Jimmy, maybe it had been.

'He'll be gone soon, I promise you. He'll be gone.'

Jimmy laughed half-heartedly. 'Gone, Freddie? In what way? Dead gone? What?'

Freddie was silent once more. He was trying to gather his thoughts but it was hard, so hard. He wished he had not snorted so much gear. It was point nine, the best you could get and he had been hoovering it up like it was going out of fashion.

'He can't help it, Jimmy. I told you that before, he can't help it.'

Jimmy dropped his wife's hand and it fell on to the bed with a soft thud. Then he grabbed Freddie by the scruff of his neck and pulled him towards him roughly so they were eye to eye, and he said through gritted teeth, 'You brought up an animal. Someone was going to pay for his madness in the end, and you knew that. I have sat here and remembered you learning him to swear, and learning him to fight, and it hit me what you did to him. That boy never had a chance, Freddie, you and Jackie made sure of that. You thought it was funny when he attacked his sisters, when he didn't sleep at night and watched those violent films all the time. You created him, and then suddenly he was a *big* kid and he wasn't so fucking funny any more, was he? He was in trouble with the school, with the courts, and you *still* didn't get him any help. You left him to it, and now he has killed my baby and you know he has.'

He threw Freddie away from him then, as if frightened to keep up any kind of contact with him. As if he was tainted.

'We don't know that for sure . . .'

Freddie was desperate to try to make some sense of it, find some other explanation.

Jimmy shook his head at Freddie's denial. 'Jimmy

Junior would never have dreamed of putting that bag on his head. Why would he? And it was *tied* there to keep it in place. The police will be back, Freddie, you know that because it was tied under his little chin. Joe told me that, because he was the one who ripped it off in the end to save Lena seeing it. The bag was stuck to his little face. That took *time*, Freddie. It was a fucking premeditated act. My little Jimmy couldn't tie his *shoelaces*, so how would he have managed to tie that bag up under his own little chin, eh? The *cunt*, why did he do it, Freddie? Why?'

He was nearly crying again. He was so angry and so sad and he was trying so hard to keep a lid on his emotions.

Freddie shook his head. 'I don't know, Jimmy, I really don't know.'

'You have a lot to answer for, you have *so* much to answer for, Freddie. *Stephanie. Lenny.* I gave you a pass every time, and now this is the upshot, ain't it? You and him are like two peas in a pod, you have no care for anyone or anything. It's only my Maggie lying here that is stopping me from screaming the truth from the roof tops, because she would never be able to cope with knowing what had *really* happened. I don't know if I can, either. All I do know at this moment in time is that Maggie must *never* know what happened, that her little boy had been forced to put that bag over his head. It would *kill* her. *I* can't handle it, Freddie. I keep picturing it in my mind. My little Jimmy would have trusted him, would have wanted to please him, he was *scared* of him. But I am warning you now. If I even catch a glimpse of your boy, he will know what fucking scared really is, because I will not be responsible for my actions.'

Freddie was crying silently and Jimmy could see him wiping away his tears, but he felt nothing for him or his suffering.

'I've sorted it, Jimmy, I swear to you that I've sorted it.'

Jimmy wanted to laugh again, but he didn't have one laugh in him, and he doubted that he ever would again. This wasn't something that could ever be sorted.

'Just go, Freddie, will you? I don't want to be around you any more.'

Freddie didn't argue with him, he stood up and walked quietly from the room. Jimmy didn't even bother to watch him go.

This was the end of his life, and his wife's life. Oh, they would carry on as normal eventually, they had to. It was what happened after something like this, but that would be it. They would be going through the motions, that was all. No more and no less.

Dianna was scared. She was still seeing her Danger Man and he was still mucking her about. She had slipped away to meet him and he had not arrived.

Now, here she was waiting by the side of the road in the dark and she felt certain that he was not going to turn up. He had done this to her before, and she should be in the pub with her family now, where she belonged. They had experienced a terrible tragedy and she should be with them, not out here waiting for a man who treated her like dirt. Terry Baker was like a drug. She needed him, wanted him and without him she felt as if she was nothing.

She had waited over an hour for him, and she had finally had enough. Now she just wanted to be back inside with her family, in the warmth of the pub and sharing their grief together. She was wrong to have left them at all.

She started to walk back slowly. Her heels were high and her feet were killing her, and she was nearly back at the pub when he pulled up.

She decided to ignore him. Just once, she felt she had the right to make him come after her. She walked inside with her head held high and her feet giving her serious gyp.

Terry Baker followed her inside, and it was the biggest mistake of his life.

Roxanna and Kimberley were talking about her pregnancy, and Kimberley was a little bit jealous, but only in a nice way. She envied her sister her life. Dicky was a real diamond and anyone with half a brain could see that he worshipped her sister. Kim didn't have a man. She was still trying to keep herself clean, make a life for herself and she was doing that well enough to please everyone.

The death of little Jimmy had made them all reassess their lives in one way or another and the girls were talking about Roxanna's baby because they couldn't discuss the tragedy any more. It was far too upsetting. The thought of poor Mags having to wake up and find out it was true was playing on both their minds. Dianna came back inside and they nudged one another. They knew Dianna had a fella, but no one could get anything out of her about him.

Jackie was completely gone, and she shouted out gaily, 'Here, Di, where you been, then?'

Dianna smiled and went over to her mother. She noticed that Patricia was also the worse for wear.

'I just popped out for some air, Mum, that's all.'

Jackie laughed her dirty laugh that annoyed the girls with its innuendo. 'Is that what they call it now, Pat? I've come up for air a few times. So have you and all, I bet, Freddie can go all night!!'

She was shrieking with mirth now and Dianna could have clumped her. Imagine her saying that to Pat, as if they were all girls together. Terry must have heard what she had implied about her own child too, and this upset her.

Pat laughed with Jackie as was expected, but she didn't really think it was funny. She had enough on her mind without listening to this crap, but she had to stay. She wanted to see Freddie, hear what had happened from him. She actually needed him for once and this was a real departure for her.

'Hello Terry!' Jackie's voice was loud, and it was friendly.

Terry Baker walked over to the bar and said jovially, 'Is that Jackie Summers as was?'

It had been so long since anyone had called her by her maiden name, and tonight Jackie was pleased to hear it. *Jackie Summers.*

It seemed like a lifetime since she had been called that.

'Terry Baker! As I live and breathe.' She looked round at her daughters to show them off. Now they were off her hands she enjoyed people seeing these good-looking girls of hers. She knew she had no right to take any of the credit at all really, but that didn't stop her.

'Here, girls, this was my first boyfriend. We was in the juniors and I went out with him to make your dad jealous.'

They were laughing together and Dianna wanted them to drop down dead, she wanted them to disappear. She could tell Jackie, her mother, had been on the okey doke, as Terry was himself. Like her mother, once he had snorted a few lines he got outrageous, he forgot what he was saying and, more to the point, who he was saying it to.

'Nice-looking girls, Jackie, but then you were a looker in your day, eh?'

Jackie ignored the inference that she was a bit battered

around the edges, and ordered more drinks for them. She liked Terry and he had been away for a long time on an armed robbery, so she allowed for him talking out of turn. Fifteen years with no one but a load of other men and his right arm could do that to a body, she knew.

Dianna was blushing and she was convinced everyone in the pub knew her secret. All she wanted now was for the floor to open up and swallow her.

'So what brings you here, then?'

Terry shrugged. 'Same thing as you, I assume. A drink, Jackie.'

Jackie smiled. 'Oh, we've been in here for a while—'

He interrupted her and said unpleasantly, 'I guessed that one, love, you're fucking well gone.' He laughed at his own joke. But no one was laughing with him.

Jackie was still unaware of the undercurrent around her, but Paul and Liselle were making eye contact. This could be more aggravation and they knew it.

'Have you heard, Tel?'

'Heard what, mate?' He was all ears now, pretending to be interested in what Jackie was saying, holding out his hands in a theatrical flourish.

Pat and the girls had picked up on him immediately. He was wacked out of his head and he was after a row, was looking for a scapegoat. He was disrespecting Jackie Jackson, and that alone said he had to be on a death wish.

Jackie, though, was oblivious to the fact he was taking the piss. It had not even occurred to her.

'Poor Jimmy Jackson lost his son today.'

Terry frowned as if the weight of the world was on his shoulders, and then he said sarcastically, 'And where did he lose him exactly, Jackie, in the public bogs? In the Amazon jungle, up Jack's arse and round the corner? Where?'

He was staring into her face and he was half smiling a nasty, sarcastic smile that was daring her to answer him.

It finally penetrated Jackie's brain that he was having a rise out of her. She was hurt, and she was upset. He had made a fool of her and she had not noticed it happening, but she knew now that everyone else had.

Dicky was watching carefully and she knew he was waiting to step in. But Terry was an old mate, why would he want to mug her off like that in front of everyone? He knew who her old man was, and to take the rise out of the child's dying would never be forgiven by any of the people within earshot, let alone Freddie and Jimmy when they heard about it. And they *would* hear about it.

She felt a hand gently guide her away from Terry.

'Why don't you take your drink and fuck off, mate, learn a bit of respect?' Dicky was fuming, he wasn't going to have this, especially not off an ice cream like Terry Baker.

Terry turned towards him and said menacingly, 'Why, are you going to make me, then?'

Dianna was mortified. Why was he doing this? Why was he causing all this trouble? She was on the verge of fainting with fright.

'With pleasure, mate. You want a fucking row, you just got one.' Dicky was well up for anything that was going now.

Jackie turned back.

'Stop it, Terry. What's the matter with you? What is your fucking problem?'

He looked at Jackie then and she saw complete and utter disgust in his face as he said loudly, 'Who are you then, Jackie? Who the fuck are you to ask me what's wrong?'

He was poking his finger at her now, and Jackie being

Jackie was not about to let him get away with taking the piss out of her, let alone slagging her off like she was *no one*.

As her arm came back to punch him, Patricia grabbed her and pulled her away, and then Dicky went in like a bulldog.

Paul had already cleared the glasses from the bar, and he jumped over it wielding a baseball bat, which he brought down on Terry's head with all the force he could muster. Dicky grabbed it off him and all hell was let loose.

A pole dancer and friend of Jackie's called Pat the Pole, or Pat Fletcher, had also been on the receiving end of Terry's vicious tongue and, being the type of woman she was, she was determined to join in the fray. She aimed a kick that unfortunately hit Dicky instead, knocking him flying. Her shapely legs were her prized asset, and more than one man was pleased to get an eyeful.

Pat's husband, Harry Fletcher, a market trader from Romford, was a man who knew how to look after himself. He prided himself on the fact that he was scared of no man; the only person he was even remotely scared of was Pat's mother, known to all and sundry as Nanny Donna. As Harry jumped in and tried to remove his wife from the middle of the fracas, a large young man called Richie Smith shouted out, 'Leave her to it, Harry, she'll do a fucking better job than you.'

Even Dicky was laughing as Richie helped Harry calm his wife down. Then he turned back to Terry Baker. Terry was about to get the hiding of his life, and no one watching the event, not even young Dianna, was willing to help him out.

Chapter Twenty-Five

Terry was lying on the filthy floor battered and bleeding, and against her better judgement Dianna went to him. As she tried to kneel on the floor beside him to give him some kind of comfort, Roxanna dragged her away roughly.

'Leave him, Di, for fuck's sake. He is a fucking muppet.' Her tone showed that she thought her sister had gone mad.

But look at him, Rox, he's in a right state.'

'Fucking right and all, so he should be.'

Rox's voice was hard and without any emotion whatsoever, and it occurred to Dianna that even though she professed to loathe their so-called father, Rox was actually more like him than she thought.

In fact, it was the loyalty factor that was kicking in, no more and no less.

Dianna could hear Terry groaning, knew he had to be in terrible pain and she didn't know what to do about any of it. *She* had caused all this. He had explained about her father hating him, and how Freddie had used him in the past. If she had only waited for him outside, if only she had not walked away from him like she had, this would never have happened. Now look at him. He would never forgive her, she knew that, and who could blame him?

His forearm was shattered, it was hanging loosely at the elbow. He had been trounced so badly that he would never be able to work again. He was covered in his own blood and even though they knew he would live, that would not guarantee him a pass once Freddie Jackson heard the full story.

Terry had to have been mad to even think he might get away with mugging off Freddie's kinfolk. Jackie Jackson was renowned as a piss head, a pill popper and a wanker, and that was just what her *friends* said about her in the comfort and safety of their own homes. But she *was* Freddie Jackson's wife, even if he only stuck around because of the boy. Jackie was off limits to anyone who valued their life, their family's lives, or their credibility.

Terry Baker must be off his trolley, but then, they had heard the stories about him. Gossip was, after all, their main conversational directive. It wasn't *classed* as gossip, of course, it was classed as tipping each other the wink, or giving out the nod. They dealt in *facts*, not women's chat.

Dicky was shaking with the anger and the excitement a real heavy tear up created in a body, especially when he was the undisputed victor. He gulped at the brandy handed to him by Paul, and he felt the friendly and respectful hand that squeezed his shoulder gently. Paul was telling him he had done the right thing.

As he looked at Rox he knew he had pleased this beautiful woman of his no end. She was made up with pride, and she was beaming at him now as he tried to calm himself down.

He had saved her mother's reputation, what was left of it anyway, and defended her honour. Whatever *she* might think of her mother privately, no one outside their tight-knit circle of family would ever hear it from her. Jackie was, after all, her mother. In their world that accounted for everything.

Dicky understood that way of thinking, and he would give Jackie her creds. His own mother had been on the game most of her life, and he respected her for that. He didn't *like* it, but he *understood* it. The grief he had taken as a child over her chosen, but ultimately lucrative, lifestyle had paid off for them both. The fights that had consequently ensued as she had been called names, been denigrated by the kids he mixed with, had stood him in good stead for this kind of life. He could have a row, and he appreciated the fact that he could take on men much larger than him, because that had been a must all his life.

Fight or *die*, had been his only option then, and he had fought for his mother at first and then later on for himself, for the respect of his peers. His father had been either banged up or on the trot most of his life. She had done what she could to keep them clothed and fed, and no one would ever say anything about her that was even remotely out of order.

Now the fight was over, the doors had been locked and the place was to all intents and purposes out of bounds, especially to the Old Bill. It was taken for granted that, naturally, no one had seen or even heard anything that had happened.

Terry would be dumped outside a hospital at some point, but for the moment he could lie there and think about what a cunt he was, because that was the general consensus of every person in the building.

Rox pulled Dianna to one side and said under her breath, 'What the fuck is going on with you? He was cunting our mother and you were going to help him?'

She was trying to understand this sister of hers, who

as far as she was concerned needed a slap herself. They all knew the score, they had grown up knowing the score, so why would Dianna, *Dianna* of all the people in this place, try and help him? It didn't make sense, but being a clever girl the reason why hit her like a billiard ball in a sock.

'Is he the mystery bloke? Is he the fucking squeeze you've been hiding away? No wonder you didn't want the old man to know about him. That is Terry Baker.'

Dianna nodded. She had been sussed.

'Dad hates him, Di.'

Dianna was nearly in tears. 'Dad hates everyone.' She sounded like a petulant child even to her own ears.

'He hates him for a reason and you know that. For all his faults Dad looks out for us in his own way. Terry Baker was banged up on an armed robbery and he caused untold aggravation for the old man before he went. You would do well to remember that in future.'

Terry Baker had gone down in history as one of the only people to ever mug off Freddie Jackson and get away with it, but only because of a lucky capture while robbing a NatWest bank in Silvertown. No one knew what had caused the barney in the first place, only that Freddie had been looking for him for days before the fatal blag. The lump Terry had incurred had in fact been a lifesaver.

He was handsome, a man with panache, and he was also what was commonly termed an arsehole. He had gone down in local folklore as a man who had blagged with no rhyme or reason, except for a pump-action shotgun and two mates as stupid and naïve as he was. He had always been a person with a personality deficit, which was caused by his complete lack of one in the first place.

He would argue over a pound, and with drink or drugs inside him he became morose and aggressive and he was also under the mistaken impression that he could take on all comers. Terry Baker was a lot of things but a fighter was not one of them. He was a weapons man, a machete king, not a fisticuffs person, regardless of what he might think to the contrary.

But women *loved* him. He knew how to push all the right buttons and his handsome face was adept at hiding his utter contempt for the female population. He had seen Dianna as nothing more than a bit of fluff, some fun. He was shagging his biggest enemy's daughter, and what more could any man in his position want?

'Dad, please, Dad . . .'

Freddie sighed as he stopped the car. As he looked as his son, his boy, he was not surprised to find that he had no feelings for him whatsoever. He had felt a lot of emotions about this child over the years, anger, love, sorrow. Even he was susceptible to a child's ability to make you love them, make you protect them, but even Freddie Jackson had his limit.

No matter what he had done in his own life, no matter how badly he had treated Little Freddie and even Maggie over the years, he could not, in any way, shape or form countenance his son's actions.

Little Freddie frightened him. This was a child who, without knowing it, had taken away the son he had secretly loved.

Jimmy Junior had been everything he had wanted in a child. He was also his trump card in a war that he had caused by himself and which he was also fighting by himself. Every time Jimmy had made a new deal, had cranked his power up another notch, Freddie had been able to console himself that he had the upper hand, that he knew something Jimmy boy didn't. He had needed that power.

Then something had happened that he would have believed impossible, and after a long time of fighting it, had eventually had to accept it.

Jimmy Junior had got *under* his skin, had made him *vulnerable*. And this child of his, Little Freddie, had somehow *sensed* that, had *resented* that, and like his father would, he had taken steps to prevent it from going any further.

In one way, a detached part of him could see the boy's point of view, but it was wrong. Little Freddie was far too young to be removing anyone from his orbit. Far too young to have countenanced even *letting* the thought cross his mind.

He kept seeing that little boy fighting for his breath, and it was the knowledge another child had wilfully and purposely brought that suffering about that was so hard to stomach. He desperately needed to make some sense of it all. He loved Little Freddie in his own peculiar way, and he knew this child loved him, *really* loved him.

He had proved that by his actions.

He also knew that this boy of his was a time bomb. One day he could be at risk from his son, and Rox's child could easily be what he saw as the next threat to his security.

Driving along, he had told Little Freddie that he knew what he had done and that he was going to give him up. Not to the filth, that would be too much even for Freddie Jackson, but he would put him into care and leave him there to rot.

But now he had actually stopped the car, had made himself stare into Little Freddie's eyes, he wondered whether he could in all honesty go that far. This boy had kept him in a house he hated, with a woman he had not wanted since before he had been sentenced and shut away from the world for years, and he had been dragged up by his wife, the child's own mother, the person who should have been the one to make sure he was secure and cared for. Jackie had a lot to answer for, and he had a lot of things to make good somehow, to *mend*.

It was this simple fact that was stopping him in his tracks now. He knew what it was like to be unwanted. His father had never cared for him, not really, and he understood his son's fear that someone else might be more important than him. Might be snatching the little bit of love and affection he was given as and when it suited the parent in question.

Freddie was more than aware of his failings, and he wanted to put this night, and this son, as far away from him as he could, but he was responsible for Little Freddie.

He knew he should do what he had promised, but it was easier said than done. This was his legal flesh and blood, and he wasn't so sure he could dump him now.

It wasn't just his face and the fear it was displaying, though. He could feel the genuine terror coming off his only son in waves. It was also because Little Freddie was his only son, and he knew how it felt to be ignored, knew how it felt to be unwanted, seen as nothing more than a bind. Freddie's mother too had used him and made him the be all and end all of her married life. Like Jackie, Maddie had known that his father would have gone on the trot. It had been left to Freddie to make sure he finally did the right thing, and he had. Freddie had been there for his father from the beginning to the end of his chequered and pointless life.

So he wasn't sure he could turn this child away now the anger had subsided and the knee-jerk reaction of earlier in the day had all but worn off.

He had a duty to his only son. He should be standing

by him, trying to make sense of what had happened and try to stop it happening ever again.

He wanted to wash his hands of Little Freddie and punish him for his actions, and until now he had been determined to do just that. But now, looking at him and seeing the child's deep unhappiness he really was not so sure he should give up on him. Jimmy Junior was gone, but this boy was still here.

His mobile went off and cursing silently to himself he answered it.

Lena and Joe had come back to the hospital because they didn't really know what else to do. They felt so guilty, so responsible. Their daughter was prostrate with grief and they decided they should be beside her no matter what.

Joe, especially, felt the full force of what had happened. He felt it so acutely that he wondered if he would survive this feeling he was carrying around in his chest like a lead weight. It wasn't just that the boy had died, it was also because he knew it was not the accident everyone thought it was.

He should have opened his mouth as soon as he had realised what had really gone on. That mad bastard Freddie had finally killed someone, and he had killed the dearest, the most important person in their lives.

But, for all that, and as big a fucker as that child was, Joe's natural loyalty made him unsure about bringing this into the public domain. Little Freddie was his flesh and blood, and Joe was also worried about Jackie's reaction.

In his heart he was worried about Freddie knowing the score, though he was even more worried about Maggie finding out. It would bring his whole family down in an instant.

He also knew, or rather *guessed*, that Jimmy knew far

more about this than he was letting on. So he sat with his wife and son-in-law by the bedside of his lovely daughter, who he knew would never recover from this tragedy.

Jackie snorted her line of coke, sniffing noisily as she brought the white powder through her nose and into the back of her throat. The bitter taste made her gag but she brought her head forward and sniffed loudly once more to make sure she got the full monty inside her head. Then she looked into the dirty mirror that adorned the wall of the pub toilet and for the first time in years saw herself as others saw her.

She was yellow, not yet jaundiced, but well on her way. 'Sallow skinned' was how her mother described her.

Her hair was lank and greasy, her eyes were sunken and bloodshot, and her body was aching and bloated. She had waited for her Freddie, and she had longed for her Freddie, and when he had finally emerged from his prison cell he had looked younger than ever and fitter than ever.

That was when she had *really* needed a drink.

Deep inside, her condition frightened her, but like many an alcoholic before her, until the symptoms were up and running and kicking her arse she would ignore them. What else could she do? Drink made the days bearable and the nights pass.

Freddie didn't want her, he wanted the Pats of this world and the young girls, and she couldn't compete with them. She was too far gone now. Since Kimberley's birth she had been ruined. Her belly was saggy and she was marked all over. Even the backs of her knees and the backs of her arms had been stretched. The little confidence she had possessed had deserted her like her husband had.

Jackie hadn't had the advice that was given out these days – use a lotion, don't put on too much weight. She had been told she was eating for two! No one was expected to look like a fucking beauty queen when they were in the club, no one had told you then how to avoid the wrecking of your body. Magazines were not read for those kind of tips. She had only ever bought *True Crime*, sometimes a *Woman's Own*. When the recipes had been the hook, and she had not even known about healthy eating until it was all too late.

The first birth had ruined her all right, and when you had someone like Freddie, you were more than aware that there were trollops lining up to be on his *arm*, the *villain's* arm. Freddie, like most of his counterparts, needed the approbation those girls afforded him, needed to be seen with those young girls. Her father had been the same, but in a much smaller league of course.

Freddie had broken her heart and she had never recovered from it.

So stopping drinking was *not* an option for her. With a few drinks inside her, she could pretend her life was great, convince herself that her husband loved her really, and with a few shots in the morning her hands stopped shaking long enough for her to light a cigarette.

It was so *easy* for everyone else to condemn her, talk about her *drink problem*. Especially her girls, who were still relative virgins where men were concerned and still believed in happy ever after. But they would learn, as all women learned eventually. Life took its toll on women far quicker than it did on the men.

Jackie had a few drinks because without the crutch of alcohol, her life and all it entailed absolutely terrified her. It had helped her sleep when Freddie had been banged up, when the utter loneliness had been more than she could bear. A couple of shots had brightened her day when the pressure of being alone with three kids had been so intense, and the need of her husband had been *so* acute, she had felt as if she would die from the want of him.

When a man was sentenced to prison, the judge, the lawyers, barristers, whoever was involved in the court process, never realised that a *whole family* was often sentenced along with them. The *bad* man was put away, and so he should be, he had broken the law. Society could sleep easier at night, but what about the mothers and the wives and the kids that were left behind, mourning someone they loved who was gone for a lifetime, but who was not dead? What about the *love* they had for them? The person being accused in the courts was often like a stranger to their family members, and was often made to look far worse than they actually were by over-zealous policemen and the Crown Prosecution Service. So the family didn't think that justice had actually been done, because they missed the person they *knew*, the person who had loved them, and who they *loved* in return, the person who had always stood by them, or who had walked the floor with them when they were babies, sat beside them when they were ill. Loved them whatever.

No one thought of people like her, whose whole life was over in minutes because of a jury verdict, who had two little girls and a belly full of arms and legs when her husband had been placed so far away from her. Who had been left on her own and without any kind of support whatsoever. Who had given birth alone, and with tears running down her face because the baby would not see her father for months, and could only be parented from afar, on visits, and by a man who she didn't know from Adam. So a drink had been her salvation in the end, had been the one thing that could stop the ache inside her and ensure she slept at night.

By the time Freddie had been on the out she had been

consumed with the habit, and even his presence had not been enough to make her stop.

Now she looked into this grimy and scuffed mirror and she saw what Freddie saw. Terry Baker had proved to her the truth of her life, that she was a nothing, a no one and that she was only a joke to people.

He had destroyed her in front of nearly everyone she knew, and it didn't matter that Dicky boy had stepped in to defend her. The damage had already been done.

She cut another line quickly and neatly. She needed total oblivion tonight and she was determined to achieve it. If she was going to walk out there again and face everyone she needed all the Dutch courage she could get. She might be a piss head, she might be a prescription drug queen, but the great thing about it all was, with a few drinks inside her she could laugh about it, in a way she'd never manage if she was straight and sober.

Now that was a state of mind she hoped she never experienced again, because it was only the drink that kept her from jumping off the nearest bridge she could find. *Drink problem*, well fucking whoopee. For all their whispers, they were actually confusing her with someone who cared.

'Can we go home, Dad, please?'

Freddie shook his head. They were on the way to Paul and Liselle's. He had just received a call to say they were experiencing a *soupçon* of trouble from a local bully boy. His Roxanna had rung him, before it all got out of hand. She said that the usual faces were in there, but she felt he should come and have a look see. Freddie was annoyed now. Paul and Liselle were good people and he was not about to have them disturbed by what amounted to the equivalent of a fucking lager lout. A few of the local fucking ice creams had tried to get an in, and they had been sorely disappointed. So an event like this was not unheard of, though he would not normally deal with it personally. Any other time he would have made a call, he would have delegated the job out to a lesser person on the payroll.

He was good at that, delegating, but he had decided to sort this lot out for himself, to show willing, he supposed. The pub was Ozzy's and so he had to make sure the punters' nights were untouched by any kind of aggravation. They expected to drink in a trouble-free environment. He was also going there personally because he needed an excuse to delay his decision about his boy.

Without looking at his son, he said, 'I have to sort out a bit of business. Now just be quiet and let me concentrate on me driving, eh?'

Little Freddie was for the first time in his life unsure of what he was going to do. He had no remorse in him, he was incapable of it, but he was frightened of his father because this time he might actually put him away. The social worker had been harking on about it for ages, and he knew that one word from his dad and he was guaranteed a lock-up somewhere, without any chance of kiddie parole. It was his mother who was keeping the wolf from his door, and he made a point of keeping *her* sweet.

This man, though, his father, who walked in and out of his life at a whim, finally had him well and truly sussed out. For a moment there, Little Freddie had been convinced he was off to the land of the psychologists. Now, though, he had seen a little chink of light, and he was going to milk that for all it was worth.

He was learning the hard way that he had to keep on the right side of everyone, especially his father, and his days of saying and doing what he wanted were long gone. He had to keep a low profile, do what was expected and wait until he could safely and securely be himself to do what he wanted, when he wanted. And he was shrewd enough to know that even then he would need the protection of his family around him.

Since he could first understand his surroundings, he had known on some level that he was different. He had no real feelings for anything or anyone. He had thought his father was like him, but now he was not so sure.

Jimmy Junior had been a severe irritation for a long time, and he had been determined to rid himself of the boy's constant presence. He was disappointed in his father because he was only trying to emulate him. He had not wanted him to find out what he had done, but he had not expected his dad of all people to make such a song and dance about it.

Now it was all about damage limitation, as governments said when they fucked up big time. And he was more than aware that he had fucked up what had been a very relaxed and very protected lifestyle.

Damage limitation was definitely the order of the day.

Freddie walked into the bar and the first thing he saw was his girls surrounding their mother in a protective cocoon. After the revelation about his boy, he was pleased that they were such good girls, even poor old Kimberley was a diamond, problems or no problems. He saw how protective they were of Jackie and he was heartened to see it. She was going to need them in the future, he would lay his last pound on that.

As soon as he'd entered the pub he'd sensed that there was something drastically amiss, and he was right. Paul motioned with his head and he followed the direction of the man's eyes. What he saw put the seal on what had already been a strange few days.

Terry Baker, his one-time friend and the archenemy, was lying in a pool of blood by the back doors.

He had been dragged there by Paul and Dicky until such time as someone decided to take him to the hospital on their way home. Some of the regulars were debating on whether they should just dump him at the train station, always a good place to dump people, but seeing Freddie Jackson in the doorway they were saved from any more pointless conversation about it. He would sort it out, so they could get back to the serious business of the night, drinking and talking.

Mug bunnying was the order of the day, coke was dispensed liberally, and the tragedy that had befallen Jimmy was as good a topic of conversation as any.

Taking a drink from Liselle, Freddie walked over to his family and for the first time in years he was not scanning the room for strange. He noticed that his wife looked crestfallen and guessed that whatever had happened with Terry Baker had involved her in some way.

Looking at the girls he was reminded of how attractive they actually were. Even his Kimberley, who had been a big girl when she was young, now had a trim figure and a sweet, heart-shaped face like the other two.

He was told what had occurred quietly and succinctly, and he amazed everyone once more by shaking Dicky's hand, thanking him, and not bothering to go over and finish the job young Dicky had started. Pat had received nothing more than a curt nod and this everyone knew must have been annoying for her. Freddie didn't even look at her after that, he had other things on his mind.

Terry was unconscious now, and that was how he would stay until he was delivered back into the outside world.

'What a ponce, eh? You all right, Jack, you OK?'

Jackie looked at this husband of hers in speechless shock. He was genuinely concerned. Young Dicky was also amazed and he could see that Rox was thrilled by the reception he had received from her father.

Freddie had just finished his drink when young Freddie knocked on the doors to be admitted, and there was nothing his father could do to stop him. Jackie, full of her own self-pity and still smarting from the insults she had received, hugged her son to her tightly. For once in his life, he was quite happy to let her.

The girls made a fuss of him, pleased he was on his best behaviour, and he was all smiles and big eyes as he charmed them.

Freddie watched him closely as he interacted with his family, aware that his son was sensible enough to know that he was going to need all the friends he could get.

Chapter Twenty-Six

Maggie had hardly spoken to anyone since she had woken up in the hospital with her head heavy from the drugs used to calm her and her whole being numb with shock. She had left with her husband the next morning with a prescription for the tablets that had kept her from feeling anything too acute. And since then she had just gone through the motions.

She was pale and she looked delicate. Other than that she was her usual pretty self, but all the happiness had gone from her face. She looked tired out, sad-eyed, and she was acting almost normally except she barely uttered a word.

Her hair was perfect, and her clothes were, as always, immaculate, and she even cooked a meal for Jimmy as she had always done.

Jimmy watched his wife now as she made coffee for him, and observed her as she laid out a tray, with a plate of biscuits, a napkin and a small coffee pot. The caterers were working around her. She had not even acknowledged their presence, but he knew she was aware of them. He had been relieved when he had seen her dressed in black. He had been dreading having to force her to go to the child's funeral.

She filled the little white china pot with coffee, and she wiped the sides delicately before placing it on the tray once more. It was like a work of art, and he had no stomach for it.

She had a knack for making things look smart, stylish, she always had done. Their homes, even the little rabbit hutch they had first owned, had looked like something from a magazine. Now this house, which had finally become like the home he had always dreamed of, the house that had finally rung with the sound of childish laughter, was suddenly like a mausoleum.

He couldn't bring himself to go in the boy's bedroom. He knew that Maggie did, he had listened to her sob there in the night, the only time he had observed a proper reaction from her. When he had gone in there, though, she had pushed him away. She wanted to be alone with her grief and her hurt.

But he couldn't bear it. He knew he was not ready to see all the paraphernalia that constituted a child's life, the toys, the little slippers, the trains that had been painted on the walls so carefully.

He had gone to get a plate from the kitchen the day before and he had picked up his Jimmy's Thomas the Tank Engine bowl and he had stood there, in the huge room with its Aga and its American-style fridge and cried his eyes out.

When did the pain stop?

Maybe today, once the funeral was over, he would finally be able to make some sense of it.

Jimmy could hear the tables being erected in his front room, knew they would be covered in white damask and that the food would be exemplary. It was the least he could do for his boy's sendoff.

The place would be packed out, and he just wanted the whole thing over with so he could grieve in peace.

* * *

Freddie was already dressed in his funeral garb and having a drink with Paul in the pub. Even Paul had noticed that Jimmy was blanking him, and any sympathy Freddie had felt was all but gone now. He knew that Jimmy was treating him as if he was a nothing, a no one, a fucking ice cream.

Jimmy had not returned any of his calls, he had not tried to contact him about work, he was getting what amounted to orders from Paul here, who was now a fucking go-between, and he knew Paul felt this himself. Was obviously wondering what the score was.

Freddie was fuming now, absolutely fuming. He was back to his old self. He had tried being the nice guy, and what had it got him? A fucking humungous mugging off, that's what, and he was not standing for it. Jimmy Junior's death was terrible, but his boy wasn't going to take the fucking fall for it. He had slung Little Freddie back on his pills, and he was making sure the fucker took them this time, but at the end of the day, whatever had happened in that room, Freddie felt that Jimmy should respect him and all he had stood for over the years no matter what.

The old animosity was back, and Freddie was annoyed with himself over his weakness and the fact that Jimmy had used it to take advantage of him. Well, he had learned a lesson here. He had nearly turned his back on his son, and for what? For whom? A man he had raised from the fucking gutter and who had slipped in like a snake and taken all that, by rights, should have been his.

He had seen the change in his boy. He was *adamant* he had not taken part in what had happened, and Joe had admitted to Freddie that he had not actually seen Little Freddie go into the kid's room that night. So he had nothing really to go on, they had just *assumed* it was his

Freddie. He had, in effect, allowed Jimmy to cloud his judgement.

Jimmy Junior could have tied the bag himself, he was a bright little spark and Jimmy was trying to blame his boy for his own failings. They should never have left him with Lena and Joe. They were old, they weren't able enough for a lively kid like him.

He had taken his Little Freddie under his wing, and he was now of the opinion that the boy had been grievously maligned. He was only a kid, and he was now back on the happy pills and like a different person.

Jimmy, even allowing for his grief, was not making all this any easier with his fucking attitude. He was acting like he was something special, someone better than him. He was giving Freddie fucking orders as if he was a novice to the game.

It was an insult of momentous proportions. And Freddie Jackson, with his knack of rewriting history to his advantage and convincing himself that his was the true and accurate account of what happened, was once more after revenge.

Jackie was wearing a black skirt and jumper provided by Roxanna, who had also been over that morning to blow-dry her mother's hair. As Jackie applied her make-up, she wondered at the day that was overcast and chilly, and on which they would be burying a small child. It was unbelievable that such a tragic occurrence could hit their families. It must be doubly hard for Maggie, who had not expressed an interest in her child for three years. The guilt must be eating at her like a cancer.

Freddie was adamant that Little Fred must not go to the funeral, in fact, the child had been almost tied to the house. She was aware that his little cousin's death had hit him hard, and since it had happened he was a changed boy. Polite, friendly and almost annoying in his quest to be helpful and useful. It was as if he had been given a personality transplant.

Freddie had felt the change in his boy and they were now like that. She mentally crossed her fingers in her mind.

After the terrible events, Freddie had seemed pleased to see his son not only alive and well, but also trying to make up for his past behaviour. He was a model son now, and even the social workers had been amazed at his changed persona. Freddie made sure he took his pills every day as specified. *She* had never been able to get that child to take them, yet for Freddie he was as good as gold about it.

Freddie, though, had hardly been near poor Jimmy and Maggie, and that had confused her. Even though Maggie didn't want anyone round the house, and Jimmy said she was best left alone, Jackie had at least expected Freddie to be there for Jimmy. Yet from what she could make out he had basically left him to it.

When she had tried to discuss it with him, he had bitten her head off and the only thing she could deduce from his behaviour was that he was also grieving for the little boy. Freddie had always made such a song and dance about that child, and it had annoyed her because he had rarely done that with his own kids. She knew it had upset Maggie too, and she had seen her almost wince when Freddie had picked the child up and thrown him into the air. Jimmy Junior had screamed with laughter, and been thrilled at all the attention. Her own son had sat there watching the little display with his usual stoic demeanour, and she had felt Little Freddie was probably wishing his father had bothered to shower him with so much love and attention.

She had to admit, Jimmy Junior had been a lovely little kid. She conveniently forgot the times she had accused her sister of ruining the boy, had felt that her mother and father had preferred him to her son, had accused them in her drunkenness of favouritism and used any excuse to make out the child wasn't right.

Now she was the perfect sister, or at least she had tried to be, but even at this terrible time Maggie had not wanted to see her, and that had hurt.

The official story was that no one had been able to get across the doorstep, but she knew in her heart that the girls had been allowed access, especially her Rox, who was closer to Maggie than she had ever been to her own mother. Jackie swallowed down her anger at her thoughts, and then she gulped at her glass of vodka to calm her thoughts, and quickly washed down a few Valium before spraying herself with Giorgio perfume and slipping on her old black suede slingbacks. Her feet were spilling over the edges, but once she had worn them for a few minutes they moulded into her shape and were comfortable.

As her old nan used to say, get yourself a good bed and a good pair of shoes, because if you ain't in one, you are in the other. Wise words.

She had also said many times, never drink to forget, because no one ever forgets the ramblings of a piss head. For Jackie, that had been proved to be true.

Maggie stared at the small white coffin and wondered at a God who could have given her a child in such terrible circumstances and had then seen fit to take him away from her. It was cold in the church, and she was aware that everyone was watching her as if waiting for her to do *something*.

All she wanted to do was die. How would her little

Jimmy get on all alone? But then, he had been given plenty of practice at being alone, hadn't he? She had left him to his own devices enough times.

The pain hit her once more. It came in waves, washing over her like an icy wind, making her bones ache and her jaw numb. Maggie was freezing with pain, she was almost stiff with the cold knowledge of her son's death and the awful suspicion that this feeling inside her would never be eased, it would never get any better, that it could only get worse.

She felt suddenly as if she was floating up into the air, like she was suspended over the crowd of people all singing their hearts out.

She felt Jimmy grab her hand and squeeze it tightly, and she fought back the urge to snatch it away from him, make him stop this charade. She wanted to scream out the black, putrid hate that was building up inside her.

Freddie, she noticed, was not crying. Jackie was, a loud, heavy, liquid sound that made her want to retch. They were in the pew opposite them. It was Glenford who was sitting with them, and she knew that some people must have been questioning that fact.

Roxanna, who was sitting beside her father in a smart black two-piece that must have set her back a small fortune, was also crying, but her tears Maggie appreciated. Rox's tears were clean and salty looking, she even cried in a tidy, designer way. Dabbing at her eyes daintily with a snow-white handkerchief, unconsciously making sure her make-up wasn't ruined.

Dicky, the love of Rox's life, was sitting on her right side. He had a handsome profile. He was a good-looking man, and they would produce a lovely child. She envied them, not in a nasty, jealous way, but in a wistful way. She envied them their love and the newness of everything.

She had been like that once with Jimmy, and she had believed, as they probably believed, that their life would be charmed somehow. That nothing *bad* could happen to them, that they were *different* to everyone else, their love could only bring them *joy*.

Of course life had a habit of kicking you squarely in the teeth, and she prayed that those two young lovers would not find that out for a long time.

Jimmy was shaking with his grief. He was sitting beside her with his head down and his shoulders hunched over, and she could almost feel his pain, it was so acute.

Yet she now felt nothing, she just wanted this over.

Behind her she could hear her mother sobbing and her father's inadequate words of comfort whispered in the quiet of the church. It was too little, too late.

She felt like screaming once more but she forced herself to keep quiet, forced herself to people-watch, to take her mind off her troubles.

Jackie was slumped in the pew. Her fat legs were crossed and her black skirt had ridden up over her knees to display varicose veins and milk bottle white calves that wouldn't have looked out of place on Geoff Capes.

Maggie wanted to laugh, but she didn't. She wanted to stand up and ask the people in this packed church why they had even come. Most of them had only glimpsed her little Jimmy. Many were here to show their friendship, a good few to show their respect for her husband and his employer, but she also knew there were people attending her son's burial who would brag about it. Who saw it as an event not to be missed.

But Jimmy was well able for the hangers-on, always had been. It was Freddie who had trouble keeping them at bay like normal people. He *embraced* them, *needed* them and their approbation, and their sneaky little ways of carrying on.

The priest was saying the Gospel now. Soon she could go, soon she could make her escape from the kind people who thought that shaking her hand and kissing her cheek would make everything all right.

They were all back at the house and the main crowd had finally gone. It was early evening, and the only people left were close family and a few friends.

Jimmy had been pleased with the turnout. It was reassuring to know that so many people cared about Jimmy Junior, knew him, wanted to pay their respects. Even his little friends from his playschool had been represented by the owners and the young girls who had worked there.

Maggie had sat through the whole thing without a word or a tear.

She had not accepted any condolences and even her old friends had found themselves being blanked. Seriously blanked, in fact. She had not even returned their phone calls or acknowledged their black-edged cards, cards that she said spewed out their own fear of death while pretending to sympathise with her loss.

The service had been beautiful, and the tears from the women present had been heartfelt. Burying a child was difficult, no one wanted it to be happening but they would rather it was someone else's child than their own.

Freddie was drinking heavily, but then so were most of the people in the place. Even Jimmy was the worse for wear, but on a day like this what else was there to do? He just wanted to try to anaesthetise the pain inside him, that was all.

His parents were both at a loss, and he felt, as he often did, that he was completely apart from them and their life.

Lena and Joe were in pieces. Joe was hammering the whisky and, if it helped him get though the day, he was glad of that. Lena had aged so much in such a short space of time, and he was heart sorry for her.

She had said a very true thing to him that afternoon. She said that this kind of heartbreak made you realise what was really important in life, and when you experienced it, then thought back to what you had seen as important before the event, you suddenly understood that really, you were as nothing in the grand scheme of things.

It showed you that life was just a series of events, that was all, and you had no real power over it whatsoever. You just thought you did.

Jimmy had nodded his agreement, and it had occurred to him that he loved Lena Summers. She was a lovely woman and he was lucky to have her as his mother-in-law.

That thought made him glance at poor old Dicky, who would soon be lumbered with having Jackie as his. What a terrifying thought that was.

He watched Jackie. She was drinking, he noticed, in constant yet very large quantities. She should by rights be floored by now, unable to string a sentence together and unsteady on her feet. But not Jackie, Jackie the animal. She was still sober in comparison to everyone else.

He knew Little Freddie was on the prowl, was still walking around as if nothing had happened. The verdict on his son's death had been misadventure. 'A tragic accident and my heart goes out to his parents and family.' Those had been the stupid old bastard in the coroner's court's exact words.

Jimmy understood on one level Freddie's need to protect his own flesh and blood. He knew Freddie had wanted to make the boy pay but blood, it seemed, really was thicker than water.

But not Jimmy's blood, he had no feeling any more for the man he had adored, the man who he had kept employed for years. He had watched him make his son into the animal he had become and they had all stood back because Freddie was Freddie, and he was a *nutter* and he used his anger and his hate to control everyone around him.

Freddie was feared by some of the hardest men in their world, Freddie was feared as a head case, a nut nut, a Looney Tunes. Freddie had made a point of ensuring his reputation guaranteed him respect, but Jimmy was not scared of him. He hadn't been for a long time, he had seen through him like a pane of glass.

Freddie was just stupid, he barrelled through life and he had been given a pass because he was useful to Ozzy. But Jimmy had Ozzy's respect, it was *him*, James Jackson, who was trusted, who had been chosen to run the different businesses and who was now party to Ozzy's deepest and darkest secrets.

Jimmy had kept Freddie sweet because they were kin, their wives were sisters, he had once looked up to Freddie, he had once been his role model. But he had carried him long enough, Freddie was out, and he was out for good. After today, Freddie was going to get his marching orders and he was not going to give him any kind of warning.

Freddie was about to find out just how much power his younger counterpart actually wielded. Jimmy was determined to bring him to book over his little son's murder. He was not going to let him walk away from this one. By the time he had finished with him, Freddie wouldn't be able to get a job as a doorman, let alone anything else.

Jimmy wanted to wipe him and his boy off the face of the earth. The absolute need for revenge was something he had never experienced until now. It had started with his little Jimmy's death and it had taken him over when the coroner had ruled it an accident.

Knowing Joe had his suspicions made it all slightly more bearable. It wasn't an accident that had taken his child from him, and he knew that when this was all over and the pain had subsided enough for him to function once more, he would make sure that Freddie Jackson Junior would never harm anybody again.

Kimberley was watching her sisters as they chatted together, and feeling left out. She picked up her orange juice and walked out to the garden. It was a cold day but she was well wrapped up.

She loved this place, and she felt the hole that Jimmy Junior had left behind. It was unbelievable that he would not run up the lawn again, or swim in the pool.

She was on the verge of tears once more. He had been a lovely little boy, and Maggie and Jimmy had doted on him. He had everything a child could possibly want and he was dead. It was beyond belief.

Now the crashing silence of a house without a child's presence was overwhelming. It was this that had really driven her out into the garden and towards the summer-house. It was constructed from old yellow stock bricks that had been reclaimed from one of the other outbuildings, and the windows had been hand-made to ensure it was in keeping with the rest of the house.

She was about to slip through the door when she heard Maggie's voice. Instead of going inside, she stood outside the window and listened.

'I am not going anywhere, Maggie.'

The bully was back in control, and Maggie knew that he was never going to let her be, never going to let her forget what had happened to her. She closed her eyes tightly, hoping against hope that when she opened them again Freddie would have disappeared.

'Go away from me.'

Her voice was low, and he could hear the underlying anger that was bubbling away below the surface of her mind.

'Why don't you just answer me, Maggie?'

Maggie shut her eyes once more, and she listened to the man who had stolen years of her life, stolen her son's early years from her, because of his threats and his hatred and his jealousy. He was still trying to manipulate her, even now. He was still using his hatred to make her miserable, was trying to force his will on her even after today's event. If it wasn't so outrageous it would be laughable.

Maggie had no intention of answering him, she just wanted him to go away. He had followed her out here when she had wanted to be alone, had just wanted to gather her thoughts together.

'He was my son. Admit it. Go on, admit that to me now.'

He was being hurtful now. He wanted her to finally admit that it was his child, to say it to him and Maggie's contempt for him was wiping away his sympathy.

'Will you go away.'

Her voice had regained some of its strength, and was much louder than she had meant it to be.

'Maggie, say it.'

She interrupted him then. 'Oh, fuck off, Freddie. You *raped* me, and now, even on the day of my child's burial, you have to try and make my life miserable. Will you leave me alone now he's *dead*? Can I breathe easy now because the thing you held over my head for all those years has been buried, and you have no power any more. Is this your last attempt at breaking me?'

He was shaking his head at her now.

'Go away, Freddie, before I scream for my husband and tell him what you did to me.'

Kimberley heard a scuffling noise, and she quickly walked behind the summerhouse. After a few seconds she poked her head around the corner, and saw Maggie stumbling over the lawn as she tried to make her way back to the house. Her father was still in the summerhouse, and when he finally emerged about fifteen minutes later she was amazed to see that he was crying.

Jackie was listening to her mother and father talking about when they had been young. This was always the way when they were at funerals or weddings. Any family gathering ended up with her parents telling them all tales of times long past and the things that had happened to long-dead relatives.

She lapped it up. It was so comfortable in Maggie's lovely front room with its deep soft sofas and cream-coloured walls. The girls were ensconced on the largest of the three sofas with her, and she was actually enjoying the evening so much she had forgotten they were all there for a funeral.

Lena was telling the girls about her own grandmother now, how she smoked a pipe and never missed Mass, how her grandfather had battered her nearly every day, and how she had followed him only weeks after his death.

'Silly cow, how could she love someone who gave her a clump on a daily basis? When he finally popped off she should have had a bleeding party!' Rox's voice was annoyed, and they all smiled at her.

Freddie, who was now sitting on the floor in front of the fireplace, laughed out loud.

Jimmy was sitting opposite him and he stared at him for long moments as Freddie laughed, that irritating, sarcastic laugh he had.

Seeing Jimmy looking at him, Freddie said in a friendly way, 'By the way, don't worry, Jimmy, I will sort out the takes tomorrow.'

Jimmy knew this was meant to be his chance to take the olive branch, to try to resolve their differences.

He had to be joking.

This was the day of his baby boy's funeral and he was only letting Freddie and his kin inside his home because of Maggie, because Maggie was finding some kind of peace having the girls around. She was sitting with her mother now, holding her hand tightly, and he knew she was looking for comfort and that, like himself, she would not find it.

'Don't bother, it's already sorted.'

Joe heard the exchange and saw the look on Jimmy's face. His sudden angry countenance seemed almost demonic.

He was looking at Freddie with such contempt Joe expected his burly son-in-law to take umbrage, to leap up from the floor and confront Jimmy.

Instead he sat there and took it. But Joe guessed that soon these two men were going to collide, and he knew who his money would be on as the victor.

Chapter Twenty-Seven

'I want him out, Oz, and I want him out sooner rather than later.'

Ozzy nodded, forgetting that Jimmy couldn't see him since they were on the phone. As always, Ozzy liked his young protégé's straight talking and he was pleased that Freddie was being aimed out at last. Personally, he would have seen the back of him years ago.

Since the boy had died he had felt a marked change in Jimmy. He was harder, and he was also easier to nark. This was to be expected, he supposed.

When the news had been broadcast to the wing that poor Jimmy Jackson had lost his son in tragic circumstances, Ozzy had seen the reaction of the men who had children, especially the ones with young families. He had understood Jimmy's grief much better then. Never having had a child himself, he could only imagine what it felt like to lose one.

Jimmy, like many a man before him, was focusing on his work to get through this terrible time. Everything in life was geared around it. It was working in Jimmy's favour, anyway, helped him escape all this grief. Ozzy had watched men in prison dissolve after an event like that.

Maggie, he understood, was not coping with it at all, and he also guessed that Jimmy couldn't even scratch the surface of her grief. How could he? Women were a different species and as they were the ones who grew the children inside them anyway, he assumed they felt the loss far more than the fathers. Though the newspapers and the TV news told him, some women had no feelings for their offspring, and he knew Maggie had not taken to the child at first.

Ozzy sighed inwardly. He was distressed for Jimmy, felt for him, but Ozzy could still see the personal opportunity that his grief was affording him. He was going to overhaul the businesses and he was starting off by getting rid of the dead wood.

'You do it, Jimmy, you have a good old clear out, son. It's long overdue anyway.'

'All right, son?' Freddie slowed the car down to the annoyance of the drivers behind him, and he waved at his son through the open window.

Little Freddie smiled and waved back, and his father tooted the horn of his car as he drove past him and the two friends he was walking to school with.

Freddie smiled. He was all right, there was nothing wrong with that boy. He was highly strung like his old man, that was all. It was temper, and *he* also had a temper, as those who crossed him found out to their detriment. Well, his boy had inherited it from him, so he couldn't be all bad.

His sorrow and shock had completely gone and Jimmy was the new focus of his attention. Jimmy was the bad bastard, and Jimmy had better watch out.

Freddie was weaving in and out of the early-morning traffic and he was cursing and gesturing to all the other, less-capable drivers who had the audacity to be on the road. He was driving to Jimmy's suite of new offices in a purpose-built block in Barking. Jimmy was working from there exclusively now, and they really looked the part.

Freddie was disgusted about them, seeing the use of them as a front as a mug's game, and he told anyone who would listen to him that Jimmy was heading for a fall. Filth raided premises as it was – their homes, their safe houses. Why put yourself in the frame by advertising your existence?

But Jimmy was running legitimate businesses from there, and the other stuff was only ever discussed in the place. Nothing tangible could ever link any of the employees to anything that was not above board and taxable. Jimmy was moving with the times while Freddie was still stuck in a time warp.

Freddie was fuming because he had not heard from Jimmy for a week, and then he'd got a message telling him to come to his office. Well, he was on his way, and he was going to sort it out once and for all. This showdown had been a long time coming. He was more than ready for it, and he was prepared to go to any lengths to see that it happened.

'Maggie's bad, Mum. I am really worried about her.'

Rox was sitting on her mother's bed and trying to get her to drink some tea and eat a piece of toast. The girls took it in turns now to force Jackie to get out of bed and to eat. They were worried about her and her escalating drinking problem.

'She'll be all right, now will you piss off, Rox, and let me sleep!'

Rox sighed. 'Imagine it was one of us, Mum, who had died. How would you feel?'

'At this moment, Rox, I would be over the moon. Now will you sod off and leave me be.'

Kimberley, who was on the landing, listened to her mother and wondered at a woman who had no real feeling for her sister's grief.

Rox tried again. 'Will you sit up, Mum, please, and eat this toast we've made you?'

Jackie was getting really annoyed now. This was becoming a regular thing and at first she had loved it. The attention and the knowledge her girls were looking out for her had been lovely. Now it was getting a bit over the fucking top. They were here every day like a gaggle of bloody witches, and all she wanted to do was have a kip.

Kimberley walked into the bedroom and, pushing Rox out of the way, she grabbed the quilt and dragged it off her half-naked mother.

Jackie went ballistic. She sat up in the bed and screamed in anger, 'What the fuck is it with you lot? Why can't you just leave me alone!'

Rox was trying not to laugh, but then she looked at her mother properly and saw the way she had bloated out again over the last few months and any thought of laughing vanished.

Jackie's legs were a mass of bruises and scratches, because her kidneys were gradually breaking down and causing an itchy rash. Rox and her sisters knew this because they had looked it up on the internet. They knew what was happening to Jackie and they wanted to try to help her help herself, before it was too late. Their mother was a textbook case for a female alcoholic and they wanted to stop her from drinking herself to death.

Rox looked around the bedroom. It was filthy. The bedding was rotten, the carpet was a mass of cigarette burns and coffee stains, and the whole room stank of sweat and stale perfume. But the saddest thing of all was that it didn't look half as dilapidated as the woman sitting up on the bed amidst all the squalor.

Jackie had pulled the quilt back over her, but any thought of sleep was long gone, and her anger was being expressed as vindictive personal insults.

She lit a cigarette and said loudly and sarcastically, 'So what is this about, then?'

She spoke in a high, sing-song voice, the utter contempt for her children's do-gooding evident. 'Rox is having a baby, so now she is a fucking fountain of wisdom. Well, you know fuck all, Rox, you never have.'

'She knows more than you ever will, Mother.'

Jackie smiled as she looked at Kimberley. 'Oh, now me *junkie* daughter is giving me the benefit of her experience as well, is she? Well, shove it. Go and have a fix, Kim, at least you were smiling on the skag.'

Rox walked to the door. She had heard enough.

Kimberley said quietly, 'Look at yourself, Mum, and your life. It stinks, *you* stink and you drink yourself stupid so you don't have to accept that. But you do, you have to try and stop destroying yourself and everyone around you.'

Jackie laughed nastily, and pushing her hair back off her face she hollered, 'At least I have a life, what have you got, eh? No man, no *nothing*. Who'd fucking want you, Kim, with your miserable fucking boatrace? You tell me that.'

'Listen to yourself, Mum, I don't need a man to make me feel like a valid person . . .'

Jackie was laughing again. 'Kimberley, go and score, go and get pissed, jack up, snort, I don't give a fuck. Just get out of my fucking face!'

Rox and Kimberley looked at her, and the expression

on their faces told Jackie all she needed to know about herself.

Kim spoke up, the disgust evident in her voice. 'You ain't got a man, Mum, you ain't even got Dad. You know what? He *loathes* you. He is out and about all the time . . .'

Rox was trying to make her sister leave the room, trying to prevent the blow-up she knew was about to erupt. 'Leave her, Kim, we're wasting our time . . .'

Jackie laughed again.

'"Leave her, Kim,"' she mimicked her daughter's voice. 'Go round Maggie's, she loves all this shit. You get it from her, the lot of you . . . another fucking drama queen. That poor child, she wouldn't give it the fucking time of day for years. Neglected him—'

Kimberley laughed with utter contempt. '*You*, to talk about neglect! You've got some nerve, Mother. Little Freddie's arse was always red raw because you couldn't be bothered to change him, he never ate a decent meal unless we provided one, and you talk about neglect!'

Jackie knew this was true, which just annoyed her more.

'I was always there for him, and whatever I am or I ain't, I've never not loved him! Maggie had it all, the house, the car, even the fucking dog! But no baby, and when she got one, finally got one, she didn't even know what to do with it! She is only off her trolley now because she fucking well knows she had no time for that little boy. She's feeling *guilty*, and so she should be after all those years of neglect.'

Jackie was shouting now. 'Even your father had more time for him than she did, and she couldn't stand him even touching the child! I used to watch her when he played with the poor little sod, her face screwed up, like we was all nothing. She hated him near the boy, yet she didn't fucking lay one finger on him herself unless she had to, did she? That poor child was neglected, and even my mother said it. My Freddie loved that boy and she wouldn't even let the poor child have the benefit of him making a fuss of the poor little fucker, let alone anyone else!'

'And just why do you think that might have been then, Mum, eh? You know so much, why do you think she hated him touching him, then?'

Rox could hear the inflection in her sister's voice and knew that something was going to be said that was going to cause trouble, big trouble, serious trouble.

'Shut up, Kim. Come on, let's go.'

Jackie leaped up on the bed, she wanted to hear this. 'You keep out of it, Rox. Come on, then, what are you getting at, Kim? Fucking spit it out. He loved that little boy, he doted on him, and thanks to him at least the child had a few good memories to take with him—'

'It was *his* child, you stupid bloody cow!'

Jackie was stunned and wondered, briefly, if she was hearing things. 'What did you say?'

'He *raped* her. Dad *raped* Maggie!'

Maggie was sick inside, and the pain she felt could not be relieved with the tablets her mother was forever trying to get her to take.

'Please, Mum, leave me, go home, I just want to be on my own.'

The strange thing was she was *fine* on her own, but no one believed her. Alone, she could gather her thoughts, pretend that things were OK, all right. She could relax, try to rest. She could forget what had happened.

Forget how her son had been conceived, remember him as the little boy he was, the son she loved. She would let Freddie Jackson rape her every day if it would bring her son back to her. He was a child of rape, he had been brought on to this earth because of an action that was so heinous, so evil, and yet she had learned to love him. He had been the innocent party, he had been the catalyst for her life being destroyed, and then he had been the catalyst that had given her life meaning, and given her marriage the kick-start it had needed to survive. Jimmy had loved him and that had allowed her to love him as well.

Now, her own company was preferable to anyone else's. Her own company afforded her the luxury of pretending he was still alive, that her son was still near her. Alone, her life could be what she wanted it to be, instead of what it was.

Alone was now a good thing.

Lena was at the end of her tether. Nothing she did seemed to make any difference. Maggie was determined to be alone and she knew that she couldn't get through to her, knew she was wasting her time.

But the guilt she carried around with her was weighing her down, and she needed to make her daughter better, needed her to need her.

If only they had looked in on him properly that night, checked him, protected him, he would still be alive.

Lena would never know another happy day, so how could she expect her daughter to? Her Maggie was dying inside. It was not something that you could look at her and see, instead it was more subtle. Maggie's eyes were sadder by the day, she looked at you and the bleakness was terrifying because somewhere inside you knew she was right. Her hurt and pain were right, the only option left to her daughter.

Without it, she felt nothing.

* * *

'You sure about this, Jimmy?' Glenford's voice was sceptical. He knew the Jacksons fought between themselves, but this anger from Jimmy was out of the ordinary, and unusual.

'As sure as I'll ever be, Glen. He is out and that's the end of it.'

Glenford was nonplussed for a few moments. 'There'll be murders and you know it. You can't row Freddie out, that would be outrageous! He will want to kill you, he will go mentalist.'

Glenford said it all in thick Jamaican, but he meant every word.

Jimmy grinned. 'Let him bring it on, as much fucking hag as he likes. Like I give a fuck.'

Glenford was surprised, but not *that* surprised. This had been a long time coming, he had just not expected it now, and not in such a voracious way. Freddie must have fucked up with honours this time, and caused untold aggravation to cause this upset. Freddie, in all honesty, must have been picking the pockets of the damned to get Jimmy this fucking aerated.

Jimmy was the *good* guy, Jimmy always looked for the best in people, looked for the easiest way out of things, tried to keep the peace, tried to make it all better.

Not any more by the looks of things.

Glenford had to question, though, the logic of aiming him out now. Freddie collected quickly, without arguments. He gave people ten hours and they never failed to deliver, they always paid up on time. He did the job, he talked the talk and he earned for them. He might not be the greatest mind they had on the payroll but he knew how to frighten money out of the biggest wankers in recorded history.

Freddie was a nutcase and people like Freddie were

worth keeping around if for no other reason than that.

'You *can't* aim him out, Jimmy, think about it. He'll never rest if you do that. He'll go fucking mental. Who would employ him other than you? All he *has* is you.' Glenford was trying, in his own way, to warn Jimmy about reckless actions. 'Freddie Jackson is far more useful to you if he is in your good books. *Use* him as a heavy, let him have his moment, let him have his creds, but don't put him out altogether. He'll never live that down, he'll *never* get over it.'

He was actually wary of anything happening, because he knew Freddie spent his life on the edge. Looking for trouble was his forte, it was what Freddie did for kicks. Freddie would love an excuse to widen his circle of hatred.

'But that is just what I want, Glenford. I don't *want* him to get over it, I *want* him to know how I feel. I am going to finish him once and for all, I am going to wipe his fucking name off my pension plan, he is history. He is *out* of everything he ever wanted, everything he has always *felt* he was entitled to. Freddie is *over* and the sooner he realises that the better off he will be. I have carried that cunt from day one, and now he can start earning for himself, earn a fucking living like all of us.'

Glenford snorted in derision and annoyance. 'This goes deeper than that, Jimmy, this is far too personal. What the fuck has he done, *fucked* your wife?'

Jimmy didn't answer, and Glenford wondered what the upshot of this day was going to be. Life was a series of unavoidable events – until now he had not understood what his father meant by that. But he had known what the score was all his life.

His father was a handsome Jamaican called Wendell Prentiss, who had travelled over to Britain in the fifties with nothing but a Rasta hat and a sense of humour. He had a posse of outside children, from a gaggle of different white women, but his legal wife had unfortunately only ever produced one son, Glenford. Wendell had always argued with him, saying that you had only one life, and it was up to *you*, what you did with *it*.

Of course, Wendell would say, in his thick Jamaican accent and with a grin, there would always be the *unexpected*, you needed to allow for them kind of thing, mentally and monetarily, that would cost you dearly. Deaths, births, and more often than not, a serious prison sentence for the majority of Jamaican boys, because the British police don't like us one bit as a race, there *too* many of us now. Always remember, son, he had said with all the dignity he could muster, while drinking white rum and banging his dominos on the kitchen table, those things cost money, time, and the *serious* use of brain power. But other than that, he would say on a laugh, your life was your own, to waste or make the best of.

Jebb Avenue in Brixton, Wendell would say, his deep voice making his words as dramatic as possible, could be the marketplace you visit for a sheepskin coat in the *darkest* days of winter, or where you could end up *queuing* to visit your friends or family. Funky Brixton, as the prison there was called, was the place where white boys had eventually become the niggers.

Glenford had laughed with his father when he had philosophised about those things, yet he knew he had actually been stating facts.

Wendell had died ten years ago, still believing he was a prince, a walking flag of Ethiopia, and still smoking the weed that had actually prevented him from fulfilling his dreams. He had always been too stoned to do anything constructive.

'Life is what *you* make it,' he would say on a daily basis, loudly and seriously. 'You have a blank piece of paper, Glenford, and what you eventually write on it is of your own doing. Good or bad, you have to decide for yourself.'

Glenford had adhered to his father's teachings all his life, and they had kept him in good stead. His father had taught him that sometimes you *had* to hurt people, be cruel to be kind, but Jimmy Jackson, he was a different kettle of fish. He had always tried to make other people's lives *easier*, and the responsibility had weighed on him from day one.

Glenford had few real friends. Like his father before him, he was fussy about who called him by that name, to him friends were people you trusted as much as your family. In this case *more* than your family. Jimmy was a *real* friend. Freddie, on the other hand, was just *treated* like one. It was a subtle difference, but there all the same.

But to Jimmy, Freddie Jackson was family, and in their world *family*, no matter how big a cunt they were, got a wage. That went without saying, but they were supposed to be grateful. They were supposed to understand their fucking good luck that someone close to them had the nous to earn a crust, a crust they were willing to share out.

Now Jimmy was threatening to remove that wage, was going to drop Freddie like a stone. It was Jimmy's call, and Freddie was one dangerous fuck, after all, but Glenford knew that in one way Freddie had a point and was within his rights to believe he was owed a job.

He also knew, by the way Jimmy was talking, that Freddie had irrevocably fucked up any relationship they had ever enjoyed, and Jimmy, whatever Freddie might think, was the better man in more ways than one.

The Jacksons had fought before and nothing had come of it. They had been the talk of the town, especially after

Stephanie's death. Best-kept secret in London that was. But Jimmy had always accepted Freddie back into the fold. He still could, and Glenford hoped that would be the case.

He hated Freddie, but he knew they were better off with him in front of them, acting as a friend, than away from them, out of their orbit, and, knowing Freddie, planning their demise.

Glenford knew that Jimmy must have his reasons for what he was determined to do, but Freddie was going to go what was commonly referred to as ape shit.

Roxanna felt sick and she wasn't sure if it was the baby she was carrying, or her sister's revelation. Even her father could not be capable of something like *that*, of raping Maggie. It couldn't be true.

Maggie was *strong*, she would have fought him surely, stopped him, and she would have screamed it from the rooftops.

Wouldn't she?

But somehow Rox knew that Jackie would have made any kind of accusation impossible for Maggie, and she also felt certain that Maggie would have kept it quiet for their sakes as much as for her mother and Jimmy. Jimmy could never have been told something like that. Maggie was sensible enough to know that her Jimmy would be capable of murder if he had even suspected that something like that had occurred.

Kimberley *must* be wrong, *must* have got the wrong end of the stick. And if her dad *had* raped Maggie, did that mean Jimmy Junior had been his child, as Kim had insinuated? Was he her *brother*? One sexual act, and they had produced a child – it was too off the wall. She knew she had other half-brothers and sisters, she had heard the gossip over the years, but she had never felt the urge to see any of them. Why would she want to?

Jimmy Junior could not have been her father's child. It could *not* be true, it was an absolutely outrageous suggestion. Maggie wouldn't have let that happen to her, she would not have let him near her, no way, it was not feasible.

Not her aunt Maggie, the person who had been like a surrogate mother all their lives, who had always been there for them, and who was still their shelter when their lives got too stormy for them. When this excuse for a mother got pissed and caused fights at Christmas and New Year, they had gone to Maggie because she sorted things out.

Had he raped her? Was her father really that bad, capable of such an act?

The worst thing of all was, deep inside her, she knew it was *true*.

Kimberley had spoken the truth, and even her mother, her dad's biggest fan, his only alibi, and also the only person on the planet who actually *really* cared what happened to him, knew it. It was almost as if Jackie had been expecting to hear it, or something like it, at some point in her life. She had looked almost as if she was being told something she had always known, had looked almost smug because she had finally found out the truth, finally had an understanding of something that had been bugging her.

But Rox just couldn't let herself believe it, didn't want to believe it. She just didn't want to deal with it. Didn't want to look at her aunt Maggie, who she loved, and know that her father had intruded so violently into her life.

Jackie Jackson, however, had finally found the last piece of a puzzle she had been trying to solve for many years. When Freddie had made a fuss of Jimmy Junior she had known in her heart that something was off, that there was something underneath his smiling demeanour, and his grinning face. He had never taken much notice of his own children, and she had always felt a deep jealousy about his treatment of that boy.

'Jimmy Junior', what a fucking pantomime that was. But then the two men looked so alike and the kids all had a look of one another. Her Rox was like a clone of Maggie. Jackie knew that Freddie had always had a penchant for her little sister, but what about Jimmy? What would Jimmy think about it all, especially now the boy was dead? She had to have had an affair, that was all it could be. Maggie had to have things, had always wanted what she had, Freddie included. But raped? Kimberley said it was a rape, that Maggie had said it to Freddie in no uncertain terms when he had tried to make her admit little Jimmy was his child at the funeral. And Jackie knew Freddie was capable of something like that. Was Maggie really raped?

Freddie had a way with women, maybe she had come on to *him*. He could be so charming when the fancy took him. She remembered how he had gone on about her, Maggie this and Maggie that, nearly driving Jackie out of her mind with jealousy. And look at how pleased Freddie had been when she had been delivered of a son.

Maggie had finally got pregnant, after all that time, and she had been thrilled for her. Pregnant Maggie was not supposed to have been a *threat* any more, she was supposed to have been out of bounds, and now Kimberley was saying that Maggie's boy, that poor little boy, was her husband's child.

Well, he was dead and gone, thank God. That was all she needed now, a living reminder of Freddie's infidelity, and in her own family this time.

The bastard.

But *raped*, not a chance, what *crap*. Freddie had women after him all the time, he didn't have to force anyone. If this was a true story then Maggie had to have been gagging for it.

She was crying rape in case it got back to Jimmy, and he would not listen to reason. Like everyone else, he thought that Maggie was a *blinder*, a *good* girl, well, she had shown her true colours now.

She wasn't the first tart Freddie had shagged and she wouldn't be the last, and Jackie had seen off better women than Maggie. But she would play this hand close to her chest, for now. Until Jimmy found out about it, she would keep stumm.

In her heart she didn't want this out in the open. Maggie was too close to home, and far too lovely for Jackie Jackson to allow herself to ever be compared with her. She knew that the majority of people would not blame Freddie for straying with her younger, more beautiful sister.

She could hear him brag that he had married the wrong sister, that he should have waited a few years until Maggie was old enough. He had said those words to her in this very room many times.

Kimberley listened to her mother as she went on and on about Maggie always wanting what she had, Maggie always taking whatever she wanted, being the favourite child, and instead of anger, she felt a deep and abiding pity for the woman who had borne her.

Jackie had already blamed poor Mags for what had happened, and her father was as always the innocent party. Maggie had lured him into her bed to get back at her. Jackie was actually believing her own lies now.

Kimberley now knew that when she had opened her

big mouth, she had started something that would haunt them all down the years.

Her father was the innocent in all this, her mother had tried and already condemned poor Maggie, and the only thing her stupid revelation had achieved was more hurt and more unhappiness for her lovely aunt. As if she didn't have enough to contend with.

Chapter Twenty-Eight

Jimmy was nervous, not frightened, but he was *nervous*, because he knew Freddie was not going to accept his expulsion from the business with easy grace.

Freddie had been given a message to come and see him, and he was psyched up and ready for him. Freddie was a wild card. He had seen some of the stunts he had pulled over the years on people he had seen as doing him down, or, as was more often the case, because he had no further use for them.

He would take this personally because of the blood tie and also because he saw Jimmy as taking what he saw as his by rights. Jimmy was in effect banishing him from what had always been his world, and he was not wavering at all. In fact, he was going to relish telling him.

Jimmy had given him opportunity after opportunity to redeem himself and Freddie, being Freddie, had thrown them all back in his face. Now he was going to find out that he was on the lowest rung of the ladder that denoted their particular food chain, and *he* was the one calling the shots, not Freddie.

Jimmy had swallowed his knob over the years but that mad bastard he had reared was the final straw. He couldn't tell Maggie what had happened, and he couldn't ever let on to anyone else, but Freddie had known what was expected of him and he had not kept his end of the bargain, so he was out.

Not just out of the business but out of his world completely. He did not want to clap eyes on him ever again. If that meant he had to remove him from the face of the earth, then so be it. Jimmy only wished that he had made a point of taking him out sooner.

How Freddie coped with it was up to him, but anyone who employed him would not be able to deal with Jimmy or his workforce ever again, he would make that known everywhere.

Freddie was going to be a pariah and no one except the two of them would know why, and Freddie would understand that he was not going to let him walk away from his problems any more.

He should have done this when Freddie had done Lenny, but he had given him another pass. Well, he was all out of family loyalty now, so fuck him and fuck his poxy kid. Freddie Junior was his father's son all right, another mad cunt had been unleashed on the world. Well, Freddie Jackson had better take the boy as far away from him and his family as he could, because if he ever saw him he would run him down without a second's thought.

It was only Maggie that was stopping him from blowing Freddie and that mad little bastard wide open. Maggie had enough to contend with without knowing what had really happened to her boy, and he would protect her as long as he had breath in his body.

She must never, ever know.

Freddie was finished in their world, and that would be punishment enough for him because he lived and breathed his reputation. Well, let him try and muscle in on

Jimmy after he had delivered the bad news, and Freddie Jackson would find out exactly what he was dealing with.

He couldn't wait for that to happen. He was shaking with anticipation, and he was high with adrenaline. Freddie had the shock of his life coming to him, and Jimmy was getting impatient with the waiting game he had been forced to play because he had not wanted to hurt anyone's feelings.

Family loyalty was a load of old cods. Who in their right mind wanted to be related to those two-faced lying ponces anyway? He had carried them for years, lent them money, sorted out their problems. He was like the Bank of Jimmy.

Well, not any more. Let them stew in their own juices and let them go to their so-called friends in the future.

They were takers, professional takers and they had taken the thing he held most dear to him, and for that alone, he would *never* forgive, or, more importantly, *forget.*

This was for his Jimmy, for his own peace of mind. Like Freddie Jackson before him he now held a grudge and that grudge would see him through the dark days ahead.

Jackie was looking at her eldest child but she was not seeing her. She was seeing what she had ignored over the years. Even when she was a young girl Freddie had coveted her sister. He had watched her, and he had wanted her, thought about her, desired her.

These thoughts were not registering on her face. As Kimberley looked at her mother she knew that she was in a state of shock.

Roxanna was also shocked, in fact she'd been almost at fainting point since Jackie had insisted that Maggie must have seduced her father. 'You can't believe what you are saying, Mum. Like Maggie would want him anywhere near *her*.' The inference being that no woman in her right mind would want her husband, this girl's own father.

Jackie's head snapped towards this beautiful daughter who at this moment she could happily strangle. The truth was screaming inside her skull, but being the personality type she was, she could never admit out loud that Freddie wanted her sister, even though she knew it was the truth. Freddie wanted anyone who came near him and was in the least bit shaggable.

Jackie had laughed about it over the years, she had been forced to. It was how she had saved face. Especially when she had found out about him with her friends, with her neighbours, when she had seen young girls looking at her in the pub, and finding her lacking. She had endured knowing that they had intimate knowledge of her man, and that some of them had produced children for him.

She had accepted so much because she could not in any way envisage her life without him somewhere in the background, no matter what he did or how he treated her. And in his own way he *had* stood by her. She was the *only* woman he had ever stood by, even though it was in a callous and often degrading way.

Jackie was going to be Freddie Jackson's wife until the day she died. It afforded her the only kudos she had ever experienced, and it also guaranteed her a level of protection that enabled her to drink and drug with impunity.

Since the turnout with Terry Baker, her confidence, which had never been in abundance, was at rock bottom. Another humiliation was more than she would be able to endure. Freddie was everything to her, he made her a valid person. From the first moment she had been with him, she had felt like she was somebody, and she was, she was Freddie Jackson's bird, his woman, eventually his wife.

The money was only a small part of it all. She loved him with every fibre of her being, and if Maggie thought she was going to change that she would find out how wrong she could be.

He had lived his life hunting out strange and she had accepted everything, but she could not in all conscience accept this.

She knew this ought to be kept quiet, she actually wanted it kept quiet because the thought of anyone knowing made her feel almost suicidal. But she also knew she could not keep this to herself. A few drinks and it would be blurted out in temper, or worse, she would throw it at Freddie and he would turn it back at her, making a terrible situation even worse.

She needed to strike first, make this common knowledge, cause trouble for Maggie. Jackie knew better than anyone how to play the wronged wife – she had had enough practice over the years after all.

Maggie, dead child or no dead child, had betrayed her. Rape be buggered, the truth would be out there in seconds.

Her mind was made up.

Freddie had decided to make a short detour on his way to Jimmy's office. He pulled up to the pub, and after standing for a few moments, as if surveying his realm, he decided that Jimmy Jackson could come to him, so he sauntered inside and ordered a large Scotch.

Paul and Liselle were pleased to see him, at least as pleased as anyone who knew him could be. Paul refilled his drink as soon as it was empty and the two men smiled at each other. He could feel the usual animosity off Freddie, but today there was a new feeling, an undercurrent of menace that was not usually so evident.

'You heard anything from Ozzy?'

Paul shrugged as he always did when asked that question. 'A few lines, that's all. He doesn't confide in me, Freddie, you know that.'

This was said in a flat monotone voice, a voice that brooked no more questions and told the enquirer he was keeping his own counsel but also that he knew far more than he was letting on.

He knew it irritated Freddie, even though he never expected a different answer. Today, though, there was an added annoyance that caused Paul to keep close to the shotgun he always kept underneath the bar. It was a weapon that was there mainly for the threat factor, but he would use it if necessary.

'And you ain't got no new fucking messages for me from Jimmy, then? After all, Paul, you are normally far more aware of what's going on than I am, ain't you? Jimmy, the cunt, tells you much more than he tells me.'

This was said so as to cause the maximum aggro, but Paul smiled carefully before saying quietly, 'No one's told me anything about you, or given me any messages, but if I hear anything you'll be the first to know, OK?'

He was watching Freddie while making sure his hand hovered over the shotgun.

Freddie had been gearing himself up for a while now, and Paul guessed, rightly, that it was all about his discontent. Freddie was being mugged off big time, everyone had noticed that, but that was not Paul's problem, that was Freddie Jackson's. Freddie was like a fucking big wet balloon, and he was due to burst soon.

Even the little boy's death had not softened the edges. In fact, since then Freddie seemed to be even worse, if that was possible.

Poor Jimmy had taken it badly, but that was to be

expected. He had lost a child, an only child, a loved and wanted child, but it was Freddie whom the knowledge had seemed to age. As Paul watched him drinking now, so early in the day and so heavily, even though he knew he would insist on driving, he wondered what the added aggravation was this time.

As far as Paul knew, he was still pissing about on the take, and Freddie, being Freddie, that was all he would ever be doing. He never kept anything up for any length of time and he had ideas that were good and which he talked about for days but never came to fruition.

He had seen Freddie looking for a fight before and he was suddenly glad that he was not the recipient of Freddie's obvious anger and resentment. But that could change, he knew. Freddie Jackson could turn on a coin, and that meant no one was ever really safe from him until he had left the building.

Glenford and Jimmy had lunched at the Ship and Shovel on sandwiches and a few beers, the mainstay of men in their line of work.

They were both aware of the unspoken agreement between them, Glenford was going nowhere, he was sticking it out for the duration. Jimmy was more than aware of what he was taking on but Glenford knew he had a far more intelligent outlook on the situation. Unlike Jimmy he wasn't that close to the enemy.

Jimmy, for all his hardness, was liable to relent and give Freddie, as usual, the benefit of the doubt. Freddie, however, was never going to let this affront go without a serious fight, and Freddie fought well, it was all he had ever been good at. Glenford was frightened that this friend of his was making the mistake all great men eventually made – they underestimated their enemy, or, even worse, they assumed their enemy possessed qualities that they themselves had. Were far more decent people than they actually were.

Jimmy Jackson had always played the white man, while Freddie had always talked one way and acted another. It was the very nature of the beast he was. Freddie Jackson did not have a decent bone in his large and overly strong body. Of that much, at least, Glenford was sure. He also knew that Jimmy Jackson was not intending to go back on his decision. His worry, if he was honest, was that Jimmy might relent at the last moment and leave himself wide open to attack.

'Mum, for fuck's sake . . .' Kimberley had just realised what she had actually caused and the knowledge was frightening her now.

Jackie was getting dressed and any thought of sleep was long gone. This was now a woman on a mission, a dangerous mission that entailed murdering her sister in cold blood if necessary.

'Stop it, Mum, and listen to me. I heard them at Jimmy Junior's funeral, Dad was baiting her even then, he was being *hateful* to her even though she had just buried her child—'

'Oh my heart's bleeding for her, the cunt, and don't you mean *their* child?'

'Mum, Maggie would never hurt you, not intentionally. Why do you think she kept it quiet all these years?'

'If you were shagging my old man wouldn't you keep it quiet? Jimmy might not be too thrilled when he hears either, love, has that occurred to you yet? All my life she has wanted what I have, she had been jealous of me since day one! I had what she wanted!'

Kim laughed now. 'You can't seriously mean me father,

can you? Maggie wanting him, are you off your fucking trolley, Mother? And even if she had, Maggie wouldn't do that to *you*, she loves *you* even though you treat her like shit.'

Jackie sighed and then said in a friendly yet sinister way, 'She is dead, Kimmy, get that through your thick fucking head. She *fucked* my old man, she had a baby with *my* old man – your words not mine, Kim – and if you think I am listening to all that old fanny about rape you can get stuffed. I will take her fucking head off her shoulders, and yours with it if you interfere any more.'

Kimberley was absolutely terrified now. 'Stop this, Mum, and think about it. Why would she be telling him to leave her alone, eh? Why would she have fucked him off out of it?'

Jackie sighed heavily. Her daughter was just what she needed to start off her campaign of hate. No one was accusing *her* husband of rape. He was a fucking babe, and Maggie had wanted him because he was *hers* and she was *jealous.* In Jackie's mind everyone she fell out with, or had a grudge against, was jealous of her. In her mind she was really something else. Her home was a cause of jealousy, her husband, their lifestyle. It never occurred to Jackie that it was her own vindictive jealousy that caused most of her problems.

To her now, Freddie had been duped, had been led up the garden path by a femme fatale who had been a virgin till Jimmy and who she knew would not have given Freddie Jackson house room if the four-minute warning had just sounded. And they had produced a child – well, for once Maggie could hurt like she had hurt as she watched her little sister make a success of her life, watched her go on to bigger and better things!

Jackie was the eldest, it should have been her who had

the salons and the big houses, not Maggie, not little Maggie who she had always used as and when it had suited her and who had suddenly, overnight, become the rich bitch of the family.

How *dare* she think that she could get one over on her?

Freddie had joked that Jimmy was a Jaffa, and maybe he was right. No other kids had arrived and she knew it wasn't for want of trying. Maggie was desperate for another one, had been since the birth of little Jimmy Junior. She went on about it enough.

Jackie had, it seemed, cried over her husband's bastard, and she would not let that go lightly. Baby be damned, little Jimmy *had* been her husband's child. He had taken more notice of that boy than he had of any of his own, and she would not forgive that bastard Maggie for that. It was the ultimate betrayal as far as she was concerned. No wonder she had not wanted the poor little fucker, guilt did that to a body, and even her own mother had called her unnatural over her treatment of him.

'Please, Mum, think about what you are doing. He raped Maggie, raped her. Jimmy will kill him, Jimmy will believe her . . . Like I do, and other people will.'

The truth of these words didn't escape Jackie but she fronted it out as always. 'Oh, Kimmy, what's the matter, eh? You want me to score a few pills for you, calm you down, like? Or maybe you want me to take back my fucking fist and wipe that pathetic look off your face once and for all? She is a fucking husband-stealing whore and she is me own sister, me own fucking sister. Well, she's dead, as are you dead if you get in me way.'

She grinned as she dragged her clothes on to her cumbersome body. 'Come on, sweetheart, it's your call.'

Roxanna was watching the scene before her and she still had a feeling of terrible doom on her. It was like the first few days before her period, when everything had a weird aftertaste, when she could make 'Good morning' sound like a declaration of war.

She knew that if what Kimberley said was true then Maggie had been raped by her father. There was no other way that it could have happened. Maggie would sooner bed down with the local tramp than Freddie Jackson, and she couldn't blame her. If the boot was on the other foot she would have felt exactly the same. But how was this going to affect her? Her and her Dicky boy? What would happen when all this shit hit the big fan that had now metamorphosed into her mother's big trap?

She didn't want Dicky's mother and the rest of his family finding out about anything like this, it was too extreme even for the Jacksons. It was now her reputation she was worried about, but any reasoning with Jackie about this little lot was likely to be about as much use as a handbrake on a fucking canoe.

Kim had opened up a can of worms, and these were evil worms, vindictive worms and they were worms that were in her mother's mouth and would therefore be spewed out sooner than any of them might actually believe.

Jackie was still dressing herself, and as she did so Kimberley was trying to convince her that Maggie, poor Maggie, had been the victim. Rox knew that this was the worst thing her sister could do. If her father took an axe and murdered all the neighbours in front of a film crew from Channel Four, her mother would convince herself that it was not true, or that they had done something so heinous his murdering of them was justified.

Roxanna could cheerfully wring Kim's neck.

She would have to warn poor Maggie and as she wondered about Maggie's reaction to this news getting out, it hit her that Jimmy, her lovely uncle Jimmy, was as big a force as her father was. In fact, she was aware that he was now a bigger, better-connected force. Dicky was enamoured of her uncle Jimmy to the point of adoration.

This was so serious, she knew it would smash the family apart, and she wished that Kimberley had kept her big nose out of it. Like her mother, Rox liked everything on an even keel and if that meant keeping things swept under the carpet, pretending things were OK, then that was what she was prepared to do.

She wanted to cry. Everything was going to be destroyed, and she knew that life would never be the same again for any of them. But it was her loyalties that were really disturbing her, because if she was pushed to choose, her mother and father wouldn't stand a chance.

Paul had answered the phone three times and each time it had been Glenford asking if Freddie was still there, and what condition he was in.

He had said each time, 'Yes and not good.'

He knew something was going down and he was terrified of it happening in front of him and his wife. Liselle had been dispatched off to their flat with a warning that no matter what she heard, she was to keep a low profile.

Freddie was on a roll now, and his handsome face belied the evil that lurked so near to the surface. A girl had arrived an hour earlier, when Freddie had finally been about to depart. The girl was in her twenties with long hair, a crooked smile and a skirt that defied gravity. She was also, to add insult to injury, Liselle's niece, and she had taken one look at Freddie and love had been born.

What was it with women and Freddie Jackson? The worse he treated them the more they seemed to want him. She was all perfume and mint chewing gum, her clothes were New Look mixed with Dot Perkins and the stomach she was baring was not as washboard as she liked to believe.

She was Freddie's cup of char all right, up for it, been about long enough to know the score, but still young enough not to have the hard bitter look that Jackie and her cronies had acquired. Jimmy was gone from his mind now. Freddie was on the pull and in an extravagant and exhilarating way, much to the delight of Melanie Connors.

Melanie was funny, she had the chat, the look and the experienced way of young girls who had been at it from too young an age and still hadn't sussed out that sex was not a bargaining tool for most women.

Her witty ripostes were hilarious, and Freddie was enjoying the arrogance of her youth and her complete confidence in her good looks. But that could all change in seconds if she said something that he considered was disrespectful or downright challenging.

On Melanie's part, Freddie Jackson might be old enough to be her father, but she wasn't worried about that. He was, to her, gorgeous, with his dark hair and blue eyes. He also, she was pleased to note, had a wedge that could hold her mother's front door open in a hurricane, and she knew instinctively that he was hung like a horse. All in all, she was pleased with the way the day had turned out.

Paul, however, was absolutely gutted. He knew that Freddie was on the edge and poor little Melanie had not experienced Freddie with the hump just yet. As she was a relative of his wife's he would have to step in at some point and that was not something he was looking forward to.

At the moment, though, Freddie was like a sniffer dog in a crack house, happy as a sandboy and enjoying the afternoon's events. He hunted strange like other men hunted deer. He was quiet, he was watching her every move and when the time was right he was going to shoot this fucker down. If she was good at her trade she might get a second airing, if not she would be forgotten in the time it takes to find a new one with bigger tits and the pure attraction of unknown territory.

It was the chase he loved, the conquering of the girls. Once that was achieved they were history.

Dianna was in bits as both her sisters shouted simultaneously and with equal anger and annoyance, 'Oh shut up, Di!'

Maggie stared at the three girls she loved with all her being and then she turned to her sister and said quietly, 'Don't be so silly, Jackie. Kimberley heard wrong, that was all.'

Kimberley grabbed the branch she was being offered and hoped that it would stop her drowning in her own guilt. 'That's right, I was not sure what I was going on about, Mum. We were arguing, and I wanted to hurt you, that's all.'

'You fucking lying whore, you fucking junkie slag! You know what happened, I ain't fucking stupid!'

Maggie was under no illusions about how this knowledge was going to be received by the main antagonists, but she was past caring. Nothing could ever hurt her again and she wasn't sure she was even capable of keeping the peace with her sister. If push came to shove she was willing to annihilate her. If that's what it took to shut this slob up, then that was fine by her.

But she forced her voice to sound calm and civil once more. 'Come on, Jackie, have a drink, a coffee or a vodka, you choose.'

Jackie knew she was being offered a face-saver, a chance to stop this madness before it got out of hand, but Maggie's utter calmness was her undoing.

Even though she knew without a shadow of a doubt that this girl, and Maggie still looked like a girl, had been *raped* she could not for the life of her let that fact seep outside her closest circle.

'You are offering *me* vodka? Sure *you* don't want one now your fucking secret's out?'

Maggie looked into her sister's bloated face, remembering when she had been everything to her, had been the mainstay of her life. And she had been, there had been a time when Jackie had been the whole of her world, when she had always included her little sister in everything.

Maggie was more than aware that loneliness had been the real reason then, but it had also been because Maggie had taken on the kids for her.

She had practically brought the girls up, and she had to admit she had enjoyed every second of it, unlike this sorry item in front of her who only saw her kids as a wage each week, people to chain their father to the floor and make him cough up in more ways than one.

Maggie had played with them, bathed them, tidied up for Jackie and listened to her as she had run down everyone within a five-mile range – family especially, mates, and anyone she was jealous of. Since that encompassed everyone in the world she could get very irate. Jackie slaughtered everybody, and she did it in such a way that it was ages before you realised exactly what she was doing.

By the time she had been fourteen Maggie had stopped wanting to be like her, and instead become adamant that her life would be the complete opposite of Jackie's. She would pay her *own* bills, look after herself if needs be, but she was determined not to become a part of the man she was with like Jackie had.

Jackie's biggest fear was being left without a man, her man, but it was the man she loved so much, who had reduced her to the fat, scruffy wreck she was now. She was living proof that love was not the wonderful emotion young girls thought it was going to be. The man she loved had raped her little sister and yet she still had the power to delude herself, because everything was *always* about Jackie, never about anyone else.

'Was little Jimmy Freddie's son? I need to know.'

Jackie sounded so self-righteous and so fucking banal all at the same time, it was better than a play as far as Maggie was concerned. This woman had always been an innate coward, and this was being proved to her once again. Jackie only kicked off when she knew that the fight she had caused would be stopped.

Maggie laughed, but it sounded forced and it also made her sound like a woman who had had enough, enough of life, enough of the world and enough of the woman in front of her.

'If you really thought that there was anything remotely true in what you are saying, me and you would be rolling around the floor fighting now, Jack, and you know it.'

'Too fucking right.'

'But we ain't, are we, Jackie?'

The sarcasm was evident and Jackie Jackson had to acknowledge that her little sister was a force in her own right.

'There's still plenty of time for that, lady.' She pointed a grubby finger at her sister as she said loudly and in a voice full of her own self-pity, 'You always had your eye on my fucking Freddie, you always got what you wanted out of life. I was never good enough for Mum and Dad, it was always you! Now, the one thing I have and you fucking think you can take it!'

'What are you on about, Mum? Maggie is the best thing that ever happened to you, or us!' Dianna realised immediately she should have kept this gem of wisdom to herself, and Kimberley pushed Roxanne out of her way as she went to her mother and said angrily, 'I was winding you up, Mum, please listen to me.'

Jackie wanted to take the exit and leave the madness of her world, but she couldn't. This would eat at her now and she knew she had to sort it out today once and for all, no matter what the cost.

'Either go home and sober up, Jackie, or talk to me properly, OK?'

There was a steely quality to her sister's voice that Jackie had never heard before. In fact, she would go as far as to say that it was distinctly disrespectful.

'I will break your fucking neck, you cunt!'

Maggie sighed once more. 'Is that really the best you can do, Jack? Call me names, call *me* a cunt, the one word that I hate more than any other? I just realised, Sis, it sums you up lovely, doesn't it? I lost my child and you think you can come round here shouting the odds, because you think I wanted the piece of shit you married. You had better sort yourself out, mate. Listen to yourself now and again, you selfish, drunken fat bitch!'

Maggie waved her hand at Jackie like she was nothing and turned to the girls, who were huddled together in various stages of shock.

'Take her home, for fuck's sake. Get her out of my sight!'

The animosity was almost tangible between the two women now.

'I'll fucking kill you, Maggie Jackson. You'll fucking regret taking the piss out of me, lady.'

Maggie turned back towards her sister. She spoke quietly, and with menace, enunciating every word slowly and clearly, her own well-manicured finger poking her sister in the face.

'You lay one hand on me, Jack, and I will *wrap* you around this house. I am capable of it and all, mate. You *don't scare me any more*, you haven't scared me since I was at school. You are a big, fat, bloated, mouthy, fucking no neck, and that is your problem. You know that better than anyone else does and that knowledge kills you.'

Maggie was shaking her head in disappointed anger. 'I buried my baby and you would still bring this shit to my door? If there's any killing to be done this day, it will be done by me, get it? And you remember that if you bring this little soirée into my Jimmy's world, Freddie and you will both be finished, and I will see to that personally. You are not welcome here, Jackie. I have carried you for years and I don't fucking need this *crap* in my life any more. Now fuck off home before I really lose my rag.'

Chapter Twenty-Nine

'Please tell me what the fuck is really going on, Jimmy. Me nerves are nearly busted with all this.' Glenford was laughing as he spoke but Jimmy knew he meant it seriously.

'I told you, I ain't carrying him no more. I have had enough of him. Not before time, is it? Anyone else would have aimed him out the door years ago. But he was family, and I swallowed because of that. End of story.'

'Beginning of the story, more like.'

Jimmy shrugged, and Glenford knew that he would not get any more from him. Instead, he asked, 'Is he still on a promise?'

'From what I gather, yeah.' Jimmy grinned now. 'Freddie and his skirt, eh? I remember when he was released and he was clocking anything with a pulse.'

Glenford laughed loudly now, his new gold teeth glinting in the weak afternoon sun. 'It his hobby. Strange is what keeps the man alive.' Then he sat down on the comfortable leather sofa in Jimmy's office and said seriously, 'What is this about, man? I can feel your anger, feel your body rhythms are all out of sync. I just want to help you, man, you are me best friend and you know that. I think there's a good chance that I am yours as well, you know.'

Jimmy nodded in acknowledgement.

Glenford was shaking his heavy dreads in consternation now, and, picking up half a joint from the heavy white soapstone ashtray in front of him, he relit it. Puffing on it heavily he said, 'Since Jimmy Junior, you ain't been right, you specially ain't been right with Freddie. It's almost like you blaming him.'

Jimmy loved this man like a brother, and he wasn't surprised that he had worked out the cause of his problems so easily, but he could not say out loud what was still careering around his head every second of every day.

Freddie's son had killed his baby, his boy, his life's blood.

Freddie was on the laughing gear. The girl had provided a decent bit of sniff and, mixed with the whisky and Freddie's bad humour, he was now rocking.

Melanie thought she was the height of sophistication, she sniffed as loud as possible and with dramatic hand gestures so that everyone around her would know she had taken cocaine.

Freddie didn't have the heart to tell her that it was cut so badly, if it was a geezer it would have a face full of Mars Bars. He had scored some decent shit for himself off a mate that lunchtime, and he had just slipped it to Melanie who was now about to fly higher than the Hubble spacecraft.

Her eyes were already glittering and, he had to admit, coked-out birds before they hit the deck had a certain charm about them. This little bird really believed she knew her gear, knew a snort and knew a puff.

What an embarrassment she really was. A fucking babe in arms to him, and that was just how he liked them.

In a few minutes she would start to talk the hind leg off a table. He would find out all her business, and Freddie was looking forward to that. She was a lamb, and lambs like this one needed slaughtering badly. This was going to be a life lesson for her. He only hoped she realised how lucky she was that he was taking such an interest in her, even if it was mainly to kill a few hours and see if Jimmy came to him for a change.

He forced another drink on her and she gulped at it, as he knew she would, because her mouth was now drier than a nun's tits, and the whole bottom of her face had gone numb. As she leaned forward he saw she was about to stumble and he grabbed her in his arms, in a tight bear hug that made her feel cared for, made her feel safe.

'Steady on, girl, you sure you're all right?'

He was jovial, he was on his best behaviour, and he was also copping a feel of her very adventurous-looking Bristols. He guessed from her smile that they had been handled more times than a footballer's dick but he didn't care about that. He fancied a bit of soft, and big bouncy ones were always good for a bit of soft.

Judging by her belly, which she was now forgetting to hold in, she usually drank lager.

Well, she was in for an education today, and he was just in the mood to start educating her.

Paul was worried about the condition of his wife's niece and knew without a doubt that he was going to get the blame for it. 'Leave her alone, Freddie. Come on, Mel love. Go on up to Liselle.'

Melanie pushed her long straggly blond hair out of her face and said belligerently, 'Piss off, Paul, I am over eighteen, you know.'

Her hostility was rubbing off on Freddie now as he watched the little scene unfolding before his eyes. 'What the fuck's it got to do with you anyway, Paul?'

Paul shrugged. 'It's Liselle's niece.'

Freddie bellowed at the poor girl, 'Are you? Really?'

She nodded and they both started to laugh.

Paul knew when he was beaten but he tried once more, knowing Liselle would get a blow-by-blow account off the regular punters. 'Come on, you're off your nut. Let me take you up to Liselle, eh?'

Freddie pushed Paul's arms away from the girl, nearly knocking her over in the process.

'Fuck off, you prick, she is all right with me.'

Paul sighed. 'Come on, Freddie, how would you feel if it was one of your girls? Liselle will do her crust, and you know it.'

He was the voice of reason, the nice bloke. None of which cut any ice with Freddie Jackson, who only saw his afternoon's shag disappearing before his eyes. 'Fuck off, Paul, and I mean it.'

The menace was evident, as was the way he suddenly straightened up, pulled back his shoulders and bared his teeth, making him look almost feral.

'Why don't you go and ring Ozzy, or even Jimmy, his chief arsehole licker, and grass me up, tell them what I've been doing all day, eh? You fucking snotbag . . . Tell them, right, that I think they are a pair of cunts. Go on –' he was laughing now at his own words – 'tell them that. Go on, I dare you.'

Everyone in the pub had gone quiet as he shouted out his insults and Paul knew his ravings were going to be all over the place within hours. Freddie should have known better than to let his mouth run away with him like that. It wasn't the first time it had happened, though, lately it had been a frequent event. He was more annoyed that Freddie was mouthing off like that to impress a little girl who was destined for everything their world had to offer, except of course greatness.

Melanie was her mother's daughter, and he gave her three years before she really was old before her time. Paul could have launched his wife's niece out of the door and through Barking Park. Instead, he shook his head sadly and watched the girl as her screeching laugh became a very deep and very nasty smoker's cough.

She was eighteen and three months and she was listening to Freddie Jackson as if he was the oracle and looking at him as if he was something the cat had dragged in just for her.

Well, fuck her now, let her make her own mistakes. He had just about had enough. If Liselle stayed upstairs he was safe enough. If not, she could sort this lot out herself.

Jackie was alone in her house and as usual she was drinking vodka mixed with wine. She had been so sure that she was going to lay Maggie out once and for all, but she had ended up leaving with her daughters and her shame at her predicament was growing by the second.

Her daughters should have seen her confront and conquer the woman who had accused their father of rape, yet she knew they believed it of him. Her own kids thought that little of their father, and she knew they thought even less of her.

It was this that was troubling her so much. In a few hours her whole world had come crashing down around her ears and she knew that there would never be any going back now. Her mother and father would be in bits about it, especially after the kid dying. He was the kid now, because she knew in her heart that Freddie was his father. Freddie had fathered that little boy.

If Maggie told Jimmy what she had said there would be murders. Maggie had denied it all but she had known her sister was lying through her teeth. Maggie was trying to save her, trying to save the family and on one level she understood that. But looking at Maggie today, with her perfect hair and her perfect home, the usual jealous animosity was to the fore.

Even with the grief she knew her sister was having to cope with, Jackie still found it hard to feel any pity for her. In fact she felt that Maggie had all the luck, even her bloody kid had died and she was once more a free agent.

What she wouldn't have given to have offloaded hers over the years. Especially the girls, who had driven her mad with their backchat and their constant sniping at her.

She picked up the bottle of vodka and saw that she had downed over two thirds of it, and she wasn't even starting to feel drunk. It took longer and longer now, she was just topping up. She was half pissed all day every day. But instead of her usual happy feeling she was experiencing an incredible anger. It was bubbling away and the more she thought of how she had humiliated herself at Maggie's, the more she felt she should do something, something spectacular, to make amends.

Rape! She was having a laugh if she thought that old flannel would wash. The hate was inside her once more. She could never allow herself to believe that her husband had done something so monstrous. It was, she decided, the most ridiculous thing she had ever heard of, and she was not going to let that fucking skank get away with the accusation.

She swallowed down the rest of her drink and poured herself out another, larger glass. She was feeling in the mood for revenge now and she had a good idea how she was going to achieve it.

Jimmy needed a rocket up his arse and she was going to see that he got just that. She would make Maggie think twice before she threw around those kind of allegations.

She was almost out of control now, she knew the signs, and she knew she was on the verge of losing the little bit of rationality she possessed.

Everyone was the enemy now, including her slag of a husband, and especially that skinny bitch who had the nerve to call herself a sister.

Paul was on the phone to Jimmy. 'He is cunting you up hill and down dale. Everyone is blanking him as best they can, but you have to come and get shot for me, Jim. He is fucking out of order.'

'Start clearing the pub, Paul, on the quiet, OK?'

Paul sighed and whispered angrily, 'I have had enough of him. Liselle is like the fucking anti-Christ, walking round with a face like a fucking Rottweiler chewing on a hornet's nest, and blaming me for her niece being out of her fucking box. And to add insult to injury, he is accusing me and you of being arse lickers for Oz. Who will not be in the least impressed when he hears about this lot.'

Paul sounded worried. Freddie was not a man anyone would take on lightly, and Paul, even though he had his shotgun, would much rather leave the man's removal to Jimmy Jackson.

Jimmy sighed. 'You're like a fucking old woman, Paul. Get a fucking grip, you nonce. Just do what I say and clear the pub. Leave everything else to me. I want a car and I want peace and quiet, do you get my drift?'

Paul didn't answer and Jimmy knew then that he was finally taking the seriousness of the situation on board.

'When I arrive, I want you to fuck off, and I don't want to see you until the morning, all right?'

Paul was nodding in complete and utter consternation. 'OK.' Only that morning he had said there would be murders. He had not, however, meant it literally.

Freddie was calling out to him from the bar, 'Phoning your boyfriend? Tell him I am ready when he is.'

Melanie was laughing her head off and this alone was annoying Paul. He knew Jimmy could hear it all as well. He felt like a kid who had been caught out grassing, but then again, he knew that was how Freddie wanted him to feel.

'Ignore him, Paul. Just get yourself out of there, OK.'

The line went dead then and Paul stared at the phone as if he had never seen it before. As he replaced the receiver, he saw his wife standing at the top of the stairs. The fear on her face was evident as he said quietly, 'Pack a bag, we are out of here.'

'What about Melanie?'

Paul shrugged in exaggerated boredom. 'What about her?'

Maggie was alone, and as always since her baby had died she let the quiet envelop her. She liked being on her own. It gave her a feeling of security because she could still pretend that he was alive, that he was going to walk through the door laughing with his daddy. Only poor Jimmy walked in by himself and the bubble burst and she became more aloof than ever.

All that wasted time, all those years when she had not been able to even touch the child without a feeling of revulsion. Freddie taunting her with his eyes and with his smiles, how had she lived through that?

She wondered at times how she had coped with it all. Now she would put up with anything to have him back beside her, no matter how much his presence might hurt her.

And Jackie – the balloon would be going up soon there. She knew her sister too well. Now she had this big black secret that she could use as a big stick, and Jackie would take great pleasure in beating her with it.

Maggie hated her at times, and she never wanted to see her again, but it was still second nature to her to try and protect the woman who would happily destroy her and her life.

She waited patiently for her husband to return.

'This is between me and Freddie.'

Glenford sighed, much like Paul had a few minutes earlier. 'Let me come with you, eh?'

Jimmy shook his head. 'Nah, I have a lot of sorting out to do. You get yourself off home, mate. You've been stuck to me like shit to a blanket all day.'

'Is this as serious as it feels, Jimmy?' Glenford's voice was soft. He had a deep brown voice and it was a kind voice, unless the person he was addressing had upset him in some way. Then his voice sounded deadly, and the listener was aware that their days were liable to be numbered unless they did *exactly* what he was asking of them.

It was this determination, which Jimmy also had in abundance, that had made them such good friends.

'Do you remember all those years ago, Jimmy, when Freddie tried to have me over with that shit grass?'

Jimmy nodded.

'I knew even then that you were to be trusted and Freddie was nothing but a piece of shit. A lucky piece of shit, he had been lucky enough to have been banged up with Ozzy who saw a worker and utilised him. But without you he would not have lasted a month, and do you know the worst thing of all?'

Jimmy shook his head.

'Freddie knows that as well, and that, my friend, is why this day had to come.'

Jimmy grinned. 'I never begrudged him a thing, always a fifty-fifty split, and I still had to fucking bail him out. Do you know how much we have collared over the years? Fucking fortunes, and I watch him putting on his thirty-grand fucking bets, and his fucking cars that he runs into the ground and then fucking dumps. He don't even bother to fucking insure them half the time, a sixty-grand motor and he can't even be bothered to insure it. All that dough and he is still scratching a fucking living. I ain't giving him a fifty split any more. I haven't for years, and he has never once questioned it. He gets twenty per cent now because I couldn't bear to see that money being spunked. He ain't earned it anyway, I earn it. I use me fucking nous, he just threatens people, but it shows you how much working knowledge he has of the businesses that he ain't ever questioned it. It has never occurred to him that the wedge is huge for us. He has no concept of the real world whatsoever.'

Glenford listened carefully, and then he said, 'In all these years this is the first time you have ever said anything like that. This is really serious, isn't it?'

Jimmy smiled. 'Nah, it's just long overdue, that's all.'

He jumped into his motor. Glenford watched him as he sped away and he wondered at a man who was so relaxed when going into what was, in effect, the lion's den. Freddie was a nutter, Freddie was not all the ticket, and that meant you never knew what he was going to do next.

He only hoped Jimmy bore that in mind when he confronted him.

He made a mental note to ask around some of his cronies to see if he could shed any light on what had occurred between the two men. He didn't hold out much hope. He knew Freddie cunted Jimmy at every available opportunity, but Jimmy was aware of that and so it couldn't be starting to bug him now.

No, whatever this was it went deeper than anyone could imagine.

'Oh, Jackie, you're drunk as a lord!' Lena was furious and Jackie enjoyed the effect she was creating.

Joseph shook his head at Maddie, who was in the flat for her weekly chat and shop with Lena. It was hard to believe that those two had once been enemies over their children marrying, and yet now were like bosom buddies.

Joseph raised his eyebrows and Maddie pursed her lips primly. Jackie sober was bad enough, but drunk she was a nightmare. It was as if she grew with the drink, somehow. She was a big girl anyway, but with drink in her she seemed enormous. Maddie knew it was a silly way to think and that it was only because Jackie was so accident-prone while in her cups.

As she barrelled through the small flat into the kitchen, she caught sight of her mother-in-law and said loudly, 'Have you heard?'

Joseph sighed in annoyance and even in her drunken state Jackie saw the toll the boy's death had taken on her parents. They seemed much older, and her mother's usually spotless home was grubby, unkempt and uncared for.

'Heard what?' Joe sounded irritable and this irritated his daughter in turn.

'About your darling daughter Maggie.'

No one spoke, and Jackie felt on the verge of screaming. As usual, none of them thought the marvellous Maggie could do any wrong.

'You leave poor Maggie alone, she's enough to contend with.'

It was her mother's tone of voice, the reverence with which she spoke about Maggie, that set Jackie off and she hollered as loudly as she could, wincing at her own inebriated ramblings, 'She reckons my Freddie raped her. Have you ever heard anything like it?'

She now had what she always wanted, the attention of the whole room, and as three pairs of eyes looked at her in absolute disdain she bellowed, 'And she reckons, or *so* she told my Kimberley anyway, that Jimmy Junior was his baby, Freddie's son, not your fucking precious Jimmy's.'

'Get out, Jackie.' Her father's voice was harsher than she had heard it for years. He grabbed her by the hair and he physically dragged her to the front door. Opening it he threw her with all his might out into the small lobby.

'Fuck off, and don't you ever come back here again, you hear me?'

Jackie was unsure exactly what had happened until the door slammed and she scrambled to her feet. Her father's voice was so final, so full of dislike, that she understood that any last chances she might have had were long gone. Kneeling on the floor, she cried as she had not cried in years.

Melanie was aware that they were alone in the pub. Her uncle Paul had put a bottle of Scotch on the bar and Freddie was pouring it out for them both in huge quantities. The coke had made her higher than she had ever been, and the sudden exodus around her was making her feel uncomfortable for some reason.

She put it down to coke paranoia. She had experienced it before, but this stuff Freddie had was out of this world. Each snort had made her feel more and more adventurous, in fact she was almost willing to strip off and go for it as Freddie kept urging her. If her aunt had not been upstairs, she knew the temptation would have been too much for her.

This was the life she dreamed of, being with someone like Freddie where every day was a holiday and every night was just a round of pubs and clubs and getting out of it, and making yourself up for your bloke.

No job, no real income, just an endless round of enjoying yourself.

If she played her cards right, she knew she could find herself right on her feet with Freddie Jackson. She wasn't silly, she knew he was married and she knew his wife was a right headcase. But she would cross that bridge when she came to it.

She only wanted to be his bird. He was far too old to think of marrying, he was almost Jurassic, bless him.

She was still congratulating herself on her catch of the day when a younger, much better-looking version of Freddie walked into the pub.

Freddie, who had been regaling her with his tales of derring-do whilst in prison, was suddenly aware that the place was empty, quiet.

Even the jukebox was silent.

'Well, well, if it isn't fucking Livingstone.'

Jimmy smiled. 'Pissed, are you? What happened to you this morning? I was waiting for you.'

Jimmy was talking nicely, almost conversationally. But Melanie picked up the nuances in the conversation and a fright took hold of her. The two men were so alike, but the younger one, he had the stature and the standing of someone important, someone who was listened to.

Freddie Jackson, beside him, looked like the poor relation and she guessed that Freddie felt the same way as she did.

The younger man had on a smart pair of trousers and

a smart shirt, his gold watch was thin-banded and obviously expensive. He had well-cut hair and manicured hands, and even his voice was modulated. He sounded educated, sounded like someone who, as she had first thought, was listened to.

Next to him Freddie looked what he was, a dishevelled and bloated also-ran. He had the button eyes of a grifter and the sneaky look of a con man. In her heightened state of awareness it occurred to her that Freddie Jackson was not such a prize after all. This man was a prize, though, this man was someone to aspire to.

She smiled at him as he stood in front of her.

'Fuck off.' His voice was cold, calculatingly cold, and it unnerved her.

She immediately looked at Freddie for his reaction to the man's rudeness. Freddie grinned and she now saw the nasty glint in his eyes, the sallow skin and the redness around his cheeks that told her he was a drinker.

She raised her eyebrows at him to see what she was supposed to do, and he kept his eyes on the younger man as he said nonchalantly, 'You heard the man, Mel, fuck off.'

She was shocked at the callous way he spoke to her. A few minutes earlier she had been contemplating stripping off and doing whatever he wanted, she had even contemplated a relationship of some kind with him.

Now he was pushing her away, discarding her without a backward glance. She was also aware that she was letting this man talk to her like she was dirt, letting him look down his nose at her.

Freddie was laughing now. The look on Melanie's face was priceless, and now that Jimmy had come to him he was feeling an adrenaline rush.

'Come on, girl, chop chop. The big man has spoken

and everyone has to do what you tell them, don't they, Jimmy?' This was said quietly, like a schoolboy to a teacher.

Then, passing her a drink, he took Mel's arm gently and led her to a table by the stained-glass window. After she was seated Freddie smiled at her and said, 'Wait here, this shouldn't take long.'

Jimmy watched the man he had admired all those years ago and wondered at what had happened to him. He had no respect left for him whatsoever. Freddie was dragging this stupid girl into their argument, into their business, because he could not do anything without an audience.

Walking over to them, Jimmy took her bodily by the arm and walked her through to the living quarters of the pub.

'Piss off, love.'

As he walked back he saw Freddie pouring out more drinks, and he sighed. Freddie was drunk and as always he was mean drunk.

'You came, then?' Freddie seemed to think that this was hilarious, and once more Jimmy was aware of how little esteem he now held this man in.

'I knew you'd come to me eventually.' This was said smugly, as if he had won something.

Jimmy didn't answer him for a few seconds, and then he said seriously, 'You're out, Fred.' He was gratified to see Freddie's look of complete astonishment.

'What do you mean, I'm out?'

Jimmy grinned. 'What I say, you are out.' He said the last few words distinctly as if talking to a small child, or a deaf person. Enunciating every word.

Freddie was nonplussed for a few moments. Then he said, 'Out of what, Jimmy?'

Freddie sounded as if he was in a padded room, narked

up with Dospan. He sounded amazed and also as if what he was hearing was unbelievable to him. Which of course it was.

Now Jimmy laughed, as he said in a clear voice, 'You are out on your arse. You are *finished*, Freddie, and you had better get that through your thick head once and for all.'

Chapter Thirty

Little Freddie was at school and the novelty of being the perfect child was starting to wear off, but he knew that to keep on his father's good side he needed to act the dutiful son. As he looked around him at the classroom and at his classmates, he wondered how people didn't die of absolute boredom.

He was aware, though, that if he didn't keep this façade up he would be put away somewhere. His father had been on the verge of it, he knew, and Little Freddie had been reduced to giving him a load of fanny about it all just being a game that had got out of hand. Neither of them believed it but it was there, out in the open, for his father to use for his own benefit.

The annoying thing was, he was fed up with this act. It was wearing, being nice all the time.

He imagined the people around him in his power, imagined them in his complete control. They were all marks to him, nothing more, with their please and thank yous, and their fucking politeness. He was forceful enough to get them where he wanted them, he liked to manipulate people, liked his rep as a bad boy.

The fear of real violence could do that just as well, his

father had taught him that much. He liked to remember things when he was alone, and he liked to fantasise about people around him.

He looked in the mirror every day and saw himself, and he knew that he was a handsome boy. Tall for his age, he had his father's looks and his father's build, though his dad was starting to run to fat. Young Freddie saw himself as apart from everyone else. He had friends but they were his friends, he wasn't theirs. He ruled them, they were wary of him, and his father's reputation got him an out on a daily basis.

He felt nothing, and when his friend's mother had died of cancer a few weeks earlier he had not understood the boy's crushing grief.

She was dead. Crying wouldn't bring her back. What on earth was the problem? She was a miserable old bitch anyway, always fucking carping on, silly cow.

Yet, as young as he was, he had already sussed out that he had to at least emulate the emotions of other people, and luckily for him soap operas filled this gap in his education. In fact, they were fountains of wisdom as far as he was concerned.

He knew how to act out emotion now and thanks to *EastEnders* he was happy in the knowledge that in East London you fought and argued to get what you wanted.

Little Freddie also knew that he got away with murder because of his looks. Beautiful people were treated better in the world than the ugly bastards were. His father had always said that, and it was true.

'Go home, Jackie, and don't come back here any more.'

Jackie was completely hysterical and the mother in Lena wanted to go to her, try to comfort her, but her husband had for the first time in years put his foot down.

'If you let her in, I will fucking walk out of this house, and I swear on that poor child's grave that I will never come back, and that is fucking swearing to it. I am sick to death of Jackie and her fucking problems.'

Lena knew he meant what he said, because now he was ranting and raging all over the small flat. Lena and Maddie shrugged at one another like conspirators.

'I am fucking sick and tired of her and that fucking boy of hers, that mad bastard she bred. When she was carrying him she was either pissed out of her brains or drugged up to the eyebrows. She lost one because of her fucking drinking and drugging and I wish the same had happened with him, because he ain't all the fucking ticket. I don't want him near or by me or mine, and the same goes for that fucking muppet she saddled herself with. Freddie Jackson is another fucking awkward ponce. Jimmy is outing him anyway, he gets the bad news today, and if you ask me not before fucking time.'

He looked at his wife as he said through gritted teeth, 'It's a serious out and all, Lena. There ain't been one like this since the fucking Krays walked the pavements. Freddie will be a fucking *outcast*, he will be like a fucking leper, and consequently it means that he won't be welcome *anywhere*. Any mates have to either blank him or lose their own livelihoods. That cunt is all but finished, and not before fucking time, I say.'

Lena had never seen him so angry before, and in his day he had given her more than her fair share of rows, black eyes and fat lips. But they had been passionate fights, at least that is how she remembered them now. Not as the vicious hidings they had really been from a man who was taking out on her his own guilt because he had pissed up every penny they had on some old sort he had picked up in a pub. Those had been the days, of course, when all women got a clump off the old man, especially if they nagged, and Lena was the first to admit that she could nag expertly and for hours at a time if the fancy took her.

Nowadays she would not take that off anyone, let alone a man, though in the past she had expected a shiner or two, like her mother before her. They had been stupid enough to think that a jealous man loved them, that a man in drink was not responsible for his actions. And that they, the women concerned, were somehow lacking, or the men would have come home on time.

But this hate-filled ranting was new, she had never seen Joe like it before. And if Freddie had the serious out, that meant her daughter would have to pack up and move away. There was no other choice, they would be social outcasts, and even family would be wary of seeing them. There may not have been an out like this since the sixties, but it would still be enforced. It was the criminal equivalent to being put away, except in nick you could have visits. Her daughter would be gone from her and she felt awful because the news made her feel relieved, and that was wrong. But she was so sick of all the trouble that came with Jackie and she was getting too old for it.

Joseph started raging once more, and Lena could see the absolute hatred he felt for his son-in-law in his wrinkled-up face.

'That big vicious ponce Freddie Jackson, thinking he can do what he likes to whoever he fucking likes, and that fat bitch out there who was demented enough to go and get married to him, shouting about rape. This shower of shite are all fucking barred now, the out is already in force as far as I am concerned. They will not cross this bastard, poxy, fucking doorstep and he can come round here with a fucking army-surplus flame-thrower and I will still tell him to get fucked!'

He was spitting in anger and Lena knew that he had something terrible on his mind. She had assumed it was the poor little fellow's death but now she wondered what he knew. If Jimmy boy had confided in him, what trouble was going to come to their door? She was worried herself now, and, putting on the kettle, she decided to make a cup of tea, not that she wanted one particularly, but for something to do.

Jackie's crying was going through her head and she assumed rightly that it was also going through her neighbours' heads. What she had to put up with from that girl and her husband was no bloody joke. She was now looking forward to the out, although she wouldn't admit that, of course.

She closed her eyes in shame as she heard Mrs Faraday, a very clean-living Protestant with a blue rinse and varicose veins, who resided on the ground floor, shouting up to her daughter.

'I am phoning the police, this is an absolute disgrace. You're drunk, woman, now go home and leave your poor mother in peace.'

Lena hated Mrs Faraday with her bloody cardigans and the annoying way she had of looking down her nose at people because they were Catholics, Irish, a mixture of both or Scottish. She liked the Welsh, apparently, and Lena gathered this was because they went to the correct church. That said, a Jehovah's Witness never knocked on another door in the block once they had experienced Mrs Faraday, and in that respect she could be very handy.

Lena had spent the best part of thirty years trying to look, outwardly at least, respectable to Mrs Faraday and two other tenants of the council block who acted as if they lived in Kensington Palace. Between her husband and Jackie she had fought a losing battle over those years.

Now, though, with the grief inside her and the voice of Mrs Faraday bringing back memories of long-ago days when she had been humiliated by her, Lena suddenly lost all her maternal instincts and bolted from the flat like a banshee. Physically picking up her daughter by her clothes, she pushed and dragged her down the stairs, then she threw her out on to the pavement.

'Go home and sober up, you drunken mare, and don't come here any more. We've had enough of you for one bleeding day.'

She was pleased with herself for not letting a string of expletives come out of her mouth as was usual.

Mrs Faraday, who had been watching from her doorway, said primly, 'And about time too.'

To which an overwrought Lena answered, 'Oh, fuck off back inside, you nosy old bag.'

'Do you think Mum will be all right?'

Dianna shrugged. 'Who cares? I have had enough of her, to be honest. Drop me at the hospital, will you?'

Kim sighed. 'You're not going to see that Terry, are you?'

'Mind your own business, and ask Rox if I can stay at hers tonight. I think there's going to be fucking murders at home.'

'That's nothing new.'

Both girls were wary now of talking too much about Maggie and what their father had been accused of. It was too raw for them, too much out of their experience, so they decided to leave the adults to it and then just pick up the pieces afterwards, as was usual in the Jackson household.

But they were both frightened of what the outcome was going to be.

Jimmy and their father were both hard men, both were

capable of taking care of themselves and both were due to have some kind of tear up because everyone knew that Jimmy had overtaken his mentor years before.

Maddie listened in silence as poor Joseph vented his spleen, and she knew it would do him the world of good to let out some of his anger and his sorrow. He looked awful.

As she got up and poured the boiling water into the teapot, he seemed to remember that this was Freddie's mother sitting at the table, and suddenly all his fight left him and he said sadly, 'Sorry, Maddie, it's nothing personal to you, love, but I fucking hate him. Everywhere he goes he causes upset or trouble of some description.'

She sighed then and patting her as always immaculately coiffed dark hair she said regretfully, 'I feel the same way about him meself.'

Lena thought she was going to drop down dead at the table in shock. Maddie had said *him*, in a voice drenched in hatred, and she knew she was talking about her son. Her Freddie, the love of her life.

Lena went and shut all the doors in the flat, and she closed all the windows too. Jackie had resumed her crying in the street, but this time it wasn't going to wash. She was not going out to her. She always ended up going to her house to sort her out, or picking her up from a pub because her mother's phone number was the only one she ever seemed to remember when drunk, or dragging her in from the street outside after an argument had gone over the top, and she was fed up with all the bloody drama of it.

Maddie poured the tea and as she sat down in the chair once more she said quietly, 'Freddie killed his father, you know.'

Lena and Joseph stared at the tidy-looking woman opposite them, and both wondered if they were hearing things.

She nodded at them as if to confirm that what she was saying was true.

'He was never the same after the beating Freddie had doled out to him. That's what he does you see, my Freddie, he beats you down. He sucks all the confidence and the life out of you and before you know it you are like that poor child who's screeching for England out there.'

She lit a Kensitas cigarette and sipped at her tea in the ladylike way extremely thin people seem to possess naturally, before saying softly, 'To be honest, I wouldn't put it past my son to have slashed his father's wrists for him. My husband had the blood count of a man five times over the legal driving limit, the coroner told me that to try and make me feel better. But I know Freddie was responsible, and he knows I know. Whatever happened in that room only happened because Freddie *wanted* it to happen, because Freddie *made* it happen.'

She smiled weakly at her two friends then, and Lena wondered how long this poor woman had wanted to get that family secret off her wheezing chest.

'You can't fucking *out* me, what about Ozzy?' Freddie was still gobsmacked. He had expected a row, he had even convinced himself that he might even have to take this lairy little fucker out.

He was more than aware, though, that if he offed Jimmy for whatever reason his days on this earth would be numbered. Jimmy had too many friends in their world, real friends and he gave them all a good living, himself included.

The one thing he had not expected today was to be told he was out of a job, out of the firm and out of all that entailed for him, from birds to money to a decent fight when he wanted one. But if Jimmy thought he was going to lumber him with a serious *out*, well, that was not going to happen, he was determined not to let that happen.

Jimmy shrugged nonchalantly. 'Oz has given everything over to me. When he dies, and I hope that is not for a long time, it's mine, Freddie. I am to all intents and purposes Ozzy, and everyone answers to me. That, unfortunately, once included you, Freddie, but not any more. Ozzy, if you are interested, is right behind me.'

He could see the way the pupils of Freddie's eyes widened at his words, and Jimmy admired the way he recovered himself so quickly.

'You are finished on this manor, mate, and you had better accept that. If anyone employs you then I don't deal with them any longer and, ergo, neither will anyone else. It's as simple as that. No one works anything here without my express say-so, remember. I have a touch off everything and everyone, the blags, the clubs, the pubs, the dealers, even the late-night fucking burger vans are indirectly run by me or mine. I rowed you out fucking years ago, Fred, and now you are really out, out in the freezing-your-gonads-off cold. You and that animal you spawned with your piss head of a wife are dead to me. All that is left for you now, Freddie, is to pick up and start over somewhere else, because you ain't welcome here.'

He picked up his mobile and his car keys and made to leave.

Freddie grabbed him by the shirtsleeve. 'You can't do this to me, Jimmy.'

Jimmy shrugged him off aggressively. 'I just did, Freddie. You had your chance and you blew it, like you've blown every chance you've ever had.' He shrugged once more and then smiled happily. 'Bye.'

Freddie had envisaged many things on this day but not to be outed. Out of all this meant he was a complete no one, it meant all he had ever known would be gone from him. He would have to move away, he would have to disappear because the shame would kill him otherwise. No one would even acknowledge him if Jimmy outed him. He felt almost sick now with apprehension and dread.

He had to keep his wits about him, he had to try to talk his way through to Jimmy, Jimmy who had loved him once. The enormity of what had happened was hitting him like a ball-peen hammer, and he felt fear, real fear, for the first time in years.

'He is my son, Jimmy, don't forget that. I got him help, he's on drugs . . . It was a game, that's all, a tragic game that went wrong.'

Jimmy looked into the face so like his own and said with absolute incredulity, 'He needs locking away and I tell you now, once this is all over, if you ain't fucked off out of it somewhere new, I am telling a few choice people what the score is with him. Joseph knows, he always said Little Freddie was a fucking few paving stones short of a patio. If I see him I will fucking kill him. He might be a kid but he is a big cunt and he's a dangerous cunt, and he is for the out along with you and that fucking scab you married. I don't ever want to clap eyes on you, that retard you fucking fathered, or the fucking moron you call your wife, ever again.'

Freddie tried for the sympathy vote. He could not be outed and he could not bang his boy up. He had been banged up and he knew what it was like.

'You can't fucking tell me what to do with my child. He is a kid. He is a big fucker I admit, but he ain't got the brains he was born with. Jackie was always out of her box when she was carrying him, you know that. That's what happened to him, Jimmy, that's why he is like he is . . . He is on the pills now and he is a changed boy.'

For the first time in years Jimmy heard a real emotion in Freddie's voice. He grinned. 'You don't honestly believe that I am going to swallow that load of old cods, do you? Let you off with another caution like I did with that poor Stephanie and fucking Jewish Lenny? You're a fucking animal and you bred an animal. You live like fucking animals in that filthy shit hole you call home. You are a man whose card has been well and truly marked, mate. No one will touch you with a fucking dodgy DVD now, Freddie. The word is out. You are *finished*, and if you are foolhardy enough to think that you can fucking resume your usual skulduggery, under my nose, then you are even more stupid than I thought.'

He poured himself a Scotch then, and he sipped at it before saying quietly, and without passion or even a hint of smugness, 'Do you know the funny thing, Freddie? No one defended you, not *one* person even asked what you had done to get a punishment like this. No one has been outed for years, yet no one was curious about why you were being blanked. They were all more relieved than anything else, and I can understand that, because I am *relieved* meself that I ain't got to fucking have you hanging round my neck like a cast-iron fucking albatross any more. And I made it perfectly clear that you are to be treated like a fucking pariah, and everyone from Glenford to the Blacks was over the moon about it.'

Freddie was once more in mortal agony at his words and it occurred to Jimmy that he had expected violence, extreme violence. In fact, he had placed a small axe in the back of his trousers. But Freddie was too busy trying to think his way out of the total blanking he was going to get when this all came to fruition.

Jimmy had taken Freddie's very livelihood from him, a serious step in their world where compensation was paid out liberally if anyone happened to accidentally tread on someone's toes, either by encroaching on their scams, or even something trivial like dealing in the same clubs. This was a world where your reputation was only as good as the firm that you worked with, drank with or was employed by you. Freddie was past killing him, because once Jimmy was dead he would lose all chance of ever getting another in, getting another *take*, and their *take* had been huge and yet he knew that Freddie was probably boracic lint as per usual. He just spunked it all up as he got it.

He had worked out one night that Freddie had spent over half a million pounds on his house over the last fifteen years and yet it was one of the scruffiest in the street. They had not even bought it on the Right to Buy Scheme. They were still on the fucking council and he knew they were still in rent arrears. It would be laughable if it wasn't so very sad.

The man he had visited all those years as a young boy had been a figment of his imagination. His boyhood hero was now reduced to less than nothing and he felt not one iota of compassion for him.

Freddie glared at him now, and Jimmy knew that the implications of what was going to happen to him in the future were starting to sink in properly.

'You would do this to me.' It was said without menace, it was said without a questioning tone, it was a statement of fact.

Jimmy nodded silently.

Freddie finally understood then that Jimmy would do it, more to the point had *already* done it. He had a nasty feeling that his predicament was being discussed by people even as they were standing here. He looked at the two of them in the bar mirror and saw they were evenly matched protagonists, except, as he looked properly, Jimmy, being of lighter years and larger build, looked already like the victor.

Freddie saw then, for the first time, what he could have been, should have been.

Jimmy looked the part, acted the part, he *was* the part.

'Have you served my boy up, grassed him?' This was said with accusation, with the disrespect that would normally be reserved for a grass, a supergrass in fact.

Jimmy didn't answer him. His face told Freddie what he thought of the accusation and that he would not give the question any credence by honouring it with a reply.

But *he* could grass. Freddie knew he could take the fucking lot down if he wanted to and the filth would reward him, he was sure. The idea took root as he knew it would, and he filed the thought away for future reference.

He stood there for long moments with his huge hands clenched into fists and an almost electric charge going through him as he gradually allowed the predicament he had caused to sink into his brain.

'Well, I ain't going quietly, Jimmy. I'll fucking kill you before I will let you do this to me. You'd fucking humiliate *me*, you fucking scumbag. When everything you got, you only got because of me!'

He was poking himself in the chest now as he began to lose his temper once more. 'I was the one who done the lump and set all this up. I was the one who had to listen to that boring cunt's stories of the old days over and over again, and set the meets up, and I brought you in with me because I loved you, and now you are snatching it off me. But you remember, Jimmy, that it was me, it was *me* who laid the foundations of everything we have now and you know it. I want my fucking compensation, because without me you would still be nicking fucking cars and selling dope on the side.'

Jimmy refilled his glass with whisky and sipped it once more. He was almost enjoying himself now. 'Without *you*, Freddie, I can grieve for my boy in peace without wondering if that mad cunt of yours will be nearby. I can work my living now, without worrying about what trouble or upset you are going to cause with your fucking big trap. Without you, I don't have to listen to your crap fucking stories or feed and water your fucking ugly wife. I know what you've said about me over the years, Freddie, you treacherous cunt. I hear *everything*, and do you know what? I expected better off of you, but deep inside somehow I always knew you were just a two-faced, jealous and fucking incompetent wanker. Without me, Freddie, it's you who are nothing, mate. You, not me.'

Freddie knew he was beaten and yet it just would not register in his brain. His life as he knew it was over, he would be suspect now that Jimmy was giving him the cold shoulder, and if no one knew the real reason, and he was confident that they didn't, then they would assume the worst. That he was a grass, or a fucking nonce, a poxy kiddy fiddler, or worse still that he had stolen off his own.

He suddenly realised with a stunning clarity that he had to kill Jimmy, if for no other reason than to make himself feel better, and also to make sure his son was safe for the future. Little Freddie might not be the child of his dreams but he was the child of his loins and as such he would see him all right.

He tried one last time to appeal to Jimmy's better nature. If it all went well he was back in and he would keep a low profile for a while until this all died down. If he was out then he would get his money's worth from this long streak of paralysed piss he had once called his kin.

'It was all a terrible tragedy, Jim, but he is my son. Can't you understand that?'

His voice sounded broken, and Jimmy had to give it to him, he was in the wrong profession. If ever anyone was born to be an actor it was Freddie Jackson.

'He is me boy and he has his whole life ahead of him. He is my son.'

Jimmy grabbed Freddie's jacket with such strength that Freddie was reminded of just how big this man actually was. Pushing him back against the bar he said angrily, 'And Jimmy Junior was my son, remember, and he's fucking dead. And you are dead as well, aren't you, dead and gone? You might as well be pushing up the fucking daisies now because I have already put the word on the pavement that you are to be blanked by one and all, and believe this, Freddie, you will be.'

Freddie knew he meant it, and he was still struggling to think how the fuck he was going to walk away from this train wreck without a scratch. He grinned then and, pulling himself up to his full height he backed away from Jimmy. Smoothing his clothes down as if he was the most fastidious person on earth he said snidely, 'You sure about that, about him being *your* son, I mean? After all, we all know he's dead, don't we?'

He was laughing and Jimmy felt the air leave his stomach as the words sank in.

Freddie picked up his drink and toasted Jimmy before saying, 'At least I hope he's dead, we planted him after all . . .'

His laughter was loud and it was genuine. Freddie actually thought that was funny, that it was a joke. Jimmy stared at the man he had loved and loathed over the years and realised suddenly that this was the real Freddie, that he had always been like this, this was exactly who he was. And he had produced another one just like him, a selfish, violent bully. He was suddenly thrilled to be Freddie's nemesis, thrilled to be able to dismantle this ponce's life and enjoy his decline from the security and safety of his own large gated residence. The less Freddie had going for him, the further he dragged him down, the more Jimmy knew he would feel better, and if not exactly assuaged, then at least compensated for his grief.

Freddie was roaring with laughter, and then he started shouting, 'Let me out, Dad, it's dark down here!'

He was imitating Jimmy Junior's voice, and as he listened Jimmy felt as if he was going to go mad with grief. 'You are unbelievable. Nothing is too low for you, is it, Freddie?'

'You got that right, and remember that for the future, won't you? But *dad*, now that's a good word, ain't it, Jim. *Dad*, help me, Dad, it's dark and damp and full of worms in this box.'

He kept repeating 'Dad' under his breath until he said jovially, 'But which one of us should be the one to help him, I wonder? Women talk see, and you two ain't produced any more chavvies, have you, Jimmy? A bit *suspect* that, don't you think? I have four with Jackie alone. That's without me "outside kids", as your pal Glenford would call them. You sure you ain't a fucking Jaffa, mate?'

His mirth was almost demonic in its intensity, and Jimmy knew Freddie was enjoying this, that he was really loving it. 'Remember when you announced to the world that Maggie was finally in the club, and I said to you then, if you remember rightly, "Are you sure you didn't have any help?"'

He was grinning. He was getting his revenge now, and it felt good. 'Why do you think Maggie, the little homemaker, rejected him, Freddie? You don't think it was because of who the father was, do you? All the time you thought you were stitching me up, I was *shafting* your old woman, mate.'

He was laughing again, louder this time, as if this was the most hilarious thing he had ever witnessed or heard.

'You cunt, Freddie, you fucking vicious cunt! But dream on by all means. My Maggie wouldn't touch you with a fucking barge pole.'

Freddie stopped laughing then because he knew he had him on the ropes, and he said seriously and demurely, but with that evil smile he had perfected over the years, '*Ask* her, Jimmy, ask her about our little *tryst*. It was on your anniversary. You were licking the Blacks' arses in Scotland, and I was licking your wife. Got lovely tits, your Maggie, nice and plump and full, just how I like them.'

The heavy glass whisky bottle was smashed down on to Freddie's head in a split second. The strength of the blow was such it knocked Freddie on to his knees, and it had been so unexpected that he had not even had time to react to it and protect himself. This, he knew, was because Jimmy was at the peak of his anger.

Jabbing at Freddie with the broken bottle, Jimmy felt the warm spray of blood as he severed the carotid artery, and then he stabbed viciously over and over again.

He was swimming in a red mist of blood, and the smell was overpowering.

The anger in him was so acute that even when he knew Freddie was dead he still slashed at his face and head until he was unrecognisable. The need to hurt this man was so overwhelming that he actually felt sorrow when he realised that Freddie Jackson was really dead. It was too quick a death for him, but it had been gruesome, and that was some consolation.

Freddie's blood was everywhere, all over the bar area. The ceiling had been sprayed liberally with it and the floor, the dirty old pub carpet laid there in the late sixties and still maintaining a faint blue and gold pattern, was drenched in deep red sticky blood.

Jimmy felt lighter in himself than he had done in years.

He stopped, as suddenly as he had started. The high piercing screams of Melanie finally alerted him to what he had actually done. She had witnessed it all.

Now, standing there covered in Freddie's blood, Jimmy Jackson finally understood the immense power of anger and hatred. For a few moments, he knew, he had become Freddie Jackson.

Chapter Thirty-One

Maggie had been sitting in the police station for hours, but they were being very nice to her, which meant tea and coffee was offered at appropriate intervals.

Now, after five hours, she was finally being allowed to see her husband.

As she walked through to the interview room she felt a deep coldness inside her. The policeman smiled at her as he opened the door, and the heavy sound of it closing behind her made her jump, grated on her nerves.

Her husband was standing by a table and chairs. There was video equipment set up all over the place, and she was so on edge that she could actually smell the cup of coffee he had been given minutes earlier.

He looked well, and that surprised her, but he looked older somehow, which for some reason, made him look even handsomer.

This was such an alien environment for her that she was frightened at seeing him here, surrounded by all this electrical equipment and looking, for the first time ever, vulnerable.

Jimmy looked at her for long seconds before saying, 'I am sorry, babe.'

She smiled as best she could before she went into his arms and enjoyed the feel of him once more. 'Have they charged you?'

She felt him shaking his head and her heart started pounding in her chest, she felt faint for a few moments, and then it passed.

'They ain't got nothing. Don't worry, sweetheart, after forty-eight hours they either charge me or I am free to go.'

He was staring into her eyes and she was terrified that she wouldn't be able to hold his gaze. The guilt she was feeling over everything was weighing on her with a crushing heaviness that was almost physical in its pain. This was what she had been dreading for all these years, Jimmy finding out what had happened to her.

She knew for certain when she had looked at him that he was finally aware of what Freddie had done to her. Nothing else could have caused this much mayhem. If he had wanted Freddie dead for any other reason, then it would have happened quietly and without any kind of fanfare.

The fact he was holding her tightly told her he was still with her, still loved her, and so she said quietly, 'What happened, Jimmy?'

Jimmy looked into her eyes once more, then he kissed her softly on the lips. The feel of his gentle mouth was nearly her undoing.

'Remember this, Mags, little Jimmy was *my* son. I know that and *you* know that.'

She smiled sadly, 'I know that better than *anyone*, Jimmy.'

'He tried to break us, but he won't, mate, he weren't worth a wank, and neither is anything he ever said.'

She squeezed him to her then, knowing he had killed

the person he had once loved more than anyone else in the world.

She only wished now she had let this all come out years ago. Her silence had ruined everyone's lives in the end, yet all she had ever wanted was to keep the peace, to protect everyone she loved from a man who she hoped was burning in hell at last.

Jackie was looking down on the body of her husband, and she was without tears. She had insisted on seeing him, even though she had been warned that he was not in a fit state to be seen, that he had serious head and neck injuries, and she would be well advised to let her father identify his body, so she could remember him how he *was.*

She had been on the verge of outright laughter, as the only thought that popped into her head was of her saying to these nice people, 'What, you mean, dirty, scruffy, drunk and drugged, and with a fucking bird on his arm?'

But she had not said it, she was aware she was getting the sympathy vote, and she was not about to fuck that up for herself. Her father was being lovely, and she wasn't going to do anything to upset him or anyone else for that matter.

But her first glance at Freddie's body had not sent her into convulsions or tears, as she had thought it would, it had just sobered her up. Now, as she looked at him and the obscene wounds that had been inflicted on him, she felt nothing but an odd calmness.

Looking down at him, *knowing*, *seeing for herself*, that he really was dead, she felt a weird elation washing over her. It was as if everything in her life had been careering at full speed towards this moment in time.

She felt the strangest feeling, as if she had *won* something.

She had known instinctively, from the first time she had kissed him, that she would one day have to look at his dead body. His temper would be his downfall, and his luck would eventually run out.

She had always assumed that he would pick on the wrong person one day, and either find himself up against someone with a will, and a temper much stronger than his, or someone with a huge fear of him and a sawn-off shotgun in their hand.

She had never in her wildest imagination dreamed that that person would be Jimmy.

She had also believed, that when it finally happened, and Freddie was gone from her, she would be destroyed. But she wasn't. In fact she was surprised with herself, because all she felt looking at his lifeless corpse, was a deep and abiding sense of euphoria.

She felt free.

She had always said to friends that it would be easier for her if Freddie died, rather than if he left her for someone else. She always joked that she could *cope* with that, with not being with him as long as no one else was.

While he was alive, and breathing, she could not bear the thought of him with anyone but her. Yet now he was gone, and his shagging days were over, she was almost happy inside, because he had died *her* husband, and that meant she was now his widow. All the women he had pursued over the years and all the girls he had given kids to were nothing to her now, because Freddie was gone, and he had gone while she was still his legal, his wife. Now she would never again have to worry about him, or where he was, or even wonder what he was doing.

All this business with Maggie could be conveniently forgotten, and her mother and father would have to allow her back into the fold. She would watch her P's and Q's, and make herself likable. She was no good on her own and she was going to need her family, and Maggie especially, as she had plenty of dosh as well as a very forgiving nature.

These were wonderful thoughts, and she was enjoying them.

Freddie would have left her eventually, she had always known that, and her life had been blighted because she had wondered, every day, if that was the day he would meet the love of his life.

And it would have happened in the end. He would have hit an age where he needed to prove himself, needed a young bird on his arm to make him feel young once more. He would have met one, the usual blaggers' bird, a tanned no neck with a council flat, who would be only too willing to play him, because he needed her youthful adoration and she had a killer body and a desperate need for the criminal limelight. Freddie would have succumbed to one of them in the end. All women in her position knew that.

She had *been* his bird once, many years ago, but four kids and Freddie Jackson as a husband had aged her before her time. Even if she had kept herself nice, had all the treatments, fought off age with a fucking hatchet, youth always won in their world.

It was what she had dreaded more than anything else. Without Freddie she was nothing, but as his widow, she would still have the honour of his name and the respect due to her because of his reputation.

Over the years she had socialised with sixty-year-old men who had children younger than their grandchildren and wives younger than their daughters. She had also observed many of the first wives as they were pushed aside like an old crisp packet. These were the women who had borne their husbands' children, visited them in prisons all over the country, who had loyally lied to the police and in some cases under oath for their men, and been happy to do it. Then suddenly, some little bird enters the frame, *thin*, with a fake tan, no stretchmarks, a Gossard bra and the conversation of a retarded orang-utan, and she was now the new significant other in his life.

Overnight, it was as if the first wife, the one who had struggled to keep things going when times were hard, and the kids were small, the one who had borrowed money off her family when things were tough and spent her youth defending her husband to everyone who told her he was a waster, and who should now be enjoying the benefit of her husband's hard graft, was dumped unceremoniously and it was suddenly as if she had never existed.

The older children either accepted the new bird because she was a permanent fixture now, not a quick booty call (those girls knew their place and had the sense to ignore the man when he was out with family), or they ended up not talking to their fathers, and by taking their mother's side they then put themselves up for a life of hurt and betrayal.

It was awful seeing the look in the women's eyes when you met them out shopping, or at their children's weddings. You could see the bewilderment and the pain and, worst of all, you could see the way people treated them now they had been discarded. They were barely tolerated. She had witnessed first-hand the humiliation on their faces if the husband was there with the new wife, who Jackie had noticed nearly always got drunk and caused a scene because even the woman he had left for them was seen as a threat.

She had been pleased to see that once the girl had got the man off the wife, she then had to live with the knowledge that it could easily happen to her too, and she did not have the benefit of the years together that the first wife did.

The pain in the women's faces as they watched the men they still loved with their new and improved models had always been painfully evident to Jackie, no matter how brave a face they put on it. These women, like her, eventually realised that they had devoted their lives to, and showered all their love on, a man who had no concept of what they had gone through over the years, and who felt no actual guilt for casually smashing their lives to pieces.

That had terrified her for years, the prospect of Freddie discarding her with about as much care and attention as he would a cigarette butt, or a used Durex.

Now all her fears of that happening were gone. All her worries were gone, and she felt as if she had just thrown off the weight of the world from her shoulders.

She was glad he was dead, because dead meant that she could finally love the rotten bastard in peace.

Kimberley and her two sisters were outside the police station having a cigarette with a very subdued Dicky.

They had brought their aunt something to eat. She had accepted it gratefully, and they were pleased to see that she was not treating them any differently than she had before this awful day.

The fact their father was dead had not really sunk in yet. They were still trying to get their heads around the knowledge that it was Jimmy who had murdered him.

They had all been questioned and had all said the same thing, that they had no idea what could have happened. Until they were given the nod, that was all they were prepared to say on the subject.

'Poor Dad.'

Dianna sounded so sad, and Kimberley hugged her younger sister tightly. 'Yeah, as you say, poor Dad.'

She looked at Rox and they exchanged glances that told Dicky they were not going to be mourning the man they called father for very long.

'Let's get back to Mum, eh? Look, Glenford has just pulled up in a black cab.'

Dicky walked over to him and the two men shook hands.

'It all being taken care of. Get the girls home now, OK?'

Dicky nodded. 'The brief's here at last, and she ain't half got some trap. We could hear her bollocking them all from out here.'

Glenford grinned. 'She good all right. They been looking for me all over me work places, so I am going in voluntarily now and get it over with. From what I can gather from a friend in the Met, they are pulling in all his known associates.'

Glenford threw his joint away carelessly and said on a laugh, as he walked off, 'Better not bring that in with me, eh?'

Dicky laughed with him. He was absolutely thrilled to be a part of something this big, and he knew that this was important to his standing in the future. He would be watched and judged by them all to see how he handled this event.

Well, like most people he had never been Freddie Jackson's biggest fan. He had to deal with him because he loved his daughter, and she was being a blinder.

She was upset but not surprised by the news her father had been found in Epping Forest naked, beaten and partially burned. He was still smouldering when a man out dogging had tripped over him while walking back to his car after an enjoyable time watching couples having sex on their back seats. A fitting end for Freddie Jackson, when you thought about it.

Melanie was still crying, and Liselle, who loved her niece dearly, was on the verge of smacking her one.

This was her own fault, and Liselle was bloody annoyed that her niece was at the centre of this mayhem. If Mel had not chased the bloody glamour of criminals and all they entailed, she would not be in this predicament now. She was a nice girl, and she had a lovely nature, but she was only ever going to be bird material. She had too much trap and too much flesh hanging out to ever be anything else.

She only hoped that this had taught Mel a lesson on life, and about fully comprehending the world you chose to live in, both the good bits, and the bad. You had to be a certain type of woman to survive in their world, and she knew that from personal experience. You had to understand the men, and you had to understand what they did, and what drove them to do it. If you didn't grow up in their world, or know the unwritten laws, you were no good to them. You had to have complete acceptance of how they lived their lives, so no matter what they did, or what they were accused of, you only cared about them getting off with it. Nothing else mattered.

You also needed to be able to keep your mouth shut, and never, ever volunteer information about any part of your husband's life to anyone, no matter who they were.

It was a good life if you knew how to play the game. She had been doing just that for many happy years with her Paul, and she wouldn't change a second of it.

Now that Melanie had an insight into what could happen when you were in the wrong place at the wrong time with the wrong person, she might have a serious rethink about what she actually wanted out of life.

Paul sighed, and said to the distraught girl in as calm a voice as he could, 'Stop this, and listen to what I am telling you.'

Liselle went to the girl and slapped her across her face with all the force she could muster. 'For fuck's sake, will you stop fucking crying and listen to us. Do you understand how much shit you are in, girl?'

Melanie stared at her aunt with terrified eyes, and she finally stopped crying. Paul turned her to face him. 'Jimmy Jackson is a bad man. I would lay money on him being the baddest man in London, and you might be Liselle's niece, but that won't cut no fucking ice with him if you ever breathe one word of what you heard in the pub. This is serious, Melanie. You have to forget everything about what happened, right? It never happened. You are going on a long trip to Spain with Liselle tonight, and you will use the time there to empty your fucking brain. But I warn you, if you ever even hint that you saw or heard anything . . .'

He didn't finish what he was saying, because he could see from the utter terror in her big blue eyes that she would not repeat a thing to anyone. He only hoped she never forgot the fear she was feeling now, because she was in a very dangerous position. It was only the bit of blood she shared with his wife that had allowed her to pass go and collect two hundred.

Jimmy had not asked him to do anything, he didn't need to, Paul was a clearer-upper of unavoidable messes. That was what he was paid extremely well for and in the normal scheme of things he would have got someone to take care of this girl to guarantee her silence.

Liselle, bless her, was very tolerant of his work, but he

knew she would draw the line at her niece going on the missing list.

Still, the girl had learned a valuable lesson. He hoped so, anyway. Liselle would talk her round over the next few weeks and reiterate the danger she would place herself in with a careless remark or a drunken statement.

It was late and he was tired. It had been a long old day.

Lena and Jackie were sitting together in Jackie's house, and for once Jackie was almost rational. The girls were in the kitchen making tea and sandwiches, and they were trying to digest the events of the last couple of days. They all knew that they had to keep any thoughts they might have to themselves. It was better for everyone that way.

It was nearly morning now. The light was creeping across the sky, and Jackie was pissed, but she was happy pissed. Lena said to her quietly, 'Tell me the truth, did you speak to Jimmy about you know what?'

Jackie looked at the woman she loved, and whom she had always felt treated her as second best and she said, scornfully, 'You know what?'

Lena closed her eyes in distress. 'Listen to me, and listen good, Jackie. You and the girls have to forget about what was said, do you hear me?'

Jackie sighed heavily and slumped down in the chair, her ample breasts suddenly lying on her belly.

Lena saw that she looked older than her years, that in itself was nothing new. But she also seemed a lot more relaxed somehow.

'Don't worry, Mum. I won't cause any trouble, I promise you.'

Lena was surprised at her daughter's answer and this showed on her face.

'I know he did it, Mum, I know what he was better

than anyone, but it didn't matter to me. I loved him, see.'

Lena grabbed her daughter's hand and squeezed it tightly. 'I know you did, love.' She didn't add, God knows why, but the thought was in her head just the same.

'Now he is dead, I feel all light, as if a weight has gone off me. Does that make sense, Mum? I ain't glad he's dead, but I ain't sorry about it either.'

Lena understood what she was saying far better than her daughter realised.

'The newscaster on the telly said it was a gangland murder. He looked awful, Mum. Whoever did it done a fucking good job, I can tell you.'

Lena sighed again at the things this daughter said, but kept hold of her hand.

'I will miss him, but I feel really strange, Mum. I feel almost happy, and that is wrong, but I can't help it. I feel like I can finally *relax.* I realised today that I never ever relaxed, Mum, not properly, and now I just *am* relaxed. Does that make sense?'

Lena nodded and hugged her daughter. 'It's because you were so besotted with him. The love you had for him was almost like a mania, and you know something, Jackie? I would watch you sometimes, and my heart would break for you, because I knew you were hurting, and you were hurting because of your love. Love is supposed to make you happy, child, and your love for Freddie never did that. Now he's gone, of course you can finally relax, because for the first time since he came out of nick, you will know exactly where he is twenty-four hours of the day.'

She hugged her daughter gently to her again. 'I won't be a hypocrite. I never liked him, you know that, but I am heart sorry for *you*, for losing him, and I will always be there for you, and so will your dad. We might fight and argue, but we are family at bottom, eh?'

Jackie smiled sadly. 'I wonder if they've let Jimmy out yet.'

'We'll know as soon as anything happens, don't worry.'

Little Freddie watched his mother and his nana and wondered at the way everyone in this house seemed to thrive on emotional outbursts. His father's murder had not affected him at all, but he would still milk it for all it was worth. He would also keep a low profile where his granddad was concerned. He felt as if he could look right through him, and this made Little Freddie both wary and nervous, two emotions he had never experienced before.

But he knew that his granddad had sussed him out, and he was sensible enough to play this new development very carefully. Caution was his new watchword.

The girls came in and made a fuss as they fed him bacon sandwiches and drinks of Diet Coke. He looked suitably upset, and managed to watch his favourite videos in relative peace and quiet.

Jimmy got out of the shower and walked through to the huge bedroom. This room had once filled him with pleasure, and the house had been the culmination of everything he had ever wanted from his life. Now it was just a house, like any other.

Homes were not just bricks and mortar, they were about the people who lived inside them.

Maggie was sitting on the giant bed. She looked very small and very vulnerable, and he loved the very bones of her, more now than at any other time in their life.

She passed him a glass of brandy and he sipped it before saying happily, 'Am I glad to get the smell of that police station off me. It stank in there.'

She didn't answer him, and he sat beside her on the

bed, and grabbing her leg in a jovial way, he said loudly, 'Are we not talking, then?'

Maggie knelt up and pushing her hands through her hair she said quietly, 'Stop this, Jimmy, we have to talk about what's happened. I know you killed Freddie, I knew it was you as soon as I heard about it. Now you are acting like it's a normal day, and it ain't, you can't go through the rest of your life pretending that nothing *happened*. You think that if you pretend it didn't happen you won't have to deal with it, or the consequences. But I can't do that. I need to get this all out in the open once and for all.'

Jimmy got up and walked to the window. It was going to be a nice day, it was the best time, he always thought, the early morning.

'He *raped* me, Jimmy, and you have to look at me and tell me you don't hold it against me because I didn't tell you about it.'

He didn't turn towards her and she felt the sickness inside her once more. But she couldn't do this any more. She would rather he went and left her than pretend they were OK. Secrets had nearly destroyed her and her family, and she was not going to live like that any longer.

'Who told you about it, Jimmy? Jackie?'

He did turn then. 'Jackie knew about it and I fucking didn't?'

He was angry now and she was shaking her head in denial. 'She found out by accident the other day. Kimberley told her, she had overheard him taunting me at little Jimmy Junior's funeral. Kim let the cat out of the bag in anger, she never meant to cause any trouble. Did Jackie tell you, Jimmy? I have to know.'

He shook his head and the droplets of water were cold as they hit her bare arms. He was everything she had ever wanted, and now he was all she had left.

'He was taunting you at the boy's funeral?'

She nodded brokenly. 'I was terrified of what you would do if you knew, and of Jackie's reaction. You know how jealous she was of him, Jimmy, she would have lost her mind and caused trouble for us all. I was only trying to keep the peace. I was doing what I thought was best for everyone involved . . .'

He retied the towel he was wearing around his waist and then he walked out of the room without a word.

She heard him as he padded down the stairs. She lay down on the bed, the bed she had shared with him for so long, and she was so upset, she couldn't even cry.

In the kitchen, Jimmy opened the fridge and got himself a beer. He was angry again. The thought of Freddie touching his Mags was hard enough, but to know he had taunted her with it was too much to bear. All those years they had been together, all the time he had spent with Freddie, helped him out, drunk with him, had him in his home, and he was laughing at him, he was laughing up his sleeve at him because that silly bitch upstairs had tried to keep the peace!

Her and her getting it all out in the open . . . if only she knew what had happened to her little boy. She wouldn't be able to live with that, so he was not going to force the knowledge on her, unlike her, who wasn't happy unless she was dragging the guts out of everything, analysing every fucking sentence that was said to her.

He didn't want to talk to her about it. Why couldn't she understand that, for him, it was too much information? He was better off not talking it over, not fucking knowing all the ins and outs of the cat's arse.

Once things were said out loud they were out there for ever, and some things were best left unsaid. It didn't mean that he didn't care, or that he didn't understand. It just meant he could cope with things better if he was allowed to digest it all in his own time, and at his own pace.

He couldn't look at her now, not in the same way. She had spoiled herself for him, and she should have known that. She was his wife, and she should have known him well enough to leave well alone. He had felt sorry for her, he had felt so very sorry for her, but now he felt nothing but anger and spite towards her.

He knew as soon as Freddie told him about his so-called tryst that he had to have forced himself on Maggie, there would not have been any other way for him to take her. But it had been the way he had insinuated that Jimmy Junior was his child that had caused his death, because he had believed him. It didn't matter, he had loved that boy and that would never change, but Maggie going through all that for years, living with him and his innuendos and his fucking laughing face, that was, at this moment, too much for Jimmy to bear.

He raced up the stairs and Maggie jumped in fright as he stormed into the bedroom. Grabbing her roughly by her arms, he shouted into her face, 'Thanks to you, that ponce was laughing at me for years. I was the butt of his jokes and I was not in any way aware of it. I had no fucking idea that he was taking the piss out of me, you stupid fucking mare.'

He threw her away from him and she lay there terrified as he dragged on his clothes. Then he looked at her and said, 'You weren't doing it for me, you were doing it for that scab you call a sister. I fucking done him, you believe me when I tell you I done him up like a fucking kipper, and I was *all right* about what had happened. I knew he would have to have forced you, I knew that without a second's doubt. But I tell you now, Maggie, you and him between you have fucking destroyed me. You spent all this time knowing what he meant and listening to him saying all those things to me, and you still didn't fucking feel like you should tell me what was going on. I feel like the cunt of the year, and you took me for the biggest cunt of all. If for no other reason, you should have let me in on your big secret at the time it happened, so I would at least have been aware of it when he was taking the piss out of me.'

Maggie was sitting up now and shaking her head in distress. She understood that all his real feelings were coming out.

Jimmy was good at hiding things, that was why he did so well in his chosen occupation. In the police station he had told her in no uncertain terms that he knew everything, and that he never wanted to discuss it. If you didn't talk about it, then it never happened was an old maxim of his.

Now she had forced him to confront what had happened, it had backfired on her and she wished with all her heart she had not started this.

She saw it now from his point of view. He was suddenly remembering every little thing that Freddie had said, all the slights, all the innuendos, and putting them in their proper context. For someone of his dignity and his self-belief, that would eat at him, gnaw at his very soul, and she had caused this pain. She had kept it secret and it had nearly destroyed them. Then she had forced it out into the open and that had been the catalyst for the total destruction of their lives.

He looked at her as she sat there crying, and he felt the urge to strangle her. He was angrier with her than he had ever been in all their time together.

'Jackie was all you cared about, all your life it's been about her. I have had to put up with her every fucking Christmas, every fucking holiday. It was her you were more worried about, and that is what I am so fucking angry about. I can't face the truth like you, Maggie. I would rather do me ostrich impression. You should have left me alone. Stopped fucking pushing me. You wanted this all out in the open, well now it is. I hope you are fucking happy now. You got what you wanted, Mags, you finally know what I really think.'

With that he left the house and she heard his car screech off the drive.

Chapter Thirty-Two

Jimmy woke up to the feeling of a soft moist mouth on his erection, and he sighed tiredly. He didn't have the heart to tell the girl that it was only a morning glory, a piss proud. She tried her hardest but he was deflating at an alarming rate. In the end she looked up at him, and he smiled as he said, 'Better luck next time, eh?'

She grinned and jumped off the bed. He watched her lazily as she grabbed her belongings and slipped from the room.

That was the beauty of prostitutes, all they wanted was what *you* wanted, no more and no less. No long-winded fucking conversations, and no fucking harping on about their families or their problems or their poxy lives.

He felt bad now, though, and that annoyed him even more. He was sleeping with anything that moved, and that was only accomplished with the aid of alcohol and, more recently, Viagra.

He yawned again, and he realised he could smell himself. Jumping out of the bed he slipped his clothes on and made his way downstairs.

Patricia shook her head at him as if he was a naughty

boy. 'I hope you fucking paid the poor whore, they ain't working for nix, you know.'

Jimmy gave her a lazy, annoying smile. 'What's it to you, Pat? This is my place. I own them all in one way or another.' He didn't mean it, he was just trying to antagonise her.

'Are you going to Freddie's funeral, then?'

He shook his head nonchalantly. 'Why, are you?'

Jimmy left the house then, pleased he had got a rise out of her. He drove back to Glenford's quickly. He was desperate for a shower and a change of clothes.

Jackie and her girls were all together in the church. Little Freddie was still outside, and Jackie knew he was chain-smoking cigarettes.

The body had finally been released, and his murder was just another crime that was classed as unsolved. Hardly a soul had turned up for the funeral. Her mother was coming, his wasn't, no surprise there. Nor was her father, and no wreaths had been delivered anywhere. This didn't upset her, it annoyed her. There was a subtle difference.

But once the day was over she could start a new life, that was what she kept telling herself. It was all that got her through the nights.

She surveyed her daughters. They were beautiful girls and she was proud of them. She had never really bothered with them before, but now she saw them all the time and she actually knew about their lives and their thoughts.

Freddie's influence over the house was gone, and she was enjoying the freedom that not being in love brought her.

She would pop over Maggie's tomorrow, see how she was faring. She did not expect her here today anyway, but she had offered to go if that was what Jackie really wanted, and she had been pleased about that. Been pleased that Maggie cared enough to do something like that for her. But she had assured her sister that she would be all right with her girls, that they would see her through it.

She wished they would hurry up and get started. She was dying for a drink and she had a lot to do today. This was the most important day of her life, at least that was how she felt about it though she wasn't so sure her family would agree. She had never buried her husband before. This was a definite first in her book.

The priest was looking at his notes and she hoped that he got Freddie's name right. It was not as if he had known him, after all.

Glenford was leaving the house when he saw Jimmy's car racing up the road. So he went back inside and put the kettle on. He had time for a coffee, that was the good thing about their lives. You never had to live by the clock like most people did. You could pick and choose your hours. It was one of the life's main attractions.

Jimmy walked into the little kitchen and his bulk took up the whole room. 'All right, Glenford!' He was smiling and laughing as usual. 'You know Freddie gets planted today?'

'No, never heard a word. Who told you?'

'Ugly Pat. She ain't going, anyway.'

Jimmy yawned loudly, and taking a joint from the ashtray he lit it up and toked deeply on it before saying, 'I am fucking knackered. I have to get me head together today, though. I am going to visit Oz tomorrow and I have a few things to get sorted first.'

'You look like shit, Jimmy.'

He grinned. 'I feel like it and all, don't worry.'

'You spoke to Maggie yet?'

Jimmy looked at his friend and shrugged. 'No point, nothing to say.'

'It's been two months, Jimmy. What the fuck you and her argued about I don't know, but if you leave it much longer there will be no going back. The longer you leave things the harder they become.'

'You are preaching to the converted, mate. Now let me drink me coffee and smoke me spliff without feeling like I am on the sofa with Lorraine Kelly. Not that I would knock her back if she gave me half a chance!'

Glenford laughed despite himself. 'Have you been to the pub yet? It's nearly finished. Paul said it looks too nice for his usual clientele, which includes us, I suppose.'

Jimmy laughed with his friend once more, and a few minutes later Glenford shot off. His smiling façade slipped away immediately.

'You need anything else done today, Mrs Jackson?'

Lily Small had been cleaning Maggie's house for five years, and she felt that they had a rapport. She came in five times a week and she cleaned the place from top to bottom, and she had sussed out ages ago that Mr Jackson had left his wife.

Mrs Jackson was putting a good face on it all, but Lily had seen the weight drop off her and the frown lines appear as if by magic. Losing that lovely little boy was hard enough, and maybe the strain had been too much for them. She could understand that, it was still too raw even for her, so God knew how this poor cow must be feeling.

She would give her eye teeth to know what Mr Jackson had done, if he had done anything of course, but trying to get anything out of this woman was impossible. She was tighter than a duck's arse that had been superglued.

'Can I iron Mr Jackson's shirts?'

Maggie smiled then. She gave old Lily points for perseverance anyway. She could make Mo Slater look like a deaf mute, but before assassinating her nearest relatives or her neighbours, people whom Maggie had never met nor would want to, Lily would puff up her ample chest, pull on her cigarette and say the magic words that had made both Maggie and Jimmy roar with laughter once she had left the premises: 'I am not one to gossip as you both know, but . . .'

Now, as she stood there trying to glean even a smidgeon of information on her employers' predicament, she repeated her question, eyebrows raised and cigarette hovering near her orange-painted mouth. 'Well, shall I iron Mr Jackson's shirts? I know just how he likes them.'

'If you like, Lily.'

Maggie knew she was annoying the poor woman but it was the principle of it all. Her life was hers, and she had no intention of gossiping with anyone, let alone Lily, whose lips, Jimmy used to joke, were looser than a Scandinavian whore's. Even her poor mother had given up trying to find out what was wrong, so Lily had no chance.

Maggie understood what Jimmy had meant now. If she didn't tell anyone then it had not happened. If he came back, no one would know anything and they could just get on as normal. He was right, sometimes things were best left unsaid, it made it easier to live with them somehow.

She poured herself a cup of tea and took it through to the conservatory. She had piles of paperwork to get done and now was as good a time as any. The salons were all doing well, extremely well in fact, and this knowledge didn't have the normal effect on her. Instead of a quiet pride, she had no real interest in anything. Every day he was away from her, she died a little bit more inside.

She had not heard one word from him, and she had not attempted to contact him either. Money was still piling up in the bank so she just carried on as usual, but the loneliness was getting to her, and no matter how tired she felt, as soon as she got into bed, her brain went into overdrive and she relived two separate days of her life, over and over again.

Her son's death, and the absolute grinding grief that it caused, and the day her Jimmy had walked out on her.

She imagined how she should have played it, reminded herself that if she had only kept up the pretence as she had until then, he would still be with her. They were both grieving for their child, and she should have left it all until they were feeling stronger emotionally. Until they could walk into his little room without breaking down, until the raw pain had eased.

For the first time in her life, she understood her sister's jealousy of other women. She tortured herself with visions of him making love to another woman. Loving them, as he had once loved her.

She couldn't eat, she couldn't sleep, and she couldn't rest.

And she had no one to blame but herself.

'Come on, Mum, eat something.'

Kimberley was looking at Jackie with that worried frown she had come to love. She was a good girl, her Kim, and she had not been as good a mother as she could have been. That bothered her these days, and she tried to be nice to them all, nicer than usual.

Since Freddie's death, the girls had been like proper troopers, they had really taken good care of her and their little brother. She was amazed at how well they had turned out.

She knew in her heart that it was Maggie's influence that had helped her girls become what they were, but she didn't feel the usual anger or the jealousy about that. She no longer felt as if she was being compared to everyone, and she didn't feel the pressure of her failings either.

Now, she had made her mind up. She had made decisions and she had been pleased with herself for finally taking control of her life.

'It was a lovely service, weren't it, Mum?'

'It was lovely, darling, and you were all lovely as well.'

Dianna's face was gorgeous, she was a real little sweetie. Even Kim had never looked better. And Rox was getting a nice little lump and, unlike herself, she was making sure her body was not going to be blown out of all recognition, she was taking care of herself. Rox wouldn't hear the man of her dreams, her child's father, saying, 'Fuck me, girl, you look like something from a Hammer horror!' Her girls, they were like film stars, and Jackie only wished now that she had taken up Maggie's offers of beauty treatments and slimming consultations years ago. But even her sister's offering of them had felt like criticism, and so she had not gone. She had cut her own nose off, and now her face was well and truly spited! She wanted to laugh at her own thoughts, but she knew she mustn't.

Once this day was over, she would finally be able to sleep, a real deep and comfortable sleep like she had experienced as a child, she was sure of that. It was what she needed and she knew it would do her the power of good, because in her dreams Freddie was back with her, and they were happy. They were deliriously happy, and she was slim, and didn't drink, and he had eyes for no one but her.

That was why she wanted to get the sleep back. She needed those dreams to help her heal.

As she smiled at her son he nodded at her, and she watched as he left the house. He would be missing his dad. He had loved him so much, unlike his feelings for her. She was painfully aware that the child had never liked her and, if she was honest, she didn't really like him that much either.

Freddie Jackson Junior was walking to a friend's house when he saw two of his little neighbours walking on the pavement opposite. He hated Martin Collins. He was eleven years old and small for his age, but he had a way with him that made him popular with everyone. His brother Justin looked after him, and Freddie was interested to see how far he was willing to go to achieve that end.

Little Freddie crossed over the road and caught up with them. Martin Collins looked at him warily.

'All right?'

Martin nodded cautiously. 'Yeah, you?'

Little Freddie grinned. 'Got any money?'

Justin Collins was nervous. He was older than Freddie Jackson, but he was not as big and he was not as aggressive.

Martin shook his head. 'No, I ain't got any money, Freddie.'

Freddie stared at the boy for long calculated moments before he drew out a long, thin-bladed knife. He watched in glee as the two boys stepped back in fright, and when Justin pushed his little brother behind him he laughed. 'Looking after the wimp, are you?'

'Leave him alone. I mean it, Jackson, go and pick on someone your own age.'

'And if I don't, what are you going to do about it?'

Cars were flying past them and the smell of diesel was thick in the air.

An old man was watching the little tableau from his flat window. He was deciding if he should call the police when the bigger boy, that Jackson lad whose father had been murdered, stabbed the blond boy in the heart.

Martin was screaming in fear as his brother lay on the filthy pavement clutching his chest. Blood was everywhere and Freddie Jackson was watching it flow as if he was in a trance. Then he snapped his head towards Martin and said quietly, 'Now give me some money.'

Martin handed over the two pounds fifty his mother had given them to go and get her a paper and ten cigarettes from the corner shop.

As Freddie Jackson Junior walked away the shrill sound of sirens could be heard coming over the Barking flyover.

Justin Collins died ten minutes later in the ambulance.

'Are you sure you will be all right, Mum?'

Jackie forced a smile on to her face and only just managed to prevent herself from screaming at them. She knew they meant well, but she wished they would leave her alone sometimes.

'I just want to get into bed and have a sleep, that's all. I am exhausted, it's been a hard few months and whatever he was or he wasn't, I loved your father more than anything. I want to lay here *alone* and think about him, all right?'

The three girls nodded in unison, and then they all took turns to kiss her good night even though it was only three o'clock in the afternoon.

Downstairs they saw their nana on a mobile and the sight made them all laugh. She hushed them all with a hand gesture as she walked out the front door to finish her call.

'That was so funny.'

The girls laughed again, and Kimberley sighed. 'She ain't right, is she? She is almost *nice*.'

Roxanna grinned. 'I know it's a bit disturbing at times, but it can only be a good thing. It seems weird thinking we buried our dad today, don't you think?'

She was pouring herself a mineral water, while her sisters were drinking white wine. They all sat on the large, battered sofa and looked around the room which, thanks to their hard work, was clean and shiny.

Dianna started to cry again.

'Oh, come here, you poor little mare.'

Kimberley hugged her sister, who said, through her tears, 'What a terrible way to die. I keep thinking of him being murdered . . .'

Rox shook her head. 'We told you not to read the papers or listen to the news. You can't let what happened to him get to you, babe, he was not a saint, as we all know. In his world, it's almost an occupational hazard, and you have to accept that or you will never get back on track.'

Since the revelation about poor Maggie, any feelings Rox might have harboured for the man who had sired her were long gone, but she was not going to make her sister's grief any worse than it already was.

'But who would do something like that to our dad? Why ain't the police out looking for them?'

Rox and Kimberley exchanged looks over Dianna's head. They had their own ideas about that but they were keeping them close to their chests. They were upset about what had happened, of course, but unlike Dianna they were realists and they privately wondered how it had not happened long before. Freddie had more enemies than Vlad the Impaler and he made a point of goading them at every opportunity. Dianna was like their mother. She saw only what she wanted to see in people, especially when she was dealing with her father, who in fairness had loved her more than the other two since the moment he got out of prison.

As Kim and Rox had started to see their father for what he really was, they had been pleased that no real connection had ever been made between them. He was a vicious bully who had destroyed everyone who came into his orbit.

They were glad he was gone. Now they could all finally live in peace.

Jimmy drove along at a snail's pace, and pondered the call he had received from Lena two hours earlier. It was the first time he had heard from any of the family since his departure, and he had initially felt very awkward because he had practically lived at her house as a kid. He was wrong to have blanked her and Joe along with Maggie. He thought the world of them, and they reciprocated that affection.

Lena had not said anything about that, but her call had thrown him into a quandary. He also knew that she was right when she had made him promise never to tell Maggie she had contacted him. Maggie was like him in that respect, her pride would not appreciate the gesture, however well meant.

As he turned off the M25 and made towards his house he felt nervous. The feeling was alien to him these days, but as Glenford had said, the longer he left it, the harder it would become.

Now he was ashamed of his silence – she was his wife after all. But after a week's angry silence, he had not heard from her and so he had done what most men do. He had fed his anger, nurtured it, and eventually it had been a month and more and he could find no excuse to call her and he convinced himself that she could just as easily call him if she wanted him. But he knew that he had walked away from her, and in their marriage that meant he had to make contact.

If Lena had not called him he would never have made the first move, and if what Lena said was true, he would have regretted it all his life.

Once he saw Maggie, looked at her, he would know finally whether he could ever live with her again in peace and happiness. The flip side was that he might instead realise instinctively that he couldn't. If he couldn't put the images that tortured him out of his head their marriage would be finally and irretrievably over.

He pulled into the car park of his local pub. He needed to think this through, and he needed a drink to help him muster up some courage.

The knock on the door was heavy and unexpected. Even on the day of their father's funeral no one had bothered to come to offer either their condolences or respects, and the girls had been sensible enough not to have expected it anyway.

Roxanna assumed it was Little Freddie back from his jaunt. She opened the door wide to see two uniformed policemen and two CIDs. Plain-clothes police had always been referred to by her father as coppers in disguise, dressed up like real people. The thought popped into her head and she wanted to laugh. Her natural-born animosity for the police was straight to the fore though and she said sarcastically, 'If you are after me father, you're too late. We buried him today.'

The taller of the two plain clothes stepped forward then and, flashing his badge, which for all she knew could be a bus pass he had done it so quickly, said in a deep and serious tone, 'I am DCI Michael Murray, and I am looking for a Freddie Jackson all right, but it's the son this time.'

Roxanna said in annoyance, 'Oh, have a day off, will you, and leave us to grieve in peace.'

'Is he on the premises, Miss Jackson?'

This Murray was starting to get on her tits. 'What is he supposed to have done now? He was at his dad's funeral most of the day so I think you will find he has a cast-iron alibi.'

Roxanna was feeling incensed. Of all the days to come knocking . . . and then she noticed there were three squad cars parked up and they were all holding uniforms.

'What's going on? He is only a kid, what are you doing round here mob-handed? Don't tell me he's being accused of robbing a fucking bank! Come on, what's he supposed to have done?'

'He is wanted in relation to a fatal stabbing that occurred earlier this afternoon by the Roundhouse public hostelry.'

His convoluted language made it hard for her to work out what he was saying, but two words stuck out like moose horns. 'A stabbing?'

The incredulity in her voice was communicating itself to the policewoman standing behind Murray, and who was sorry for this pretty girl who had just buried her father. 'We sympathise with your loss, miss, but it is imperative that we locate him as soon as possible. We have a warrant to search the premises.'

Murray looked at the WPC with open hostility. Her civil tone and friendly approach were highly unsuitable when dealing with this particular family. He couldn't wait until the girl had her first experience of Jackie Jackson. Now that would be a sight worth seeing.

Jackie had stood on this very step with a baseball bat before now. Even his most hardened officers were very loath to approach her and they had done their time keeping the peace at Upton Park. They would rather face a herd of screaming West Ham supporters than Jackie Jackson with a few drinks inside her.

Still, the warrant had got them an invite, so he walked in warily, expecting a lunatic in a black dress in honour of the occasion, and wielding some form of weapon. Instead he was pleasantly surprised to see Lena Summers, whom he had known since his beat days, and the other two Jackson girls.

'Where's Jackie?' All formality was gone from him now. This was serious and he wanted to know the answer so he could take the appropriate precautions.

'She is asleep upstairs,' Lena told him, watching as the house slowly filled up with the uniforms. All she could think of was her husband's predictions concerning their grandson. He said Little Freddie would end up killing someone and she had no doubt whatever that he had finally done it. Filth didn't come round this quick, with a warrant and enough uniforms to have a séance unless they had one eyewitness at least.

Poor Jackie, today of all days.

'Go and wake your mum up, Kim. They will be tearing the place apart soon looking for him or the weapon. Bless her heart, as if she ain't got enough to contend with.'

Murray grinned then. 'I think this WPC can have that honour. The main bedroom is the third door on the left.'

Rox smiled as the young woman walked up the stairs. Like Murray and the other old hands, she was intrigued to see how her mother took this latest interruption from the police.

They were not disappointed. The girl screamed loudly,

and Murray only stopped chuckling when she bent over the landing and vomited all over him.

Lily brought through a pot of decaffeinated coffee and a sandwich. Smiling her thanks, Maggie finally sat back in her chair and stretched her aching muscles. As always Lily sat opposite her, ready to give her an update on all the people she now knew intimately but had never met.

Paperwork was Maggie's friend these days. It was the only thing that took her mind off her troubles, and she delayed Lily's chat by busily gathering all the papers together in a neat pile.

The phone rang and she picked it up, saying in a tired voice, 'Hello.'

Lily was amazed to see her drop the phone a few seconds later, then lean back in the chair with her hand over her mouth, rocking herself back and forth. An awful wailing sound was coming out of her, and as Lily was to regale to her family later that night, it sounded like nothing on this earth. It was frightening to see her employer reacting so strangely to what was obviously bad news of some kind, and poor Mrs Jackson had had more than her fair share of bad news these last few months.

A few minutes later she was relieved to see Mr Jackson come through the front door. He rushed to his wife and, as Lily later told her gobsmacked family in as dramatic a tone as possible, Mrs Jackson clung to him as if her life was dependent on him being there. Though Lily Small didn't know it, that was a very true and accurate statement.

Rox was still trying to hold on to the contents of her stomach, and Dicky was holding her tightly while at the same time trying to drive the car to Maggie's house.

Dianna and Kimberley were in the back with poor Lena who should never have had to witness the sight of her daughter dead in her bed, her wrists cut and a plastic bag over her head.

What was it with this lot and fucking plastic bags? First little Jimmy, and now her.

Dicky was starting to get a bit shirty now. These Jacksons made fucking Job look like a lottery winner. Now Rox was in the club, he was working for Jimmy, her favourite uncle, and who also happened to be the local Mr Big, and he was starting to think that they were all fucking jinxed. He was now wondering if he should have given himself a bit more time before he got so involved with them all. But he could hardly walk out on Rox now she had a belly full of arms and legs.

As much as he loved her, this was all getting a bit too mad for him, and he considered himself a hard nut, able to deal with anything that life threw at him. Well, it was throwing fucking missiles at this lot at the moment, and he was not happy about putting himself in the line of fire.

He was gratified to see Jimmy's car on the drive. At least another man would be there and he could get himself a few more Brownie points with him, so the whole day wouldn't be fucking wasted.

Poor old Lena, though, his heart went out to her. She had shown no real reaction at all, and he hoped that old Joe arrived soon because she looked distinctly iffy. All he needed now was for her to drop down dead with shock and they could keep the match ball.

This was fucking outrageous, the most outrageous day of his life. Dicky had never really experienced the Jacksons' intricate and dangerous family connections, and now he was getting an insight into them he was wise to be wary.

Maggie was crying when he brought Rox indoors. The girl was still clinging to him for dear life and it was only when she peeled herself off him and sank into her aunt's arms that he could finally have a fag in peace and rub his aching neck muscles. His watchword for today was definitely fucking outrageous. It was all he kept saying, over and over again.

Epilogue

Ozzy was pleased that the visit had gone so well the day before, because he knew his time was nearly up. If he was offered parole because of his illness, he would cheerfully kill again to make sure that never happened. It was weird really. He had taken to this life, and he knew that was because something deep inside him was off kilter, was broken.

But now his time was drawing near he was happy. He had enjoyed these years, the solitude, the camaraderie of his fellow prisoners, and the excitement of making a fortune while ostensibly being punished by the Queen.

He liked the Queen. When the younger lads cunted her over being pursued and eventually convicted in her name, he had always pointed out that she was only a figurehead, she was not the scab involved. She left all that to the scabs on the police force and in the law courts. They should remember that, and respect her for winning the fucking case against them, otherwise they wouldn't be here. If they had used their loaf, they would not have got a capture in the first place.

This was urban warfare as far as he was concerned, us against them. Them being, of course, anyone who had the nerve to uphold the law when he was trying to earn a crust by breaking it.

Even Ozzy expected them to put fucking gas-meter bandits in jail. And fucking muggers, they were a stain on society. But he saw himself and others of his ilk as businessmen, which of course they were.

Now he was seeing that young lad happy again and for that he would have given the last few days of his life. The Jackson family had been decimated. All their problems had stemmed from one member, Freddie Jackson, and Ozzy felt at times responsible for all the trouble that Freddie had caused over the years. It was he who had given Freddie the dreams of the big time, and his first big take, and it was also he who had gradually worked him out, and young Jimmy in.

So he had inadvertently caused the chaos that had ensued, and he would always regret that. But Jimmy had looked good today and he was happy with his life, and for that alone, Ozzy would be eternally grateful.

He had never wanted a family, even his sister Pat got on his tits, but Jimmy had somehow touched a chord inside him. He knew that Jimmy had never once tried to collar a penny over and above his wedge, because for years he had made sure the books were looked over in private. He had known in his heart that Jimmy would not touch a bean that wasn't his, but you never could be a hundred per cent sure about anyone. He was now, though it had taken many years before he had finally admitted that the boy was completely straight.

This knowledge pleased him. When he finally shook off this mortal coil, Jimmy Jackson was going to be a very rich man indeed, and he deserved every penny he had coming to him.

Ozzy felt he was paying him serious compensation,

because by raising him in their world, he had inadvertently given Jimmy a powerful enemy, and this enemy was twice as dangerous because he was related to him by blood. Family, he knew, could be far more treacherous and far more vengeful than any other adversary you might have acquired along your merry way. Their strength lay in the fact that they knew you so well, and knowledge, as they say, is power. And you had *no* reason *not* to trust them, until it was too late of course and they had tucked you up big time.

Ozzy sat in his cell, and he congratulated himself for having the sense to leave the outside world alone. Inside he didn't have to deal with anything too pressing unless the fancy took him. He turned on his little portable TV. Richard and Judy were on and he loved the way they interacted with each other. He enjoyed this little bit of contact with the outside world through the glass screen of his antiquated black-and-white TV.

He had only one thing left to do and he had arranged that a few weeks earlier. He was going to give the nod for that to go down tonight, when a tame screw brought him in his mobile as usual so he could make any necessary calls in relative peace and quiet. He also brought him in a bottle of Glenfiddich every few days as well. It was a lovely treat last thing at night with a drop of hot water and plenty of sugar.

He wouldn't tell Jimmy what his last act for him was going to be, he would be far better off never knowing anything about it. But it would be worth more than all the money in the world because it would help Jimmy Jackson to sleep better at night. And it would make Ozzy feel that he had done everything in his power to compensate young Jimmy Jackson, the new Face of London.

* * *

Glenford Prentiss was smoking a joint as was usual, and smiling at a young coffee-coloured lap dancer with high breasts and a very expensive smile.

His phone rang and he answered it with a frown. 'Hello, Ozzy.'

The girl could hear the respect in his voice and the sound alerted her to the fact that everyone had someone they answered to, no matter who they were.

'Of course it's all arranged. The boy checks out tonight.'

Libby, as she was known, watched as Glenford turned the phone off, then put it down on the table with a sigh. He then drank his Bacardi and Coke in record time before saying, 'Now, where were we?'

But she was sensible enough to know that he had a lot on his mind. 'You OK, Glenford?'

He shrugged. ' 'Course I am, girl.'

She smiled then, and he smiled back, happier than he had been for a long time.

Maggie was actually laughing, really laughing, and the sound made Lena and Joe smile at one another.

'He is a lovely fella, old Jimmy, eh?'

'A blinder. Fuck me, Lena, pour that tea out before the Christmas rush starts, eh.'

Lena grinned. They spent a lot of time at Maggie's now, as did the girls. Jimmy didn't mind, but she guessed that sometimes he would have liked his wife to himself. He would get his wish sooner than he thought.

The girls were gradually starting to accept what had happened, and she knew they were stronger than they thought. Jackie's suicide note had not helped them, she knew. She had just written plainly, to no one in particular:

> Sorry. But I can't live without him. Be happy one and all.

It had been so short, so poignant and so lonely she had wanted to die herself. Her poor daughter, who even in death remained in the grip of the man who had deliberately and systematically chipped away at her until she had forgotten how to be happy, forgotten how to live her life.

Lena prayed every day that her poor Jackie had found some kind of peace at last.

'Here they come, Lena. Go and refresh that tea, girl, it's older than I am.'

Joe loved Maggie, and he loved Jimmy, but as they walked into the large conservatory and placed the baby in his arms, his face lit up like a Belisha beacon.

This was the miracle child as far as they were concerned, and the family had been brought closer together with his birth and his cousin's birth.

Rox had also been blessed with a boy child a few months earlier, and they looked like two peas in a pod. Both were strong and dark haired, and sometimes a shadow crossed over Lena's face because they looked like Freddie and Jimmy all over again.

But these two were not going to be like that. Jimmy would ensure that they were brought up properly, and little Dicky was gutted that Rox had given theirs her maiden name so they were both Jacksons. Rox had decided that marriage was out of the question now, she wanted to wait until her life was back on an even keel. The papers had had a field day, and they had all had to suffer the humiliation of their private lives being played out on a daily basis, and being branded criminals and anything else that guaranteed sales for the gutter press.

Lena looked at the two little Josephs and she knew that the names of these boys had given her old man more pleasure than anything in his life before.

'The girls coming over tonight?'

Maggie shook her head. 'No, they are all going out, and about time too. What do you think of their house, Mum?'

Lena smiled again at her daughter and she said earnestly, 'It's beautiful, and they love it there. You are very good you know, you two.'

Jimmy shrugged. 'What can you do, they are family.'

Joseph nodded his head in agreement. 'What's left of it anyway, eh?' He held his grandson tightly as he said it and he prayed that this boy, and his great grandson, had inherited nothing from Freddie Jackson.

Family was a blessing and it was also a fucking curse. He knew that better than anyone else in the world.

Joseph had taken a call that morning from the secure unit that housed his other grandson and it seemed Little Freddie had hung himself in the night. He had felt a wave of joy wash over him at the news. He still loathed the boy and the news he was dead had cheered him up no end. That was another mad bastard out of the way.

He would tell them all eventually, when the time was right. Until then he would let them enjoy the lovely summer days.

Maggie lay on the chaise longue at the end of her bed and breast-fed her little son. It was her favourite time of the day. She counted her blessings now. God had seen fit to give her this child and she was not going to let anything mar her happiness.

She would never forget her little Jimmy, but Joseph was like a life belt and she had held on to him for dear life, until now, at long last, the fear was gone. Freddie and his poison was in the past. He had ruled too many lives and it was time for them to stop allowing him to dictate their feelings and their thoughts.

She was still young looking, she knew. Her body was not as good as before but she didn't care and neither did Jimmy. He still took her with the same passion he had taken her with when they had first come together.

Jackie was often in her mind. She missed her, but she knew the girls were always going to be there for her in the same way she had always been there for them.

It felt strange, this return to normality. It had been so long since she had felt like this, she had forgotten what it was like to just sit and think like other people.

Just to be.

She was happy again, but this was a happiness based on the truth. Like her Jimmy had said, all that time ago, sometimes things are best left unsaid, and she was now a devotee of that herself.

She kissed Joseph's head as she swapped breasts, and the smell of him alone filled her with delight. She was happy, really happy and no one was going to interfere with that.

Jimmy never tired of this spectacle. He could watch Mags feed his Joseph all day and all night, it was to him the most beautiful sight in the world. They had been given a second chance and they were determined to make it work.

Freddie Jackson had blighted all their lives in one way or another and now he was long buried and the wounds he had inflicted on them all were healing over.

He felt the difference more and more every day. Even the girls were coming to terms with the devastation that had passed for their lives. They were closer than ever before, and they were gradually fleeing the nest that he had provided for them with Maggie.

He had achieved so much in his life, he had worked for his family, he had tried to live a good life, and it was his duty now not to let Freddie Jackson spoil his happiness in any way.

If Freddie had left a legacy, it was to push the remaining family closer together. As Ozzy had always told him, find a positive instead of a negative, and you will find your life is much easier to bear. The Jackson clan was still strong and new recruits would be added all the time. Rox had already started the ball rolling for the girls.

The Jackson empire would live on, and he was determined to pass it over to this little lad here. Otherwise, what the fuck was it all for?

He smiled at his lovely wife and basked in his own happiness, because being a Jackson he had learned the hard way that you never knew how long this feeling was going to last.

The Business

Martina Cole

LOVE YOUR FAMILY. HATE YOUR ENEMIES.
KNOW THE BUSINESS.

Imelda Dooley is scared. Really scared. She's played hard and fast and now she's been caught. She's pregnant and she's on her own. So Imelda Dooley tells a lie. A lie that *literally* causes murders.

When Mary Dooley's husband is killed, she knows she must graft to keep the family afloat. And graft she does, becoming a name in her own right. But she still has to watch her daughter's life spiral into a vicious, hate-fuelled cycle of drugs and prostitution.

Caught up in the carnage that is Imelda's existence are Mary's adored grandchildren, Jordanna and Kenny. Pretty little Jordanna isn't yet three and she already knows far too much. All the little girl can do is look after her baby brother and try not to draw unwanted attention to herself.

Set in the heart of London's criminal world, from the tail end of the seventies up to the present-day, THE BUSINESS is a gritty, disturbing and haunting tale of drugs, prostitution and a young girl's fight for survival – against all the odds.

Praise for Martina Cole's phenomenal No. 1 bestsellers:

'Terrific stuff from a terrific lady' *Daily Mirror*

'Intensely readable' *Guardian*

'Martina Cole again explores the shady criminal underworld, a setting she is fast making her own' *Sunday Express*

'One of the most popular novelists of our time' *Literary Review*

978 0 7553 2867 3

headline